"Another Whiskey Creek novel is just what readers need to satisfy their craving for a romance that tugs at the heartstrings."
—*RT Book Reviews* on *A Winter Wedding*, Top Pick

"[*This Heart of Mine*] had such beautiful details that it captured my full attention—and had me sniffling and smiling while waiting to board my plane."
—*First for Women*

"*This Heart of Mine* is a potently emotional, powerfully life-affirming contemporary romance that can be read and enjoyed on its own, but it also serves as an excellent addition to Novak's popular Whiskey Creek series."—*Booklist*, starred review

"Another engrossing addition to Novak's addictive series."
—*Library Journal* on *This Heart of Mine*, starred review

"Novak's Whiskey Creek novels are a favorite among romance readers because of their small-town charm… Novak never disappoints."—*RT Book Reviews* on *This Heart of Mine*, Top Pick

"Once again Novak's Whiskey Creek springs to life in all its realistic, gritty Gold Country glory as two determined, likable people come to terms with their pasts and give love a chance. This poignant, heartfelt romance puts a refreshing spin on the classic reunion/secret baby theme."
—*Library Journal* on *Come Home to Me*

"One needn't wonder why Novak is a *New York Times* and *USA TODAY* bestselling author. Just read *Come Home to Me*."
—*Examiner.com*

"The Whiskey Creek series is an absolute delight and this newest installment is…so satisfying I ran out of superlatives. Brenda Novak outdid herself in *Take Me Home for Christmas*."
—*Fresh Fiction*

"It's steamy, it's poignant, it's perfectly paced—it's *When Lightning Strikes* and you don't want to miss it."
—*USATODAY.com*'s *Happy Ever After* blog

Also by Brenda Novak:

BRENDA NOVAK

Discovering You

ISBN-13: 978-0-7783-1880-4

Discovering You

Recycling programs
for this product may
not exist in your area.

www.MIRABooks.com

Printed in U.S.A.

To Kay Myers, who read my very first book
before it ever came out and told me it was good.

Dear Reader,

Dylan Amos is probably my favorite character in all of Whiskey Creek, so it is with great pleasure that I return to his family to write about another one of his sexy brothers. There's just something special about a family of rugged men who've managed to pull together in the face of adversity. The Amoses are tough, able to carry the weight of the world on their shoulders. I love that they have a hard edge to them, because, as much as they may not want to admit it, they also have soft hearts (way down deep). I think Rodney rises to the occasion when he meets his beautiful new neighbor, who so desperately needs his friendship and support. Only he would be right for her. I hope you'll agree.

If you're just starting the series, don't worry. The books are written to stand alone, so you won't be lost jumping in at any point. And if you'd like to go back to the beginning and catch up, I have a list of the books in order on my website at brendanovak.com. There's even a pdf you can download and take to the bookstore (or use to order online).

Next up, I'll be veering away from Whiskey Creek for a bit with the publication of *The Secrets She Kept*, my second Fairham Island book. It'll be released at the end of July, but if you join my mailing list at brendanovak.com, I'll send you an email whenever I have a book coming out. At brendanovak.com, you'll also be able to enter monthly drawings, contact me with comments or questions or join my fight to find a cure for diabetes by purchasing a copy of *Love That! Brenda Novak's Every Occasion Cookbook* (with Jan Coad). My youngest son has this disease. Thanks to the support of so many, I've been able to raise $2.5 million for the cause so far (which has gone to both JDRF and the DRI).

Best wishes always,

Brenda Novak

Discovering
You

1

There was a bloody man walking down the middle of the road.

India Sommers's heart leaped into her throat the moment her headlights fell on the tall, lean figure. Had she been more familiar with the area, she might've come racing around the bend in her quiet Prius and accidentally mowed him down, but he didn't seem to give a damn about the danger. He looked too angry to care. And judging by his rumpled clothes, she thought she could guess why. This guy had been in a fight.

He seemed determined to flag her down. But she'd seen enough violence to recognize that he was no helpless victim, which made her far less sympathetic to whatever he needed than she might otherwise have been.

She started to slow; she didn't want to hit him. But neither was she willing to leave herself vulnerable. She was alone on a winding road in the foothills of the Sierra Nevada Mountains, and she'd moved to Gold Country only this week. She hadn't had a chance to meet more than a handful of people. For all she knew, this man could be some kind of crazed lunatic who'd just committed murder!

He *looked* menacing, with his hands curled into fists and his jaw set as if he'd like to take another swing at someone.

Who had he tangled with already?

She edged to the right so she could squeeze past him. Once it seemed safe, she planned to punch the gas pedal and get out of there. Whatever he'd been involved in, she wanted no part of it. Since she'd been using GPS to get home from the art show she'd attended in another town, she had her cell phone in the passenger seat. She'd call the police as soon as she was well away, so she wouldn't leave him stranded, and be done with this.

But the minute she slowed and he started to approach, she recognized him. It was her neighbor! She'd seen him out with his brothers, throwing a football the day she moved in. The three of them—all equally tall, dark and muscular—had even hauled her potter's wheel into the screened-in porch at the back of her house, where she'd decided to work through the summer.

Although still a little reluctant to stop, she couldn't just drive off, not if her neighbor needed help. So she stepped on the brake, and Rod—she remembered his name because he was the type of man a woman wouldn't easily forget—came to the side of the car.

A chill ran through her as he waited for her to lower the window. Was she a fool for trusting him? Just because he lived next door didn't make him safe, especially if he was high on something. And even if she could normally outrun him, which wasn't likely, she was wearing a long dress and heels.

Cursing her desire to be helpful and polite, which occasionally overrode her good sense, she pressed the button.

"It's you," he said as soon as they no longer had a barrier of glass between them.

"Yes." She wasn't sure he remembered her name, so she added it. "India Sommers."

"Right. My new neighbor. Listen, India, I need you to call the cops."

He seemed quite matter-of-fact. She didn't get the impression that he intended to drag her out of the driver's seat and into the woods—or steal her purse or her Prius. But she'd been correct when she guessed he'd been in a fight. His knuckles were scraped.

"What happened?" she asked.

He wiped the drop of blood that was running from his mouth. "Some bastard got out of line."

And Rod had put him back in line? Where was that *bastard*?

Butterflies danced in India's belly as she squinted to see down the road, as far into the darkness as she could. "Where is this person?"

"Back that way." He jerked a thumb over his shoulder.

The other guy hadn't driven off? Why? "Is he seriously injured?"

Rod stretched his fingers, as if his hand hurt. "Probably not *seriously*, but he's out cold."

She still wasn't clear on why he'd been walking in the road. This remote location wasn't one you'd arrive at on foot. "So…why are you without transportation? Were you traveling together?"

"No. He wrecked my motorcycle when he came up from behind and ran me off the road. Now it's undrivable. And somehow in the scuffle I lost my phone. I looked for his, but he doesn't seem to have one on him."

"It's a miracle you're alive!" she said as she reached for her cell. "What would make someone do what he did?"

Obviously irritated, Rod gestured as if too much had happened to explain. "It started before, at the bar. I should've kicked his ass then."

"Oh, God." Her hand shook as she dialed 911. She didn't do well with violence; she'd seen too much of it. That was part of the reason she'd come to Whiskey Creek—to start over in a place that still felt innocent. Her past was littered with dangerous yet attractive rebels, men a lot like this neighbor of hers. The rough, outlaw type used to fill her with excitement, with desire. They made her feel…*alive*.

She'd learned a few lessons since then about what really mattered. It wasn't a reckless disregard for the rules, or a handsome face and rock-hard abs. These days she understood that in more than a cognitive sense; it'd sunk deep into her emotional memory. But whether she'd learned her lesson or not, she was still paying a terrible price for having associated with the wrong people.

As she waited for the dispatcher to pick up, she eyed the tattoo—a snake slithering up a tree—that covered the sinewy contours of Rod's right arm until it disappeared into the sleeve of his white T-shirt. Yep, this was *exactly* the kind of guy she would've liked once upon a time. She wouldn't have cared that he could be volatile. She wouldn't have cared that he probably didn't have a college education or even a decent job. Physically, he was everything a woman dreamed about.

And he'd probably be good in bed—although she had no idea where that thought came from. Just the casual way he held himself, his lack of self-consciousness and natural confidence, she supposed. He stood out from other men. But the intimacy she'd shared with Charlie, who was *nothing* like this guy, had been sweet and fulfilling. What Charlie had brought to the rest of her life was even better. She needed to find another man like *him*—when she was ready.

"911. What is your emergency?"

At the sound of the operator's voice, she snapped to attention. "Hello... I'm out on..." She looked up at Rod for help. She'd forgotten the name of the street. She wasn't familiar with anything other than the few blocks that constituted the center of town and Gulliver Lane, which led from town to her place.

"Old Church Road," he said.

She'd begun to repeat that when he took her phone and spoke into it himself. "There's been an incident about a mile before you get to Sexy Sadie's outside Whiskey Creek. A man's down, so send an ambulance."

The operator must've asked for more details, because he said, "I'm not a doctor. All I can tell you is that he's not moving."

"Sir? What caused his injuries? Are you still there? Can I get your name?"

India could hear those questions, since Rod was handing her the cell. "Um, just get someone here quick," she told the dispatcher and disconnected.

"Would you mind giving me a ride back to my bike?" he asked.

India wasn't sure she wanted him in her car. But he had to know she was going in that direction; they lived next door to each other.

"Okay," she said, because she didn't see how she could refuse.

When he walked around the front of her car, she

noticed that he favored his left leg and figured he had a few injuries of his own, in addition to the scraped knuckles and busted lip.

"You could use some medical attention yourself," she said when he opened the passenger door.

"I'm all right," he responded as he climbed in.

"But your leg—"

He stretched it out through the open door to have a look. "When he hit my bike, I came down on it pretty hard." He lifted his torn jeans away from the scrapes. "Skinned it up is all," he said, as if that wasn't anything to worry about.

"Are you sure you didn't break it?"

Shifting gingerly, he managed to bend his hurt leg far enough to get it in the car. "I wouldn't be able to walk if I had."

She gave him a skeptical glance. "That's not necessarily true. It would depend on the kind of break. You should have it x-rayed." She felt confident that was what her husband would've said, and he *had* been a doctor— on his way to becoming a world-class heart surgeon.

Rod closed the door. "There's no need."

Having him in the same confined space made her slightly claustrophobic. Or maybe he made her uncomfortable for other reasons. Like the fact that he reminded her of Sam, the boy she'd married straight out of high school only weeks after her mother's death. Unlike Charlie, Sam had been a terrible husband. He'd possessed no more life skills than she had at that age, so the marriage didn't last a year. But being with him had had its high points, including a certain giddy I-can't-keep-my-hands-off-this-man attraction.

She felt some of that attraction now, just as she had the

other day, when Rod had carried her potter's wheel from the back of her Prius. She also felt wary—more wary than anything else. But she couldn't complain about the way he smelled, like warm male and fecund earth. She saw some leaves sticking to his shirt and hair and assumed he'd taken a tumble when he fell from his bike. Maybe the fight had even turned into a wrestling match. Most fights went that way, at least the ones she'd witnessed.

Pushing her silver bangles up her arm, she pressed the gas pedal.

They rolled carefully around the next bend, but she didn't see any sign of a bike, a car or another person.

"It's farther down," Rod said before she could ask.

Apparently, he'd walked a greater distance on that leg than she'd expected.

The road took several more twists and she still saw no sign of where the incident might've occurred. "Where were you going?" she asked in confusion.

He looked over at her. "When he hit me? I was on my way home."

"No. When I saw you. You were walking *away* from town. You do realize that?"

"Of course. I've lived in Whiskey Creek all my life. It's not likely I'd get turned around. I was heading back to the bar so I could use a phone or get help."

She'd driven past a saloon-style tavern, one with a big neon sign out front. That had to be the place he was talking about. "Are your brothers there?" She'd gotten the impression the three men were close, that they did a lot together.

"They were until they got tired and left."

"They must be wondering where you are."

He was too focused on the road to look at her again.

"Doubt it. I'm sure they're asleep." He pointed ahead. "There it is."

She hunched over the steering wheel until she saw a flash of shiny chrome reflecting the moonlight. "So this guy knocked you off your bike, and then he came back to...what? Fight?"

"I think he was planning to taunt me, to celebrate what he'd done. Or kick me while I was down. The way I fell... he had to believe I'd be more hurt than I was."

"He must've been surprised when that wasn't the case."

"Yeah, he would've been smarter to keep going, although I would've caught up with him eventually."

That last bit sounded ominous, but at least the other guy seemed to have been the aggressor.

"Do you have any idea *why* he'd run you down?" she asked.

"I guess he didn't like what I had to say to him at Sexy Sadie's."

They'd reached his Harley, which was black and lying on its side. She parked on the shoulder between it and a white compact car that was still running. The car had its back end in the road, as if the driver had slammed on his brakes and hopped out. The door was open, and the cabin light cast an eerie triangle on the blacktop.

India wanted to ask Rod what he'd said at Sexy Sadie's that might've incited the driver of that car to violence, but she didn't get the chance. He got out right away and, despite his injured leg, strode confidently over to a dark shape lying off in the bushes.

She hurried behind him, even though she wasn't sure she could stomach what she was about to see. It used to be that the sight of blood didn't bother her. But, like the rest of her life, that'd changed eleven months ago. Now she had nightmares in which she was drowning in blood.

And it wasn't just anyone's blood...

Shoving that memory from her mind, she focused on the gravel crunching beneath her high heels until they reached the inert form of the guy Rod had fought. There were no streetlights, but the moon was full. The man seemed to be about thirty-five and was dressed in a polo shirt, jeans and cowboy boots. A dark streak suggested the brawl had taken place in the middle of the road and someone—Rod, no doubt—had pulled him to the side when it was over so he wouldn't be struck by a car.

It was a point in her neighbor's favor that he'd had the presence of mind to take that precaution. But, as he'd mentioned, his opponent wasn't conscious. India guessed the blood on the road had come from the man's head, since that was where he was bleeding the most.

Was he even *alive*?

Holding up her dress, she crouched to find his carotid artery. Then she backed slowly away. He had a pulse, thank goodness. She didn't want to touch him beyond ascertaining that. She was already having flashbacks, could hear her own voice screaming Charlie's name...

Instinctively, she covered her ears—then lowered her hands when Rod gave her a funny look. "Do you know him?" he asked.

She shook her head and was relieved when he didn't press her.

After throwing the man a disgruntled glance, he began to pace back and forth across the road.

"Shouldn't we search for your phone?" she asked. "I could call it, if you give me your number."

"I put it on silent. I hate it when you go out with some-one whose phone is always ringing."

"It'd light up, at least," she said.

They gave it a try. They even used her flashlight app to comb both sides of the road—all to no avail.

"I'll come back in the morning, when it's light," he said and returned to pacing.

India held three fingers to her forehead as she watched from the shoulder. "Can you please get out of the street?" she asked when he didn't move to a safer place.

His gaze swept over her as if he was wondering why she was so dressed up. But he didn't ask. Neither did he comply with her request. He continued to prowl while she stared in the direction of Whiskey Creek, wishing the police and the ambulance would arrive.

"Can you stop?" she finally muttered. "You're mak-ing me nervous."

"Don't worry about it," he grumbled.

Obviously, they were both agitated. She could feel the anxiety flowing through him. "I can't help worrying," she said. "Not everyone is as cautious as I am. I get that. But a car could come tearing around that bend any sec-ond and—"

"Fine!" He cut her off and came over to the shoul-der, as if arguing with her was more of a hassle than it was worth.

She reined in her temper. "Thank you."

He didn't acknowledge her thanks. "You don't happen to have a smoke, do you?"

She almost walked back to the Prius for her purse be-fore it occurred to her that of course she wouldn't have a smoke. She hadn't bought a pack of cigarettes since she'd gotten pregnant with Cassia nearly six years ago. "No."

He touched his mouth and looked at his fingers, checking to see if his lip was bleeding again. "I never smoke unless I'm drinking," he explained. "It's been a year since I've done even that. But I'll be damned if I couldn't use a cigarette right now."

"I quit when I was twenty-four." She hadn't been the same person in those days...

He raked his fingers through his light brown hair. It was a little too long, but she admired the way it fell loose and went curly at the ends. "Can I use your phone?" he asked.

The moment she handed it to him, he turned away and kicked a pebble from foot to foot while waiting for the person he'd called to pick up.

She knew someone had answered when he straightened and forgot about messing with that rock. "You're not going to believe this," he said. "It's me...Our new neighbor's...Yes, *that* neighbor...Stop. Listen, I need some help. Remember that guy who was bothering Natasha? The one we warned to stay away?...Yeah, him. He wrecked into the back of my bike."

Rod didn't explain that he'd been driving it at the time, which seemed like a salient point to India. He could've been killed. But she wasn't about to get involved in his conversation.

"No, I'm not kidding," he said. "Uh-huh...Don't worry, I doubt he'll ever mess with her again." He slowly gravitated over to the man he'd knocked out and nudged him with one foot.

No response.

"I can't leave yet," he said, stalking off in the other direction. "I'm waiting for the ambulance...Yes, *ambulance*. The asshole's out cold...What would *you* have done? He had no business hitting my bike. I'm lucky I can still walk...*Of course* I was riding it at the time! I was driving home."

There, the information had finally come out. India took a deep breath and told herself to relax.

Usually, it cooled off at night when the Delta breeze swept in. That was what she loved about Northern California. But they'd been going through a terrible heat wave since she'd moved to Whiskey Creek. Part of her discomfort had to be due to the stress of the situation, but it felt like a hundred degrees outside, as it had been earlier in the day.

"Right. So can you bring the trailer and get my bike?" she heard Rod say. "How would I know? Chief Bennett's going to give me hell. He might even take me down to the station to get a statement or try to lock me up for the night...True...No, don't call Dylan or Aaron. I can handle my own problems."

He disconnected and was about to return her phone when he saw he'd gotten blood on it. After wiping it on his jeans, he gave it back. "Sorry."

"No problem." She held on to the phone, since she didn't have a pocket and her purse was in the car. "That was...one of your brothers?"

"Yeah."

Still no headlights coming from Whiskey Creek. What was taking emergency services so long? She and Rod—and the man who needed the ambulance—weren't that far from town. "Which one?"

"Grady. He's driving over to get my bike."

"Is he older, or..."

"Dylan and Aaron are older. Grady and Mack are younger."

"Would you mind if I asked how old *you* are?" They were both young enough that she couldn't imagine it would be an offensive question.

"Thirty-one. You?"

She considered taking off her heels but was afraid she might cut her foot on a rock, nail or piece of glass. "Thirty."

"I guessed we were about the same age."

"When?"

"The other day."

She ignored that, didn't want to think about the implications. She'd noticed more details about him than she cared to admit; knowing he'd done the same with her didn't help keep her mind where it needed to be. "So there're five kids in your family, not three?"

"Right. Dylan and Aaron are married. They live in town with their wives. You met Grady and Mack, who live with me."

Finally, the faint wailing of a siren drifted to her ears. "And this Natasha? She's your…?" She knew better than to ask. It sounded as if she was probing, trying to learn whether he had a romantic interest. And yet she was too curious to let it go.

"Little sister. Actually, she's my *step*sister, ever since my father married her mother a few years ago."

"I see. You have a big family," she said to shift the focus away from the fact that she'd wanted to find out if Natasha was his girlfriend. "I think I've seen your father and stepmother. Are they living with you, too?"

"For now. It was supposed to be a temporary arrangement, but it's been a couple of years and they don't seem too eager to leave."

"You've got a big house. Having them there wouldn't be too bad if they're helping with the mortgage."

"They aren't."

"Then I could see how it might be an imposition."

His gaze slid over her, taking in every detail of her long, slinky black dress—including the slit up her leg. "What's your story?"

She cleared her throat. "I'm an only child."

"From the city?"

"What makes you think I'm from the city?"

"That dress," he replied. "Women around here don't wear that type of thing very often."

"I was born and raised in Oakland." She'd been living in San Francisco since her marriage to Charlie, however. An art exhibit in the city was a fancy affair. She knew she was overdressed for the small towns along Highway 49, but she'd felt the need to clean up, to feel attractive again, the way she used to feel when Charlie took her out.

"And now you live alone in Whiskey Creek, except for your little girl," he said.

She stiffened in surprise. "How'd you know I have a little girl?"

"I saw a photograph of her in your car the other day."

"Oh." She smiled at the thought of her five-year-old daughter. She missed Cassia so much.

He waited for her to look him in the face again. "Is she staying with her father right now, or…"

"She's with her grandparents. They offered to keep her until I could get settled." And because they missed Charlie as much as she did, India had felt obliged to allow it.

There were other reasons she'd felt she had to let Cassia stay with the Sommerses, but those reasons made her stomach churn.

Rod stuffed his hands in his pockets. "So where's your husband?"

She refused to flinch despite the sting that question caused. "Not everyone who has a child has a husband."

He raised his eyebrows. "You're wearing a ring."

It'd been so long since she'd been anyplace a man might bother to ask, she hadn't even remembered, probably because her ring didn't mean what it was supposed to. Not anymore. Charlie was dead. She'd sold their lovely home because she could no longer bear to live there. She couldn't divest herself of her ring, too. That symbol of his love meant too much to her. Besides her mother, he was the only person who'd ever treated her as though she mattered, as though she was special enough to deserve any kind of devotion. She'd since figured out that was a reflection of her own self-esteem at the time, but he'd somehow been able to look beyond that to see what she could be, to help shape her into what she was today.

"Right. My ring," she said. "Of course. But—" she stared down at her 1.5 carat diamond, remembering the night Charlie had given it to her "—my husband's... gone."

Fortunately, a truck came from the direction of the bar, interrupting their conversation before Rod could follow up on that. Two men rode in the cab, both of whom knew Rod.

The driver stopped and lowered his window, and the passenger called out to him. "What's going on, man? You okay?"

They exchanged a few words. Then the guys in the truck asked if Rod needed any help and Rod phoned his brother to say he could send his bike home with Donald and Sam. By the time the three of them had used a wooden plank to roll the heavy motorcycle up and into the bed, a policeman arrived—Chief Bennett, according to his name tag.

"Stand back," he told them, pushing them even farther to one side of the road. "I'll talk to you once I get some flares out so no one else gets hurt."

The ambulance came just as Rod's friends drove off with his bike. India watched from about ten feet away while two paramedics knelt by the man on the ground and Chief Bennett gave Rod a sobriety test—which, thankfully, he passed.

India hated to interrupt the paramedics, but they were beginning to load the injured man into the ambulance and she hoped to get some word of his condition before they left. "Is he going to be okay?"

"Most likely," one of them replied. "Even minor head injuries bleed a lot. I think he'll be fine."

"He was an idiot to pick a fight with Rod Amos," the other paramedic piped up.

The first guy jerked his head at the wallet resting on the unconscious man's chest, which Chief Bennett had used to ID him. "Liam Crockett's from Dixon. Mustn't have heard."

India wanted to ask if Rod was a professional fighter, but they were in too much of a hurry, so she backed away and let them go.

Ever since the police chief had determined that Rod was sober, Bennett had been grilling him on how everything had happened. They were still talking, and India didn't know whether to get in her car and leave, or wait to see if Rod needed a ride home.

"Damn it, Rod," she heard the police chief say. "You are *so* damn wild. It's always something with you."

Rod was obviously not pleased by that reaction. "I told you. *He* started it."

"Yeah, well, we'll see if that's what *he* says."

"You saw my bike! How do you think it got wrecked?"

When Bennett refused to commit himself, Rod continued. "We could've settled our differences at the bar. Instead, he followed me and tried to run me off the road. What kind of pussy tries to run someone over instead of fighting like a man?"

"Wait. What do you mean, handle it at the bar?" Bennett said. "You bust up Sexy Sadie's again, you won't be allowed to go there anymore."

"What are you talking about?" Rod cried. "I've never busted up Sexy Sadie's! You can't hold me accountable for what my brothers do."

"One of you is always raising hell," he said in disgust. "Anyway, I'm going to look into this further. That I can promise you."

"Fine," Rod told him. "I hope you do. When that bastard wakes up, he should go to jail."

"*If* he wakes up," the police chief grumbled. "God, I'm exhausted. Do you need a ride or—" He looked at India, obviously hoping she'd relieve him of that duty.

"I can take him," she volunteered. "I'm going that way."

"Maybe you should drive him over to the hospital first," he said, "see if he has any broken bones or needs stitches. It shouldn't take long. They've got to be on a first-name basis with him by now."

Rod shot him a dark scowl. "Quit trying to make me look bad."

"I don't need to *try*," Bennett said. "Since you can't stay out of trouble, you make yourself look bad."

Stepping between them, India touched Rod's arm to get his attention before he could spout off and get himself arrested. "Should we go to the hospital?"

He shook his head, suggesting it'd been a ridiculous idea to begin with.

"Can't hurt to get checked out," Chief Bennett said, attempting to persuade him.

"No way," Rod told him. "I'm going to bed."

"Suit yourself." With a sigh, Bennett adjusted his heavy belt and trudged over to his car.

All the excitement was over. India raised the hem of her dress to keep it from dragging on the ground as she returned to the car. She was halfway there before she realized Rod wasn't following her—and glanced back to see why.

"I can't even begin to guess where you've been tonight," he said, "but that dress…" Letting his words fade, he ended with a whistle.

"Thank you." She felt her face heat and wished she didn't find his appreciation so gratifying. He was definitely *not* the type of man she needed. She needed Charlie, but Charlie was gone and he wasn't coming back. The vacuum created by his death, as well as the reason behind it, had left her feeling…abysmal. It was terrible to be so lost and lonely that a stranger's attention felt like a lifeline.

"What happened here really wasn't my fault," he called out. "I hope you believe that."

"Of course," she responded, and yet she'd heard Chief Bennett say he was always in trouble. That confirmed her first impression of him, didn't it? He still wasn't coming toward her, so she crossed her arms and looked back at him. "Are you ready to go home?"

Finally, he started walking. "I'm ready, but…maybe we could clarify a few things along the way."

"Like…?"

"That ring on your finger," he said and threw her a sexy grin.

India felt a corresponding shiver of desire, which scared her. *No!* she told herself. Not *this* guy. She couldn't screw up again.

2

Rod had never particularly liked red hair. He usually had a preference for blondes. But India's hair, which fell long and straight to her shoulders, was between a bright orange and a dark mahogany, and somehow it worked with her pale skin and almost translucent blue eyes. She was different, unique, delicate in appearance.

The more he looked at her, the more he liked what he saw. But based on what he'd gathered from their conversation since she'd started to drive, she was still in love with her dead husband. She teared up when she talked about him, and yet she wouldn't say how he died. When Rod asked, she told him she didn't want to "go into that." Then she fiddled with her wedding ring the rest of the way to town. The only thing he could get out of her was that it'd been eleven months since the "tragedy" that'd taken Charlie.

"When will your daughter be back?" he asked, hoping she'd be more comfortable if he changed the subject.

"After the Fourth of July," she replied.

He shifted to ease the terrible ache in his leg. "That gives you three weeks on your own."

"Yes, too long for me, but I plan to make good use

of that time." She turned toward the river, where they both lived.

"Doing what?"

"Using that potter's wheel you helped me carry into the house."

"You do ceramics for a living?"

"Hope to," she said. "To be honest, I haven't made much money on it in the past, but I've never seriously pursued my art. I plan to open my own studio one day."

The smile that curved her lips when she said that— as if it had always been her dream—lit her whole face.

"Here in Whiskey Creek?"

"Yes."

"Not out of your house…"

"No. I'm picturing a cute little shop downtown. But first I have to build up my inventory."

He was glad she didn't expect folks to find her place along the river. He didn't think she could be successful there, not tucked away as they were. "Don't you have stuff already? I mean, haven't you been doing it for a while?"

"Since high school, but not with a business in mind. What I created before belongs to a different era in my life. Now that I'm starting over, rebuilding, I'd like to take my work in a new direction."

Her husband must've left her well-off, Rod decided. She'd essentially told him that what she planned to do wouldn't cover her bills—and he knew she'd paid quite a bit for her house. Although it'd once been a cheap rental, some investors had purchased it and renovated with the intent of reselling. They did a lot of work and put some key upgrades into it, so it'd been pricey by the time they were done.

Of course, Rod would've been able to tell by her clothes—or that rock of a wedding ring—that she wasn't hurting for money, even if he hadn't known how much she'd paid for the house, or noticed the expensive furniture the movers carried in when the van arrived a few hours after he and his brothers had helped set up her potter's wheel. "So you'll work from home every day?"

"For the next year or so, until I can determine if I have any chance at succeeding."

"You can make it," he said. "There're quite a few artisans in Gold Country. There's a glassworks place not far away, in Sutter Creek, if you haven't seen it."

"I have. It's wonderful." She stopped at the four-way, the last turn before the route home took them along the river. "What about you? What do you do?" she asked. "From the way the paramedics were talking, I wondered if you're a professional fighter."

"No," he said with a chuckle. "My oldest brother, Dylan, used to do MMA. Made good money at it, too. But he didn't want the rest of us to get involved in it. He needed us to work in the family business, which started doing well after he took over."

"From…"

"My father." Rod didn't state the reason or say anything about the circumstances. He knew how his history would sound to someone who wasn't familiar with it, especially someone who came from a better class of people—and India's clothes, her interest in art, even her language, suggested she came from a better class of people.

She tucked her silky-looking hair behind her ear. "What kind of business?"

"We own the auto body shop."

"And you work there?"

He could smell her perfume. That, too, seemed to hint at money. "I do. Probably always will. But that's okay. There isn't anything I'd rather be doing. Maybe you've seen it. Amos Auto Body. It's a couple of blocks off Sutter Street."

She shook her head. "Don't think I have."

"I've been fixing smashed cars, trucks and motorcycles pretty much all my life."

"Given the state of your bike, that experience should be useful," she said wryly.

He opened and closed his right hand, which was beginning to swell. "I rebuilt it the first time. I can do it again."

"It was insured, wasn't it?"

"Oh, yeah."

"That should help."

He leaned over to check her speedometer. He felt he could push the damn car faster than she was driving. "You realize you're ten miles under the speed limit."

"I'm a little rattled."

"Why? *I'm* the one who got into a fight."

She gave him an exasperated look. "Which proves there's no telling what you might come across out here!"

He chuckled. "This is a quiet area. I think you're safe for the rest of the night. And I *would* like to get home before morning," he added, just to rib her.

Her jaw dropped open. "You have no shame," she said. "Here I am, being a good citizen and helping you out, and you're criticizing the way I do it."

"Nope. I'm only suggesting you make more of an effort."

She hit the gas, and the car surged forward. "Happy now?"

"Happ*ier*."

"I aim to please."

He studied her profile. "India's a different name. You're the first India I've ever met."

"My mother loved *Gone with the Wind*. Named me after India Wilkes."

"Shouldn't it be Scarlett or something like that?"

"India was a secondary character."

"I guess I skipped that book," he joked. He'd skipped a lot of books, hardly ever shown up for class. It was surprising he'd graduated from high school. He wouldn't have, if his big brother had been willing to accept anything less. "Where does your mother live these days? She still in Oakland?"

"She died when I was eighteen."

She'd had to deal with *two* family deaths? "I'm sorry. So it's just you and your father now?"

"No, my father died before she did, but I didn't know him very well. They were divorced when I was three. He was an alcoholic, wasn't part of my life."

He could relate to her situation there. His own father had turned to alcohol. "So neither of your parents knew Charlie?"

"No, we were only together the last six years."

"Where did you meet?"

He expected her to say college. The timing would've been about right. But she didn't. "I was waiting tables at a restaurant near the hospital where he worked. He and some of the other doctors used to come in quite often."

"Doctors."

She nodded. "He was ten years older than me."

"And he was a doctor." Rod repeated that because it

wasn't good news. It confirmed that she was, indeed, way out of his league.

"A heart surgeon," she said.

Shit. Just what a guy wanted to hear when he'd never even attempted college.

"If he'd had another fifteen or twenty years, who knows what he might've accomplished," she said softly, almost reverently. "I believe he would've made a real difference in the world."

Rod knew then that it didn't matter if Charlie was six feet under. An auto body technician couldn't compare with a renowned heart surgeon, even the memory of one.

"Was it a car accident that killed him?" Rod hoped it wasn't a heart attack. That would be too ironic.

"Please. Like I said, I'd rather not talk about his death."

He didn't understand why she had to leave him wondering. She'd told him other things, like how long Charlie had been gone. Why couldn't she say it was an accident or an illness or whatever?

"I shouldn't have asked again," he said. But his curiosity couldn't be entirely unexpected. Someone dying that early was unusual.

They were silent for a moment. Then Rod spoke again. He didn't want his question about her late husband to be the end of their conversation. "Can't be easy to work on art with a child underfoot. Is that part of the reason your in-laws are keeping your daughter? To give you a chance to get started on your pottery?"

"Not really. Having her around helps fill the hole Charlie left behind. They have a daughter, but her job took her to Japan two years ago. They don't see her often."

"A family of high achievers, huh?"

"Yes. They can be a bit intimidating."

"You didn't feel you fit in?"

She hesitated. "They were fine. Anyway, for the record, I'd never choose to be without Cassia." She sent him a grim smile. "When she's gone, I hardly know what to do with myself. I can't work *all* the time."

She'd recently lost her husband, and she was new in town. He could see why she'd want her daughter to keep her company. But at least the kid had grandparents who cared about her. Rod hadn't been lucky enough to get decent parents, let alone anything more. If not for Dylan, his oldest brother, who'd raised him, he would've been put into foster care when he was in middle school.

Now that they were older and able to take care of themselves, life was easier. Rod was glad of that. He was also determined not to do anything that might make it hard again. Intrigued though he was with his new neighbor, he'd be better off moving on to other prospects.

"You've been through a lot of changes," he said. "But I'm sure things will eventually improve." That was a throwaway statement. He was backing off and letting her have her secrets and her space. Considering what his mother had done and how it had affected his whole family, he had no desire to get involved with an emotionally inaccessible woman. He wasn't about to try to break down what he considered a locked door.

When India glanced over, he could tell she'd noticed the change in his tone. That glance was filled with uncertainty, and maybe a tinge of regret. She understood that he'd disengaged; he could see it in her face. It surprised him that she didn't seem completely convinced she wanted that. But what else could he do? *She* was the one who'd thrown up barriers.

"You're quiet," she said at length.

Now that he no longer had any romantic interest to distract him from his injuries, he discovered that his leg, his mouth, his hands—almost every part of his body— hurt like hell. He needed to take a shower, swallow some pain pills and fall into bed. "It's late. I'm not in the best shape. And there's not much to say."

"I may not be open to a relationship. I'm still in love with Charlie. I hope we can be friends, though."

That was direct, but he'd been direct with her. He preferred open communication, didn't see any reason to play games. "Of course."

"I'm sincere. I could use a friend."

He shrugged. "Sure, we'll be friends *and* neighbors."

That must've sounded trite, because she frowned, apparently not pleased by his response.

Bed, he told himself. He needed sleep. This woman was sending him mixed signals. She said she was still in love with her late husband and yet she kept looking at him as if…well, as if she liked what she saw. How was he supposed to react to that if she wouldn't give him a chance?

As soon as she pulled into his drive, he reached for the door handle.

"Rod?"

When he looked back, she seemed about to speak.

"Yes?" he prompted.

She pressed her thumbnails into the padded steering wheel. "Maybe if…if you're not too tired, you should come over to my place."

"Right now?"

When she raised her eyes, she seemed nervous—but she nodded.

"What for?" he asked.

She kept making those indentations in her steering

wheel. "Well, I've got some salve and bandages. I could help get the dirt and gravel out of your leg."

Except she'd just told him she wasn't interested. What the hell? "It's okay, I'll manage."

She caught his arm. "You could—" her voice fell to a whisper "—shower at my place."

He stared down at her pale hand against his darker skin. "I thought you didn't want to be with me."

Releasing his arm, she looked away. "I never said that."

"You shut me down. Immediately. I let you know I was interested, that I wanted to take you out, and got a no."

She went back to making those marks in the steering wheel. "Because I'm not available for a relationship. I think it's important to be honest about that up front."

"So what's this about?" He peered at her a little more closely. *"Sex?"*

Her nails dug deeper. "No! I just thought…maybe we could get to know each other a little better."

"Then this *isn't* about sex. You want me to shower at your place…as a friend? For company or something?"

"Sort of. I guess we could…talk."

They'd been talking. He didn't believe that was what she had in mind. But whatever she was asking for wasn't easy for her to put into words. "You're missing your husband," he ventured.

"Of course."

"The way he touched you."

She briefly closed her eyes. "Yes."

"And you haven't been with anyone since."

Her face flushed. If he could see her cheeks in the light, he suspected they'd match her hair. "Right."

He felt his breath seep out, hadn't even known he was holding it. "Then you *do* want to fuck me."

When she blanched, he regretted stating it so baldly. But he didn't want to wind up at her house and have her bail on him. This night had been bad enough.

"It doesn't have to go that far," she said.

"You just want to make out?"

"I'm…open to ideas. I guess with Cassia gone, it felt like a good opportunity to…" Finally, she glanced up—and then she seemed to lose her train of thought because she stopped talking again.

"Be with a man," he filled in. Did *that* put it nicely enough?

She slid her bracelets up her arm, something she'd been doing the whole drive. "If…if you're interested. But you're injured and…I'm basically a stranger to you, so…I'll understand if you're not up for that kind of… *encounter*."

"I'm trying to get this straight. You won't let me take you to dinner. But you'll let me take off your clothes?"

She would no longer look at him. "I know, that sounds crazy," she said with an awkward laugh. "I'm not thinking straight. You can go."

"This back and forth is confusing," he told her. "I've been getting conflicting signals since I got in your car. So why don't you tell me exactly what you're after?"

Her eyes widened. "You liked the dress," she said helplessly, as if she couldn't frame it any more clearly than that.

He chuckled at her lame attempt. "I like what's *in* the dress, and I'm not ashamed to admit it."

She said nothing. Staring straight ahead, at his house, she nibbled at her bottom lip.

"Look at me," he said and waited for her to comply. "Are you really committed to going to bed with a man you've barely met? Have you ever done that before?"

"No. I've been with some rather...unsavory characters, but I always *knew* them before...you know."

"And that means..."

"It wouldn't be a good idea."

"That's a no," he said. "Okay. I'm glad I clarified. Because if I'd had to guess, I would've gone the other way."

He started to get out, but she caught his arm again, and this time when he looked back, she gripped her forehead with her free hand and squeezed her eyes shut. "Yes. It's a yes."

Suddenly, Rod didn't feel all the aches and pains that'd been bothering him. Opportunities like this didn't come around very often. Although there'd never been any shortage of women in his life, there'd been no one like India Sommers. She was refined, educated, classy—not the kind of girl who typically tried to pick him up.

Lowering his gaze to her lips, he leaned across the console to get a sample of what he could expect at her house. He could tell a lot about a woman by the way she kissed—and he wasn't disappointed. She wasn't too assertive or overeager, despite the fact that she was the one who'd extended the invitation. She was still struggling with her decision to do something so reckless. He could feel the tug-of-war inside her—between her idea of what was appropriate and her desire. But she was responsive in spite of that, and her mouth meshed so comfortably with his that he had no doubt he was in for a special treat.

He could use a few hours with a woman, especially a woman who kissed like this.

When her hands touched his face, and her tongue gently probed the cut on his bottom lip before she allowed him to deepen the kiss, he could sense an inherent sweetness, and that caused his excitement to skyrocket. He'd found her to be different and attractive from the start. But she'd acted so aloof when he helped her unload her Prius, Rod had decided she thought she was too good for him *and* his brothers.

He'd never expected *this*.

"That's nice," she murmured when he kept it soft.

It *was* nice. Her kiss told him she wasn't nearly as cold and unreachable as he'd assumed.

Soon his heart was pounding almost as hard as when he'd gotten into that fight. But as she relaxed and began to sink into the kiss, he could tell she was investing a great deal of emotion, as if…as if she knew him better than she did.

He pulled back to look at her, but she didn't open her eyes. He was fairly certain she didn't want to see him. She wanted to feel what he was making her feel so she could pretend he was someone else. Someone she loved and missed. Charlie.

A strange reluctance hit him, slowing his pulse. Two minutes earlier he hadn't cared that she wanted him only for his body. He'd known she wasn't inviting him over for his personality; they weren't well enough acquainted for that. But now?

His gut told him to stop. He'd been with plenty of women, knew he could give her an orgasm. But she'd experienced what it was like to feel something deeper for the man who was making her tremble. A hit-and-run, even a successful one, would only convince her that their time together had been a mistake.

Finally, she opened her eyes. "What's wrong?"

He wasn't sure he could explain the disappointment he felt, wasn't sure he should try. Since they'd barely met, it probably wouldn't make any sense.

"Are you...in pain?" she asked. "Hurting? I have ibuprofen at my house."

"That's not it." He had so much testosterone flowing through him that, once again, he could hardly feel his injuries. He wanted her; he was rock-hard. But she didn't want *him*, and that disconnect was something he'd never experienced before. His previous one-night stands had involved women who admired him and were anxious to be with him—or what they perceived him to be. Even if he couldn't count love as part of the equation, there'd been the hope of something more, a certain openness that wasn't present here. It was almost as if India had chosen him because she didn't feel he could ever be a threat to her heart. He was just a cheap substitute for the man she'd married.

"I'm sorry," he said.

"You're *sorry*?" she echoed. "What does that mean?"

"I didn't intend to get your hopes up and then disappoint you." On the contrary, that was the one thing still goading him to continue. He felt he'd made a commitment, even though he'd barely touched her.

"Is that what you're doing?" she asked.

"I guess it is," he replied.

"What'd I do? You...you don't like the way I kiss? Or my perfume reminds you of someone else? Or—"

"Nothing like that."

"Then what?"

Should he tell her that he'd figured out why she'd chosen him? That he understood she'd defined him as a "troublemaker," thanks to what she'd witnessed tonight and what Chief Bennett had said, and saw him as the perfect guy to use?

"I'd go home with you if that'd fix anything," he said and meant it. "But you'd be every bit as lonely and miserable in the morning. The guilt might make things worse."

Her troubled eyes met his. "If you're stopping for *my* sake, don't. I see it as an hour or two during which I won't have to feel what I'd otherwise feel." She pressed her lips against his, trying to engage him again. "I can take care of myself," she said when he resisted. "I'll accept responsibility."

Catching her hands, he leaned away from her. "But there's no way I can compete with the man in your mind."

She looked befuddled. "You don't need to compete. I'm not asking you to."

"That's just it. Because you've already counted me out. Why would I get involved?"

"Surely a guy like you—"

"A guy like me? You don't even know me."

"I'm guessing you've had other casual encounters."

"Of course. I'm not pretending to be a saint."

"Then…how am I different?" she asked. "I won't expect anything from you afterward. I promise. I may live next door, but I'll keep to myself."

"Maybe that's the problem." He could feel her surprise when he got out, knew she was watching as he walked to his house and went inside. He was stunned himself. Was he crazy to refuse what she'd offered him?

He knew what Grady and Mack would say. They'd think he'd lost his ever-lovin' mind. They'd all been admiring her, and she'd just invited him into her bed!

If he were a few years younger, he would've said yes

to something quick and dirty like that, he told himself. But he was thirty-one. It was time to take life more seriously, time to earn more respect. If India wanted to be with him, she'd have to give him an honest shot, not relegate him to the category of "good for a midnight ride but nothing else."

Just because he'd had so little in life for so long didn't mean he had to accept less forever—even if he was an auto body technician and not a heart surgeon.

If she closed her eyes, India could taste Rod's kiss, could easily feel the way his lips and tongue had moved with and against hers. It wasn't often that a man could kiss with such perfect pressure tempered by control. She'd just decided that she'd picked an ideal partner, one who could actually carry her away, when he'd pulled back and brought all that positive sensation to a halt.

Why had he changed his mind?

What he'd said led her to believe he wasn't satisfied with the limitations she'd imposed on their encounter. Perhaps he didn't like that she was the one dictating the terms. Or she'd ruined the challenge by offering. The men she'd been with before Charlie had liked having something to conquer. Love, or what passed for it, was a game to them. Considering what she'd learned from those early experiences, she'd played Rod entirely wrong. But she was an adult now, no longer interested in all the pretense and posturing that so often went with the single life.

Besides, she hadn't *intended* to proposition him, hadn't intended any of what had happened tonight. It'd been a desperate, spur-of-the-moment attempt to numb the dull ache that echoed through her body with every beat of her heart.

"Congratulations, you've fallen to a whole new low," she muttered to herself. She needed to get her little girl back home. Cassia was the only anchor she still had in her life. She wouldn't have made this mistake if Cassia was with her.

Getting her child back early wouldn't be easy. Charlie's parents wouldn't welcome the idea. They'd likely start a fight as soon as she mentioned it.

Tears burned her eyes as she entered her drive and parked. Then she sat there, staring at her new house. She needed to hang all the art waiting in the detached garage, make this place her home in the truest sense. But some of those pieces were so heavy they'd require a helper, which she didn't have, not unless she went to the trouble of hiring someone.

Anyway, the paintings would only remind her of Charlie, she told herself. He was the one who'd bought them for her—and she already thought of him far too often. She'd *never* get over him if she didn't do what she could to move on.

She saw a light go on next door and realized it was probably coming from Rod's room. The window that glowed in the darkness was on the second floor, and it had a small deck with stairs that led to the backyard and overlooked the river. She grabbed her purse, but just as she reached for the door latch, he confirmed that it was his room by coming out onto that deck and looking down at her car.

She wished she'd hurried inside while she'd had the chance to do it without being observed. How could she be so desperate as to proposition her new neighbor?

He must've thought she was pathetic…

Blinking back the tears that'd threatened a moment

before—the situation would only get worse if he believed she was crying over his rejection—she forced herself to climb out of the car. She wanted to offer him an apology for being so forward, and to promise she'd never approach him like that again. But he was too far away to hear her, and she wasn't about to walk any closer.

Better to prove it, anyway.

So she acted as though she didn't notice him standing there and said nothing.

Once she was safely inside, she breathed a sigh of relief, locked the door and went to lie on Cassia's bed, where she could hug one of her daughter's stuffed animals while she waited for morning. Although she knew she wouldn't be able to sleep for some time—she'd had trouble getting a solid eight hours ever since *that* night—she didn't bother turning on any lights. She just stared at the moonbeams filtering through the window.

3

The next morning Mack walked into the kitchen. "What happened last night?" he asked.

Rod glanced up from his cereal bowl. He wasn't feeling any better for having slept. As a matter of fact, he was worse. He wasn't bleeding anymore and some of the scrapes he'd sustained when he fell from his bike were starting to scab over, but every muscle was sore. He could hardly move without wincing. He was beginning to wonder if he should've listened to Chief Bennett and gone to the hospital—not for his leg but for his hand. It was almost twice its normal size and hurt whenever he tried to use it.

"Last night was freaking crazy," he said. And Mack didn't know it, but the fight wasn't the only crazy part. Rod felt terrible about what'd taken place between him and India. He should've gone to her place. So what if she wanted to pretend he was her dead husband? It wasn't her intention to be hurtful or selfish; she was just looking for an escape from the pain. He'd had low moments like that in his life, hadn't he? When he'd needed to be with someone?

Besides, there were worse tasks than giving a woman a little pleasure and comfort...

"Grady woke me up, said you'd been in a fight with the prick who was giving Natasha so much trouble." Mack walked over to the cupboard to grab himself a bowl. "When I opened my eyes this morning, I thought maybe it was a bad dream. But now that I see you..."

Rod used his left hand to bring the spoon to his mouth. "I wish it *were* a dream."

"Tell me the other guy looks worse."

"He should. He's the one who's in the hospital."

"Good for you," Mack said. "I don't feel the least bit sorry for him. Sounds like he's where he deserves to be."

Rod rested his elbows on the table. "Whether he deserved it or not, I wasn't trying to hurt him *that* bad. He can't fight worth shit, but he doesn't seem to understand his own limitations. Every time I'd step back, thinking he'd had enough, he'd take another swing at me."

"Stubborn son of a bitch," Mack grumbled. "So how'd it end? Did someone call the police or what?"

"*I* called. The fight didn't happen outside the bar. It happened on the road when I was on my way home. And he needed an ambulance."

Mack whistled. "Which officer came out? Hope it was Howton. Far as cops go, Howton's not too bad."

"None other than Chief Bennett. Just my luck, right?"

"He's not a big fan of yours, not since your ex-girlfriend filed that complaint claiming you beat her."

Rod grimaced at the reminder. "I never touched Melody." He'd never even been *tempted* to strike a woman, but if he ever did, he wouldn't have the police to fear as much as his older brother. Dylan would beat him to within an inch of his life—and Dylan was one of the few people who could do it. "She was pissed off that I was calling it quits and was trying to get back at me."

"I know that, and you know that. But once this kind of accusation's been launched, the dude never gets the benefit of the doubt. There'll always be people who wonder, and I think Bennett's one of your skeptics."

Rod thought so, too. What Melody had done still enraged him. It was *so* unfair. But the more he protested, the guiltier he looked. He'd had to let it go. He could only hope that someday she'd come forward and tell the truth.

Maybe when she was over him. Until then…

"Bennett's not a big fan of any of ours," Rod said as he shoveled another spoonful of cereal into his mouth. "But at least he's not as bad as the former chief."

"You would've gone to jail if Stacy was still in charge," Mack agreed. "He loved to yank Dylan's chain, and he knew he could do that by harassing one of us." He poured himself some of the Wheaties Rod had on the table. "Does Natasha know you wound up fighting the guy who kept coming on to her?"

"Not unless Grady woke her, too. Why?"

"She won't be happy about it. You heard her last night. She thinks she can fight her own battles."

"Yeah, well, it got personal when he crashed into my bike."

"I'm sure Grady didn't wake her. He only came into my room to ask me to go with him, in case you weren't in any shape to help load the bike."

"Then we won't mention it," Rod said, but he knew there'd be no keeping it from her. Not only did she live with them, when she wasn't in school she also worked at the shop, doing the bookkeeping and other administrative tasks. She'd see his scrapes and bruises and know *something* was up.

"So what now?" Mack asked. "What're the chances this incident will just…go away?"

Rod dropped his spoon in his empty bowl. "Not very good. If that guy—Liam Whatever—decides to press charges, it could be a problem."

Mack scooped up a spoonful of cereal. "He started it. But that might not matter. You've been in too many fights to get the benefit of any doubt."

Rod didn't appreciate the candor. "You've been in as many fights as I have, little brother."

Mack didn't argue. He grinned, completely unrepentant. "Have you heard if the jerk's going to be okay?"

"Haven't called the hospital yet."

"He had no business trying to cop a feel off a nineteen-year-old girl."

That was true. She'd asked him to leave her alone several times. He wouldn't, which was why they'd stepped in. But talking about Natasha always brought up something Rod didn't like. He sometimes got the impression that Mack cared a little *too* much about their stepsister's love life. Or, rather, he cared in the wrong way. Natasha was nothing like her insufferable mother. Rod was willing to look out for her as a big brother should, or he wouldn't have stood up for her last night. But Mack was the family pet. Surely there was someone else out there, someone better, as much as Rod hated to use that term, for his kid brother. Natasha was basically a decent person, but anyone who'd been raised by Anya would have issues, and to say she could be prickly was an understatement.

Fortunately, Natasha was heading off to Utah to attend college in the fall, so they only had to get through the summer. With any luck, Mack would meet another new girlfriend—he went through quite a few—while she was away, and Rod's concerns and suspicions wouldn't amount to anything. Then, if their father ever divorced the freeloading drug addict he'd married, they'd all be done with Anya.

"I need to go out and find my phone," he said.

"I could help with that, if you want," Mack volunteered.

Rod gave him a wry smile. "Nice try, but I think you'll be more useful at the shop. We're always busy on Saturdays. I'll get there as soon as I can."

Mack scowled. "Why bother? You can't do anything with a broken hand."

"It's not broken," Rod argued and hoped to God that was true.

The creak of footsteps told them someone was coming down the hall. Rod expected it to be Grady. Unless there was some reason not to, they usually drove to the shop together.

But it wasn't their brother. It was Natasha, still sporting the X on the back of her hand that told the bartenders she was underage and couldn't be served last night. Her bleached blond hair was spiked and she wore a nose ring, but no one could deny she was attractive in spite of everything she did to hide her natural beauty. Rod could see how Mack might like her. A lot of guys did. Despite her wild hair and her piercings and tattoos, she had a certain…raw sex appeal. But that didn't change the many reasons it'd be stupid to get romantically involved with her.

"Thought I heard you." Her gaze settled on Mack first. It had a tendency to do that—and to return to him again and again. When she finally shifted her attention to Rod, she gasped. "What the fuck happened to your face?"

He walked over to put his bowl in the sink. "Watch

your language. We've talked about that before. You're a girl, not a truck driver."

"Oh, stop with the misogynistic bullshit. I'm of age. I'm not just a girl anymore, and I'll say exactly what I want," she told him. "Fuck, fuck, fuck. So what happened?"

He rolled his eyes. "You're hopeless."

"Does that mean you're not going to tell me?"

"Grady'll have to explain. I gotta run."

"Why can't Mack?" she asked.

Rod took Mack's bowl and dumped it into the sink.

"Hey!" Mack cried. "I wasn't finished!"

"You can eat later," Rod said, messing up Mack's hair just to piss him off. "Let's go."

Mack knocked his hand away, then halfheartedly tried to comb his hair back into place with his fingers. "Go where?"

"You told me you'd help me find my phone, remember?"

Rod thought Mack might give away the fact that they'd already decided he should go to the shop and *not* help find the phone, but he didn't. He didn't speak until he'd passed Rod's smashed bike, which Donald and Sam had set to one side of the driveway, and climbed into Rod's truck. "First you don't want me to go. Now you do. What's up?" he asked once Rod had started the engine.

Should he try to explain? Probably not. If he brought it up, his brother would only deny feeling any attraction to their stepsister. To Mack's credit, he did his best to avoid her. Rod had noticed the effort he put into that. But…as hard as his brother was fighting whatever he felt, there was still a kind of tangible energy whenever he and Natasha were in the same room. "You've never touched Natasha, have you?" he asked.

Mack's eyebrows slammed together. "What the hell are you talking about? Touched her in what way?"

"You know what way."

"Unless you're looking for a better fight than you got last night, don't ever ask me that again," he snapped, instantly furious. "That's too screwed up for words."

"I know she's attractive, but…she's off-limits." They weren't related by blood, and they hadn't grown up together, so Rod could see where the confusion might come in. Two people from different families meeting after adolescence because their parents had married through some prison website could cloud the "related" issue. But Rod couldn't stand the thought of his brother being tied to someone who'd make Anya a permanent part of their lives. There were too many other women out there who didn't have an addict for a mother, didn't bear the stigma of ever having been called their *sister*—and didn't have the emotional problems Natasha did.

"You think I'd ever be able to forget that?" Mack said.

Rod felt like shit for even asking. He should've gone with his first instinct and kept his mouth shut. "No, of course not," he replied and peeled out of the drive.

When India heard the sound of an engine, she peered through her plantation shutters. She knew it had to be one or more of the Amos brothers. Other than a handful of houses half a mile down the road, they were her only neighbors. She liked the countryside, with its wide-open spaces. That was why she'd chosen this location.

Sure enough, someone was leaving in a big blue truck.

She recognized Rod immediately. He was in the driver's seat, which was closest to her as the vehicle rolled by. She was fairly certain he had Mack or Grady with him, but it was difficult to see. The passenger didn't matter, anyway. Knowing that Rod wouldn't be around for a while eased her anxiety. She hadn't *begun* to get over her embarrassment about what she'd done last night. The fact that they could bump into each other if she so much as went out to weed the front flower bed made her reluctant to leave the house.

God, what had she been thinking?

Rod had to be scratching his head, too, wondering what kind of woman had moved in next door. The further she got from that moment, the more horrified she became. It bothered her so much that, when she couldn't sleep last night, she'd gotten up and baked him some cookies. She had a special snickerdoodle recipe that had been her mother's. Besides a few pieces of jewelry, some photo albums and a handmade sweater, that recipe was about all her mother had left behind. Charlie would often take platefuls of her snickerdoodles to the other doctors and nurses at the hospital, so she thought Rod might like them, too.

In any case, they were her peace offering. She'd just relocated, planned on starting over. She didn't want the first person she'd met in Whiskey Creek to hold a terrible opinion of her. She and Rod could be neighborly even if they weren't exactly friends, couldn't they?

As she watched his taillights disappear around the bend, she breathed a sigh of relief. Now she had the chance to make her delivery when he wasn't home, which was the opportunity she'd been looking for—if only she could figure out what to say on the accompanying note and get it over there before he got back. She didn't want to write anything that might make him think this was another invitation. That was why she'd driven to the

Gas-N-Go early this morning, before the closest super-market was open, to buy a package of paper plates—so she wouldn't have to put the cookies on a dish he'd feel obliged to return. She was merely acknowledging that she'd screwed up and was promising it wouldn't happen again. She preferred to leave it at that.

She imagined seeing him in the future, out in the yard or on the road, and giving him a polite wave. She wasn't sure they could get to a polite wave from "Will you take me to bed?" Especially with just a plateful of cookies. But she'd already made them. She figured it was worth a try.

Dear Rod, she wrote. Then she made a face at the words. "Dear" sounded both too familiar and old-fashioned. Unfortunately, "Rod" without the "Dear" didn't seem right, either.

After throwing that note away, she started over and skipped the salutation completely:

> *I wasn't myself last night. I'm sorry. Please accept these cookies as my apology and know I will never cross that line again.*
> *Sincerely,*
> *Your neighbor—who is cringing at her behavior but promises she's not as bad as you must think.*

She didn't allow herself to analyze what she'd written or change it again. She slipped the card into its envelope, grabbed the cookies and a roll of tape and hurried over to the stairs that led up to the deck outside his bedroom. She couldn't go to the front door and ring the bell, or his brothers would know she was leaving him something. If he had to explain, she was afraid of what he might say.

"With any luck, he'll forgive me, and we'll just go on

as if it never happened," she mumbled and put the foil-covered plate on the railing.

As she searched for a place to tape the note, she saw that he hadn't closed his door all the way. He didn't seem to take much care when it came to protecting his personal property, but she could understand why he might not be too concerned. There wasn't a lot of crime in Whiskey Creek; that was one of the reasons she'd moved there. Also, for the most part, everyone knew everyone else, which would make a man like Rod an unlikely victim.

He was an idiot to pick a fight with Rod Amos. That was what one of the paramedics had said.

Since she had such easy access to his room, India wished she could put the cookies on his bed or dresser, so she wouldn't have to worry about ants, rodents or other animals finding them before he did. But entering his house wasn't a serious consideration until she heard someone outside, around the front.

"You'll have to drive over later," a male voice called out. "I'm late as it is."

Damn! She was afraid she was about to be spotted...

"It won't take me long to shower," a female voice responded. "Rod's hand is jacked up. Mack texted me that he doesn't think Rod'll be able to work, but Mack will be at the shop in an hour or so."

"We'll manage. See you there," came the response.

An engine started. India had to do *something* or whoever was driving that car would see her the moment he backed up, and she definitely didn't want to be caught lurking outside Rod's door.

Snatching up her cookies, she stepped into the room.

"Hey, keep it down!" someone shouted, this time from

inside the house instead of at the door. "What do you think this is? I'm trying to sleep!"

That was a woman, too, but not the woman India had already heard, a fact that became more apparent when the first woman snapped an equally irritated response. "Yeah, well, *some* of us have to work."

Half expecting an argument to flare up, India held her breath. Neither woman seemed to be in a good mood. But nothing else happened. The younger one must've gotten in the shower so she could go to work, because everything fell silent.

"Thank goodness," India whispered. She thought she could leave now, but she couldn't help taking a look at Rod's room while she was there.

He had a big bed, which he hadn't made. His torn and bloody clothes from last night lay on the floor, along with some cleats and a football. Other than that, the place was clean. It was even sort of decorated, which came as a surprise. Twenty or more baseball caps lined the dresser, and a collection of grilles and hubcaps from old cars hung all over the walls.

India was tempted to throw away the clothes he'd left—they couldn't be saved—and straighten the bedding. She supposed it was the mother in her...

Actually, if she was being honest, it had nothing to do with the mother in her. She liked him enough to want to touch the things that were most personal to him...

A door opening and shutting somewhere else in the house reminded her that she needed to get out.

She set her cookies on the railing, where she'd put them before, taped the note beside the foil-covered plate and hurried down the steps and across the lawn.

Once she reached her screened-in porch, she knew

she was safe. But then she turned to give the cookies and note a final glance and realized she'd left his door open a little wider than she'd found it. She hated that he might guess she'd invaded his private space—especially since she had—but she wasn't going over to correct it. In the future, she planned to keep her distance from Rod Amos and anything or anyone associated with him.

Now she needed to figure out a way to approach her in-laws about getting her daughter home, so she could bring some normalcy back into her life, or the loneliness that dogged her every step would completely destroy her.

Before she could commit herself to that course of action, however, she had to call the detective who was handling her late husband's case.

4

"Are you going to get it x-rayed?" Dylan asked, his voice sounding a bit tinny through Bluetooth.

Rod glanced at his swollen hand. He'd been driving with his left; it hurt too much to use his right. But at least he'd found his phone, way off, under a bush. The fact that it had traveled so far from the point of impact showed how hard he'd come down, which made him angry all over again. "I think I'll give it a few days. See how it feels."

Mack frowned at him from the passenger seat. He, too, had been telling Rod to stop by the hospital—and now that Dylan was starting in on him, Rod wasn't sure he'd be able to refuse. He loved and respected his oldest brother more than anyone in the world. Dylan was more of a father to him than their own father had ever been.

"I'd rather you got to a doctor right away," Dylan said.

Mack, who could hear everything, since Rod's Bluetooth worked as a speakerphone, smirked at him. He knew how hard it was to say no to Dylan. They all had the same problem—except maybe Aaron. Although Aaron and Dylan got along now, they'd fought like crazy over the years, probably because they were closest in age and too damn much alike.

"What will it hurt to wait?" Rod asked.

"I need you at the shop," Dylan replied. "If it's broken, let's get it fixed so you can use it as soon as possible."

Rod rolled his eyes. "Fine."

When Mack laughed to see him crumble so easily, Rod sent his younger brother a look that said he'd better not provoke him any further, and Mack, of course, ignored that and slugged Rod in the arm.

"Want me to meet you over there?" That came from Dylan before Rod could slug Mack in return, an interruption that was well-timed. Since he couldn't use his right hand, it would've been too awkward to reach across his body with his left.

"You kidding?" Rod said. "It's Saturday. You're needed at the shop. Besides, I'm a big boy. I can handle seeing a doctor on my own. I'll drop Mack off first, so you'll at least have his help."

"Thanks."

"I'll check on Liam while I'm at the hospital," Rod went on. "See how bad off he is." As angry as he was that this guy wouldn't leave Natasha alone at the bar, not to mention everything the bastard had done afterward, Rod didn't want to be responsible for seriously injuring anyone. It wasn't as if he lived for violence. He also didn't want this incident to escalate. He knew *he'd* probably get the worst of any repercussions. Although Liam had started the fight, he'd been hurt worse, so it meant Rod looked like the bad guy.

"No need," Dylan said. "I've already called over there. Liam Crockett has a broken jaw, a broken nose and a concussion."

"Damn!" Mack said. "You busted him up good."

"What'd you do?" Dylan asked. "Slam his head into the pavement?"

Rod wasn't even sure. It'd all happened so fast—and when someone pushed him that far, he fought to win. "I honestly don't remember. After I went flying from my bike, I got up, saw him charging toward me and... unleashed. But it wouldn't have been like that if he hadn't asked for it."

"Might be a few days before we find out what he has to say," Dylan informed him. "I talked to Chief Bennett this morning, too. Called him as soon as Grady filled me in. He's not even going to take Liam's statement until the guy gets out of the hospital."

"When will that be?" Rod asked.

"Tuesday or Wednesday," Dylan replied. "At least, that's what his sister told me, who's with him."

Rod scratched his neck. "Stupid bastard shouldn't have run me off the road."

"I doubt he'll ever make that mistake again," Dylan said wryly. "Call me after your X-ray."

Dylan had his own son to worry about these days. Little Kellan was nearly eighteen months old. Dylan doted on him, but Rod figured he'd never stop taking care of his brothers, too. Their father was out of prison and living at the house with his wife and her daughter, yet J.T. hadn't replaced Dylan. Dylan had been there for them too many years to suddenly stop playing that role.

Rod considered it a blessing that Dylan retained some interest in them. Their father was more of a liability than an asset, even now.

"Okay," Rod said grudgingly. "But it might be a while before you hear from me. You know how long the hospital takes."

"Cheyenne can bring Kellan over and sit with you, if you like," Dylan offered.

"Kellan doesn't need to be in a hospital waiting room," Rod said.

"They can keep you company, help you pass the time."

Mack cut in, raising his voice so Dylan could hear. "Hey, Dyl, I can always send some toy trucks with Rod, if you think that'll make the wait any easier."

Rod shot Mack another warning glance for being such a smart-ass but spoke to Dylan. "You're getting soft in your old age, big brother. You know that? You're treating us more like little girls every day."

"Just get yourself back to work," Dylan snapped.

"That's better," Rod teased and hung up.

"So you'll go to the hospital if Dylan asks you to but not if I do?"

"I'd walk through fire if Dylan asked me to, and so would you," he replied. As far as Rod was concerned, Dylan had earned it.

India had tried to reach Detective Flores three times and received his voice mail every time. She wanted to talk to him. But when she saw his number flash across her screen, she drew a deep breath. There was so much she needed him to say, so much he never seemed able to say. Her disappointment in the criminal justice system and the lack of information and closure she received from the police could be crippling. Sometimes it took days to recover.

"India, Detective Flores," he said when she answered. "How are you?"

He always sounded so warm and friendly. But she didn't trust the encouragement and hope his tone offered.

His voice had the same inflection the day he'd told her that the crime scene analysts hadn't found any of Sebastian's DNA in her house—and on the day he'd told her that Sebastian's wife, despite the way he'd treated her, was providing him with an alibi.

"I'm good. Better." To a point, that was true. She had some bright moments, usually when she was working or feeling grateful to still have her daughter in her life. At other times the memories flooded back or she missed Charlie so much she could scarcely breathe. Then the questions would start. Could she have saved him if she'd called 911? Or would Sebastian have shot her, like he'd said he would?

"I've moved to Whiskey Creek and set up my pottery workshop in a lovely screened-in porch overlooking a small river," she told him. "So that's nice."

"Sounds like you'll be able to open your studio soon."

"I hope so—when I find the right spot."

"I can't tell you how happy I am to hear that you're moving on."

She cringed as she thought of the mistake she'd made with Rod Amos last night. Was that a sign that she was making progress—or backsliding? Her behavior would shock Detective Flores; it would shock anyone who knew the person she'd become once she'd managed to gain some self-esteem and change her life, and that included Charlie's parents. "Thanks. How are you?"

"Busy, as usual. My wife and kids are actually at Disneyland. I was supposed to go, too, but something came up here at work. With any luck, I'll be joining them tomorrow."

"You work hard, and that's a blessing to every single person attached to the cases you handle."

If only he could do more… As kind as he was, she hated to think that, but it was the truth. She'd seen firsthand how difficult it could be to hold anyone accountable—even when that person had committed a horrendous crime and she had a diligent detective investigating the matter.

"I appreciate that," he said. "I'm guessing you called to see about Sebastian's new trial."

"Yes." She wanted to know when it would be taking place, although she wasn't sure she'd attend the whole thing. The first trial had dominated her life after Charlie died, what with waiting and wondering and preparing—and then testifying and listening to everyone else testify, including the infuriating witnesses called by the defense.

She'd have to testify again, of course. There was no way to avoid that; she didn't even want to. She had to do her part, for Charlie's sake. But she didn't have to sit in court day in and day out and see all those gruesome photographs of the man she loved. The morning the first trial ended in a hung jury had been almost as painful as the night Charlie was shot.

The prospect of going through it all again was too daunting to consider.

That didn't mean she wouldn't keep abreast of what was happening, however. Only once she knew Sebastian Young was back in prison—this time for the rest of his life—would she feel entirely safe.

"Yes. When's the new trial? Have you heard?"

Once she had the date, she'd have a legitimate reason to call her in-laws, and then she could approach them about having Cassia come home before July. India had escaped San Francisco and all the people and places that reminded her of Charlie. She had fresh scenery and the promise of reestablishing her life—but now she was too alone. She thought that was the reason she was flailing around, grabbing on to strangers, like Rod Amos, who had no reason to care that she was drowning in a sea of loss and regret.

"The district attorney called me a couple of days ago," Flores said.

She curled her fingernails into her palms. She could sense that, once again, she was about to be disappointed. "And…"

"It's not good news."

"Don't tell me the DA has changed his mind!"

"I'm afraid so. He doesn't want to try Sebastian again for fear the state will lose. He's decided to wait until we can gather more evidence."

Unable to continue standing, India sank into a chair. "What does that mean?"

"It means we'll keep at it—and when we have more, we'll bring him back to trial."

"But that isn't a certainty."

He hesitated. "No."

"Then…*you're letting him go.*"

"We *had* to release him, India. We couldn't hold him once we dropped the charges."

"*He's out?* And you didn't tell me?"

"I've been meaning to, but…I knew how heartbreaking this would be for you."

"It's more than heartbreaking! He could find me again, Detective Flores. And what about Cassia? He knows she's the reason I wouldn't go with him when he tried to drag me off that night. Next time he won't take the chance. He'll *kill* her."

"I understand the fear and pain you must feel," he responded. "But please try to understand our dilemma. If we go back to trial and Sebastian gets off, we can't try him again. We've discussed it at great length. After what happened with the last jury, we feel it would be smarter to wait and see if we can build a stronger case."

India felt as if she'd been shot herself. As terrible as the past eleven months had been, as slowly as justice seemed to crawl, she'd still had faith that Sebastian would be convicted eventually. How could he not? She'd *seen* him shoot Charlie. There was no confusion in her mind about who was responsible or how it had happened.

She dropped her head in her hand. "What are the chances that you'll find some new piece of evidence? They've got to be slim, at best. That means he might never have to answer for what he's done."

A long silence ensued. Finally, Detective Flores cleared his throat. "I hope that's not the case," he said. "And we have to hang on to that hope. It's the only way to keep our sanity in the face of such a horrendous act. A lot of things could change, India. This isn't over."

But he hadn't been able to deliver on *anything*. How could she trust what he told her? "You won't get any more evidence from the house," she said. "You went through it and released it. The place has been sold. You already subpoenaed Sebastian's cell phone records. You searched his house and his car and didn't get what you need. What could you possibly come across in the future that might strengthen the case?"

"Maybe we'll receive a tip from a neighbor who hasn't come forward yet, or someone will turn in the gun. It's even possible his wife will leave him. If she does, she could change her story. I've seen that happen a number of times. If she'll admit he went out that night, that they weren't together, we might have what we need to get a conviction."

"Sebastian shot Charlie!" India insisted. *"I was there."*

"I believe you. However, your background...the mistakes you made in your youth..."

He let his words trail off. She could tell he didn't want to come right out and say it, but the defense had assassinated her character. They'd painted her as a woman who couldn't be trusted, someone who'd managed to get her hooks into Charlie, then killed him for his money and his life insurance.

Thinking about all the things that'd surfaced while she was on the witness stand made her sick—especially since her in-laws had been in the courtroom, staring up at her. She'd never forget the expression on her mother-in-law's face when the defense claimed that Charlie's wife was the person who had the most to gain from his death.

"I had very little parental support growing up," she said. "My mother meant well, but she had to work two jobs just to keep a roof over our heads. And my father was an alcoholic who stepped out of a bar when I was seven and was struck by a car. I was wild in my teens and early twenties. I hooked up with the wrong crowd. I dated the wrong men. But I put all of that behind me once I met Charlie and realized what I really wanted out of life."

"I understand. People change. Still, your past doesn't look good on paper. You were once an 'old lady' to a man in a biker gang—and drove the getaway car when Sebastian robbed a liquor store."

"Sebastian didn't tell me he was going to rob that store! I was waiting for him to pick up a pack of cigarettes!"

"Money is motive."

Tears began to roll down her face and drip into her lap. "So is obsession. Sebastian was obsessed with me!"

"I get that," he agreed. "But it isn't motive we need so much as evidence."

Charlie was dead, and yet Sebastian was free to go anywhere he wanted. How had it come to this? "What if Sebastian somehow finds out where I live?" she asked. "He could turn up at my house again."

"I wish we could keep him behind bars," the detective replied, "but we can't."

She was glad Flores didn't point out that *she* was the one who'd given Sebastian her address the night Charlie was shot. She'd felt sorry for him, wanted to help an old friend get into rehab. She'd never dreamed Sebastian would read more into her actions, that he'd start trying to reconcile with her. *I'll never be happy without you*, he'd said that night.

So he'd made it impossible for *her* to be happy...

"Have you told the Sommerses?" she asked dully.

"Not yet. I've been trying to figure out how to break the news to both of you. I knew how it would make you feel."

She felt there was no justice in the world. That was how it made her feel. Then there was the helplessness. What now? How would she defend herself—or Cassia—from Sebastian if he tracked her down?

"I doubt he'll bother you," the detective was saying. "He'd be crazy to risk his freedom again."

"You mean since he's gotten off once," she said. "Criminals do that all the time. They're given a second chance, and then they reoffend, right?"

"If I were you, I'd get a security system. And keep an eye out. But try not to let this ruin your peace of mind."

She had to laugh. Could he be serious? She'd get a security system, but that wouldn't stop Sebastian from getting to her if he was determined enough. All he'd have to do was follow her to Cassia's preschool or the store, where she'd be defenseless.

"India?" Detective Flores said when she didn't respond.

She couldn't answer him. What was there to say? They'd let Sebastian go, and now he'd come looking for her. She'd testified against him. In his world, there was no greater sin, no greater betrayal.

"When?" she said as she wiped her cheeks.

"When…what?" the detective asked.

"When did you release him?"

There was another long moment of silence. Then he said, "Yesterday."

Now she didn't want Cassia to come home, not when the child would be so much safer with her grandparents.

That meant Sebastian hadn't cost her only Charlie; he'd cost her Cassia, as well.

5

Rod cursed as he stared down at his new cast. The doctor had indicated that the worst of his injuries hadn't occurred during the fight. He'd busted his hand trying to break his fall from the bike, but hitting Liam after had led to a second fracture—a stress fracture. The doctor couldn't believe he'd been capable of using his fists, although Rod didn't remember feeling he'd had any choice. When Liam came running back to him, he'd assumed he *had* to get up and defend himself. He wasn't about to let Crockett, or anyone else for that matter, beat his ass.

So now he was looking at six weeks without the use of his right hand. He knew the routine, had been through it before—with a broken ankle from a waterskiing accident, a broken left wrist from when he'd been hit by a wild baseball pitch and a broken transverse process, one of the small bones coming off his spine, from when he'd rolled his four-wheeler.

Fortunately, his leg wasn't broken, too. It just felt like it.

I could help get the dirt and gravel out of your leg...

As Rod passed India's house on the way home, he remembered that offer and wished he'd taken her up on it. Maybe then he'd be able to go back there and get lost in her all over again. He was eager for any distraction absorbing enough to take his mind off his aches and pains—as well as the ominous news he'd received a few minutes earlier, when Chief Bennett had called to warn him that Liam Crockett's sister was urging her brother to press charges.

If they sued for medical expenses, he'd have another fight on his hands, and this wouldn't be physical, so he wasn't as likely to win. His reputation—and the reputation of his family—would work against him, which was doubly unfair, since he hadn't done even half the shit he'd been accused of doing.

Once he'd parked in his drive, his phone buzzed. He'd received a message from Cheyenne, Dylan's wife. She was planning to bring him dinner tonight. He liked it when she cooked. She tried to mother them the way Dylan fathered them. But she wasn't coming until six, and it was only two. Rod supposed that if he couldn't spend the afternoon with India, he should try to get some work done. Dylan had sent him home, wouldn't let him stay at the shop, but that didn't mean he couldn't mow the yard. At least he'd have something to show for the day.

He went inside to change into a pair of basketball shorts, which wouldn't be as hot as his jeans. But then he noticed his laptop sitting on the coffee table and decided to take a minute to see if he could learn a few details about his new neighbor. He was more than a little curious, especially after last night.

Groaning as he eased into a recliner, he logged on to the internet. When he typed the name "Dr. Charlie Sommers" into a search engine, he thought he'd be lucky to find a brief obituary that would tell him how India's husband had died.

But he got a lot more than that. Link after link filled the screen.

> *Renowned Heart Surgeon Shot in Bed*
> *Wife Knew Gunman Who Killed Husband*
> *Dr. Sommers's Parents Hire PI*
> *Secret Affair or Spurned Lover?*
> *Sebastian Young Charged in Sommers's Murder*
> *Doctor's Wife Claims Innocence*
> *Wife's Ex-Boyfriend Murders Heart Surgeon?*
> *Surgeon's Murder Trial Ends in Hung Jury*

"Holy shit," Rod muttered as he read the accompanying articles. No wonder India didn't talk about how her husband had died. Her ex-boyfriend had broken in late at night and gunned him down while they were both sleeping and their young daughter was in the other room. According to one journalist, who'd reported on the trial, India stated under oath that she'd awakened to the sound of her ex-boyfriend's voice demanding Charlie get out of bed. When she realized it wasn't a nightmare and managed to open her eyes, she saw Sebastian Young standing at the foot of the bed, holding a gun.

Charlie, disoriented and barely awake, had reached for his cell—and was shot. The gunman then threatened to kill India's daughter if India didn't pack a bag and leave with him. She complied as far as gathering her things but pleaded and argued with him for the next few hours. It wasn't until the housekeeper arrived the following morning, and the carpet cleaners rang the bell shortly after, that Sebastian dragged India out the back door. India claimed that he demanded she leave her child, which she wouldn't do. She thought he was about to shoot her when the housekeeper stumbled on the bloody mess in the bedroom and started to scream. Fortunately, Sebastian didn't pull the trigger. At that point, he panicked and ran.

What a story! Rod rubbed his chin as he searched through even more links. The trial had lasted for three weeks but ended in a hung jury. Some questioned whether India could've been involved, whether she might've killed her husband and blamed Sebastian, or manipulated Sebastian into killing her husband for her. Although there'd never been any charges filed against her, the suspicion lingered, which became more and more apparent as he continued to read.

Rod hoped to learn the DA's decision on whether to try Young again, but he couldn't find any word of it. The most recent articles were over a month old.

What had happened since? Was this Sebastian still in jail, awaiting a new trial? Or had he been released? And if he'd been released, where the hell was he? Was India worried that he might come back? Was that the reason her in-laws had her daughter?

She must have been severely traumatized. Not only had she lost her husband, she'd been villainized by the press and her detractors, too. "It's always the spouse," one neighbor had said.

At first, no surprise, the police had focused on India. The money she stood to receive, and the value of Charlie's life insurance policy, had given her more than a million reasons to get rid of him. There was even some mention of the type of people she'd associated with before her marriage, as if the friends she'd once had proved that she wasn't a good person.

They weren't the sort Rod would've expected. One had belonged to an outlaw biker gang. She'd been with him for about a year—until he tried to run her over with his truck and she had to get a restraining order against him. Then she'd gotten involved with Sebastian, who'd robbed a store and spent four years in prison for it. Everyone pointed to that as proof that she must've known he was dangerous, that she must've wanted to get back with him when he was released from prison.

But robbery wasn't murder. Sebastian had threatened the liquor-store clerk by saying he had a gun in his pocket; he hadn't really had one. Nobody had been hurt, and he'd served his sentence for that crime. Those were important distinctions, and yet her detractors hadn't cut her any slack. What the detective on Charlie's case had to say was important, too. He told one reporter that she'd never written Sebastian or visited him, not after she met Charlie. There were no texts between them that included anything questionable or suggestive and only a few calls, which was consistent with her story that she'd merely been trying to help him. Also, Sebastian had been out of prison for a year before he even reached out, and he did that on Facebook, so they had proof of first contact.

Rod didn't believe India had anything to do with Charlie's murder, and the police must not have found any evidence to the contrary because they'd dismissed her as a suspect early on. Plenty of people continued to doubt her, though. Rod came across several articles that pointed a finger at her. But he understood what it was like to be judged on the basis of the past. There was no getting rid of the stigma attached to certain mistakes.

Maybe he and India weren't so different, after all.

Setting his computer aside, he pulled his cell out of

his pocket. He had her number from when she'd called last night, trying to find his phone. He'd nearly added her to his contacts list several times today, but he'd stopped himself. Now he went ahead. She was innocent of her husband's death. She truly loved Charlie. Rod could see that last night. She'd *told* him as much.

She'd also said she could use a friend, and he'd blown her off.

He felt bad about that now.

He felt even worse once he found her cookies.

India was concentrating so hard on her work that it took several seconds to realize someone was watching her. When it finally occurred to her that she had company, she jumped. She was so afraid Sebastian would appear out of nowhere, like he had before. But this time she knew who it would be. She'd heard Rod come home less than an hour earlier.

"Hey." He had a toothpick in his mouth and a cast on his right hand. He hooked his left on the wood overhang as he gazed through the screen.

When she'd jerked, she'd messed up the pot she'd been throwing, which was unfortunate. She'd already started over several times. After what she'd heard from Detective Flores, she was too upset to have steady hands—and yet she'd needed something to do. She couldn't sit there and worry indefinitely.

She wouldn't start over again now, however. Having Rod so close made it virtually impossible to focus, especially since she wasn't prepared to see him. She didn't have any makeup on, or shoes—or even a bra. In deference to the heat, she'd stripped down to a pair of high-waisted cutoffs and an old button-down shirt of Charlie's that she'd tied under her breasts.

"Hey," she echoed and, after pushing the clay into a big lump, turned off her wheel.

He gave her a sheepish look. "*I* didn't cause that, did I?" he asked, indicating her ruined vase.

"No," she lied. Then she bolstered her response with the truth. "Mistakes and do-overs happen all the time. This was actually my fourth try today."

"Really?"

"Really," she said. "Don't worry about it."

He lowered his good arm to move the toothpick to the other side of his mouth. "You ever seen the movie *Ghost*?"

She had. That steamy scene with Demi Moore and Patrick Swayze was one of her all-time favorites, but after last night, she was surprised he'd bring it up. "Yes."

"That's what finding you covered in clay and not much else reminds me of."

Ignoring that comment, she got off her stool and walked over to him. "You broke your hand, huh?"

"Yeah." He frowned at it. "In two places."

"I'm sorry about that. But I'm glad you saw a doctor."

"Yeah, it's a good thing. It would've had to be rebroken if I'd let it heal on its own, so…better to go this route from the beginning."

"Is this your first cast?"

He chuckled without mirth. "'Fraid not."

"They're no fun."

"You've had one?"

"Broke my arm once."

"How?"

"Motorcycle accident."

"Who was driving?"

Sebastian had been driving. He'd been angry with a friend and going too fast, and he'd pulled out in front of a semi that clipped their back tire. It was a miracle they'd lived through it. Because of that, he had a scar going half-way around his back, and she had two pins in her arm, but it could've been so much worse.

"A friend," she said to avoid mentioning Sebastian's name.

Rod studied her until she felt too uncomfortable to allow the silence to continue.

"So…what can I do for you?" she asked.

His mouth quirked to one side. "I just found a plate of cookies on the railing of my deck."

It was almost impossible not to return his smile, but India fought the impulse. She had to remain on guard at all times. He did something to her she couldn't explain—probably because it didn't make any sense. She'd barely met him. "I hope the ants didn't find them first."

"Not that I could see. Although I wouldn't have let that stop me. They were delicious."

"Were?" she repeated. "You ate them already?"

"Was I supposed to wait? If my brothers came home and found me with homemade cookies, they'd be gone in seconds. And my father and his wife are always there."

"So to prevent sharing, you ate all twelve?" she said with a laugh.

"They were for me, weren't they?" he responded with a wink.

He made her feel better. She preferred not to contemplate why. "Yes, they were for you, and I'm glad you liked them." She sobered. "I hope you also got my note."

"I did."

Then why was he here? Didn't her note say it all?

She crossed to the sink in the corner. "I'm really sorry about last night," she said as she washed her hands. "I've made my share of mistakes, but I've never done anything like that."

"I'm not here for another apology. I just wanted to tell you not to worry about it. I can understand why you might want to feel good for a change."

"Thank you. I appreciate your forgiveness. But I'm really not as bad as hitting on you made me seem."

"I know."

After drying her hands, she used the same towel to mop the beads of sweat running down the sides of her face. "Then...can we pretend it never happened?"

His gaze slid over her like it had last night, and she suddenly realized *why* she'd propositioned him. Just the way he looked at her—as if he was undressing her with his eyes, even though they weren't talking about anything remotely suggestive—made her too aware of him. He exuded sex appeal, and as a young, lonely widow, she was vulnerable. It'd been eleven months since she'd felt a man's touch; she missed Charlie's gentle caress.

"'Course. I'm not holding anything against you," he said, giving her the impression that he wouldn't have thought twice about what she'd done, with or without the cookie offering.

Maybe he got hit on all the time. India knew she couldn't be the only woman to find him attractive.

She clasped her hands in front of her, partially to hide the fact that she didn't know what to do with them now that she'd cleaned them, and partially to block his view of the stains on her shirt. When she was creating, she didn't care about staying clean. She didn't care about much of anything then. Several hours could pass without her noticing. Her art was the one thing that helped her cope with life since Charlie died.

"Good. Thanks again." She gestured toward her back door. "I'd better go inside. I've still got a lot to do tonight."

"India?" He stopped her before she could reach the sanctuary of her kitchen, and his tone suggested that whatever he was about to say wasn't idle chitchat.

She turned. "Yes?"

"Let me take you to dinner."

She almost told him again what she'd told him last night. That she was still in love with her late husband, that she couldn't get involved. Even when she started dating again, she couldn't date anyone like Rod. Her in-laws would take one look at him, see Sebastian Young instead and sue her for custody of Cassia. It could easily be the final piece of "evidence" to convince them that her poor choices were to blame for the death of their son.

But instead of "no," she heard herself say, "When?"

"Tomorrow night?"

He'd lowered his voice in what felt like a meaningful way and that filled her belly with butterflies. She stared at him, willing herself to clarify that she couldn't go, but she didn't. She nodded.

"Pick you up at six," he said.

Her heartbeat seemed to travel out to her fingertips. What was she doing? Clearly, she'd lost her mind—and yet she overrode her better judgment for a second time. "Okay."

When his smile widened, she felt a bit wobbly in the knees. "See you soon."

6

Rod was mowing the lawn. India could see him from the window above her sink, where she was doing dishes. She had a hard time looking away, especially once his T-shirt grew damp and he took it off. He wrapped it around his head to block the sun, which wasn't the most attractive way to wear a shirt, so she knew he wasn't trying to show off.

That certainly didn't detract from his appearance, however. His bare chest and arms... Holy cow! As much as she'd loved Charlie and would never have tried to change him, she had to admit he hadn't looked like that. He couldn't; he didn't spend enough time outdoors, didn't do anything physical. He was too busy concentrating on his patients and his career. They'd even had a yard service.

She didn't realize she was no longer washing dishes—that she was only staring—until her phone buzzed. Then she finally looked away. She'd been trying to reach her in-laws to tell them about the DA's decision, and now they were getting back to her.

After drying her hands, she turned from the window and hit the talk button.

"Hello?" She went into the living room so she wouldn't be tempted to watch Rod anymore. Charlie was dead, but somehow she still felt guilty about the things she thought and felt whenever she encountered her neighbor. She knew the Sommerses wouldn't appreciate the fact that another man had that kind of effect on her. She'd have to remain single for a long time in order to convince them that she'd loved Charlie and wouldn't have done anything to hurt him.

"India? It's Claudia," her mother-in-law said. "How are you, sweetheart?"

The endearments Charlie's mother bandied about could be so misleading. India wished they were sincere. Since she'd never really had a father, and she'd lost her mother when she was still young, she often felt a child-like craving for the love of a good parent.

But experience had taught her that Claudia's *sweetheart*, *honey* and *darling* were mere words. Claudia tried to like her because she'd meant so much to Charlie, but on some level, she couldn't help blaming India, as India blamed herself, for what Sebastian had done. The defense attorney had made her look so bad. India had felt her in-laws' loyalties weakening as witness after witness claimed she'd called Sebastian several times, which she had, but only for moral support because he'd been talking about suicide, that she was probably still in love with him—given their history—and that they were planning to run away together once she inherited the money. As a result, relations between her and Charlie's parents were strained and had been for months, although they all tried to pretend they were as close as ever.

"I'm fine," India said, despite the fact that she felt as if she was living from minute to minute. "And you?"

"Busy. Little Cassia and I went to the thrift store today and bought an old trunk that we filled with whatever toys she wanted. Guess what she picked?"

"A ball of some kind?" India knew it wouldn't be anything too girlie. Cassia preferred to be outside playing with boys and had no interest in Barbies or dress-up.

"Yes. We got her a tee to hit off and some other sports stuff but no dolls. She's such a tomboy."

A twinge of jealousy had India gritting her teeth. Cassia was *her* daughter, damn it. India wanted her back. And yet she couldn't push, not if Sebastian was free. He could be looking for her this very minute. It wasn't as if she'd moved far away. Her in-laws had insisted she remain fairly close so they could continue to be a big part of Cassia's life.

But right now India felt they were *too* involved. A whole month without her daughter was beginning to feel like an eternity.

"I'll bet she loved that," she said, carefully modulating her voice to sound congenial and appreciative. "You're such a good grandmother."

"It's been wonderful spending time with her. I can't tell you how much fun we're having. And I'm sure it's made things easier for you. Moving is such a big job."

India gripped the phone tighter. "Yes, but I'm pretty well finished."

"You're all settled, then?"

"Except for hanging the paintings. I...I'm not ready for that."

There was a moment of silence. "Charlie bought you a lot of art."

"Yes. He knew how much I loved it." She closed her eyes. "I miss him so much."

She hadn't intended to say that last part. The words had just welled up and slipped out. They came from a place of pain and deep regret, but she could tell from Claudia's hesitation that her mother-in-law didn't know whether to trust her.

"We all do," she said. She spoke stiffly, as if she was the only one who *really* missed him.

After that India found herself gravitating to the window to see if Rod was still out. The fact that she was ogling another man almost made her believe she must be as fickle as her mother-in-law suspected. But admiring him helped combat some of her anger, disappointment and fear.

Too bad he was mowing on the far side of the house where she couldn't see him…

"Will you be coming soon, to check out my new place?" she asked Claudia.

"Not before we bring Cassia home. Steve's too busy with his new victims' charity. We've been putting together a golf tournament, and it's taking hours and hours out of every day."

India caught her breath. "You could always bring Cassia home early if you need to concentrate on other things. That would be no problem for me. I'm basically moved in and ready." She'd figure out *some* way to protect her…

"Oh, no. Cassia's more important. We won't let anything interrupt this month with our girl."

India slowly released her breath. She'd taken advantage of the opportunity to try—because she knew as soon as she told Claudia that Sebastian was no longer in jail and might never return to custody, she'd probably have to battle her in-laws in court to get Cassia back. "Can I talk to her?"

"Of course."

A momentary flash of hope shot through India, which Claudia immediately extinguished.

"But later," she said. "She's right in the middle of helping Papa make lunch. We'll have her call you after, if we get the chance."

If we get the chance... They wouldn't call, and if India ever asked why, they'd invent some excuse. Charlie's parents were so possessive of their granddaughter.

Now that India knew she wasn't going to be speaking to her little girl, at least in this conversation, she moved on to the purpose of her call. "I got hold of Detective Flores earlier."

"You did? I've called and called. I always get his darn voice mail. What'd he say? When's the next trial?"

Rod came into view, the muscles of his left arm bulging as he carried the grass clippings to the green waste can. India put her hand to the window as if she could touch his warm skin or feel the solid thud of his heartbeat—as if such a strong man could shelter her in some way. But that was ridiculous. He was rough around the edges, much more like the ex-boyfriends who'd created so many problems for her in the past than true-blue Charlie.

"They're waiting," she told Claudia.

"I couldn't hear you. What'd you say?"

India forced herself to speak louder. "They aren't convinced they have enough evidence to get a conviction. They'd rather not risk a second trial, not until they've built a stronger case."

Another long silence, this one filled with shock and anger.

India could identify with both of those emotions.

"You've got to be kidding me," Claudia said when she spoke again.

"I'm afraid not." India swallowed, trying to wet her tongue, to make it easier to speak. "But Detective Flores is hopeful that they'll be able to bring him back to trial soon."

"When?"

India watched Rod disappear around the corner of his house again. "They can't give us a date. Yet."

"Which means what? It may never happen? Is that animal going to get away with what he did to my son? He took a life! And not just any life—the life of someone who mattered!"

India winced. She'd often felt Claudia wished *she'd* been the one to die that night. There'd been times she'd wished the same thing...

"It's heart-wrenching," she said and prayed she'd put enough emotion into that statement. The Sommerses, and everyone else who knew Charlie, were always watching her and interpreting everything she said or did with such suspicion. She felt as bad as Claudia did about this most recent turn of events. But she couldn't commiserate with her on the DA's lack of action or show the doubt she had that Sebastian would eventually be brought to justice, because then her mother-in-law would start thinking about Cassia and the fact that she might not be safe living with her mother.

If India wanted her daughter back without a fight, she had to ignore her own despair and convince the Sommerses that this was only a temporary setback.

"It's *beyond* heart-wrenching," Claudia said. "There are no words for what we've suffered."

That was true. The past eleven months had been hellish.

And yet, for her own sake as well as Cassia's, India had to keep herself together. She was fighting to do that. Charlie wouldn't want them to be miserable, but this new hurdle…

India wasn't sure how she'd get past it.

"They'll find the gun," she said. "That's what they need. If they find the gun and they can link it to Sebastian, they'll have him."

"You knew Sebastian well," Claudia said. "What could he have done with it? Where might he have put it?"

That night was a jumble of terror for India, but she could trace the gun through those memories because Sebastian had it in his hand, pointed at her, for so long. She'd spent hours believing he'd shoot her, and Cassia would be an orphan. "I told you. I told everyone. He took it with him when he ran out."

"If they haven't found it by now, they never will," her mother-in-law said. "What more can they do that they haven't already done? What more can *we* do? We hired that PI—little good it did us. He accomplished nothing, and the police haven't been much better. Detective Flores will move on to other cases, and we'll be left with our lives destroyed and Charlie's killer running around free."

"Please. Don't talk like that," India said. "We have to retain hope."

"I have to go," Claudia said abruptly.

India was afraid to let her hang up for fear of what she might decide. "I'm sorry about this, Claudia. I wish… I wish Detective Flores had given me better news, but… don't assume the worst. We'll see justice yet."

"Is that what you think? Because there is no real justice. You get that, right? Even if Sebastian goes back to prison for life, we'll still have to live without Charlie."

"Which is hard to fathom. I know."

"You do? Because sometimes I can't help feeling..."

India's stomach cramped at the sudden bite in Claudia's tone. "Yes?" she prompted when her mother-in-law's words fell off.

"As if you're—"

Someone—her father-in-law?—spoke in the background, but India couldn't make out the words.

"Never mind," Claudia said instead of finishing.

That sudden reversal led India to believe Steve had anticipated what was about to come out of his wife's mouth and admonished her against it.

"What?" India pressed, but she could guess. The Sommerses had questions about her involvement with Sebastian. They didn't understand why she'd been associating with him again. If she hadn't accepted him back into her life, none of this would've happened.

India wished she could explain. She'd tried, several times. But in light of what Sebastian had done, her reasons sounded lame. Everyone thought she, of all people, should've had some idea what he was capable of. Yes, she'd known he could be angry and unreasonable, even unpredictable. He'd gotten her in serious trouble when he robbed that liquor store on a whim. But he'd been young and impulsive, and he'd done what he could to make sure the police understood she'd played no part in it. That was why they hadn't charged her. He'd apologized over and over for involving her that day.

Prison and the drugs he'd taken over the years had changed him more than she could ever have dreamed. She'd assumed he'd learned his lesson—and was just down on his luck. She'd also naively thought she could help him.

How she wished she'd never responded to that first

message on Facebook. She'd been beating herself up over that ever since. At first *she* hadn't understood why she'd allowed Sebastian to reconnect with her, either. But, unlike the Sommerses, she had no family. That made her hesitant to cast old friends aside, even if they'd once been boyfriends.

"We love Cassia," Claudia said. "She's all we have left of Charlie. Thank you for letting her stay with us."

In other words, Charlie's mother was biting her tongue in order to preserve the relationship. But the calm her in-laws affected almost worried India more than if they'd unleashed their anger and disappointment. So much turbulence churned under the surface of those "still waters," probably more than she'd ever be able to overcome.

She feared where those powerful currents were carrying them...

"Of course. Cassia loves you. So do I," she added, hoping to retake some of the ground they'd lost.

Her mother-in-law wasn't receptive. "Good night" was all she said.

As Claudia disconnected, India let her head fall against the cool glass. It wasn't until she heard the sound of a mower in her own yard that she remembered Rod.

She hurried out front to find him cutting her grass. "Rod!" she yelled, trying to flag him down.

When he finally heard her, he looked over.

"You don't have to do this," she shouted above the noise. "It's getting a little overgrown, but I plan to buy a mower on Monday. I'll take care of it then."

"No big deal," he said. "Won't take long."

He seemed more than capable in spite of his broken hand. And here in Whiskey Creek, neighbors probably did that type of thing for each other. But receiving even a small amount of kindness on the heels of that call with her in-laws brought a lump to India's throat.

"Thank you," she said and turned away before he could see the tears in her eyes.

That night, Cheyenne brought over some lasagna and garlic bread. While Natasha helped her serve dinner, Rod and his brothers tossed Kellan around, making him laugh and squeal. Cheyenne complained that they were getting him too riled up, but Rod could tell she liked the attention they paid him. Kellan certainly enjoyed the roughhousing.

"More," he'd say whenever they stopped. It was about the only word he knew, besides *Mama* and *Dada*.

J.T. and Anya either heard the noise or smelled the food, because they entered the kitchen just as Cheyenne asked about their new neighbor.

"She's all moved in," Grady told her.

"I'd love to see the inside of the house now that it's been renovated," Cheyenne said, interested because she used to live there before she married Dylan.

"I bet she'd show you." Mack handed out forks. Rarely were their meals formal occasions, with someone setting the table beforehand. They ate whenever they were hungry and fended for themselves or ordered out. Heaven forbid Anya would ever go to the trouble of cooking or doing the dishes, even though she didn't work.

"You *should* stop by," Grady said. "And get her number for me while you're there. She's freaking gorgeous."

Cheyenne glanced up. "She's single?"

"Not sure yet," Mack said. "She's wearing a wedding ring, but her husband hasn't shown up. So…maybe he works out of the state or country."

"He's dead," Rod announced.

Everyone looked at him.

"She told you that?" Mack asked.

"When she gave me a ride home last night." Rod felt this would be the natural time to reveal that he'd be taking India to dinner tomorrow night. He'd heard Grady's little joke about getting her number and didn't want him or Mack to go on thinking she was fair game. But he didn't speak up. He wasn't sure his relationship with her would go anywhere and decided he'd wait and see how they got along before telling anyone. His brothers could be merciless; he wasn't going to provide them with fresh ammunition.

"Why'd she give you a ride home?" Cheyenne asked. "Where was your truck?"

"She came across me after the fight, when I was trying to get help."

"What was she doing out there so late at night? Was she at the bar, too?"

"No. She was on her way back from some art show."

"Oh, *art,*" Grady said.

"Something wrong with that?" Rod asked.

Grady gave him a funny look. "Of course not. I'm just messin' around. When did her husband die?"

"About a year ago."

"So she's available," Mack said, and Rod felt himself stiffen—almost as much as Natasha did.

"She's too old for you, bro."

"But not for *you.*" Anya smiled like the Cheshire cat. "Is that why you mowed her lawn today?"

Rod hadn't realized his stepmother had seen him. She usually stayed in her room all day, playing on the computer or watching TV. "Not necessarily. She doesn't have a mower yet, so I figured I might as well do hers while I was doing ours."

"And did she show you any appreciation?" J.T. joked, sending him a meaningful grin.

Rod didn't care for the way his father talked about women since he'd been released from prison. "She thanked me, if that's what you mean."

"Is she nice?" Cheyenne asked.

"Seems like it," he said.

Cheyenne took a bottle of salad dressing out of the box she'd used to transport all the food. "I'd like to meet her sometime."

Grady sat down and dug into his meal before the rest of them could get a plate. "Why not tonight?"

Without Mack's even asking, Natasha added a second piece of garlic bread to his plate, and Rod pretended he didn't notice that whatever Mack received from Natasha was always the biggest and the best.

"Dyl's getting home soon," Cheyenne replied. "So I should head out."

"Have him join us," J.T said. "He hardly ever comes over these days."

Rod suspected Anya's presence had a great deal to do with that. Dylan liked her even less than the rest of them did.

"Can't," she said. "He has a baseball game."

"We should go watch him play," Anya suggested, but no one chimed in to encourage her.

Rod put Kellan down to accept his plate. "Thanks." Since he wanted to speak to Cheyenne in private before she left, he hoped she wasn't going to rush off.

"How's your hand?" She nodded toward his cast.

"Throbbing like crazy," he admitted.

"I made that apple crisp you like for dessert." She winked. "Maybe that'll help ease the pain."

He leaned over to drop a kiss on her forehead. "Dylan got lucky the day he married you."

"That's what I keep telling him," she teased.

"Will Aaron be at the game, too?" Mack asked.

"Should be," she told them. "Dyl talked him into joining the team."

Mack got up to get a beer and grabbed one for Rod, too. "Want to go over to the park?" he murmured so Anya and the others couldn't hear.

Normally, Rod would've enjoyed seeing the game. But after being up so late, and everything he'd dealt with today, he was ready for bed. "Not tonight."

Cheyenne put the dessert on the counter and started cleaning the spatula and serving spoons. "I'll leave the rest of this here," she said, indicating the leftover salad, lasagna and bread. "Just remember to take the dishes to Dylan tomorrow so he can bring them home."

"I will," Rod said.

She swung her son into her arms. "I'd better get going. I want to make sure Dyl has a chance to eat before he has to show up at the field."

Rod wasn't finished with his supper, but he stood. "I'll walk you out," he said so the others wouldn't find it odd when he left the kitchen after only a few bites.

He caught up with his sister-in-law at the front door. "Before you go, could you do me a favor?"

She turned in surprise. "Of course."

"Will you take a second to come up and look in my closet?"

"What for?" she asked.

He lowered his voice to make sure no one else could hear.

Fortunately, they were all so busy eating, he didn't think anyone was paying attention. "I have a date tomorrow."

"And you want me to tell you what to wear? This girl must be special," she said. "You've never asked for my help with that kind of thing before."

He'd never felt so out of his element before. "She's… different."

"Special," she confirmed with a grin. "Do I know her?"

He scratched his neck. "It's our new neighbor."

"Oh!" Her smile widened. "Why didn't you speak up a second ago?"

"It's one date," he said with a shrug.

"But you'd like to impress her." She wasn't buying his nonchalance.

"I need to dress up a little, that's all," he said. "Her husband—the man who passed away—was a heart surgeon."

"I see," she responded. "So we're going for sophisticated and respectable."

At least Cheyenne seemed to be catching on to what he needed. "Yeah. That sounds good."

She put down her son and linked her arm through Rod's. "I have no doubt you'll clean up nicely. Let's go take a look."

7

India sat in her quiet living room with a cup of tea. She'd thought some chamomile might help her relax, but it didn't seem to be working. She was wide-awake and anxious, and looking at another long night. She wished she could read a book or watch TV. But ever since Detective Flores had told her about Sebastian, she'd been checking and double-checking her doors and windows. She wanted to believe he'd had enough trouble. That he'd slink off without bothering her again, maybe even leave the area before the police could find the additional evidence she was hoping for. Most men in his situation would flee if they had the chance, wouldn't they?

But she couldn't assume anything when it came to Sebastian. If he didn't care about taking Charlie's life, or even his own—and she knew from the way he'd been talking that he didn't—he certainly wouldn't care about taking hers.

Then Cassia really would be an orphan…

The report of the gun the night Charlie was shot seemed to echo in her head and she saw, again, how her husband had gasped and clutched his chest when the bullet struck him. She squeezed her eyes shut, trying to avoid those memories, but she was too tired to fight them. The most gruesome images bombarded her repeatedly, as well as the worst of what'd come after—when Sebastian had forced her to tell him she still loved him, that she'd marry him and do…other things. That was the only way she could convince him not to harm Cassia. She'd never admitted to the rape. She wasn't even sure she could call it rape, since she hadn't refused. She'd used her body and everything else she'd needed to in order to save her child.

Maybe that was why so many people suspected her of lying. In a sense, she was. She was holding back some of the worst and, arguably, more important details. But she couldn't admit to the methods she'd employed to stall, reassure and distract Sebastian. She feared—*knew*— that there'd be people who would claim she'd enjoyed it and wasn't choking back vomit every second she let him touch her.

I'll always love you. Sebastian had told her that. Her skin still crawled when she remembered his hands on her face, forcing her to look up at him as he said it. He didn't know what love was. He couldn't, not if he could murder her husband, threaten her daughter and wave a gun in her face. He'd also let his defense attorney blame *her* for Charlie's death. Larry Forgash, attorney-at-law, had said she must've hired a killer and was now using Sebastian as the scapegoat. He'd pointed to a series of cash withdrawals from her own checking account, which was separate from Charlie's, since she'd had it before they were married, to suggest how she might've paid that person, but the cash withdrawals had only added up to about $3,300 over the course of two months.

Fortunately, his defense precluded him from telling anyone they'd had sex after Charlie died. Since the police had no forensic evidence, nothing except her testimony to say he was even there, he'd had his wife claim he was with her the entire night.

India shuddered as the old revulsion welled up, so strong it made her nauseous. *Forget*, she ordered herself. Like the river outside, life would wend its way along and someday she'd be able to put it behind her. But she doubted that would be possible unless she could forgive herself. And how could she ever do that? Her shame at having acted as if she wanted Sebastian, as if she'd enjoyed being with him, was too great.

A gentle wind stirred the chimes on her porch. She'd made them herself, planned to carry a wide assortment in her studio, but that tinkle sounded far less cheerful than usual. She missed Cassia, wished she could go and lie down next to her daughter instead of having to worry that, when the time came, her in-laws would conjure up an excuse to try to keep her longer, if not indefinitely.

Actually, they wouldn't have to *conjure* up an excuse. They had a great one, considering what they'd learned today.

India stared down at her phone. She'd received a call from Ellie Cox at dinnertime and ignored it. Ellie was the wife of Charlie's best friend. They'd been close over the past three years, ever since Ellie and Mitchell had moved into her and Charlie's neighborhood. But, like the Sommerses, Ellie and Mitchell now treated her with coolness. It was humiliating to have her friends turn on her, and yet the loss of her relationship with Ellie wasn't what concerned India about her message.

India hit the play button on her voice mail, even though she'd already listened to it several times.

*India, it's me, Ellie. Give me a call when you can.
I've been thinking about you, wondering how you're
doing. I'm sorry it's been so long, but...we've been
busy with Tyler's baseball season. You know how
that goes.*

She did know, since she'd sat through many of his
games, keeping Ellie company. Ellie could easily have
stepped away to place a call or, at the very least, send a
text message.

But that wasn't what worried her.

*We have games almost every night this month, what
with his regular team and his competitive team
going at the same time. Anyway, someone at the
park told me you'd moved to Whiskey Creek. Is
that true? I knew you were looking for a house,
but I don't remember hearing that you'd found one.*

There it was. *Someone* at the ballpark had told Ellie
that India had moved to Whiskey Creek. Who? Were her
old acquaintances still talking about her? Did they know
where she'd gone? India hadn't told a lot of people where
she planned to move, but neither had she kept it as secret
as she now wished she had.

How easy would it be for Sebastian to find her?

She was just wondering if she should've gotten a new
number, when the soft thud of a car door almost made her
spill her tea. Ready to call for help should she need to, she
gripped her cell in one hand, set her cup aside and crept
into the living room to peer through the wooden shutters.

Nearly one in the morning was late for visitors, even
on a Saturday.

It'd been after one when Sebastian broke into her house the last time...

Praying that the sound had come from next door and wasn't as close as it seemed, she studied the dark landscape, her driveway, her neighbors' driveway. Plenty of shadows danced in the moonlight as branches swayed in the wind, but she saw no sign that someone had arrived.

She decided she must've imagined what she'd heard. She'd been imagining the worst all night. Jumping at every creak or bump. Nervously staring out various windows for long stretches of time. Picturing Sebastian out there, watching her house, waiting for her to go to bed so she'd be vulnerable, like before.

She rubbed away the goose bumps that prickled her arms. She was growing paranoid, and her exhaustion wasn't helping. She didn't have any reserves, needed to sleep.

Pushing herself away from the window, she went to her room and curled up on the bed. But even after she lay down, she watched the clock and continued to listen. The harder she tried to sleep, the more difficult it became.

At two thirty, she thought she heard the approach of another car. When she jumped up to check, once again she saw no sign of anyone.

Afraid she'd drive herself mad if she didn't do something, she considered going out to sleep on the riverbank. But she knew she wouldn't feel any safer there. With her luck, she'd be dragged off by a mountain lion while she was sleeping outside to protect herself from Sebastian.

After spending another fifteen minutes positive that someone was creeping around, trying to look into her windows, she was desperate enough to consider renting a motel room. She *had* to shut down for a while.

But there were only a few B and Bs nearby, no actual motels, and she didn't want to rouse some manager from his or her bed in the middle of the night. She didn't want to drag the past into the present by making the people who lived here think she was odd. The B and Bs were probably full, anyway. It was tourist season and a weekend to boot.

Then she saw Rod's deck. She would feel safe there, knowing he was so close. As lightly as she slept, the sun would wake her at dawn, so she'd be able to leave before he ever rolled out of bed. If she kept quiet, he'd never be the wiser.

Even if she overslept, or he came out for some strange reason and found her there, she didn't care. She supposed that testified to the level of her desperation. If he discovered her curled up outside his door, she'd just ask how much he'd charge to rent his deck until she could feel reasonably sure that Sebastian wasn't on his way to kill her.

"What do I have to lose?" she mumbled as she gathered a pillow and a blanket. She'd already embarrassed herself with Rod about as badly as a woman could. She'd never forget trying to kiss him after he'd told her no. Getting caught sleeping on his deck would be nothing compared to that. At least maybe she could rest over there so she'd feel somewhat human again. A short reprieve. That was all that mattered to her right now.

India didn't wake early. When she finally felt the sun beating down on her face and heard the birds chirping in the trees, she guessed it was around ten. How could she have slept so long?

The moment she opened her heavy eyelids and realized where she was, she panicked. Then she froze, because any movement or noise could draw Rod's attention if he was up and moving around his room.

Fortunately, she didn't hear any sounds from within. The whole household seemed to be sleeping late.

It was Sunday, she reminded herself. Most people didn't get up early on the weekend. It wasn't as if there were any young children in the house.

Not that she planned to press her luck any further. Slowly and quietly, she picked up her sleeping bag and pillow and crept down the wooden stairs. Her heart stopped every time she heard them creak beneath her weight, but Rod didn't come to the door. Someone who had nothing to fear probably didn't startle at every little sound, like she did.

Her feet got wet as she hurried across the grass. Apparently, the sprinklers had come on not too long ago, and even that hadn't disturbed her! She'd passed out the second she felt safe, hadn't slept that soundly since before Charlie died. She felt so much better, she couldn't regret sneaking over. And since she made it back to her house without being seen, it hadn't cost her anything, not even the embarrassment.

"That was worth the risk," she murmured as she let herself in. Maybe now she could get some pottery done. She hesitated as she remembered that she'd agreed to go out with Rod. Spending time alone with the sexy guy who lived next door was a risky proposition. Their relationship couldn't go anywhere. She'd be smarter to stay away from him.

But she couldn't bring herself to cancel. The idea of a dinner out—during which she wouldn't be alone with her thoughts and memories and the constant fear that Sebastian might break in and shoot her—was too enticing.

She could keep the relationship on safe ground, she told herself. What was one meal with her new neighbor?

It was the first time Rod had ever considered bringing flowers to a woman who wasn't his girlfriend. He wanted to convince India that he had some class, that he wasn't as bad as the fight had made him look, and he thought flowers might help. He'd even driven over to the flower shop, but then he'd turned around. He was afraid that showing up with a bouquet might make him seem as though he was trying to be something he wasn't, so he'd backed off. If she was after another heart surgeon, or someone with an equally impressive résumé, a bouquet of flowers wasn't going to persuade her to consider an auto body technician.

He figured he was what he was. If that wasn't good enough, there was nothing he could do to change it.

When she opened the door, and he saw that she was wearing a sleeveless cream-colored dress that hit a few inches above the knee, he caught his breath. She was gorgeous. Stunning. And now he was even more grateful he'd let Cheyenne help him with his attire. As it turned out, he didn't own the type of shirt his sister-in-law had wanted him to wear. She'd brought one over earlier this morning from Dylan's closet. Then she'd insisted he match it with the pants she'd given him for Christmas, which had still had the tags hanging from the waistband.

"Wow," he said on a long exhalation.

She seemed taken aback. But surely she had to attract male attention wherever she went, had to know she was striking. "Thank you," she said. "This dress is okay, then?"

Okay? He couldn't take his eyes off her. "Of course. It's fine."

"Great. So where are we going?"

He'd contemplated many options but eventually settled on an old hotel in Jackson, famous for its prime rib. Gold Country towns weren't quite like the Napa Valley Wine region, which was famous for its food. The nicer restaurants along Highway 49 struggled. Except during tourist season, there weren't enough people to support them. But some of the local favorites managed to survive, and the restaurant in this nineteenth-century hotel had been around for years. It had a dark, romantic ambience, and Rod had always liked whatever he'd ordered there. "For prime rib—unless you're a vegetarian."

"No, I eat meat." She left the door standing open while she got her purse. "How's your hand?"

He held up his cast. "I'm already tempted to bust this off. I doubt I'll still have it in six weeks."

"Just wait until it starts itching."

"Something to look forward to."

The smile she gave him as she came out of the house made him want to take her hand. But he could tell she wasn't convinced she should even be going out with him. So he didn't try. "What have you been doing today?" he asked. "More pottery?"

"Yes. I actually got some sleep last night—"

"Actually?" he broke in as she turned to lock the door.

She hesitated as if maybe she'd revealed too much. "I've been suffering from insomnia."

He figured having someone break in while she was sleeping and shoot her husband, then threaten her daughter's life as well as her own, could easily have that effect. "So what do you do? Take a sedative?"

"No, I don't take anything."

"Why not?"

"The thought of being drugged or too sluggish scares me."

Because of Sebastian? "All you have to do is sleep it off," he said.

"True. But who knows how long that would take? I'd rather not be impaired."

In case she was ever threatened again. That was what she meant; he was sure of it. He wondered if it was what Sebastian had done or what he might do that frightened her most—but didn't ask. That could wait.

"Anyway, I got a lot of work done today," she said as they headed down the walk. "So that's good."

When they reached the truck, he opened the door so she could get in. He assumed Charlie had driven a luxury car. Rod had never even considered purchasing one of those. He couldn't take it off-road or pull a trailer behind it. But a sedan would've been nice for tonight. She looked like the kind of woman who'd feel most comfortable in a Mercedes. "Did you ever finish that piece you were working on yesterday?"

"The vase? I did. I also finished a new set of wind chimes and a cute butter crock."

He'd been about to shut her door, but he held off. "What's a butter crock?"

"It keeps butter cold and fresh when it's not in the fridge."

"Never heard of it. Do most people have one?"

She chuckled. "No. They were sort of a...pioneer item."

He wasn't sure butter crocks would sell, since refrigerators seemed to work quite well. But saying that might seem negative, so he didn't volunteer his opinion. He closed her door. Then he walked around to the other side. "How long before you're ready to open your studio?" he asked as he started the engine.

"Hard to say." She buckled her seat belt. "I'll need enough variety to make the shop interesting, with pieces that'll appeal to all budgets. It's tough to make a living at what I do, because it takes so long to create handmade things, and machine-made stuff is so cheap by comparison. I have to charge enough to cover my time and overhead and yet, no matter how good my work is, I can't charge more than the market will bear."

"Sounds like you're looking at it very practically."

"I'm trying to go into it with my eyes open. I have a daughter to support. I have to be careful to build a future for us and not lose what Charlie left us."

He backed out and shifted into Drive. "Maybe you should limit the months you run the shop to summer, when the tourists come through. Then you could work at home to restock during the winter."

"That's an idea." She adjusted the air-conditioning vent. "Is your business steady all year?"

"It is, but it's not a retail shop."

"Car repair is usually more of a need than a want," she said.

"I'm not saving lives, but…what I do pays the bills."

He regretted the reference to her late husband's profession as soon as it came out of his mouth. Quickly changing the subject, he gave the truck more gas. "I hope you like prime rib," he said. "We could always do Italian or something else if you prefer."

"I can't remember the last time I had prime rib. It's

not something you typically make for yourself. And I haven't been out in…forever."

"The past year has sucked for you. But things are going to get better. I'm glad you agreed to come tonight."

The uncertainty and concern she'd been hugging about her like a cloak began to dissipate. "So am I," she said, and she sounded completely convinced.

That was when he knew they were going to have a good time—and he relaxed, too.

Rod was easy to talk to and he could be funny, which came as a surprise to India. His wit was more sarcastic than Charlie's, but she liked it. As they sat across from each other in the dimly lit restaurant, drinking a glass of wine while waiting for their food, she hid a smile at the fact that he'd dressed up tonight. He'd gone to the trouble of getting a haircut since she'd seen him last, but the changes didn't really suit him. She preferred him in faded jeans and a simple T-shirt—even missed the wild, untamed curls he'd had lopped off—but she got the impression he'd made an effort to look nice for her. That felt so good she wouldn't let herself think of all the reasons she shouldn't be spending time with him.

"So what did you tell Dylan?" she asked, returning to the conversation that had started outside.

They'd passed a sports car when they were parking on the street, and that had triggered a story about a wealthy vineyard owner who'd brought his red Ferrari into Amos Auto Body when Rod was barely fifteen. It'd had a small scratch on the front bumper, which the owner wanted fixed. But Rod had been so excited to see such a fast and expensive car, he took it for a joyride—and totaled it. "I didn't tell him anything. I couldn't. I'd been arrested for driving without a license," he said with a laugh.

"I can't believe you weren't hurt!" she cried.

"I had a few bumps and bruises, but nothing like it could've been. If I hadn't hit that tree, if I'd hit another car instead, it could've turned into one of those stupid things you do as a kid that you regret for the rest of your life."

"You were lucky."

"I don't think Dylan's ever been so mad at me."

She cradled her glass as she watched the candlelight flicker across his face. "Did you have to pay for it?"

"It was a hundred-thousand-dollar car. There was no way I could. Dylan couldn't, either. We had so little back then. Fortunately, our insurance took care of it. But there was a huge deductible, of course, and the wreck made the premiums go up." He shook his head. "For the next six months, we ate nothing but bean burritos for dinner. I don't know why Dyl didn't kick my ass out right then and there."

She chuckled as she imagined Rod so young and unruly, making life even harder for his beleaguered older brother. "He must love you a great deal."

"He does," he said unabashedly. "But I had to work two years of overtime to make up for what I cost the company that day."

She took a sip of her wine. "Did you resent Dylan for that?"

"How could I? I was the one who screwed up. I deserved worse."

The fact that he took responsibility for his mistakes showed more maturity than her first impression of him had suggested. She liked that. She also liked the way he made her feel every time he looked at her. In the six years she'd dated before marrying Charlie, she couldn't remember a man being quite so transparent in his appreciation and found it surprising that Rod would be the first, since he was possibly the prettier one between the two of them. He was willing to build *her* ego instead of waiting for her to build his, and that made him seem more like Charlie than she would've expected. Her husband had been so generous with his compliments, always saw the best in others.

"You speak with such reverence when you talk about Dylan," she said.

Rod grew silent, contemplative. Then he said, "I owe him a lot."

She'd figured out from the way he talked about his older brother that Dylan had raised him, but he hadn't told her why. "Was your father ill or something? Is that why Dylan took over?" If so, he must've recovered, because he seemed perfectly fine these days.

The waitress was hurrying over with their food. When Rod saw her, he leaned back to allow her to deliver their plates and waited for her to walk away before answering. "My father was in prison."

India had picked up her fork. At this, she put it back down. "I'm sorry to hear that."

He shrugged, but she could tell it wasn't the careless gesture he intended it to be.

"How long was he...gone?" she asked.

"Sixteen years."

Almost two decades! Whatever his father had done must've been serious, but she didn't ask for details. She understood how invasive those questions could be and assumed Rod would volunteer the information if he cared to discuss it. "When did he get out?"

"Two years ago. It still seems strange to have him back."

"Do you get along with him?"

He gestured at her food. "Go ahead and eat. This is old news. I'm fine. And he and I do get along, for the most part. Probably because he has no control over my life. Sometimes our relationship feels odd—that's all. What I've experienced is so different from what other people have experienced. My dad's more like a...a roommate than a parent."

Now she was beginning to understand the unusual bond he had with his oldest brother. "How old was Dylan when he...when he had to step up?"

"Eighteen. A senior in high school."

"Wow. It's impressive that he kept you all out of trouble."

His grin slanted to one side. "He *tried* to keep us out of trouble. Didn't always succeed."

Her meat, so salty and tender, nearly melted in her mouth. "What about his wife?"

"Cheyenne? She's great. I'm glad Dylan found her. They couldn't be happier."

"I meant your father's wife." India didn't want to judge someone she didn't know, but the clothes his stepmother wore were often dirty or wrinkled and were usually too revealing. She certainly wasn't the typical mother. The woman rarely even bothered to put on shoes.

"I can't stand her," he admitted. "I try to be cordial, but that basically amounts to ignoring her whenever I can. There's just nothing to admire."

She took a bite of mashed potatoes, savoring the garlic and cheese that'd been added. "So why do you allow her to stay?"

"When we made the decision to let them move in, her

daughter was still in high school. We did it for Natasha's sake, so Anya wouldn't keep dragging her around and she could get her diploma." He speared a carrot. "Now that Natasha's graduated and will be attending an out-of-state college in the fall, I'd like to reconsider. But if we kick them out, where will they go? We can't leave them homeless. Whether we like it or not, they're family."

Rod sounded tough, but he obviously had a soft heart. "Your father can't afford a place of his own?"

"No. With his record? Where would he find work? And he's too young for social security."

"There must be *something* he can do."

"If so, he hasn't found it. It'd be different if he'd been put away for some white-collar crime. But he shot a man in a bar."

She stopped chewing. Rod's father had *killed* someone?

"Does that shock you?" he asked evenly.

"It's not the kind of thing you hear every day," she said after she'd managed to swallow. "What made him go that far?"

He turned his wineglass around and around. "There was this guy, Fenley Tolson, who was convinced my father hadn't fixed his car right. My father insisted Fenley had been warned that it would be impossible to match the paint exactly, so he refused to refund the money. That caused a feud between them that went on for some time. Then, somehow, one night they wound up in the same bar. We think Fenley must've seen my dad leaving town and followed him just to get under his skin."

He sipped his wine. "The bar has since gone out of business," he went on, "which is no surprise. But it wasn't even in Whiskey Creek. It was here in Jackson. My father liked to drink outside of town because he didn't have to see too many familiar faces." He lifted his glass, only this time he merely stared at the wine. "Anyway, after they were both wasted, Fenley started getting in my dad's face. It might've been okay even then if he hadn't mentioned my mom. But he did."

India gripped the napkin in her lap. She could tell his story was reaching its gruesome climax, which made her feel ill. She understood what it was like to witness such a violent act—to be one of the heartbroken people who could appear on the latest true crime show. *Dateline* had contacted her to get her story, not that she'd been in any frame of mind to talk to them. For one thing, she was afraid someone would see her on TV and decide she wasn't as broken up about her husband's death as she should be. Then all the suspicion and accusations would begin again, and she couldn't live with that. It'd been one of the tougher aspects of what she'd been through, particularly since she *had* made some concessions that night, done things she'd rather not remember, let alone talk about. She was already prone to blaming herself.

"What did Tolson have to say about your mother?" she asked.

A muscle moved in Rod's cheek. She sensed that what he was about to say wasn't easy for him, but, after setting down his glass, he answered. "That he could see why she'd kill herself rather than live with him."

India's stomach tensed. Apparently, Rod's family had been through a tragedy even worse than she'd first thought. "Your mother committed suicide?"

His chest rose as he drew a deep breath. "A year and a half before the shooting. She suffered from depression, couldn't seem to get on top of it. Anyway, that's when my father started drinking heavily. He couldn't deal with losing her, especially in that way. So when Tolson said what he did—" his eyes took on a far-off look "—my dad went off. He rushed out to his truck, got his gun, and…that was it."

He shot Tolson in cold blood? India didn't want to say the words. Apparently, neither did Rod, because he left the story there.

"I'm afraid this isn't very light dinner conversation," he added.

It wasn't light at all. She was seeing visions of Sebastian looming over her with that gun, would never forget the dark shadow he'd cast over her and Charlie's bed. "I'm really sorry," she murmured. "About everything."

"It's in the past."

She shifted in her seat. "Now that your father's out, what does he do all day if he doesn't work?"

"*He* thinks he works—and I guess he sort of does. Dylan gave him an old car to restore. Maybe, once he's finished, he'll be able to sell it, and he and Anya will have enough to get an apartment. That's what we're hoping."

She took another bite of her prime rib. "But…how will they keep the apartment if he can't get a job and she doesn't work? Or does she have some kind of disability or other income?"

"*Anya?*" He laughed without mirth. "She has nothing. She's an addict. I don't think California doles out money for that quite yet—although, if she didn't have what she needed, she'd figure out some way to get it. She always has."

"Your father loves her, though?"

"Let's just say he's desperate enough to put up with her. It's worth it to him to have a warm body in his bed every night, and he feels a certain amount of loyalty to her, since she married him while he was behind bars."

India had cut her prime rib into small, bite-size pieces, but she was pushing them around her plate more than she was eating. Seeing that he'd finish his meal long before she did, she lifted her fork to her mouth. "If he spent so much time…out of circulation, how did they meet? Did she know him from before?"

"No. She found his picture on a matchmaking website for convicts."

"Sites like that really exist?"

"Oh, yeah. They're set up as if they're arranging pen pals, but you can imagine how it typically goes. Anya was writing quite a few inmates, sending them naked pictures and explicit letters." He frowned. "That should tell you something about her. I bet she only agreed to marry my dad and drop the others because he was getting out soon and promised to take care of her, which wasn't exactly realistic. He believed he'd come home and take over the business we'd built, even though Amos Auto Body hadn't been worth much when he went away. Dylan was the one who turned it around."

"You didn't let him take it back?"

"No. We came up with an amount we felt it would've been worth, although he would've lost it without us, and we've been paying him that in monthly installments. Gives him money for gas, what few groceries he buys, clothes and stuff. Still, it's not enough to live on, and it'll only last for another five years. But he should be eligible for social security at that point."

"Why not let him work for you until then? Pay him a wage?"

"We tried that, for a short time. It created too much

animosity. He won't take orders from us, and we won't let him run the place. So we had to make a few changes. Honestly? Most of us—except maybe Mack—don't want him there at all."

She was too full to continue eating, so she put her napkin beside her plate. "Who came up with the idea of buying him out?"

"Dylan, of course."

"I can see why you admire your big brother. He seems to be quite the businessman."

Rod finished the bite he'd taken. "He's good at everything. I don't know how he managed. *We* certainly didn't make life any easier for him."

"I bet you've worked hard over the years, though—like he has."

"It was that or get split up and put into foster care."

For a new acquaintance, he'd shared a lot of personal information with her. At first she was so surprised by what she'd learned, she didn't think about that, but then she realized he wouldn't reveal such things to just anyone. She got the feeling he didn't focus too deeply on anything that wasn't directly relevant, and that meant he had a reason for sharing what he had. Once she considered that, she was fairly confident she could guess what the reason was. "So…you know what it's like to be intimately connected to someone who…who's killed a man."

He swirled his potatoes with his fork. "I do."

She waited until he met her gaze. "And you know how Charlie died, don't you?"

He nodded. "I looked it up on the internet."

Of course. There was plenty of information online. Charlie had been an important part of the community, so his murder was big news, especially when the police thought *she* might've had a hand in it. "Wife Murders Husband for Money" was more salacious than a random killing. "That's why you told me about your parents?"

"Partly. Although what happened to our family isn't exactly privileged information. Ask anyone around here and they'll tell you all about it. I thought it might help you feel more comfortable to know you're not alone. Unbelievable, hurtful, humiliating shit happens to other people, too."

"Even here."

"Even here," he repeated. "Did you think it would be different?"

"It certainly looks different. Anyway, I wasn't trying to be secretive about my own background," she explained. "I just… I didn't want to drag it here with me."

"I can see why. People love to gossip. They've gossiped about my family since I can remember."

"You don't mind?"

"Not anymore. But it hasn't always been that way. For years, my brothers and I fought back—mostly out of pride. We were determined not to let anyone look down on us. Now I wonder why we bothered. Who cares what other people think? All that fighting was a waste of time and energy. So if what I've learned can help you…"

She leaned back to study him. When he noticed that she'd stopped eating, so did he. "Thank you," she murmured. "It was nice of you to reach out."

"Terrible things happen to good people, too. Maybe it's not fair, but that's the randomness of life."

She wanted to agree—God, did she want to agree—but she couldn't allow him to chalk her misfortune up to randomness if he didn't fully understand the role she'd played in Charlie's death. She deserved more of the blame for her situation than he did for his. He'd been a child when everything went so wrong for him; he couldn't possibly have been the cause of it.

She, on the other hand…

"But you read that Charlie's murderer was…someone I once dated, right?"

His gaze never wavered. "I did, yes."

"And you also read that *I'm* the one who let him into our lives? That *I* gave him our address?" She flinched at the crushing guilt. She wasn't entirely sure why she was presenting him with the evidence that had convicted her in the minds of so many, especially after professing her innocence to all those people for so long. She really *didn't* want to tarnish the present with the past. But she felt she was being less than honest or ducking responsibility if she kept those details to herself.

"Yes," he said.

"And that doesn't make you wonder if I did it on purpose? If I planned my husband's death?"

"*Did* you?" he countered.

She'd thought she'd cried all the tears she was going to cry. The last thing she wanted to do was break down while she was on a date. But the damn lump in her throat swelled and her eyes burned. "No. I never dreamed Sebastian would do what he did. I was trying to *help* him." A tear fell and she dashed it away. "He was talking crazy, telling me he hated his wife. That he couldn't stay with her. That he had no reason to live. I told him he had to get clean so he could think straight. That everything might look different to him then. And he agreed. He promised he'd rebuild his life, said his mother, who's dirt-poor herself, would let him stay with her until he could get into a good rehab if he could just get down south. That's why I gave him my address. So he could pick up the money to take a bus to Los Angeles and go into rehab. I thought nothing of it, you know? Obviously I should have, but I didn't. It never even crossed my mind that he could be dangerous, or that I should've sent the money to him some other way. He came and got it. But instead of purchasing the ticket, he spent the money on meth, came back to my house in the middle of the night and—" She cleared her throat to keep her voice from wobbling.

Rod broke in before she could force the rest out. "And betrayed your trust," he said softly.

"Yes." She blinked rapidly, trying to stop any other tears. "He once robbed a liquor store and was already an ex-con, so I guess I should've known I couldn't trust him."

Rod reached across the table to take her hand. He didn't speak. His fingers just toyed with hers until she could overcome her emotions. Then he let go. "Hindsight is always 20/20," he said. "Ignore anyone who doesn't believe you. You *will* get past what happened. Eventually."

Encouraged, she nodded. "I hate to bring this up, since we've agreed to forget about it and I'm still embarrassed, but…I'm glad you turned me down Friday night."

His fork froze on its way to his mouth. "Because…"

She picked up her water glass. "Because I underestimated you so badly. You're worth far more as a friend than a quick lay."

He seemed to carefully consider her words. Then, after a brief pause, he gave a little shrug. "I guess *friends* will be a good place to start."

"To *start*?" she echoed.

"I'm going to want to sleep with you eventually," he said, and when he didn't so much as crack a smile, she knew it wasn't a joke.

9

The more India relaxed, the more Rod enjoyed being with her. He'd thought she might be so overwhelmed by what she was going through that she wouldn't be able to forget it long enough to have any fun. But by the time they finished dinner, she seemed happy with the distraction he brought to her life. In any case, she didn't mention her late husband again. She talked about her shop and what she hoped to accomplish there, even showed him pictures of various pieces she'd made and asked his opinion on which ones he felt would be the most popular.

He could see that she was talented, which gave him a measure of relief. She wouldn't have a snowball's chance in hell of being successful if she wasn't good. It was going to be tough as it was. There were a lot of artisans in Gold Country, but only the best stayed in business.

She also showed him pictures of her little girl. Cassia wasn't the refined beauty her mother was, but she was definitely cute, with bright orange hair and a smattering of freckles across her nose.

India didn't just talk about herself. She acted interested in his life, too. She asked questions about his family. They weren't intrusive ones, though. Since he didn't like talking about his mother, he was grateful she didn't go back to that subject. She mostly wanted to know what his brothers were like and had him show her a picture of Aaron and Dylan, whom she hadn't met, as well as Natasha.

"She's beautiful," India said as she gazed down at his stepsister's image on his phone. They'd left the restaurant in Jackson and returned to Whiskey Creek for dessert—to the ice cream parlor. He wanted to get India circulating around town so she'd have an easier time adjusting to the move. Since there wasn't much employment in Whiskey Creek, it was great that she didn't need a job. But working out of her house kept her isolated and alone with her problems. He didn't think that would be good for her. He'd seen the worry in her face start to disappear as they talked and laughed and enjoyed their food. As far as he was concerned, she should get out more often.

"Natasha *is* pretty," he said. "But she's sort of…like me and my brothers, I guess."

India paused before taking another spoonful of her mocha almond fudge sundae. "Meaning…"

"She's had a rough past, and sometimes it shows."

"You're talking about the tattoos and the piercings?"

"I'm talking about her behavior. She often pushes away the very things she needs, tells the people she cares about most to go to hell. Stuff like that. But anyone would be screwed up after being raised by Anya." He thought of Natasha's salty language, which was worse than anyone else's in the family. "She's got a chip on her shoulder. She's also opinionated, thinks she can take on the whole world by herself."

"What's that about?"

"It's all bluster. She's lonely and trying to make sure

no one knows it. She's also angry, which means she's her own worst enemy. I understand that because I spent so many years being angry myself. You can get into deep trouble if you can't admit when you really want something or need someone."

India wiped her mouth with one of the small paper napkins they'd been handed with their ice cream. "The way you guys have taken her in and looked out for her is wonderful."

Rod thought of his concern for Mack and the fact that he suspected his youngest brother's feelings weren't quite as brotherly as they should be, but he didn't say anything. The last thing he'd ever do was make one of his brothers look bad. "Like I told you at dinner, she'll be heading to college next fall—to Utah—so our job is essentially done."

India straightened in her seat. "I'm glad you were willing to take responsibility for her. I bet it changed her whole life. But what you just said almost sounds like you're booting her out of the family."

"No, not at all," he responded, backing away from the finality with which he'd spoken a moment earlier. "The situation will change. That's all." He hoped it would change for the better—that she'd find a boyfriend and put his misgivings to rest. She hadn't had a single steady relationship in Whiskey Creek, rejected all romantic attention. Rod feared that her heart was set on Mack, but *surely* she'd forget him once she went to college and met so many other possibilities. Men she could date without the negative sentiment that would arise if she and Mack got together, especially in such a small town...

"You mean she's growing up," India clarified.

He took the out she'd given him, even though he'd actually meant more than that. "Right."

Since he'd finished his own ice cream and she was eating so slowly, he helped himself to some of hers.

She slid it closer—an invitation to take all he wanted.

"I have a question for you," he said.

"What's it about?"

"Sebastian."

She grimaced as if she didn't like hearing his name. "I thought we were done talking about him."

"I need to know a couple more things."

"Such as…"

"I couldn't find anything online about the date of his next trial."

"Because there isn't going to be another trial," she said. "I heard the news myself yesterday. The DA's afraid he won't have any better luck with a new jury. He's decided to wait and see if the police can dig up more evidence."

This was not good news, but Rod had been halfway expecting it. "How do *you* feel about that?"

Her eyes grew troubled again, the way they'd been at the restaurant when they were discussing her situation. "How do you think I feel? They've released him. He's out, God knows where."

He had another spoonful of her ice cream. "Are you afraid he might come *here*?"

"Of course. What's to stop him?"

"And yet you're acting as if nothing's changed."

"What else can I do? Quit living my life? Barricade myself in my house? Move again?" She frowned. "I might *have* to move again. I can't bring Cassia to a place where she might not be safe. But trying to sell the house and find somewhere else to go… It's not something I'm looking forward to."

"I'm just surprised you haven't said anything about it. We've been talking all night, and you haven't mentioned a word."

"You've had enough of your own problems. I figure you don't need to hear about mine."

But *someone* had to help her. She had a child to protect, couldn't stand up to the man who killed her husband all by herself. "The cops can't do anything?"

"No one can do anything. That's the problem."

"So what are the chances?"

"That he'll come here? I have no clue what's going on in his mind, if he's glad to be free and plans to stay out of trouble, or if he's angry and will take the opportunity to exact a bit of revenge. I lied to him that night. I had to. I did whatever I could to protect my child. And then I testified against him, so he knows I lied. The only thing I can be sure of is that he hates me now."

"You didn't leave a forwarding address when you left the Bay…"

"I did. My mail had to go somewhere, but for the time being it goes to a PO box."

"Does he have contact with anyone who might tell him where you've moved?" Because once he heard the name of the town, it wouldn't be hard to find her.

"Not really. But he could ask around. When I bought my house, the trial was still going on, and I was sure he'd be incarcerated for the rest of his life. I *saw* him shoot my husband. I couldn't believe he'd get off after that. So I wasn't as careful as I should've been."

"Meaning…your friends know."

"The ones who didn't abandon me before I decided

where I was going to move. Then there's Cassia's day-care lady, and a neighbor or two, as well as a handful of other people I might've said something to without realizing it."

Rod felt anxious for her. "Now I know why you're not sleeping."

"I wasn't sleeping even when he was in jail. I have… nightmares about…about what happened. Sometimes I wake up in a cold sweat, convinced that he's standing at the foot of my bed, watching me. My sense of security is completely shot—to use a bad pun. But knowing he's out there, free to go where he will, only makes it worse."

And yet…what was that she'd told him when he picked her up? "But didn't you say you were *actually* able to sleep last night? Did exhaustion get the best of you, or…?"

A guilty smile curved her lips.

"What is it?" he asked when she didn't reveal what she was thinking.

"Last night I had a little help."

"So you did take a sleeping pill."

"No. I slept on your deck."

He sat up straighter. "You…*what*?"

She rolled her eyes. "I know. It's pathetic to go creeping over to your neighbor's house. But it was the safest place I could think of, and I needed to crash so badly."

"You should've knocked. I would've shared the bed."

"After hitting on you Friday night for… Well, I wasn't about to knock," she said with a laugh. "Besides, I don't want to drag you or anyone else into this. One person's already been killed simply for being part of my life."

"Sometimes bullies throw their weight around until someone stops them."

"*This* bully is a murderer. You don't want to mess with him."

He scraped the bottom of the bowl, then pushed it aside. "What was he like before? When you were dating him?"

"He wasn't perfect, by any means. But he was never particularly violent."

The way she qualified that statement concerned Rod. "Particularly?"

"We had a few minor skirmishes," she allowed, "but nothing big, nothing that would lead me to believe he could seriously harm anyone."

"What made you date a guy like that in the first place? Or a Hell's Angel, for crying out loud? I can't see a girl like you being attracted to those kinds of guys."

"Wow, you really did your homework."

"I was interested." He was *still* interested, maybe even more so. There was something about her that got to him, made him want to protect her.

"You and everyone else since Charlie died. I feel like my past's been put on display for everyone to criticize."

"*I* was looking for reasons to believe you."

She smiled. "That feels good. It's why I'm talking about this at all, why I'm trusting you after shutting everyone else out. But I can't explain why I was attracted to bad boys. I was young and reckless, and they were…exciting."

"You can't tell me you thought they'd make decent husbands…"

"In those days, I wasn't looking for a husband. I wasn't thinking in terms of what would be best for my life."

"You were more interested in hot sex."

"Could be," she said wryly. "But it was more than that. *Every* emotion was exaggerated. Life in the fast lane can be sort of…addicting."

He leaned back in his chair. "Are you saying life—maybe sex—with a man like Charlie wasn't quite the same?"

She looked pained, as if she preferred not to answer that question. Her reluctance, as much as anything else, told him she'd had no hand in Charlie's murder. She couldn't say a bad thing about the guy. She'd have to be able to disconnect from that in order to *kill* him or even want him dead. "No, of course not. It was good. Just… different."

"Better?" he pushed. Something had been missing. What was it?

"In all the ways that're important."

She sounded slightly defensive, so he took it one step further. "But not in other ways, like maybe…you weren't as sexually compatible as you'd hoped?"

Suddenly defiant, she lifted her chin. "I loved him, so that didn't matter."

"It'd matter to me," he said point-blank.

Her eyes met his, revealing in their intensity. She felt something for him, if only that old attraction to men she thought weren't good for her. Rod almost called her on it, but then she looked away and seemed to stifle what she was feeling—as if that, too, was disloyal.

"I think what I'd been searching for before was all-consuming passion," she said. "But I've realized those types of relationships don't last, except in books and movies. What I had with Charlie was a solid marriage, especially when you compare it to all the dysfunctional, volatile relationships I'd had before. He gave me consistency, dependability, unconditional love, and he was such a wonderful father."

Rod had pushed her too far. Instead of acknowledging

that despite her love for her dead husband, she was feeling the spark of attraction right here, right now, with him, she was singing Charlie's praises. To stop her from becoming any more entrenched in the defense of her marriage, he backed off. He'd learned what he needed to know. For all the great things Charlie was, he hadn't fulfilled India completely, not in a deep-down, intimate way.

Maybe Rod couldn't fulfill her, either, but he wanted to try. He supposed that said a lot about the level of his attraction—that he'd choose to continue their relationship knowing she had a homicidal ex. "What would a *minor skirmish* with Sebastian include?"

She seemed to relax, definitely didn't feel the same impulse to defend Sebastian that she'd felt for Charlie. "An angry shove here or there. A raised fist. But until that night, he never struck me."

Rod felt his muscles tense. "He *hit* you?"

"Not as hard as I wish he had," she muttered.

How was he supposed to interpret *that*?

She must've seen his confusion because she explained. "If he'd beaten me to a bloody pulp, it wouldn't have been so hard for all our friends and his family to believe I wasn't in league with him, and I wouldn't be such a pariah."

"Charlie's family turned against you, too?"

"Not completely. Not yet. But I'm afraid that's coming."

"What makes you think so?"

"Things between us feel…different, strained."

"And if he'd nearly killed you, everyone would know you were as much of a victim as Charlie was. Is that it?"

"Exactly. And then…"

"Then?"

The bell over the door jingled as a small group of tourists entered the shop. After glancing up and taking note of them, she lowered her voice. "Then maybe I could forgive myself for not doing more. If I'd managed to call for help, maybe I could've saved Charlie."

They'd come full circle—back to the guilt she felt, which was probably why she could remember only the good things about her husband. "So why didn't you call?"

"At one point I got hold of a phone. But Sebastian told me he'd kill Cassia if I didn't put it down."

"You don't believe he would've done it?"

She bit her lip. "Could he really kill a child? I don't know. That's the thing. The threat *seemed* real. He'd just shot my husband. But I keep going over and over the events of that night, wondering if I could've done this or could've done that. And everyone else has done the same, questioned my every move."

"Let it go," he said. "You had no choice."

"I wish it were that easy."

So did Rod. The questions she was asking herself were terrible. "What if" was always hard, but it would be excruciating in this serious a situation. "You acted in the safest way you could. You need to accept that."

She opened her mouth to respond but didn't get the chance. Someone else called his name. "Rod!"

When he looked up, he saw Theresa Santiago, a girl he dated now and then. They weren't in a committed relationship. She was as aware of that as he was. But because she sometimes acted as if she'd like to get serious, she wasn't one of the people he'd hoped India would meet when he brought her out for ice cream.

Only Melody would've been worse.

"Hi, Theresa." He stood and collected the napkins they'd used, to signal that they were leaving.

"What are you doing here?" Theresa's eyes cut to India.

"Just enjoying the night," he replied. "You?"

She didn't bother shifting her attention back to him. Clearly, she wondered who India was—and what they meant to each other. "Same thing," she replied, except that she was alone, which made him think she'd stopped in because she'd seen his truck on the street. "Did you get my message?" she asked.

"About the barbecue next Saturday? I haven't had a chance to check my schedule. I'll do that and get back to you."

"Okay." She gestured at India. "Is this…a new friend? I don't believe we've met."

The garbage can was only a couple of steps away. Rod walked over and tossed in the napkins before returning to the table. "This is India Sommers, my new neighbor."

"The woman who bought the house next door?"

"That's me." Wearing a polite smile, India held out her hand. "Nice to meet you."

"Wow. I was hoping you'd be older." She looked thoroughly disheartened as they shook hands. "And I think I'd feel better if you weren't so attractive."

Rod hadn't expected Theresa to make her interest in him so obvious. She'd never been that bold in the past. He was about to say something about how she'd always been a great friend. He felt he needed to clarify their relationship, since India seemed a little confused. But India spoke while he was still trying to come up with the kindest way to phrase what he wanted to say.

"I'm no competition," she said. "Rod and I just met."

Theresa studied him, as if she was taking note of the fact that he'd dressed up—and then he remembered refusing to be her date to a friend's wedding because it would mean putting on a jacket and tie. "Well, if you're like me, it won't take you long to fall in love with him," she said. Then she nodded in his direction. "Have fun."

India remained silent until Theresa had walked out. "Please tell me that woman isn't your girlfriend," she said.

"No. We've been out a few times, that's all."

"Did you know she was in love with you?"

He scratched his neck. "I'm pretty sure she was joking when she said that."

India tilted her head to give him a "no way" look. "I'm pretty sure she wasn't."

Well, she'd certainly picked a fine time to tell him. "I've never made her any promises."

"But you have slept with her."

"Casually. And not often."

"Have you ever had a serious girlfriend?"

"I've had a few," he said, but he didn't want to talk about the last one. What Melody had to say wouldn't recommend him to any woman but would especially frighten someone like India, who'd been abused by men in the past.

"Let's go." He jerked his head toward the door. "I'll take you for a ride on my brother's bike, since mine's not working at the moment."

"You're not comfortable with this subject," she guessed, watching him closely.

"Like I said, I've never made Theresa any promises."

She said nothing.

"About that motorcycle ride…"

"I'd have to change my clothes."

"Of course."

She didn't seem convinced it was a good idea. "Motorcycles are dangerous, even when the driver has full use of both hands."

He slipped his left arm around her shoulders as they walked to his truck. "*Babe*, who do you think you're talking to?" he teased, hoping to put the melancholy of their earlier conversation, and the awkwardness of running into Theresa, behind them. He felt it was time for India to forget her problems and have some fun.

"Who *am* I talking to?" she quipped, playing along.

"Someone who's been riding his whole life," he replied. "You have nothing to worry about. I'll take care of you."

10

The rush of the wind and the roar of the engine seemed to block out all other sensation, except the feel of Rod's back against her chest. When they'd first started, India had been terrified. She'd almost insisted he stop and let her off. The last time she'd ridden on a bike, she'd been in a bad accident, and the one Rod had borrowed from Grady was about as big and powerful as she'd ever seen—not to mention that she was trusting a driver who had only one good hand. But Rod seemed to manage the bike effortlessly despite his cast. The longer she rode with him, the more she came to trust his ability and embrace the rush of excitement.

She even began to wonder if, in her fear of getting hurt, she'd become overly cautious. Had she given up too much?

Maybe, because she'd never felt more carefree than she did as they leaned in to each curve of the winding, mountainous road. She no longer felt like the wife who'd watched her husband killed. Or the wife who'd fallen under suspicion for that terrible act. Or the mother who was afraid she'd soon have a custody battle on her hands.

She was just…living in the moment, and she didn't

want that moment to end. Rod was so sure of himself. She wished she could hang on to him all night, without having to identify the reason or feel guilty for having that desire. It felt as if he was slowly bringing her back to life, or at least reminding her that life was still worth living, and that made her want to be with him more and more.

When they reached the summit, he pulled into a turnout and shut off the engine.

"You okay back there?" he asked as he removed his helmet.

She got off the bike, removed her own helmet and shook out her hair. "Yeah. That was fun," she said. "Quite an experience."

He seemed slightly surprised by her enthusiasm. "I thought you were scared to death."

"Only at first. After that I loved it." He was a big part of the reason, but she didn't let on. "Will you teach me to drive?"

"Sure."

"Tonight?"

He laughed. "No. When we have access to a bike that fits you. You wouldn't even be able to hold this one up."

He was probably right, so she didn't argue. "Someday I'll buy one," she mused. She had a lot to worry about before then, but it was fun to dream of a time she'd feel safe and secure enough to consider such a purchase.

"I can help you look when you're ready," Rod offered.

She liked that he didn't try to discourage her. Charlie, bless his conservative heart, would've told her how foolish that was, how dangerous owning a bike would be, how many other places they could and should put the money before "wasting" it on a toy like that.

And he'd be right. That was the quandary.

"It's beautiful up here," she said as she gazed at the red-and-orange sunset.

Rod beckoned her to the mountain's edge. "You haven't seen anything yet," he told her.

The vista below nearly stole her breath.

She climbed onto a rock so she could be as high as possible.

"Careful," he warned.

"I'm tired of being careful," she said. "Tired of being worried. Tired of trying to compensate for all the things that have gone wrong in my life."

"Good. Anger is the next step in the healing process. It'll make you strong."

"Is this our destination?" she asked after she'd allowed herself a few more minutes to enjoy what he'd brought her to see.

"It is if you're ready to go back. If not, I'll show you a pretty lake I found a few months ago. It's not much farther."

"I don't want to go back," she said. "I don't think I *ever* want to go back."

She could feel him studying her, but she didn't look over. She wasn't about to explain that statement or apologize for it. Of course she didn't *mean* it. She would never run out on her daughter. But this chance to escape all the bad memories was a welcome reprieve.

"Let's head out," he said.

She hopped onto the bike far more eagerly this time and slid her arms around his lean waist. "Go faster!" she yelled once they'd started.

He couldn't hear her until she put up her face mask. Then, with a grin, he nodded—and obliged.

The ride was exhilarating. India felt happier than she'd

been since before Charlie died. Whenever something her husband would've said or done came to mind, she ignored it and focused strictly on the solid frame of the man she clung to. She liked the feel of Rod so much that it was shockingly easy to enjoy his close proximity—something that, once again, she refused to think about.

After they reached the sign he'd been looking for, they parked and he led her down a short, wooded path to a small lake. It was getting dark. With the sun barely a brushstroke of gold in the west and a giant, ghost-like moon climbing into the sky on the other side, they seemed to be witnessing the day's last gasp.

That seemed…significant, as if she was also witnessing the last gasp of her old life before she allowed it to slip away for good.

"It's nice and cool here," she said and took off her shoes to wade in the lake.

Rod stood farther up the shore.

"You're not getting in?" She turned to see why he wasn't joining her.

"No. I'm happy just to watch you."

She stopped moving and stared back at him.

"You're beautiful," he said. "You know that, I hope."

"God, you're…"

"What?"

"Tempting," she finished.

His boyish grin made him even more tempting. "You act like that's a problem."

Her heart was suddenly pounding so hard she could barely speak. "It is!"

"Why?"

"Because sex between us now…it wouldn't be casual. We…we couldn't do casual. Not anymore."

"I never wanted casual in the first place, not with you."

She tucked her hair behind her ears. "What's different about *me*?"

"I don't know. Something. So what's wrong with intense?"

She wasn't ready to open herself up to that much emotion. It didn't seem fair to Charlie. And even if she wasn't still struggling to get over him, she was terrified of what she might feel with Rod—and where it might lead. She couldn't risk making another mistake. She had no more reserves, no way to rebound if it turned out all wrong. "There's no point in starting anything. I probably won't be able to stay in Whiskey Creek."

"You can stay. I won't let Sebastian or anyone else chase you out," he said. And the crazy thing was she almost believed him.

"There's nothing you can do. He's willing to go too far. You can't get involved, anyway. I don't want anyone else hurt."

"You don't have to worry about me. I can look out for myself." He came over, stepped into the water with his motorcycle boots on and took her hands.

India told herself to back away. She could easily do that; he wasn't restricting her movement, wasn't hanging on tight.

Instead, she stood transfixed, waiting for his lips to touch hers.

They did, but far too briefly. When he lifted his head, she felt a heavy dose of sexual frustration.

He knew what he was doing, she realized, knew exactly how to weaken her resolve.

"But if you want me, you're going to have to give me a real chance."

She shook her head. "I can't. Charlie was my husband! Cassia's father!"

"The man you've told me about wouldn't want you to be alone, India. If you're ever going to be happy again, you have to let go. You *have* to."

She closed her eyes. "That's easier said than done."

"I know. But he'd want you to *live* your life. Don't let the past ruin the future."

She wanted to ignore caution, respond the way her body dictated and forget everything else. But her child was at stake. What if the Sommerses learned about her involvement with another man? They'd never believe she truly loved Charlie. That she'd had nothing to do with his death.

Maybe she was even being watched by the police. Maybe Detective Flores now believed Sebastian's defense attorney and was actively gathering proof against *her*. That could be the reason they'd freed Sebastian.

Regardless, if she got involved with another man at this stage, especially a guy like Rod, it wouldn't reflect well on her.

"I can't offer you anything other than a casual encounter," she said. "Here. Now. And no one can know about it."

"I'm not satisfied with that," he said. "Quit making stipulations. Quit holding back. We go into this with at least some hope for more or we don't go into it at all."

She nearly slid her arms around his neck and pulled his mouth to hers. She craved the feel of him against her, wanted him to help her forget all her fears. But she *couldn't* start a new relationship, or she wouldn't be able to respect herself, let alone command any respect from Charlie's family or Detective Flores.

"Then I have no choice," she said.

He stepped back. "We'll see."

That wasn't the response she'd been expecting. "Excuse me?"

"Since you're going to be sleeping in my bed from now on, you can let me know when you're ready."

She felt her jaw drop. "Who said I was going to be sleeping in your bed?"

"*I* did. You can't stay at your place. It's not safe. And I won't hear of you camping out on my deck again. That puts you in my bed—" his gaze ranged over her "—right where I want you."

Mack felt his muscles tense under his blankets. He could hear Natasha moving around the TV room and was afraid she might knock. She did that occasionally. Sometimes she'd even come in and sit on his bed. That wouldn't be good, considering how hard he'd struggled to ignore her while they were watching a movie earlier. The older she got, the more difficult it became for him… She was what he pictured whenever he closed his eyes. How many times had he dreamed that he finally had her naked beneath him?

Too many. There had to be something wrong with him to want her like he did.

He was a twisted, sick son of a bitch, he decided. He was also ashamed. He could guess what his brothers would think. Rod had already brought the subject up to him, so obviously there were signs.

Maybe he should've admitted how he felt and asked for help. Except he didn't see what anyone else would be able to do. He'd done everything he could to kill the attraction—had been trying to control his thoughts and feelings from the start. Nothing seemed to work. He'd wanted her in his bed from practically the first day he'd met her.

He'd never forget how she'd walked into that restaurant with her flake of a mother, so embarrassed and angry by Anya's behavior that she couldn't look at anyone without glaring. He'd felt sorry for her. He'd also felt protective. But, God help him, he'd never felt brotherly. He'd been fighting to keep their relationship within the proper boundaries ever since.

Even if his father hadn't married her mother, she was too young for him, he told himself. Nine years was a lot. She was only nineteen!

But nothing he did seemed to change what he felt. He ignored her. He avoided her. He tried to distract himself with other interests. He'd gone out with—and slept with—just about every available woman in Whiskey Creek. He'd nearly turned himself into a man-whore trying to satisfy the craving Natasha inspired.

All to no avail.

And these days she was making it so much more difficult than it had to be! She spent every minute she could with him. Walked up to him in her bikini to see if he wanted to swim in the river. Sat next to him on the couch or at the kitchen table if he was ever stupid enough to take a seat where there was an open spot nearby. Cooked him food. Brought home whatever leftovers she thought he might like if she went out.

Once, when they'd been cooling off in the river, she'd tried to kiss him. He'd shoved her away and told her never to touch him like that again, but the hurt his rejection had caused almost made him feel worse than if he'd let her do it. She was already so defensive, so reluctant to trust. The way he was treating her couldn't be helping her feel loved or secure.

But what could he do?

"Shit," he grumbled. He couldn't wait until she left for college. Surely then he'd be able to forget her—at least in *that* way—since she wouldn't be living and working with him anymore.

Rolling over, he grabbed his phone to check the date. She'd be gone in two months. That wasn't long. But every day seemed more difficult than the one before...

Briefly, he considered getting up and going over to Sexy Sadie's. He needed to lose himself in a woman or he'd continue to lie there indefinitely, hard as a rock and thinking about Natasha.

He was just getting out of bed when his door opened. "Mack?"

Oh, God. There she was. He'd been able to tell she was restless all evening, that she had something on her mind. She'd kept sidling closer to him as they watched that action flick he'd chosen—until he'd gotten up under the pretense that he needed a beer and then sat clear across the room when he got back.

"Mack?" she said again, since he hadn't answered.

He almost growled at her to get the hell out. Didn't she know what she was doing to him? That he was tied up in knots all the damn time? She was making it impossible for him to live with himself!

"What is it?" he said, struggling to modulate his voice so that she wouldn't assume there was anything wrong.

"Can we talk?"

He hesitated. The smart answer would be no. But now she'd gotten his curiosity up, in addition to...other things. "Sure," he said and climbed back into bed so he could cover up. He was wearing boxer briefs. She'd seen him going into or out of the bathroom in his underwear before. But lately that felt different.

The way she looked at him these days…

"What is it?"

She slipped inside the room and closed the door behind her. It was too dark to see what she was wearing, but when she came closer he recognized one of his old T-shirts. He knew that was what she normally wore to bed. She snagged various shirts out of the laundry, but he'd noticed that they always belonged to him.

"Something wrong?" He couldn't help wondering what she was wearing *underneath* that T-shirt. He hoped she had on a pair of panties almost more than he hoped she didn't…

"We have only two months left," she said.

We? "Until you leave?"

"Yes."

He cleared his throat. "You excited?"

"No. Why would I be?"

"Because college is…college. It's supposed to be a blast. And you're the only one in the family to have that opportunity."

She fidgeted with the edge of his blanket. "I don't care. *You* won't be there. That's all that matters to me, so it doesn't sound like fun at all."

His heart began to knock against his ribs. "You might find it hard to be away from home at first, but you'll get used to it."

"Are you even listening to what I'm saying?" she snapped. "I don't care about leaving *home*. I care about leaving *you*. You're all I want, all I've ever wanted."

What could he say to that? "Natasha, stop. Don't make things weird between us. Our parents are married."

"So what? We were both adults when that happened. Absolute strangers when we met two and a half years ago."

"*I* was an adult. You were sixteen." That was the other problem… Maybe she'd just turned nineteen, but the age difference hadn't narrowed.

"Almost seventeen. I know what I feel. Know *who* I want. Don't treat me like a baby. You've never done that before."

"Listen, it's just a crush," he said. "You'll meet someone else once you get to school."

For a long time she said nothing, merely kept her head bent as she stared at the carpet. "So you don't love me back."

Those six words hit him like a fist to the gut. The last thing he wanted to do was hurt her. "Natasha, this isn't about love. It's about—"

"What?" she broke in. "That we've lived together for two years because our dysfunctional parents happened to find each other on some website and wound up getting married? Why should that keep us apart? We're no more related now than we were then. It's not like your father raised me—or my mother raised you."

"Trust me. It matters, whether we want it to or not," he said. "Besides, you're too young for me."

"At *nineteen*?"

"Nineteen is too close to eighteen! There's someone else out there for you."

She stood up. "That's not true. There's *never* been anyone else."

"There could be. I've seen the way guys look at you. You've had plenty of interest."

"I've never been interested in *them*."

Mack's chest constricted, making it tough to breathe. "Good. Wait until you fall in love. Sex is much better if there's love involved."

"Stop it!" she yelled. "Just…stop! I hate that you won't listen to what I'm saying."

He said nothing. She might be only nineteen, but she was the oldest nineteen-year-old he'd ever met. With a mother like Anya, she'd seen it all growing up, could never be called naive.

"Whether you want to hear this or not, I'm in love with you," she whispered harshly. "I'd give *anything* to be with you."

There. She'd said the words. What they'd both tried to ignore for months and months. And now that it was out, how was he going to avoid her for eight more weeks? Avoid giving her what she wanted—what they *both* wanted?

"You're too young to even know what love is." He knew that would start a fight. She'd never stand for such patronizing bullshit. She'd already called him on that kind of behavior once in this conversation. But he also knew if she didn't leave right now, he'd pull her into his bed and show her that she wasn't alone in what she was feeling.

She stepped closer to him. "Can you honestly say you view me as your little sister?"

"Yes. Of course," he lied, because it didn't matter how *he* viewed her. They lived in a small town. He couldn't embarrass his brothers by getting involved with the girl they'd been calling their stepsister. After what his mother had done, and then his father, his brothers had been through enough. They'd finally gained some respect in this community. He wasn't going to undermine that.

She reached over and turned on the lamp. Then she yanked off the T-shirt she was wearing and tossed it on the floor. "Say it *now*," she said, standing before him in nothing but a pair of lacy panties. "Tell me you don't want to see this, that you don't want to touch it."

He couldn't. He told himself to look away, to look at *anything* except what she'd just revealed. But it was impossible. Several seconds passed before he could subdue the desire that welled up and nearly choked him. "Put your shirt back on," he said when he found his voice.

God, when had she pierced her nipples? And who the hell had done it? She was too young for that! But she'd always been wild, and it was partly that edginess that got to him. He wanted to protect her, make her whole. Not that he could act on that desire. It wasn't his place. Eventually some other man would see her the way he did, and he hoped to high heaven he'd be able to tolerate that when it happened.

He watched her throat work as she swallowed, could tell by the way she set her chin that she was close to tears. "That's all you're going to say?" she asked.

What else *could* he say? That she was perfect? Every bit as beautiful as he'd imagined? That he was only a heartbeat away from taking her into his bed?

He got up to retrieve the shirt so he could hand it to her. He had to cover her up, before he did the opposite and removed the tiny scrap of fabric that was left. Did she have any idea what she'd just done to him? How much more difficult it would be to sleep, now that he had that image of her in his mind?

He didn't think he'd *ever* forget the sight of her standing there almost naked, glaring defiantly at him as if she knew in her heart what he wouldn't say...

"Fine. If you don't want me, I'll find someone who does," she said and, grabbing the shirt he held, stormed out of his room.

Mack felt sick to his stomach. Turning her away had to be hurting him more than it was hurting her. At least, he hoped that was true, because he couldn't bear the thought of causing her pain.

He almost went after her, but he stopped himself. That would only make matters worse. But he wished he *had* gone after her when, five minutes later, he heard the roar of an engine outside and the squeal of brakes as she tore out of the drive.

11

Rod dropped India off at her house and told her to pack a few essentials and come through the door off the deck, since she didn't want his brothers to know where she'd be sleeping. He doubted he and India could keep it secret for long, but he didn't mind giving her a few nights to get acclimated.

He went in through the front, to say good-night to anyone who might be up. He couldn't go straight to his room, though, when he found Mack sitting at the kitchen table in the light that spilled from the entry, drinking a beer. His brother had obviously come from bed. He was wearing nothing except a pair of boxers—another reason Rod was glad he'd told India she could use the deck entrance. But Mack half-naked wasn't the problem. Mack being upset was.

"What's going on?" Rod asked. The TV wasn't even on in the other room. Why was his youngest brother sitting alone in the dark?

"Nothing."

Something was wrong. He studied Mack, looking for clues, but couldn't figure it out. His hair was mussed, as if he'd been running his hands through it, and he seemed to be in a bad mood, which was unusual for him. But...why?

When Mack offered no explanation, Rod walked over to the fridge to get himself a drink. "You don't want to talk about it?"

Mack took a long pull on his beer. "There isn't anything to talk about."

"You're pissed off." Or maybe he'd had his feelings hurt, but Rod wasn't going to suggest that. It was the least attractive option for someone like Mack—for any of them—to admit to. "I think I know you well enough to pick up on that."

"Just can't sleep."

He sat down across from his brother. "Because..."

Mack's broad shoulders lifted in a shrug. "Too hot, I guess."

Hot? The air conditioner was chugging along. Rod thought it was actually a little chilly in the house. But he didn't contradict him. He cracked open his own beer. "Grady still out?"

"No. Came in a couple of hours ago. He's in bed now."

Rod paused before bringing the bottle to his lips. "His truck isn't in the drive."

"Natasha took it."

"When?"

"About ten minutes ago."

"Did Grady tell her she could?"

"Doubt it."

Rod took a swallow of his beer. "So where'd she go?"

"No clue."

That was surprising. Mack usually knew where Natasha was. That was one of the things that made Rod uncomfortable. His youngest brother kept close tabs on

her—like the other night, at Sexy Sadie's. Mack was the one who'd noticed that Liam was bothering her. And once Natasha decided to leave, Mack didn't stay much longer. It was almost as if he got bored when she wasn't around.

Rod checked the time on his phone. "It's after midnight."

"I know."

So *that* was it. Mack was worried about Natasha. Maybe they'd even had a fight. "You don't think she's in any kind of trouble…"

Mack stared at his bottle as he turned it around and around. "Who knows?"

"Well, she's not old enough to get into the bar. They only allow eighteen and up on Fridays, when they have certain bands. So she can't be at Sexy Sadie's."

"If they figure they can get away with it, they let hot chicks in, anyway."

"Those would be hot chicks from out of the area. Everyone knows how old Natasha is. So where else might she go? A friend's?"

"You might have noticed she doesn't have a lot of friends," he said with a degree of sarcasm. "None she's particularly close to, anyway. She's never really fit in with that giggling group she's had over a couple of times or anyone else at the high school. She mostly hangs out with us."

Rod *had* noticed. He also felt he knew why. "If she just left, it's too soon to panic. Maybe she'll be right back."

Mack began to peel the label off his beer. "I don't think she will."

"Then…what do you want me to do?" Rod could tell he had something in mind.

"Any chance you'd be willing to go out and drive around? See if you can spot Grady's truck?"

As concerned as he was for his brother, Rod's first thought was of India and the fact that she'd soon be in his bed. "Why don't *you*?"

When he looked up, Rod realized that Mack *wanted* to go after her. He was holding himself back, afraid of what might occur if he found her.

"Should I ask what happened between you?"

"No. I will tell you that I didn't touch her, though. I swear it."

"Okay." He didn't press for more of an explanation.

"Will you go?"

India was only coming over to sleep. Rod supposed she could do that without him. Chances were good she'd prefer some privacy. Being alone in his room would give her a chance to drift off in a safe place without feeling she needed to be wary of him. "Sure. I'll see what I can find out."

"Text me when you have news," Mack said, looking up as Rod stood. "But don't mention that I was the one who…who needed to know."

Leaving his beer on the table, he squeezed his brother's shoulder. As he'd guessed, the poor son of a bitch was so emotionally distraught he couldn't tell which way was up. "I will. Finish that for me, huh?" Rod gestured at what was left of his beer.

"Yeah." Mack tipped back his own bottle. "I plan to drink everything in the house."

Rod paused for a second. He almost said that time and separation would help. He'd never met a woman he couldn't get over. But he wasn't sure he'd ever really been in love. And he hoped love wasn't what Mack was grappling with now.

Nonetheless, he wouldn't be doing Mack any favors

by putting it into words. So he walked out and started his truck. Then he texted India to let her know he had to run an errand that might take an hour or so.

India received Rod's text while she sat on the edge of her bed. Although she'd already packed a pair of pajamas and a few toiletries, she'd been wrestling with herself about going over there. She felt too vulnerable in her own house, so the safety appealed to her. Other aspects did, too. That was what stopped her.

She couldn't turn to a man like Rod, couldn't allow herself to lean on him, not without inviting other problems into her life. It wouldn't be fair to him if she did. She wasn't *his* responsibility.

Then she received word that he wouldn't even be there when she arrived—and that made the decision for her. He'd come home later, of course, but as long as she was asleep, it wouldn't matter. She'd have one night during which she could rest peacefully, one night when she wouldn't have to listen for someone breaking in. Later on she could decide whether she should return to Rod's bed tomorrow night or the night after.

No problem, she typed and sent her message.

A ding alerted her to his reply.

You're coming though, right? I don't want you staying in that house alone anymore.

He was the kind of man who took charge and felt comfortable doing it. But India didn't mind. She liked the way he'd jumped in to help. That, along with the confidence he'd cobbled together simply by proving himself over the years, was part of her attraction to him. Maybe he wasn't highly educated or someone who would've made the contributions Charlie could've made, but, other than what he'd received from Dylan, he'd had very little support in life. Rod was street-smart—a self-made man who didn't seem to be afraid of anything because he'd already fought his way through so much. She figured there were worse things than falling under the protection of a guy like that.

She slung her bag over her shoulder and stood up.

I'm coming.

Good. Get some sleep. I'll be there soon.

She heard his truck start and wanted to ask where he was going, but he would've mentioned it if he wanted her to know.

She hoped it wasn't out to buy condoms…

Shifting her mind away from *that* possibility, she went around to all the doors and windows to make sure they were locked. Then she let herself out the back and hurried across the yard.

Natasha leaned against the brick wall of the high school gymnasium, hugging her knees to her chest as she stared out over the matted grass between the buildings. She was no longer a student here, had never fit in to begin with, so she found it ironic that this was the only refuge she could think of. But where else was there? She wasn't old enough to get into Sexy Sadie's tonight, and most other places in Whiskey Creek weren't open late. It wasn't as if she had any girlfriends she could turn to.

Boyfriends, either. The guys she'd met in high school had never held any appeal.

How could they? They seemed so young and immature compared to Mack.

She pulled out some of the blades of grass around her. She'd earned a 4.0 GPA her senior year, something she'd never dreamed she could do. Maybe that was why she'd come here. To pay tribute. To remember that she had that small bit of success to build on. She was going to college as a result—had received a partial scholarship as well as a grant from the government. It had simply never occurred to her that college would be in her future, not with what she'd experienced in the past.

But the thought of how well she'd done in school brought her back to the Amos brothers. She wouldn't have been able to do it without them and the stability they'd introduced to her life. They'd stepped in and provided a unified front, protecting her from all the crazy shit her mother used to subject her to. She'd known, almost from the beginning, that even if her mother divorced their father, she'd have a home with them until she graduated.

She was grateful for that, loved every single one of them like a brother—except Mack. The way she loved him was different. She'd never felt anything so powerful in her life.

But women in general loved Mack. While she'd been waiting to come of age, he'd entertained one woman after another. Watching that hadn't been easy. Just looking at him made her ache to touch him, and not in the way he'd always touched her, with that careful, platonic embrace—if he allowed himself to embrace her at all. She knew he felt more than he'd ever admit, could see how he tensed whenever she got too close and how his gaze trailed after her when he thought she wasn't looking, even when he had another woman over. Sometimes that was when he treated her the most warmly, as if that other woman acted as some sort of defense against his own feelings.

Too bad none of that mattered. She'd been labeled his "stepsister" because of a piece of paper that had joined her mother to his father less than three years ago, and that was all there was to it. He felt he *had* to leave her alone. He'd be too ashamed to do anything else.

A pair of headlights swung into the lot. Natasha peered into the darkness. Part of her hoped it was Mack, that he'd changed his mind.

But it wasn't. She recognized Rod's blue truck as he parked. No doubt he'd noticed Grady's SUV in the lot.

With a sigh, she stood and wiped off her bottom, which was wet from the dewy grass. She was still wearing nothing but her panties under Mack's T-shirt. She'd rushed out of the house without a thought for anything except escape, hadn't even asked to take Grady's truck. She'd found his keys on the counter and scooped them up. But as long as she didn't get into a wreck, she didn't think he'd mind. And the T-shirt was big enough that it hit her midthigh, so it wasn't as if she was any more naked than if she'd been wearing a skirt.

"Over here," she said once Rod had jumped out and started calling her name.

He stopped on the blacktop and rested his hand on his hip while he waited for her to come out of the shadows. "You okay?" he asked, looking her over carefully the moment she was standing in the moonlight and he could see her clearly.

"I'm fine," she lied.

"What are you doing *here*?" He gestured to the school with his cast.

"Just thinking."

"About…"

"I'm considering leaving Whiskey Creek early," she told him. "If I move to Utah right away, it should be easier to get a job. You know, before all the other kids arrive for fall semester. Might as well get settled in."

She could tell when he didn't argue with her, didn't mention the job she had here, that he had some inkling of what was going on. She wondered what Mack had told him. Mack must have said something. Otherwise, Rod would've gone to bed without thinking twice about the fact that Grady's SUV was gone. The brothers came and went all the time without anyone really keeping track, and they tried to ignore J.T. and Anya altogether.

"That might be for the best," he agreed.

When he said that, it felt as though he'd plunged a fork into her heart. She swallowed hard and blinked rapidly but couldn't overcome the tears that welled up.

She thought he'd ignore them. She wanted him to. She wished she could be as stoic as the rough-and-tough Amos brothers. No one dared to mess with them; they could take care of themselves in any situation. Besides, they weren't comfortable with displays of emotion, which was part of the reason she never let them see her cry.

Rod wasn't any different from his brothers in that regard, but he didn't ignore her tears. He pulled her to him and kissed the top of her head.

"I've never felt *anything* worse than this," she admitted as he held her.

He didn't request an explanation. "It won't always be this bad," he said simply. Then he released her so they could head home.

It didn't take Rod more than a few minutes to realize that he'd overestimated his ability to share a bed with India. He'd been gone long enough that she was dead to the world when he crawled in. He'd expected that, thought it would put a decisive end to the evening and he'd have to settle for just being close to her.

He *was* settling, but that didn't mean he could sleep. No matter how hard he tried to hold still and concentrate on other things—various issues at work, on the repairs he needed to make to his bike, or what he might hear from Liam Crockett—he couldn't drift off. He spent the next hour fighting the urge to touch her.

Keeping his hands to himself was hard enough when he could only smell her perfume. But as time went by, she gravitated closer and closer. Before long, she was pressed right up against him.

The feel of her soft legs against his made him so hard he knew he was wasting his time even *trying* to sleep. He'd have to move to the couch.

He was just sliding out of bed when he realized that, as careful as he'd been, he'd awakened her. She didn't speak, but he noticed that her breathing had changed, and he could feel her watching him—or what she could see of him—in the dark.

"Am I keeping you up?" he murmured.

"No."

"I can go somewhere else."

"Don't leave."

He stopped inching toward the edge of the mattress. "Okay. I'm here. Go back to sleep."

They stayed like that, beside each other without touching, for the next few minutes. But instead of relaxing and eventually nodding off, they grew more stiff and tense. He could sense her awareness of him. Being in the same bed had suddenly become as awkward for her as it was for him.

Rod was about to say he wasn't helping her out by staying when he felt her hand on his arm. "India…"

"Please…don't talk," she said.

He was still hesitating, trying to decide if he was letting his body lead him into an emotional ambush, when that hand traveled from his arm to his chest. Sucking in his breath, he closed his eyes as her cool fingers found their way under his T-shirt and moved over his stomach and pecs. "I want you," she murmured. "I've wanted you from the moment I laid eyes on you, bloody knuckles and all. I've never experienced that with anyone else."

That statement set him apart from every other man, even her dead husband. And being taken seriously by her was all he'd ever asked. He had no idea if what they felt would last. He'd never had a girlfriend for more than a few months at a time. What his mother had done had somehow damaged him, cost him the ability to trust, and without trust he sometimes feared love would be impossible. But he'd been as instantly attracted to India as she was to him, and he wanted to give what they felt an honest chance. "Rod? Is that a no?" she asked.

"That's a yes," he said and turned her onto her back.

12

India stared up at Rod as he removed the silky shorts and spaghetti-strap top of her pajamas. The sudden exposure to the air—and particularly his gaze—puckered her nipples and caused gooseflesh. She thought he'd smooth all of that away by immediately pulling her against him, but he rocked back on the bed so he could look at her.

"Gorgeous," he said with satisfaction.

India wished that didn't flatter her as much as it did, wished he'd say or do something that would turn her off. She needed to come up with some complaint she could use to build an emotional barrier between them. That giddy rush of falling for someone left her with no defense.

Was she succumbing to her own foolishness once again? Welcoming the wrong type of guy into her life?

Perhaps. But temptation had never been presented to her in a more appealing package...

"Then touch me," she said.

He slid his good hand lightly up her thigh, over her hip and waist to her left breast, where he flicked his thumb across the sensitive tip before lowering his head.

India gasped as his mouth closed over her and she caressed his recently cut hair.

"I wish I didn't have this cast," he mumbled as his mouth traveled up her neck. "It's frustrating, but my biggest regret is not being able to use both hands on you."

"You're doing fine with just one." She was so excited she could hardly breathe, but what he was doing wasn't so different from the other men she'd known. His touch seemed to hold a certain magic. Not since high school had she been this physically attracted to someone. She used to think that kind of all-consuming desire came only with first love, and after she and Sam split up, she thought the feeling would be gone forever. Since Sam, it *had* been gone. But this encounter flew in the face of all that.

"And there's still the rest of you," she said. "That feels like plenty to me."

"I'll give you all I've got," he promised and found her lips.

India loved the way he kissed. As eager as she was to experience what was coming next, she refused to rush this part and was glad he didn't seem to be in any hurry. He paid attention to every nuance, every reaction, and made the most of what he learned. She liked how he drew her out of her hesitation and her fears and managed to get her to completely relax, forget, trust. He seemed to care about what she was thinking and feeling and wanted to engage her mind before engaging anything else. The tender way he touched her face when their tongues first met was a perfect example. She almost thought she could be satisfied just making out...

"When you're so good with your lips, you don't need even your hands," she told him.

He lifted his head to smile at her. "We'll still use what we've got." He ran his fingers down between her breasts to show her that his hand could bring pleasure, too. Then he sat up to remove his own shirt. When his bare chest came into contact with hers, India blocked out any lingering doubts floating around in her head. She just wanted him to kiss her again and again.

"My heart's never pounded so hard," he whispered with a husky laugh.

Could that be true? she wondered as he began to explore the rest of her body. He acted as if being with her was special. Did he treat every woman this same way? She had no answer, but for a brief moment she was tempted to pull away and hurry home. Returning to her house, in spite of Sebastian, suddenly felt safer than staying here—and that told her a great deal.

But she'd started this. She couldn't bail out now.

Besides, she knew she'd be sorry if she left. Whatever Rod had to offer, she wanted.

"I can make it pound harder," she said and slipped her hand into the basketball shorts he'd worn to bed.

When her hand closed around him, he groaned, and that made her feel desired, powerful and as beautiful as he said she was. "What do you think?" she asked. "Do you like that?"

"I like *you*," he replied.

They were getting carried away. But any thought India had of trying to rein this in, even on an emotional level, was gone with the rest of their clothes.

"Tell me you have condoms," she whispered, already cursing herself for hoping he wasn't at the store earlier, buying some.

"I do. And I'll use one. But we're not ready for that quite yet."

"Why not?"

He held her chin as he made eye contact. "Because

we've got all night. I plan to enjoy you in other ways first, and since I can't use my hand, we're going to plan B."

India didn't mind plan B. Plan B was probably most women's plan A. She closed her eyes as he kissed his way down her stomach and had to bite her lip so she wouldn't cry out when he spread her legs.

Rod had always loved women, probably a little too much. He figured it came from growing up in a houseful of boys. All five of them were the same—a little too fixated on the fairer sex. That was part of the reason he and his brothers had the reputations they did. He'd enjoyed his previous encounters, but this…this was even better.

Rod loved the way India tried, at first, to stifle her reaction, to be reserved and subdued. She fought to keep her self-control, as if holding back would create some emotional distance. But she couldn't manage it, and nothing was more fun than watching her succumb to his lovemaking. It was almost as if they were wrestling in a swimming pool. She'd break free and start for the edge, and he'd catch her and drag her under again. Except that she *liked* going under; she just didn't know how to deal with feeling so powerless.

There were moments when guilt stood between them, when she seemed ready to bolt. But he couldn't hold that against her. If she could relegate him to the category of nothing but a cheap thrill, like she'd tried to do the night they met, she wouldn't have any reason to feel guilty. It was the guilt that told him this wouldn't be the same with just any man.

He was prying her away from Charlie, and he was using sex to do it. Charlie couldn't give her that. Rod felt bad about what had happened to the guy, but even if Rod stayed away from her, it wouldn't change the fact that Charlie was gone. Besides, when it came to India, Charlie possessed every other advantage. Sex would work, in the way Rod wanted it to work, only if there was something deeper, and it was that deeper element that made this so spectacular.

When her thighs began to quiver and she groaned despite herself, he nearly rose up and buried himself inside her so he could experience her climax more intimately. But he didn't want to frighten her by suddenly getting too assertive. He was going slow, trying to build her confidence and draw out the pleasure.

But all of that fell by the wayside after her climax. Soon, they were completely intertwined, touching and tasting each other everywhere. And she seemed as overcome as he was, no longer even tried to break free of the power that bound them together. "I can't wait to feel you inside me," she said. "Where are the condoms?"

He'd been holding off for her benefit, not his, so she could get all she wanted or needed of the other physical aspects. He wasn't too confident he'd last once he started to thrust inside her. He felt dangerously close to the edge right now, with her bare skin moving against his and her hands— God, she was talented with her hands.

He was glad she was eager to have him where he wanted to be. It was particularly gratifying that *she'd* asked for that final, intimate step, even though she'd already come.

When he settled himself between her thighs, she gripped his ass as if joining with him was the supreme moment, and within minutes he was trembling himself.

"Give me a second," he breathed, staying completely still so their lovemaking wouldn't be over too soon. "Let me make you come again," he said, but she didn't need any special effort or encouragement. They were both so aroused that bringing her to a second climax didn't take any work. Their bodies moved instinctively, in perfect rhythm, straining to get closer, to be more connected—until he heard her breath catch and felt her jerk beneath him. Then he knew he'd reached his goal, and burying his face in her neck, he abandoned all restraint, letting the pleasure he'd been holding at bay flow through him.

After that it wasn't remotely hard to fall asleep.

The alarm went off a few minutes later. Actually, it felt like minutes, but it was really four hours. Rod hated to get out of bed. He wanted to stay and make love to India again. They were all tangled up in each other, still naked, so he felt he'd be passing up the perfect opportunity.

Except he'd be late for work, and then his brothers would come pounding on his door. Even if he wasn't conscious of protecting India's privacy, which he was, he planned to avoid the ribbing that finding their neighbor in his bed would provoke. If he could...

With a sigh of regret, he kissed her shoulder and got up to shower. He didn't usually shower before going to the shop; he showered after, since that was when he most needed it. But he thought he might smell of her perfume.

"Everything okay?" she asked with a sleepy yawn.

"Fine. I've got work. But you're safe here. Sleep as long as you like."

"You're not the only one with things to do," she mumbled. But he could tell she was joking, because she didn't bother to prove how busy her schedule was by dragging her butt out of bed. She rolled over, taking the covers with her, and he chuckled as he stepped into the bathroom.

Rod showered quickly, pulled on his jeans and a clean T-shirt and was about to head down for some breakfast when he heard a knock on the door to his deck. He couldn't imagine who it could be, especially this early.

Sebastian came to mind. Even though India's ex would have no way of knowing she was with him, it was the thought of the man who'd killed her husband that made Rod walk over to see who was there. And then he wished he hadn't—although it would've been worse if India had been forced to get up and answer the door.

"Hey, Theresa." Keeping his voice down, he stood in the gap so she wouldn't be able to see there was some-one in his bed. Theresa worked as a hairstylist. She usu-ally didn't begin her day until ten or so, and yet she was completely ready. "What are you doing here?"

She raised the basket she had in her hands. "I decided to bring you some breakfast. You know, to prepare you for a long day at work."

Unsure how to respond, he hesitated. He didn't want to lead her on, but he also didn't want to be rude or hurt-ful. "Actually…"

"What?" she said. "You love scrambled eggs and bacon. I've even got some fresh-baked muffins in here. You'd have cold cereal otherwise, right?"

That was true. He ate cold cereal or a quick bowl of oatmeal almost every morning and liked nothing more than a home-cooked meal. He hadn't had the privilege of growing up with parents who made dinner—or parents at all. He'd been raised on microwave food, unless Dylan was on a health kick. Then they ate vegetables and lean meat, with no salt or sugar—nothing that could possibly be called "comfort food." Maybe that was why they all loved Just Like Mom's. There, they could get homemade chicken potpie, meat loaf and potatoes, chicken-fried steak with potatoes and gravy, and the best pies in the world for dessert—all the things Rod imagined his mother would've cooked if she'd decided to stay around. "I *do* like scrambled eggs and bacon, and it was really nice of you to go to so much trouble, but after what you said last night, I'm not sure I feel comfortable accepting it."

She lowered the basket. "I could see that surprised you. To be honest, it surprised me, too. I didn't plan to tell you how I feel when you were on a date with someone else. But it's true, Rod. I've loved you for a long time, and I feel we've had enough of a relationship that I should have the right to fight for you." She held out the basket a second time. "So please, take this. And don't worry that eating my food means you owe me anything. I'm just giving you a sample of what I can offer. What I'd *like* to offer. If you stick with me, I'll be your biggest supporter, your biggest cheerleader. Think about coming home to a hot meal and a willing woman every night."

Rod was flattered, but this was even more awkward than if she'd gotten angry. The conversation had probably awakened India. He felt certain she was listening. "You have a lot to offer any man," he said. "I'm not sure I'm the right one."

"Other women may be prettier or more exciting. I can see why you'd be interested in your neighbor. But no one could ever be more devoted to you than me."

She was really going for the close… He cleared his throat. "I appreciate that."

"Please, take this," she said. "And enjoy it. I liked making it for you. Someone with your past might not believe a woman will see it through if and when the going gets tough. But I'm here to tell you I'm not like that. I'd *never* hurt you."

Rod didn't have the heart to let her continue holding that basket, so he took it. "Theresa, I'm sorry. I...I don't even know what to say. I don't want to hurt you."

"Then don't. Give me a chance."

"But—"

"You don't have to answer now. Just...think about it. Think about *me*," she said, and with a hopeful smile, she left.

"Am I already getting in the way?" India asked when she was gone.

Rod sighed as he shut and locked the door. "No. You're fine. Are you hungry?"

"You're going to share the breakfast she made with *me*?"

"What else can I do? Let you go hungry while I eat?"

"Seems weird, that's all."

"I know. I'm sorry. I had no idea she'd show up here— or say what she did last night. Until now, she's let me call the shots."

"Because she thought she had you—or that you'd eventually get where she wanted you to go. Seeing you with me spooked her."

"I guess so, but...there's nothing I can do about that."

"Listen, I don't want to cause you any problems."

He wasn't happy to hear what she was saying. She'd raised her guard again. He was tempted to climb into bed with her, to reassure them both that what they'd shared had been real and that having the sun come up didn't suddenly put them in a new situation. But then some-one tried to open his other door and ended up knocking on it instead.

"Rod?" Grady called. "You awake? Why's the damn door locked? You think anyone here cares if we see your bare ass?"

India had jumped at the noise and pulled the sheet she clasped to her chest that much higher. But when Grady mentioned his bare ass, her lips twitched as if she was about to smile.

"I'll be out in a sec!" Rod said.

"Hurry, or you'll have to drive over on your own. We gotta go. We can't be waiting for you all day."

"Fine. Head on over. I'll be there shortly."

"Okay. See you soon."

Rod listened to his brother's footsteps recede before lowering his voice to address India. "Relax. Nothing's changed."

She still hid her breasts behind that sheet as if she was too self-conscious to do anything else. "I'm not sure we should take what happened last night too seriously."

"What *happened*? You make it sound like we played no active role in it."

"Fine. What we did. We…we're both leading very complicated lives."

He frowned at her. "Here we go."

She peered at him more closely. "What does *that* mean?"

"Are you running scared already?"

"Last night was a…a bit overwhelming."

"The hottest sex I've ever had," he admitted.

She blushed. "I liked it, too. You're amazing in bed. But…"

"But?" She'd paid him such a generous compliment, he was almost afraid to hear what came next. Was she setting him up? Would she bring up her dead husband—wimp out on him?

Fortunately, she didn't. She straightened her spine, and her nostrils flared slightly as she said, "Yes, I'm running scared. You frighten me because…because you make me feel so much, and I'm not ready."

"Because of Charlie."

"Yes, because of Charlie."

He relaxed. "Good."

She blinked at him. "Did you hear me? I said I'm not ready."

He put the basket on the nightstand so she could eat after he'd left. He was too late, didn't have time. "But you're interested, whether you want to be or not. That's what matters."

"*Excuse* me?"

"I can't make any promises about forever, India. I won't pretend I'm the most reliable man in the world. Not when it comes to love. So I'm not asking you to make *me* any of those promises, either. Life's always been one day at a time for me. All I know is, right now you're the one I want. I'm approaching whatever happens between us honestly, moment by moment. Can you do the same?"

She glanced over at the picnic basket, obviously remembering the woman who'd brought it.

"Don't worry about Theresa." He gestured as if he could erase the recent past. "It's different with you."

"*Why?* In what way?"

"How can anyone explain attraction?"

"You should stick with her."

"*What?*" He'd never had a woman tell him something like that before. "Are you serious?"

"I'm not in a position to gamble, Rod!"

"Quit thinking about tomorrow! How do you feel right *now*?"

"It's not that simple. Everything we do leads *somewhere*. We have to look farther down the road."

"No, we don't." He couldn't talk any longer; he had to go. "With this hand I'm not much good to Dylan at the shop. He wants me to swing by to get a list of parts and then drive to Bakersfield today. Can we revisit this later?"

She nodded. "Sure. Go ahead." But he wasn't done quite yet.

Grabbing the sheet, he arched an eyebrow to see if she'd willingly release her grip.

She hesitated but eventually let go, and he tugged it down. "I won't be home until evening." He gazed at what he'd revealed and felt his body react. "But I hope you'll be here, just like this, waiting for me."

13

After Rod left, India got up and went into the bathroom. As she washed her hands, she caught sight of her wedding ring and paused to stare at it. What was she doing? What was she getting involved in?

Rod had just admitted that he wasn't particularly reliable when it came to love. She'd heard Theresa say something that made sense, too—about his past making it difficult for him to rely on a woman. He hadn't been able to rely on his own mother when he most needed her, when he was young and vulnerable, and she'd been the only female in his life. It stood to reason that he'd be hesitant to allow himself to depend on other females, who, in his mind, had far less reason to stand by him.

But could *any* guy predict how he might feel in a week, a month, longer? They'd barely met. And he'd been honest with her so far. She couldn't accuse him of being superficial, of being interested in only a booty call. He could've had that Friday night, and he'd refused.

Anyway, she wasn't *asking* for a commitment from him. She couldn't be with anyone right now, least of all someone her in-laws would not approve of.

Life's always been one day at a time...

For years, her life had been like that, too. Until Charlie. Charlie had changed everything. He'd given her peace of mind, security, financial stability, even respectability. She'd be a fool to go back to the lifestyle she'd had before. Which meant she had to be decisive and cut off whatever she was feeling for Rod—while she still could.

But that wouldn't be easy…

She pressed her face into the towel he'd used and breathed deeply to catch the scent of him. She loved the way he smelled, the way he looked, the way he felt, the way he touched. Just being in his *space* was somehow gratifying. She remembered wanting to touch his clothes and bedding when she'd brought over those cookies and had known even less about him.

Too bad the kind of man her heart wanted wasn't the kind of man she needed. That'd been the case in every instance except Charlie. And she probably wouldn't have given Charlie a chance if she hadn't come to know him slowly. By the time he'd asked her out, she'd had no reservations about him…

"Rod?"

India froze. When Rod left, she hadn't thought to lock the bedroom door, and someone had come in. The voice was that of a female, but it wasn't Theresa.

"Rod?" A knock sounded on the bathroom door. "Can I catch a ride with you?"

India felt trapped. She didn't even have her clothes. Her pajamas and overnight bag were still in the bedroom.

She wished she could pretend she wasn't there, but she'd just flushed the toilet and turned off the tap. Whoever it was would've heard that, which was why this person assumed Rod was home. India had no choice except to speak up. "Rod's already gone," she said.

There was a long silence. Then, "Oh. Sorry. I didn't realize he had a...er...company."

"No problem." India held her breath and listened, but she didn't hear Natasha—at this point, she figured it had to be Rod's stepsister—move away.

"Theresa, is that you?" Natasha asked uncertainly.

Grabbing Rod's towel, India wrapped it around herself even though she was the one who had control of the lock. She felt so foolish, and being naked made it worse, even if there was a wooden panel between them. "No, it's...India."

"India?"

Shit... "Yes. India Sommers. I live next door." She almost followed up with some excuse for being in Rod's room—like the water was shut off at her place, so Rod had given her permission to take a shower—but her pajamas were lying on the floor by the bed. The condom wrapper could also be there. Whatever excuse she attempted to offer would look pretty lame.

"Oh," Natasha said. "I've been hoping to meet you. I should've come by."

Now, to their mutual embarrassment, an introductory visit wouldn't be quite the same...

"Anyway, welcome to the neighborhood," Natasha went on. "Not that it's really a neighborhood, but you know what I mean."

India took a deep breath. "I do. Thanks." She thought that would be the end of it. That she'd be able to dress and get the hell out of there. But Natasha *still* didn't go.

"Listen, since you're up...would you mind giving me a ride to work? I wasn't feeling too good last night, so the guys figured I wouldn't be going in."

India tightened her towel. It was a little odd that this

girl would ask a favor of someone she'd just met. However, according to Rod, she'd had to shift for herself in the past, so maybe it wasn't too unusual. Besides, this was Whiskey Creek. And they were neighbors.

"Sure," India replied. "I can do that." But she couldn't go anywhere as she was. "Would you mind handing me that bag out in the bedroom?"

"Oh, of course not," came the response. "Do you want the pajamas, too?"

Her underwear was tangled in her discarded sleepwear. That was the *last* thing she wanted Natasha to see—well, other than the condom wrapper. She could only hope Rod had taken care of that. "No! I mean, that's okay. I'll grab what's left on my way out. I only need the bag."

"Right. I see it." There was some rustling before Natasha said, "Here you go."

When India cracked open the bathroom door, she saw a girl with short, bleached hair styled with plenty of mousse, wide brown eyes and an oversize, expressive mouth—the girl whose photo Rod had shown her at the ice cream parlor. She was wearing a short stretchy black skirt and a tank top—an outfit that made the most of her slim figure and revealed the tattoos on her long, slender arms. There were some tattoos on her feet, too, which India could see because Natasha was wearing sandals.

Their eyes met, and they both smiled politely. "Thanks."

Natasha backed out of the room. "I'll get my purse and be waiting in front."

"See you in a sec," India said.

The moment Rod's stepsister left, India closed the bathroom door and leaned against it. "Awkward!" she whispered to herself. Then she hurried to dress. She brushed her hair, as well as her teeth, and washed her face. This wasn't the way she wanted to meet Rod's family, but what could she do?

Once she was ready, India took the food Theresa had brought so it wouldn't go to waste and let herself out via the deck entrance to avoid running into Rod's father or his father's wife. "Running into" Natasha had been bad enough.

When India came around to the drive, Natasha was there as promised. "Ready?"

With a quick nod, Rod's stepsister followed her over to the Prius. India had locked her house the night before and didn't need to go inside. She put her bag and Theresa's basket in the backseat, thinking she'd carry them in when she got home. The sooner she dropped Natasha off, the better. Then she could go about setting her world back on its axis.

"Rod told me you'll be leaving for college at the end of the summer," India said as they put on their seat belts.

Natasha stared out the window while India started the car. "Actually, I'm trying to make arrangements to go as soon as possible."

"Before school begins?"

"Might as well."

"Why? Do you have a job waiting for you?"

"No."

Then wouldn't it be smarter to stay here and earn what she could? India thought so, but it wasn't her place to give advice. "I'm sure you're excited."

"Of course. I'm *thrilled.*"

The sarcasm was as unmistakable as it was unexpected. India glanced over, but Natasha wouldn't look at her, so she said nothing.

They made small talk—mostly on India's end—while they drove. If Natasha spoke, it was only to give directions or answer a question, which she did as briefly as possible.

"Thanks for the ride," she said as they turned in at Amos Auto Body.

The shop looked like a respectable business. The property was large, and Rod and his brothers obviously took care of the building. A fair number of cars were waiting to be fixed.

India had assumed Rod would be on his way to Bakersfield, but he wasn't gone yet. She was startled to find him standing in the lot with his truck idling and his door open, talking to someone who resembled him a great deal but wasn't Grady or Mack. He glanced up when she parked, and his jaw dropped.

"Forget something this morning?" Natasha snapped as soon as she got out. Then she stalked into the office.

Rod didn't respond to his stepsister. He and the man he'd been talking to walked over to India's car and waited for her to lower the window.

Even without being introduced, India knew she was about to meet Dylan Amos. There was something about his confidence that indicated he was in charge.

"Dyl, this is India, our new neighbor," Rod said.

Dylan gave her a nod. It would've been awkward to shake hands while she was in the car. "Nice to meet you."

"Same here," she said.

"Did you know that my wife used to live in your house?" Dylan asked, shading his eyes against the sun.

"No one's mentioned it," she replied.

His smile widened. "I have good memories of that place."

"Have you been inside since the renovations?" she asked.

"No, I see these guys enough at work," he replied. "I don't get over there too often anymore."

"Feel free to come by," she told him.

"I will. And I'll bring Cheyenne, if you don't mind."

"Not at all."

Dylan gestured toward the office. "How'd you get roped into giving Natasha a ride? Don't tell me she had the nerve to go bang on your door when she could've called one of us."

"No…"

He gave her a questioning look, since that obviously didn't explain how she'd ended up in the service of his stepsister.

Rod seemed to be anticipating, with some relish, watching her squirm out of this tight spot. So she decided she wouldn't even try.

"I was sleeping with your brother," she announced. "All she had to do was come to his room."

Rod coughed as Dylan's eyebrows shot toward his hairline. "Unashamed and unapologetic," Dylan said with a certain degree of shock. "I like that."

"That's not how I would've preferred to meet her," India clarified. "But sometimes things happen."

"True. We all know Rod's pretty much irresistible." With a chuckle, he clapped Rod on the back. "Hey, bro, you might have your hands full with this one," he said and went back to the office.

Rod leaned on her window ledge, resting his cast on top of the car. "I guess you're not very good at keeping a secret, huh? What are you trying to do, ruin my reputation?"

"You're enjoying this," she accused him.

"Don't blame *me*," he said in mock outrage. "You're the one who just announced that you were in my bed."

"Your sister came in right after you left!"

"My *step*sister."

"Does the *step* part really matter?"

He looked up as Mack came charging out of the office, got in his truck and slammed the door. "It might to some people," he said as he watched his brother tear off.

India scowled. "To *you*?"

"No. Definitely not to me," he said, returning his attention to her.

She wrinkled her nose. "I'm confused."

"Never mind. It's nothing."

"Fine," she said. "Be cryptic. Anyway, I doubt last night would've remained secret after Natasha mistook me for you and came to ask for a ride."

He laughed as he kicked a small pebble across the lot. "So we've been found out. Does that mean you can come through the front door tonight?"

She sobered immediately. "Rod..."

His smile disappeared, too. "Don't say it."

"I *have* to say it. I can't let what's happening between us...happen."

"Why not? Because I'm not a heart surgeon?"

She couldn't tell him that her in-laws would look at him that way even if she didn't. "No, of course not. I'm just not ready. Like I said."

"That's bullshit. I felt how ready you were last night."

She closed her eyes. "Don't do that."

"Why? Because you don't like facing the truth?"

"Because wanting you and being able to be with you are two different things!"

"You're not doing Charlie any favors by denying yourself, India. Stop running!"

"I'm sorry, but I can't see you again," she told him and backed out of her parking space before he could see how reluctant she'd been to say those words.

14

India felt anxious walking into her house; she knew Sebastian could be waiting for her during the day just as easily as at night. On the drive home from the auto body shop, she kept an eye out for any cars that looked as if they didn't belong and walked the entire perimeter of her house with a tire iron before venturing inside.

After being shut up, her place was a lot warmer than outside, especially this time of morning, but the heat wave seemed to be dissipating. Thank goodness. Maybe she wouldn't sweat so much when she worked today.

Setting down her keys, she leaned on the counter to stare out the window, toward Rod's house. But obsessing over him wasn't helping. She'd done the right thing a few minutes ago. She knew that, and yet…it wasn't what she really wanted.

She thought it might strengthen her resolve if she could speak to Cassia, but her in-laws always acted so odd when she asked either one of them to put her daughter on the line. They usually had an excuse—she was out with Papa in the garden, she was in the bath, she was doing the dishes with "Mimi," which was what she called her grandmother. India suspected Cassia asked to talk to her, too, and was given similar excuses. Claudia was afraid Cassia would realize how much she missed her mother and ask to come home. Claudia liked to pretend that *she* was all Cassia needed and that Cassia never complained about being there or begged for Mommy, even though that would be perfectly normal behavior for a five-year-old child.

India considered calling and insisting, if necessary. But she decided that might only make the situation more difficult. She couldn't bring Cassia to Whiskey Creek if it would put her in danger, so there was no need to push. Not yet.

First she had to make sure her house was safe.

After putting on coffee, she ate some of the breakfast Theresa had prepared for Rod. Then she logged on to her computer and began searching for nearby alarm companies. She doubted she could get a security system installed today. Not where she lived. But, with any luck, she could arrange it for the next week or so.

Then she'd call and talk to Cassia.

When Dylan called for the third time, Mack finally used his Bluetooth to answer.

"Where the hell are you?" his brother demanded.

Slinging one hand over the steering wheel, Mack sank farther into his seat and looked around. "Jackson," he said, paying attention to his surroundings for the first time since he'd peeled out of the Amos Auto Body lot.

"Why?" Dylan asked. "You're supposed to be painting Sandra Morton's car. She's coming to pick it up tomorrow morning."

Mack released a sigh. He was still wearing his paint suit and didn't have a good excuse for driving off—at least not one he intended to share with his brother. "There was…something I had to do."

"Like…"

"None of your business," he snapped.

Dylan went silent. He wasn't used to having Mack respond like that. Not these days. Not *any* days. Unlike Aaron, Mack had *always* worshipped his oldest brother—and always been favored by him.

"Are you okay?" Dylan asked at length.

Mack couldn't say he was. He seemed to be losing his mind. Natasha was all he could think about, and his thoughts were becoming ever more sexual. When she was younger, he could distract himself from the attraction he felt—by helping her do homework, seeing that she had someone to socialize with on the weekends so she wouldn't feel left out by the kids who weren't accepting her, teaching her how to throw a ball. Her mother had done nothing to provide her with any life skills. He was the one who'd tried to teach her how to cook. Although he could grill like there was no tomorrow, he wasn't particularly adept in the kitchen. But he'd bought several cookbooks and muddled his way through trying to impart the basics. She'd been more interested in cooking than some of the other stuff he'd attempted to introduce her to. Like when he convinced her to sign up for dance classes and drove her over to the studio a few times. She quit that almost right away. He suspected it was because he wasn't going with her. But she liked chess. They'd played a lot over the past year, and he'd taught her so well he could no longer be assured of winning. Occasionally, she kicked his ass and took great pleasure in doing so.

But those days of being easily satisfied were over. She didn't need him in that way anymore. She was an adult and could handle most tasks on her own; she'd even taught *him* a thing or two on the computer. Now all he could think about was how badly he wanted to touch her. And after what she'd done last night, tearing off that T-shirt and letting him see her bare breasts, all he had to do was remember and he'd grow hard.

"Are you and Natasha having some sort of fight?" Dylan asked. "If you are, maybe you should come back and talk to her about it. Did she say something nasty to you? Her tongue can get sharp. I won't argue with you there. But you know what her life's been like."

Did Dylan know what *his* life was like right now—because of *her*?

"Natasha and I are getting along fine," he said. The last thing he wanted was for Dylan to learn how he felt, what he was battling. His obsession was too embarrassing to admit, especially when he could have just about any other woman he wanted. With so many to choose from, why did he have to be fixated on Natasha?

Fortunately, since Natasha had come to live at the house, Dylan had been preoccupied with Cheyenne and Kellan, and the business. Aaron was totally immersed in his little family, too. Otherwise, one or both of them would probably have noticed, the way Rod had. Grady was oblivious to almost anything that didn't directly concern him, so Mack wasn't as worried about him. Sometimes he wondered if Anya knew, but if so, she would've told J.T, who'd never said anything. Mack figured he still had a chance to get clear of this thing with no one, other than Rod, being the wiser.

Except that Natasha wasn't giving up without a fight. She could tell he wasn't immune to her, could tell he felt more than he should, and she was pushing him, testing his limits. He wouldn't have left work this morning if she hadn't caught him in the back room while he was suiting up and put her hand around to grab his junk.

"You're going to let me ride this at least once before I go," she'd murmured.

He wished he'd been appalled—or, better yet, repelled. Instead, her touch, her voice in his ear, brought him nothing but pleasure. That was why he'd set her to one side and stormed out. He'd *had* to. Otherwise, he would've dragged her into the bathroom and pulled up her skirt.

"You two are fine? Because she's not talking much, either," Dylan said. "And what she *is* saying doesn't make a whole lot of sense."

Shit, was she giving them away? Mack's heart jumped into his throat. "What do you mean?"

"She's planning to move to Utah next week, even though school doesn't start for a couple more months. Says she needs to get a job before everyone arrives for fall semester. But there's no guarantee it'll be any easier to find work in June than in August. And she's already working *here*. Doing a nice job, too. I'd rather not lose her before we have to."

The prospect of her leaving town so soon filled Mack with relief. Whittling her two remaining months down to a few days or a week would help. But he also felt a measure of panic at the thought that she'd be out of reach…

He pulled over, didn't see any point in continuing to drive aimlessly. Not when he had to go back and get that car painted. "Why's she in such a hurry?" he asked, but only because it was expected. He knew the answer to that question. She was struggling with her wants and desires as much as he was. Living in the same house had become a problem for both of them, had gotten progressively harder as the months went by.

And now they were at the breaking point.

"She thinks it'll be easier to adjust or something like that. If you ask me, she can adjust once she gets there. What's the difference? Now or later?"

"If it makes the transition easier on her, we should support her decision," Mack said, but he felt physically sick as he spoke. "She's an adult, trying to assert her will. We should allow that."

"You *want* her to leave early?" Dylan asked.

Mack let his head drop against the back of the seat. "If that's what *she* wants."

Dylan paused for a few seconds. Then he said, "Okay, I'll get on the internet over lunch today and see if her apartment complex has an opening so she won't have to move twice."

"I bet she'll appreciate that."

"She'll be pissed that I took over, like she was when I set up her housing to begin with. But it makes me feel better about letting her go. Maybe you can help arrange her airfare tonight. Aaron, Grady, Rod and I will pay for the first month, last month and security deposit on the apartment if you'll handle her flight."

Mack tapped his fingers on the wheel. "Sure. No problem."

"She claims she's going to pay for it all herself, that she's saved up. But she barely has enough to cover the hard costs, and that won't leave her with any money for food or laundry detergent or anything else. I don't want her up there broke. Who can say how long it'll be before she finds work? Even then it'll take weeks to get a paycheck."

"Thanks," Mack said. Then he realized appreciation was an odd response, since Dylan wasn't doing anything for *him*. "I mean, I'll feel better knowing she's taken care of, too."

"She doesn't like accepting any help. She's so damn independent."

Natasha *was* independent. But she also wanted Mack to see her as an equal. He understood that.

"She can pay us back when she becomes a rocket scientist or a doctor or a politician, what with all the schooling she's going to have, right?" Dylan joked.

Mack had never been prouder of anything than the report cards Natasha had brought home. Something about the fact that she was going to get out of Whiskey Creek and have so many opportunities, despite her past, made his throat tighten and his eyes burn. He needed to let her explore those possibilities, needed to let her go.

"Right. Sounds good to me," he said. Then he turned his truck around.

One more week. He could keep up the fight for one more week, couldn't he?

Rod was glad he wasn't working in the shop today. He knew his brothers would give him hell about having their neighbor over without ever letting on. And he didn't want to hear it. Especially now that she'd put a stop to whatever had started between them. Rod told himself he didn't care. He had trouble falling *in* love, not out of it. And he'd known India for only a few days.

He'd spent the whole drive to Bakersfield trying to convince himself that she'd broken it off because she was looking for someone with deeper pockets, more promise or more respect. And yet he *still* wanted to see her. That told him he might be in deeper than he thought.

He couldn't be too mad at her, though. Not after what she'd been through. She'd had an ex-boyfriend come back and kill her husband, right in front of her, and it'd happened less than a year ago. Of course she'd have scars. He could understand why she might feel jittery about being with a man after something like that, but he couldn't allow her to face the coming days and weeks alone. If Sebastian was going to seek revenge, he'd probably do it soon, while he was still angry and before he settled into whatever kind of life he was going to live.

When Rod stopped to get a bite to eat, he quit arguing with himself and texted her.

Tell me you weren't serious this morning.

Don't make this any harder than it has to be, came her response.

Stay over tonight, at least. I won't even be there until late. And when I get home, I'll sleep on the couch.

He'd tried to sleep on the couch last night; she was the one who'd stopped him. He would've pointed that out, except she hadn't had to do much to convince him. And he didn't want her to regret it any more than she already did.

He was filling up with gas by the time she wrote back.

I'll be fine.

He frowned at his phone. How could he persuade her?

Your safety has to come before any loyalty you feel to Charlie. Think about what he'd want.

We could be worried for nothing. Maybe the cops are watching Sebastian.

You don't know?

No. They won't tell me that. They can't. What if I'm the guilty one?

I'm guessing they're not watching him. Anyway, are you willing to stake your life on that?

I bought a security system today. That won't help if he follows me from the house, of course. But I might be able to sleep at night. That's worth something.

Unless Sebastian was a particularly sophisticated criminal, she'd know if someone was trying to break in before he was standing at the foot of her bed.

Good. When will it be installed?

They're coming on Saturday.

And until then?

I can get by.

Stay at my place, India.

If I don't put down my phone and finish shaping this bowl, it'll be ruined.

Does that mean you'll be in my bed tonight, where I know you'll be safe?

I'm thinking about it.

I'll stay at your place, if you prefer.

No! If it isn't safe for me, why would it be safe for you?

Then quit giving me so much trouble and be at my place, waiting for me.

He didn't think she was going to text back. He assumed she'd returned to her work. But when he stopped at the light before entering the freeway, he saw his phone screen light up in the seat beside him and pulled over.

Okay. But let me sleep on the couch. I'd feel bad taking your bed.

Trust me, you'll want the privacy. Just go to sleep where you did last night. I don't know when I'll get back, anyway.

Are you sure?

Positive. Then I won't have to worry about you.

I'm sorry.

For what?

For everything.

It's going to be fine, he keyed in—and hoped that was true.

15

After texting with Rod, India managed to build a new vase. She also fired it, as well as the wind chimes she'd created over the past week. The kiln required so much electricity she had to wait until she had enough pieces to fill it. Ceramics could be a very imperfect process. Although various glazes did unexpected things in the kiln, these had come out great. She felt good about what she'd accomplished. She was improving as an artist, could see it in her work.

After she was done, she called her in-laws to check on Cassia. Claudia, who answered, treated her coolly. And at the end of their conversation, when India finally asked to speak to Cassia, she received the same old runaround; Claudia said Cassia was outside in the swimming pool with Papa and tomorrow would be better.

India was so frustrated it was harder than ever to bite her tongue. She quickly got off the phone, but she was afraid that if she stayed home, she'd call them back and resume the argument that'd been brewing since the trial. Sitting around brooding on all the complaints she had against them wasn't going to improve her mood. So she showered, put on a summer dress and left to enjoy the idyllic town she'd chosen to live in.

Fortunately, the weather had improved. A cool wind stirred the trees as the sun slid down behind the distinctive buildings on Sutter Street. Just walking through the center of town and seeing the nineteenth-century architecture of the old Victorian homes and the many quaint shops helped her relax. She liked imagining which building she might rent for her shop—or where she might build, since there weren't too many options.

She spent a whole hour becoming more familiar with Whiskey Creek, but when she decided to eat, there didn't seem to be a lot of choices. A burger joint off the main drag, a small sandwich shop not far from the park and a diner called Just Like Mom's. The diner was almost insufferably tacky, but it was busy, which suggested the food was good. India got the impression that the purple paint and "visiting grandma's house" feel were part of its charm—or the owner did such a brisk business he or she didn't need to update.

When India entered and approached the hostess station, she was feeling significantly better than she had at home and was glad she'd opted for a change of scenery.

"Just one?" The hostess looked behind her as if she expected to see someone else come in.

"Just one," India echoed. After being part of a couple, and then a family of three for so long, she found it difficult to be alone all the time. But the Sommerses didn't seem to think that deserved any consideration.

"We're clearing off a table," the hostess told her. "Give us a minute."

India surreptitiously watched her fellow citizens as she waited. Would she fit in here in Whiskey Creek?

Would she even have the chance? A security system could provide some warning if Sebastian tried to break in, but it wouldn't stop him. *She'd* have to do that.

"Right this way." With a pleasant smile, the hostess led her across the restaurant to a small table.

India was so intent on getting seated that she almost didn't recognize the man in a nearby booth, eating with a woman. If not for the brace on his nose, India wouldn't particularly have noticed him. But someone with a broken nose wasn't a common sight. That brace caught her eye as she sat down. Then she realized who he was— the guy who'd been lying unconscious on the side of the road Friday night!

So he was out of the hospital...

"We have to do *something*." The woman who was with him leaned close, obviously intent on convincing him. "We can't let him get away with what he did."

Him? India would've focused on her menu and let them eat in peace. But that snippet of conversation grabbed her attention.

"We're not letting him get away with it. I'm pressing charges, aren't I?"

They were talking about Rod; they had to be.

"He should serve time, Liam."

"He won't serve time, Sharon. There are rapists and murderers who go to trial and get off with a slap on the wrist. Why would they put Rod Amos behind bars?"

"Because he's dangerous!"

There was a brief pause during which India held her breath. Rod *wasn't* dangerous. How unfair that they were talking about him as if he was a criminal. He'd reacted as most people would react, if they were capable of it, given the situation.

"So…what are you saying?" Liam asked.

Sharon lowered her voice so much that India had to slide over to hear. "I'm saying he must've had a weapon. Look what he did to your face. Broke your nose *and* your jaw."

A weapon? Shock and outrage made India clench her teeth.

"At least I didn't need to have my jaw wired shut." Liam spoke with his mouth full, which he certainly wouldn't have been able to do if the doctor had wired his jaw.

"Does that mean we should *thank* him?" Sharon said. "Think of the hospital bill, if you're not pissed off enough about your injuries. You have a $3,500 deductible! How will you ever pay it?"

India couldn't hear what Liam muttered next. Then Sharon started in again. "He and his brothers own a business here in Whiskey Creek. He's got money. I've looked into it."

Although it wasn't easy, India stopped herself from shooting to her feet and saying something to them.

"I'm going to *try* to make him pay," Liam responded. "But it isn't up to me—"

"Yes, it is!" she broke in. "It'll depend on what you tell Chief Bennett when you give him your statement tomorrow morning. If Rod Amos had a weapon, that would change things. He must've used *something* besides his fists to do that much damage. You're just not remembering it right. No wonder after you got beaten up so badly. You've got to take some time and think about it, get your story straight before you go in there."

The tone of Liam's voice changed, grew speculative. "What kind of weapon do you think it was?"

India could tell Liam knew there'd been no weapon. He was asking what he should say in order to get Rod in the greatest trouble. But Sharon noticed India at that moment and must've realized she was eavesdropping, because she whispered to her companion, then asked what he thought of his dinner instead of answering the question.

India sat through her own meal, trying to pretend she hadn't been listening and didn't have any idea what they were talking about. She hoped they'd relax and return to the subject, so she could learn more about their plans. But they didn't. They visited other topics, paid their bill soon after and walked out, leaving her with a sense of foreboding.

She would've been upset if she'd overheard two people planning to lie about anyone. She especially didn't want to see Rod hurt.

When she was finished, she drove over to the police station. She was nervous about drawing attention to herself. She preferred to lie low, so she could adjust to her new life and move on. But she couldn't let Liam and Sharon purposely misrepresent what'd happened Friday night.

At first she was glad she'd gathered up the nerve to go see Chief Bennett. He recognized her and treated her kindly—until he wrote down her name. Although she'd mentioned it the night of the accident, this time he connected it to all the press coverage about her husband's death. Once he confirmed that she was, indeed, the woman who'd been married to the murdered doctor, his manner changed. From that point on, he acted as if he couldn't take her quite as seriously now that he knew she'd been involved in *two* police situations in such a short time.

"Thanks for stopping by," he said after he'd made a few notes. "I'll keep your statement on file in case this goes anywhere and be in touch if I need to speak to you again."

"Okay." She stood and smoothed her dress. "I appreciate you hearing me out. I just… I felt you should know. Rod didn't have a weapon."

"You sure about that?" he asked before she could step out of his office.

Hearing the challenge in his voice, she threw back her shoulders. "I am."

"You were there when the two men were fighting? You *saw* what happened?"

"No, I…I came on the scene after, like I told you. But he wasn't holding anything. And I have no reason to lie."

"Why couldn't he have put down any weapon he might've used before you arrived, Ms. Sommers?"

She blinked at him. "Because he never had one. I'm telling you, the conversation I overheard at Just Like Mom's was upsetting. Sharon, the woman who was speaking to Liam, was clearly suggesting that he lie."

He checked his notes. "When she said he couldn't be remembering the fight correctly. That the damage to his face suggested Rod must've used a weapon."

"Yes!"

"To be honest, I'm not sure those sound like entirely unreasonable statements, Ms. Sommers. Rod has a history in this town, after all."

"For using *weapons*?"

"Not necessarily. But for finding trouble."

"It wasn't what Sharon said as much as the way she said it," India told him.

"I see. Well, I've got it all right here." He tapped the file on his desk. "Thanks for coming in."

She'd been dismissed. She had no choice but to nod and take her leave.

As she walked to her car, she was afraid she hadn't helped Rod at all. And she knew she'd have even less credibility if it ever came out that she'd been in his bed.

Natasha would barely speak to him while he arranged her airfare. Mack asked her several questions. How she'd get from the airport to the apartment complex. Whether she'd checked the surrounding area to see if there was a store nearby. Whether or not she really wanted to leave so early. But she just sat on his bed while he used the laptop he typically lent her and scowled at him whenever he turned around.

"Are you really going to make our last week this miserable?" he asked.

"Are *you*?" she retorted.

"Stop being angry. You have so much to look forward to."

"So? I'm not looking forward to *any* of it."

"Because you don't know what you'd be missing," he said, going back to the computer screen.

"Because what I want is right here. And I'm not afraid to say it."

He sent her a sharp look, since she'd spoken so loudly. The door was open and Grady was in the other room, watching TV. That was the only reason Mack had felt comfortable letting Natasha in. Nothing could happen between them; they didn't have the privacy. "You have to stop talking that way," he said softly. "You have to stop *thinking* that way, too."

She glared at him. "You'd rather I lied to myself like you do?"

He took a deep breath. "I'm not lying to myself. I'm respecting boundaries. You should try it sometime. What you pulled this morning—that can't happen again."

Her lips curved into a devilish smile. "You liked what I did this morning."

"No, I didn't," he lied.

"Yes, you did. You want me to do it right now. You want me to do a lot of things."

"Stop it," he demanded. "You're making life harder than it has to be."

"You're putting something between us that doesn't really exist—other than in your own mind!"

"And the minds of everyone else in this family and in this town!"

She folded her arms. "I don't care about anyone else."

"You should."

Grady turned off the television. In the sudden quiet, Mack raised his hand to tell Natasha not to say anything. He assumed Grady would head on upstairs and go to bed. At dinner he'd mentioned he wasn't feeling that well. But he poked his head into the room.

"What's going on in here?"

"Nothing. I'm just booking Natasha's travel," Mack replied.

Grady shifted his gaze to her. "Can't believe our baby sister is all grown up."

"*Baby?* I haven't been a baby from the moment I met you. Quit being so fucking patronizing!" she said and pushed her way past him.

"Holy shit," Grady said. "What's gotten into *her* lately?"

Mack rubbed his face. "She's going through a big transition."

"I guess so. Jeez. These days you can't say anything to her without having her sound off."

Mack remembered her hand squeezing his genitals at the shop this morning and turned toward the computer. "You remember what it's like at that age. You want so much that you can't have."

"But she's going to get it all. We've seen to that!"

"She's grateful. She's just…having a hard time leaving. Must be nervous about it."

He hooked his hands above the door frame. "Then why is she going *early*?"

"Sometimes it's easier to confront something you've been dreading, get it over with."

"I guess," he said, but he shook his head as if he still didn't understand. "She's getting harder and harder to deal with."

"She'll be fine once she moves out on her own."

"I'm going to talk to her. She shouldn't be losing her temper all the time." He dropped his hands, ready to go after her, but Mack stopped him.

"Leave her alone," he said and didn't realize until after he'd said it that he'd sounded a little too defensive.

"Really?" Grady said. "I didn't do anything, and you're taking *her* side?"

"How she's acting isn't your problem. So she's got some growing pains. Give her a chance to deal with them. She'll be fine when she comes home for Thanksgiving." Hopefully, by then, he'd have himself under control, too.

"Since when is it up to you to tell me what to do where Natasha's concerned?" Grady asked.

Mack stood up. "Since now. Leave her alone, like I said."

Grady gaped at him. "Damn, you're *both* acting like assholes," he muttered. "I'm going to bed."

16

When Rod got home, India's car was in her drive, but she wasn't in his bed. She wasn't even in his room. What worried him was that she wasn't at her place, either. The lights were on, but the doors were all locked, and she didn't respond when he knocked or when he used his phone to call her. He was going around the house, trying to figure out some way to break in so he could make sure she was okay, when he heard her voice behind him.

"Rod, I'm right here."

He breathed a sigh of relief as he turned to see her unharmed. "You scared the shit out of me," he said. "Why didn't you answer my call?"

"My phone won't pick up. I dropped it in the sink this morning, and it's been acting screwy ever since."

"You need to have it checked." What with Sebastian out and running around, a phone could be vital for getting help. She couldn't be without one if that moment ever came.

"I will if it continues. I've got it in some rice. That should help pull the moisture from it."

He studied her, taking note of her simple top, cutoffs and bare feet. She was stunning when she dressed up.

But he liked her even better like this, with her hair piled up and her face scrubbed clean of makeup. "What've you been doing?"

"Just…wading in the river."

"This late?"

"You know I have trouble sleeping."

Although he couldn't see her clearly in the darkness, he could tell she was pale and tired.

"How'd the trip go?" she asked.

"I got what Dylan needed." He leaned against the side of her house so that he wouldn't immediately reach out and draw her to him. The compulsion he felt to do that sort of surprised him. "How was *your* day?"

A flash of white told him she'd just cracked a smile. "You mean after Natasha busted me for sleeping with you?"

He returned her grin. "I can't believe you told Dylan about us." His brother must've texted him five times today: I was sleeping with your brother. Quoting her had become an inside joke between them.

She pulled on the frayed hem of her shorts. "He probably warned you to stay away from me."

"Nah, he likes you."

When she said nothing, he bent his head to peer at her more closely. "You're not upset about Natasha or Dylan, are you?"

"No."

"Then what is it? Why are you so restless? Because of Sebastian? Have you heard anything?"

"Nothing. But it's not him—at least no more than last night or the night before."

"*Something's* bugging you." Was it just that she was

undecided about whether or not she should return to his bed?

"I've got a long list," she joked. "Where should I start?"

"At the top."

She let her breath go in a sigh. "Okay. For one thing, when I called to talk to Cassia today, my in-laws put me off. Again."

He closed the distance between them, but he didn't touch her. "Why wouldn't they let you talk to your own daughter?"

"They didn't say no. They never actually *refuse*. They just won't put her on the phone very often. They always come up with some excuse."

Rod admired the creamy smoothness of her skin. "Why would they do that?"

"I'm positive it's because they don't want her to start crying and ask to come home. Then they won't be able to tell me she's as happy there as she is with me."

He ran a finger along her jawline. He thought she might step away, but she didn't. "What kind of grandparents would want to make you feel less important to her than you are?"

She stared up at him. She seemed lost in his gaze—so lost he thought he might be able to kiss her. But then she said, "I guess when you have a daughter-in-law you suspect of helping to murder your son, you don't feel she'd make a great mother for your grandchild."

He shook his head. "It's such bullshit that they can't tell what kind of person you are."

She caught hold of his wrist, since he was now moving his thumb over her bottom lip. "Why don't *you* wonder more?" she asked. "How can you be so certain I'm innocent?"

"A lot of reasons."

"Such as…"

"The fact that you haven't even tried to convince me stands out the most."

"And…"

"It's obvious that you'd never harm anyone, India." He remembered how she'd acted when she was approaching the guy he'd punched out. She'd been so queasy, he'd worried that she might faint. He couldn't imagine that a woman so sensitive to seeing someone hurt could set her husband up to be *killed*. "I can only assume that your in-laws have been blinded by the loss of their son."

"Maybe it's easier for you to accept my side of the story because you didn't have any emotional connection to Charlie," she said. "But I would've thought that I'd established *some* credibility with my in-laws. They know me a lot better than you do. Shouldn't *they* be the ones to insist I couldn't have done such a terrible thing?"

They'd hurt her—deeply. He felt bad about that. What she'd been through was difficult enough without their defection. "Tragedy does strange things to people. Sometimes it's tempting to place blame where blame doesn't belong. It's not like they can punish Sebastian, so they're punishing you for ever being connected to him."

"I suppose. But…you didn't sit through the trial."

He linked his fingers with hers and led her back to the water. "What difference would that have made?"

"You didn't hear all the awful things that were said about me," she said with a humorless laugh. "Maybe that would've changed *your* mind, too."

"I doubt it."

Pivoting to face him, she put her hand on his chest, palm flat as if she was trying to feel his heartbeat, to connect with that vital part of him in some way. But what came out of her mouth shocked him. "You don't know what I had to do to save my child," she whispered.

From what he could see in the moonlight, her eyes were filled with agony. Covering her hand with his, he lowered his voice. "I'm sure I can guess."

The silence stretched out. Then, in a hollow voice, she said, "We argued. We fought. All of that's true, but…"

"There's more."

She nodded.

Rod felt his muscles tense as he imagined what might have happened. "What'd he do to you, India?"

The question alone made her tremble. She tried to remove her hand, but he wouldn't let her. "Don't withdraw," he murmured. "You don't have to hide anything from me."

"But it…it isn't what he *made* me do." She had to gulp to get those words out, because of the tears that were suddenly streaming down her cheeks.

"Maybe it's time you told someone," he said.

"I…I can't."

He realized she hadn't expected this conversation and wasn't prepared for it. Neither was he. It'd hit them both out of nowhere. She had something she needed to say, and yet she couldn't say it. He was beginning to believe she wouldn't be able to put the past behind her until she'd dealt with whatever she was holding back. But at the same time, he didn't want to put her through the horror of reliving it.

"Then don't," he whispered. Slipping his arms around her, he rested his chin on her head. "You can always tell me later, if you want."

"You'd hate me for it," she said.

Like she hated herself? "No, I wouldn't," he said.

"More than that, if he ever returned, and you faced the same danger, I'd want you to do whatever you did again, if that's what you have to do to survive."

She buried her face in his neck and let him hold her until she quit shaking. Then, after she grabbed her phone from her house, they went to his room.

Rod fell asleep almost as soon as they climbed into bed. India was glad of that. She didn't want to make love with him—knew she'd only be disappointed in herself come morning, since she'd promised she'd pull back, be cautious, not jump into another possibly painful situation. She didn't want to talk, either. While she was wading in the river, she'd decided she wouldn't upset him right before bedtime by telling him about that conversation at Just Like Mom's between Liam and Sharon. That information was better saved until morning. So what had she done instead? She'd talked about her own problems and almost revealed the one secret that could destroy her!

What had she been thinking? That she *knew* him? That she could *trust* him? No matter how safe he seemed, she had to remember that she couldn't lean on him or anyone else. If her most trusted friends, even Charlie's *family*, could turn on her, Rod could, too. What she and Rod felt for each other now might not be there next week or the week after. She had to keep in mind how quickly circumstances and emotions could change, especially since she couldn't allow their relationship to become serious.

She had to keep her mouth shut.

When he rolled away from her in his sleep, she missed the physical contact, which worried her. She tried to convince herself that she was just lonely and stayed on her side of the bed. But that only made the wanting worse.

After lying still for several minutes, she decided she might as well enjoy the comfort of his body. She'd have plenty of nights without him as soon as the police found the gun Sebastian had used to kill Charlie—or she could get her life straightened out some other way—and she could return home to her regular life. Then she wouldn't have anything to fear, Cassia would be back and it would be easier to do what she should.

Sliding closer, she tentatively slid her arm around his waist, and when he shifted, she settled against him. Regardless of who or what he'd turn out to be when she got to know him better, he definitely made a comfortable bed partner. She loved how responsive he was—and almost everything else about him.

"You okay?" he muttered.

"I'm fine. Go back to sleep," she whispered. She said that as if she was going to sleep, too. But as soon as his breathing was regular again, she removed her pajama top and slid his T-shirt up so she could press her bare chest against his warm back. Only then did she feel safe and secure enough to drift off.

When Rod woke up, he felt the softness of India's breasts against his arm, and the resulting deluge of testosterone kicked his brain into full wakefulness without the usual groggy in-between stage. She wasn't wearing her pajama top, yet he remembered her having it on when they went to bed.

Had *he* taken it off? Or had *she*?

He turned over carefully so he could see her in the early-morning light that filtered through the blinds and pulled the blankets down a few inches in the process.

He was enjoying the view when he realized she was awake, too.

"Morning," she mumbled.

"Morning."

They said nothing else, just stared at each other for several long seconds before he reached out to touch her.

Her eyes closed as his hand cupped the soft mound of her breast, and he felt himself grow hard. He didn't have a lot of time before work, but at this point he didn't care if he was late. She'd been trying so hard to pull back emotionally, he'd assumed she wouldn't let him touch her like this. But she *was* letting him; she was even responding.

"What happened to your top?" he asked.

"I took it off."

"Because…"

"Because I wanted to feel you against me."

That was a good sign. "How about we get closer?"

A hint of reluctance showed on her face, but she didn't stop his hand from sliding down between her legs. "I don't want to mislead or…or disappoint you," she said.

"I don't want to mislead or disappoint you, either."

The satisfaction he felt when he finally pressed inside her made him smile. He'd never felt such tenderness. For a minute or two that concerned him. It suggested he could end up with a broken heart, after all—his first since his mother died so long ago.

But he didn't want to dwell on the possibility. Not when he had what he wanted right now. The moment he felt her legs lock around his hips and her mouth open beneath his, he lost himself in the pleasure of being with her. He didn't surface again until he heard her groan and let himself rush toward his own climax.

"Sorry it has to be so short," he said, pulling away. "I'll make it up to you later. I've got to go to work."

She took his hand as he got out of bed. "There's something I have to tell you."

He hesitated. Judging by the sound of her voice, it wasn't good news. "Do you have to tell me right now?" he asked. "Because I'm feeling pretty happy."

He'd meant to make her smile, but she still looked worried. "I already put it off because I wanted you to get a good night's rest, but…I think you should know."

With a sigh, he sat back down. "What is it?"

"That guy you got into a fight with?"

"Liam Crockett?" At least she wasn't telling him, again, that she couldn't see him.

"Yes. I saw him at the restaurant where I ate last night."

Distracted by her nudity, he moved his hand over her as he bent to kiss her neck.

"Are you listening to me?" she asked.

"Mmm-hmm." He took her earlobe in his mouth. "You saw Liam at the restaurant."

"I didn't just *see* him. I overheard him."

He lifted his head. "And?"

"He's going to press charges."

Rolling his eyes to show his disgust, Rod stood. "I expected as much."

"It's not only that," she said. "I heard the person he was with telling him he should say you used a weapon."

"What?"

She bit her lip. "I know. It's crazy. But his goal is to make you pay, and assault with a deadly weapon could get you arrested. It might even result in prison time."

"That's ridiculous. I had no weapon."

"*I* believe you. I'm not sure Chief Bennett will. When I went to the police station to tell him what I'd heard, he wasn't very receptive."

Rod gaped at her. *"You went to the police station?"*

"I did. I wanted Chief Bennett to know they were going to lie, before they could do it. They can't get away with that. But I don't think I really helped the situation."

Although the idea of Liam trying to get him into even worse trouble was as upsetting as India had guessed it would be, Rod was also a bit flattered that she'd immediately risen to his defense. She was trying to act aloof, to protect herself, but she had a kind and caring heart. There was no doubt about that. "Why? What'd Bennett say?"

"Basically that my word doesn't mean anything. I wasn't there when the fight occurred."

"He *knows* I wouldn't use a weapon."

"I didn't feel you could count on him to have any faith in that."

Rod checked the clock; he was running out of time. "He has no proof."

"It'll be your word against Liam's."

"What a bastard."

"Are you talking about Chief Bennett or Liam Crockett?" she asked.

"I'm not impressed with either one."

"I'm sorry."

He headed for the bathroom. "Don't worry about it. You've got enough going on."

Before he could turn on the shower, however, he heard her phone rattle on the nightstand. He waited in the doorway to see if it would work, and who was calling. He was hoping she'd get to speak to her little girl. He knew how much she missed Cassia, thought that might help keep her spirits up. But when the color drained from her face, he knew the water hadn't ruined her cell phone. He also knew it wasn't anyone she *wanted* to talk to.

"What is it?" Rod asked, coming back into the bedroom.

She waved him off in a panic, as if she was afraid whoever it was might hear his voice. Then, without even speaking—other than her initial hello—she tried to hit the end button but was shaking so badly she dropped her phone instead.

Rod picked it up and pressed it to his ear. "Who is this?" he asked.

"Who the hell is *this*?" came the cutting reply.

"Don't talk to him!" India scrambled to her feet so she could grab the phone, and this time she managed to end the call.

Rod frowned at her. "I take it that wasn't your in-laws."

Tossing her phone on the bed as if she couldn't get it out of her hands fast enough, India hugged herself.

"India?" Rod gripped her shoulders, turning her to get her attention.

Finally, she looked at him. "It was Sebastian."

17

India stood at Rod's window, looking from the number in her recent call history to her house and back to her phone. Although Rod had told her to stay at his place and said he'd check in periodically, she couldn't hide out here, or anywhere else, indefinitely. She had to free herself of the past so she could get her daughter back. But how?

India? Guess who?

Sebastian's cheerful greeting ran through her mind like ticker tape. How dare he call her! How dare he pretend she'd be pleased to hear from him! He was mocking her, gloating over his escape.

And he would do more if he could...

Did he know where she lived?

That was possible, but not a given. He'd been able to call only because she hadn't changed her phone number. The world had looked a lot different—a lot safer—when she thought he'd be going to prison for the rest of his life. So she'd taken the risk of hanging on to it. She knew that if she changed her number, many of her casual friends and acquaintances wouldn't be able to contact her. Instead of drifting away, hoping to rekindle those relationships later, when the truth came out, there'd be nothing except her memories to connect her to the existence she'd known with Charlie. But many of those people weren't the kind of friends she'd call for new information. Not at this point.

Now, if she didn't want to hear from Sebastian again, she had to change her phone number. And maybe she wouldn't really be losing anything. If her old contacts thought, even for a second, that she could commit such a heinous act, she should want them out of her life for good. It was just hard to draw that line before she could make new friends and acquaintances. She'd already lost so much.

"Damn it," she muttered and called Detective Flores. She expected to leave a message. Rarely did she get through to him on her first attempt. But today he answered.

"He called me," she said, breathless and without preamble.

There was a long pause. "Who is this?"

Taking a deep breath, India strove for calm. "India Sommers. Sebastian Young just called me."

"What'd he say?"

"I didn't give him the chance to say much of anything. I hung up."

"That was the wisest thing you could do. You don't want to provoke him."

"I don't want to befriend him, either. He killed my husband. Please tell me someone's keeping an eye on him."

No response.

"Detective?"

"We don't have the manpower to run surveillance on every person we suspect is dangerous, India. I've scheduled nightly drive-bys of the house where he used to live with his wife. I'm fairly sure he's gone back there. I doubt he has anywhere else to go. So we're doing what we can, but I wouldn't rely on that."

"You're telling me that's it? I'm...on my own?"

"I'd suggest getting a restraining order against him."

She started to laugh. "That's your answer?" She'd been down that road with an earlier boyfriend, the one from the biker gang, and it'd had no effect. Only when his mother had died and he'd moved to Maryland to inherit her house had the danger diminished. India hadn't seen him since.

"Hard as this is, it's all you can do," Flores said. "He's a free man, innocent until proven guilty."

With a sound of frustration and hopelessness, she sank onto the bed and rubbed her forehead.

"You there?" he asked.

"I was just hanging up," she replied and pressed the end button.

She was still sitting on the bed, wondering what she was going to do, when her phone rang. Caller ID indicated that it was her in-laws. A pang of longing went through her when she thought of Cassia. She had to put her life right, and she had to do it before July 4, the day she was to get Cassia back, or give up on her plans to rebuild in Whiskey Creek and go somewhere else.

More disappointment. Another uprooting. Another argument with her in-laws over taking Cassia too far away.

Closing her eyes, she answered. "Hello?"

"India?"

Claudia, of course. Steve never called. "Yes?"

"Have you heard any more from Detective Flores?"

She'd just spoken to him! The coincidence frightened her. Was this some sort of test? Did Flores phone Claudia as soon as he'd hung up with her and reveal that she'd heard from Sebastian?

He would've had just enough time, but on the off chance Flores *hadn't* called, she'd be a fool to share that information. She knew what would happen if Claudia learned that Charlie's killer wasn't just going to slink off. "Not a lot. Why?"

"Have they told you what they're doing to find more evidence? If we don't keep pushing, they'll move on to newer crimes."

"Have *you* tried calling him?" India held her breath.

"Several times."

Oh, God… "And?"

"I can't ever reach him. He left me a message yesterday. Said they're hoping the gun will turn up. Is that what he's telling you?"

"Pretty much."

"Empty words," she complained. "Flores isn't doing anything. He's giving up."

"I'll stay on him," India promised, but she was of the same opinion. She believed Flores would carry on pursuing and catching other criminals until Sebastian did something else, something for which they could prosecute him with more confidence.

She could only hope it wouldn't be *her* murder.

When Rod got home, India was gone. And this time, so was her car. He frowned as he drove slowly past her place. Then he hurried inside his own house to check his room. She might've left him a note, since he hadn't heard from her by phone…

He found nothing. What was going on? Why wouldn't she have communicated with him?

When he dialed her number, his call went to voice

mail. "Will you let me know you're okay?" he said. Then he texted her.

Where are you?

He was standing out on his deck, staring over at her dark house, waiting for her to respond, when Mack came into the room.

"Hey!"

At the sound of his brother's voice, Rod gave up his vigil and walked back toward the bed. "What's up?"

"I'm going over to the bar. Wanna come?"

Mack had been acting so strange lately. Normally, he was the life of the party, happy all the time. But he'd become sullen and withdrawn, irritable. "On a work night?"

"We don't have to stay long."

"I can't." He held up his phone. "I'm waiting to hear from India." And he was concerned about her. "Ask Grady if he's up for it."

"I did. He's too tired." Mack started back the way he'd come. "I'll just go by myself."

"Mack!"

When he turned, Rod studied him. "What's wrong with you, man?"

"She's driving me crazy," he said.

He didn't need to specify who *she* was. Rod could guess, and he wasn't sure he cared to hear the details. He was still hoping this would all go away when Natasha moved to Utah. "Maybe you *could* use a night out."

"I could use a few drinks. That's what I could use," he said.

"She even talking to you right now?"

"No."

And it was killing him. Rod felt bad, but he couldn't say he identified. He'd never felt as strongly as that about a woman. Maybe India would be different, but he hadn't known her long enough to say. Surely, given enough time and distance, Mack would get over it. "She'll be gone in a week, so…the end is in sight."

"I wish that made it easier," he grumbled and left.

Rod listened to him go, then checked his phone again. India? he prompted. Don't leave me fearing the worst.

Finally, his phone pinged, signaling a response.

I'm fine.

Where are you?

Taking care of something. Be back soon.

He didn't push. He didn't want her to think that just because she'd relented and they'd made love this morning, he was going to become possessive or controlling. And yet she was in a unique situation, one that gave him reason to fear for her safety.

What is it? Are you going to see Cassia?

There was a long pause, but her response, when it came, brought relief.

Yes. Be home late.

Okay, he wrote. Then he hurried downstairs and out the front door. If his brother was going drinking, he'd need a driver.

"Wait a sec," he called before Mack could back down the drive. "I'll go with you."

Mack had brought home a woman! As soon as Natasha heard his voice and that female giggle, she got out of bed to have a look. But she couldn't see the front entry from her bedroom. She had to slip out and peer over the railing. Only then was she able to catch a glimpse of the two of them. Mack wasn't very steady on his feet, but he was getting all the help he needed from some curvy blonde.

Fortunately, Natasha didn't recognize the woman. But that didn't make the pain any less sharp. If she didn't know better, she would've thought he'd struck her—a hard blow to the chest.

After ten minutes or so, when she was sure Rod had gone to bed and there was no danger of bumping into anyone, she crept down the stairs to the basement and listened at Mack's door. She could hear talking, laughing, a few sighs. Then everything went silent, and the woman began to pant and groan. That was when Natasha's legs turned to rubber and she slid down the wall. She told herself she was stupid to be here, torturing herself. Mack didn't care how badly he hurt her or he wouldn't be doing this. So why would she allow it?

She had no answer for that. But she couldn't leave.

India had to find some way to best Sebastian. Ever since he'd shot Charlie and she'd managed to survive, she'd been waiting, as if due process of law would eventually solve her problems. She'd thought it was up to the police or the private investigator or the prosecutor or... someone *else*.

But she'd come to the realization that there *was* no one else. She was alone in this. Not even her in-laws were completely on her side. If she wanted her daughter back—and her life back—she had to figure out how to neutralize the threat Sebastian posed.

Finding out where he lived would be a good starting point, and the first place to look would be the house where he'd been living before he killed Charlie. Detective Flores had suggested he was probably back in the same place, with his wife.

So here she was, two hours from home, in Hayward. She wasn't going to stay in Whiskey Creek, quaking under her blankets at night, wondering if and when he might strike. He'd *called* her this morning! Although she hadn't given him the chance to say much, the fact that he'd made contact told her all she needed to know. He was as vengeful as she'd feared. She'd seen the hateful glare he'd so often turned on her in court, knew he was no longer suffering from the delusion that they were friends. He'd intended to frighten her with that call, to shove in her face the fact that he'd escaped punishment for the terror and harm he'd inflicted.

But that wasn't all he'd accomplished. He'd made her angry, and that anger had galvanized her into action. Maybe it was foolhardy. She could easily guess what Detective Flores would have to say about taking matters into her own hands. But what kind of life could she have if she was constantly afraid for herself and her child, always looking over her shoulder? Flores had suggested a security system and a restraining order.

Sebastian wouldn't respect either.

Holding her steering wheel in a death grip, she drove past the address Sebastian had given her when they'd communicated eleven months ago. This was where they'd initially arranged for her to bring the money he needed to get that bus ticket to LA. If only Cassia's dance lesson hadn't gone late that night, prompting her to give him *her* address instead, maybe everything would've been different...

Careful to avoid the halo of the closest streetlamp, she parked several houses down and used her mirrors to peer back at the house.

The place seemed occupied. Dim though it was, a porch light glowed in the dark night, and there was an old Camaro in the drive, propped up on cinder blocks. India guessed the car belonged to Sebastian's brother. He'd mentioned that Eddie was living with him. So was his wife, Sheila—the woman he claimed to hate but who'd lied for him under oath. Eddie was the one who'd been supplying Sebastian with drugs, which was why India had been trying to get him out of the Bay Area.

So much for helping him. Calling herself an idiot for being so easily duped, she looked up and down the street to make sure she hadn't drawn any unwanted attention. In an attempt to simplify her life and consolidate her assets, she'd sold Charlie's expensive Mercedes, but she'd kept her Prius, so there was always the possibility that Sebastian would recognize her car. It'd been parked in the drive when he'd come to her house that night ...

But no one was out, thank God.

Besides the Camaro, two other cars sat in front. They were just as old and banged up as the Camaro, although they were probably drivable. There wasn't much else to see, except a couple of cheap lawn chairs on the front porch beside a crate that'd been turned on one side to make a table, and a few toys strewn about the weed-infested yard.

The toys made India sad, because they suggested the presence of small children.

Sheila had three kids. Were the kids who owned these toys hers?

India guessed they were; she had no way of knowing for sure. Just like she had no way of knowing if Sebastian was still living in this dump.

So how was she going to find out?

She eyed the neighboring houses. The other homes didn't look much better. She doubted this was the safest area in the world. But maybe someone would be able to tell her something. She had to ask, had to start somewhere.

"Tomorrow," she mumbled and covered a yawn as she drove off. The sun was about to come up. She needed to find a motel.

She pulled out her phone to use her Around Me app and found a text from Rod.

It's getting late. Are you driving back?

God, she missed him already. But she couldn't continue to see him. She had to retain control—of everything—especially her own emotions and the perceptions of others, or she'd only compound her own difficulties. And she couldn't retain control when Rod was around. He made her want things she couldn't have right now—made her want *him*—so she needed to stop seeing him. That was the only safe route to go.

It would be so much easier if he didn't live next door, but…she couldn't change that.

Don't expect me tonight. Might be a few days. I'll let you know when I'm heading back, she wrote, then pressed Send.

When Rod heard India's text come in, he woke long enough to check his phone. She wasn't coming home yet. That was good information to have, since he'd roused every so often to check. He was relieved—until he noticed the time. Five thirty. What was she doing awake at this hour? He knew she had trouble sleeping and nearly chalked it up to her insomnia, but there was something odd about her making the decision to stay when it was almost morning. Why hadn't she texted him at eleven or so, after Cassia had gone to bed and she realized she wasn't up for the drive home? Why would she wait until dawn?

Had she been up this whole time, fighting with her in-laws?

He texted her again.

You okay?

Fine.

Would you tell me if you weren't?

Don't worry. I can take care of myself.

That was a no.

So there is a problem. What is it? Did you leave because of that call from Sebastian? Do you think he knows where you live?

When she didn't answer, he called her, but she didn't pick up.

India, I'll help you if you'll let me. Can we have a conversation?

I can't talk to you, Rod.

Why, for God's sake?

Because hearing your voice would only make me feel things I can't feel right now. I have to be strong.

What was she talking about? Something had changed…

Tell me what's going on, damn it! Where are you? Where do your in-laws live?

No response.

Really?

I'm sorry. It wouldn't be right to involve you.

"Shit," he said and tossed his phone on his nightstand before slumping back on the bed.

She was shutting him out. Again.

18

Mack felt terrible. Somehow, last night when he'd had too much to drink, he'd come up with the brilliant idea that the best way to keep from making a mistake with Natasha would be to throw himself into the arms of another woman. Surely that would relieve the sexual frustration and longing she evoked, right? So when someone passably attractive started hitting on him, he went with it.

Now that he was sober again, however, he saw what he'd done as an act of futility. He couldn't remember what'd happened last night or whether he'd enjoyed it, but that was mostly because he didn't *want* to remember. He'd made a horrible mistake and, as a result, he had to cope with a huge dose of regret on top of the worst hangover he'd had in years.

Maybe it'd be worth it if he'd managed to change anything, he thought, but sex with this other woman had done nothing to assuage his hunger for Natasha. He wanted to take Natasha to his room this minute and make love to her for hours.

Except he couldn't, of course. For all the same reasons he couldn't do it in the first place. Even if he decided to flip off the rest of the world and be with her, the woman he'd met at Sexy Sadie's hadn't left when they were done last night. Although she had her car, she'd spent the entire night with him, was *still* there. She'd even gotten out of bed when he did, given him a deep-throated kiss that had almost made him gag and proceeded to follow him up the stairs to get some breakfast.

"I can scramble a few eggs, if you like," she offered.

Before he could answer, Natasha came into the room. His stomach twisted at the sight of her. Her red, swollen eyes left little doubt that she'd been privy to the fact that he'd had a woman over. She looked…battered.

Seeing her like that certainly didn't make him feel better.

As soon as she realized they were no longer alone, his guest turned and smiled. "Oh, hello! I'm Bella," she said, sticking out her hand. "Who are you?"

"I'm your worst nightmare," Natasha replied. "You touch me, you'll draw back a stub."

Bella's eyes widened, and she turned to Mack, so Mack forced a laugh, as if it was a joke. "Don't mind her," he said. "That's just my little sister."

The glare Natasha turned on him felt as though it could burn through steel. "Don't you say that," she said, her voice low, almost threatening. "Don't you *ever* fucking say that! I'm not related to you in *any* way. But you don't have to worry about me anymore. Do you hear? You finally achieved what you've been after. I hate you. I'm sorry I ever thought you were special. The mere sight of you makes me sick," she said, then whirled around and left.

Mack had never seen so much derision on Natasha's face. He felt eviscerated, as if all his internal organs were spilling out onto the floor. He couldn't move, couldn't speak. It didn't help that he deserved her contempt. Right now he loathed himself as much as she did.

"What was *her* problem?" Barbie asked—no, it was Bella.

He tried to think of something to say that might smooth this over but couldn't come up with anything. He couldn't claim Natasha was crazy or too temperamental, because it wasn't fair to blame *her*. This was *his* fault. Last night he'd justified his actions by telling himself he'd had other women over—quite often. But after Natasha had declared herself, her expectations had changed. What he'd done was selfish and cruel, especially since she didn't have any experience with this kind of jealousy and heartbreak, and probably didn't know how to cope with it.

Bella made a clicking sound with her tongue. "Your parents had better get hold of her, because *she's* a little monster."

"She's just..." He swallowed the word *hurt* and finished with "confused."

"If *that's* what you call it, but I've never had anyone be so rude in my whole life. I can't imagine the little bitch has *any* friends."

"Don't." He spoke softly, but when he looked up, he could tell she understood that he meant what he'd said. "Don't call her names. Don't say *anything* bad about her."

"You're taking *her* side?" she cried. "After that whole... stub comment?"

"I *always* take her side," he said.

With an appalled laugh, she shook her head. "Wow. So what if you've got a hot bod? The rest of you must be as screwed up as she is. What a way to end the night," she snapped and stomped out.

He hoped she was getting her purse and wouldn't bother to say goodbye. Fortunately, that seemed to be the case. A minute or two later she left, slamming the door behind her.

Breathing a sigh of relief that she was gone, Mack went downstairs to find his phone. Texting Natasha wouldn't do him any good, but he tried despite that.

I'm sorry.

"What are you doing?" Dylan asked. "I thought you went to lunch."

Rod clicked away from the screen he'd pulled up on the computer in the front office. "No, I'm checking something while I have a few minutes."

Dylan cocked his head. "Anything I can help you with?"

Rod could see why he might ask. Rod generally used his phone if he needed the internet at work, but for this extensive a search, he preferred a bigger screen and the ability to navigate more quickly. "I got it."

Taking one of the empty chairs, Dylan leaned back and locked his hands behind his head. "You, too, huh?"

"Me, too?"

"Maybe it's just me, but it seems like everyone's a little secretive these days."

"I'm not being *secretive*," Rod said. "Just…taking care of my own business."

"And Mack?"

"*He's* being secretive." Rod took advantage of the distraction but grinned to show he was joking.

"The question is why," Dylan pressed.

Rod shrugged and looked away. He knew Mack was

struggling, but he didn't feel it was his place to say more. "No clue."

"You'd agree he hasn't been himself lately."

"What do you mean?" Rod figured the best way to handle Mack's situation was to play dumb.

"He seems upset. Especially today. Haven't you noticed? He's hardly said a word."

Whatever was going on between Mack and Natasha was getting worse. Rod couldn't miss that. For most of the morning, Mack had kept a close eye on the clock, obviously waiting for Natasha to show up. Rod had texted her himself, since she hadn't been at the house when he went to see if she needed a ride to work. But she hadn't answered him, and she hadn't come in.

Dylan finally called her, and she did pick up, but she told him she was going to spend the day buying supplies and packing and would come over to get caught up on her work after hours.

The fact that she'd be alone at that time—and wouldn't have to see Mack—wasn't lost on Rod.

"He went drinking last night, has a hangover," Rod said to help cover for Mack's behavior.

"Mack's never been that big a drinker. He hates feeling out of control, hates what alcohol has done to our family. So his drinking is one of the symptoms, not the cause."

Rod said nothing.

"Should I have a talk with him?" Dylan asked.

"I wouldn't," Rod replied. "He'll be fine." With time, Rod believed that was true. And that time would be there once Natasha went to school.

"Okay. I'll let it go for now." Dylan got up and started to walk out but paused in the office doorway. "How's your hand?"

"I'm getting used to the cast."

"Good. Any word from Chief Bennett?"

"Not yet, but India told me something that's a little alarming."

Dylan came back toward him. "What's that?"

After Rod shared what India had overheard from Liam and Sharon, Dylan shook his head. "Unbelievable."

"Maybe he needs a refresher course in getting his ass kicked," Rod grumbled.

"Stay away from him," Dylan warned.

"I won't touch him, but that doesn't mean I'm not tempted."

"What *I* find amusing is the part of the story where India marched over to the police station to stand up for you."

"Why's that amusing?" Rod asked.

"It shows that she's defensive of you."

"She knows I didn't have a weapon."

"How?"

"Because…I'd never cheat in a fight."

"She came on the scene after the fight was over. The only thing she *knows* is that she likes you. That's all she *could* know. But since you seem to like her, too, I'm happy with her devotion. Maybe she'd be a great fit for you."

Rod studied his big brother for several seconds. Then he said, "Even if her ex-boyfriend murdered her husband and is still causing problems?"

The smile disappeared from Dylan's face. "You're not serious…"

"'Fraid so. Man named Sebastian Young shot and killed her husband nearly a year ago."

"Damn! That's rough."

"It gets worse. His trial ended in a hung jury and the DA's chosen not to retry him. They set him free sometime last week."

Dylan whistled. "No kidding?"

"No kidding."

"I feel bad for her. Why'd Sebastian kill her husband?"

"Because he's obsessed with her."

Dylan sat on the edge of the desk. "You said that in the present tense."

"As far as I can tell, it's still true. He called her yesterday, when she was with me."

Concern replaced the shock and interest on Dylan's face. "Then I take back what I said earlier. I *don't* think she'd be a good fit for you."

"Funny," Rod said.

"I mean it," Dylan insisted. "Don't get involved."

"*Someone's* got to help her," Rod argued.

"That someone doesn't have to be *you*."

"The police aren't doing anything!"

"I don't mean to sound like a prick," Dylan said. "I don't want to see her or anyone else get hurt. But you hardly know this woman. She's lived next door for what... two weeks? And you've got your own problems to deal with. This Liam thing might not go away as easily as we hope."

"This Liam thing is minor compared to what she's going through. She has a child, Dyl. I can't leave her and her little girl at the mercy of a killer. The guy has no remorse." Rod showed Dylan several of the links he'd pulled up while searching for any information he could find on the location of Charlie's parents.

"See what I mean?" Rod said when Dylan finished reading the attached articles.

"How do you know she isn't playing you?" his brother asked. "How do you know she didn't kill her husband and try to blame it on her ex?"

"Would he try to contact her again if that was the case?"

"If she lied about him, he could be out for revenge."

"That's not what's happening."

"You can't say for sure," Dylan said. "She *could've* tried to frame him, and now she doesn't know how to deal with having him out of jail."

"You're saying she's hoping I'll fight her battles for her? That she's using me?"

"I'm saying it's *possible*. She saw that you could fight. But even if she isn't—even if things are exactly as she says—you could risk your life and still not end up with her. She was married to a heart surgeon. That's a completely different lifestyle than what she'd have with you. We don't get a lot of attention or accolades for fixing cars, Rod. Neither do we make millions or get invited to swanky parties. We live in a small town, drive trucks because that's what's practical here, and we get physical and dirty every day."

Rod felt his muscles tense. Dylan had struck a nerve. "You don't think I can make her happy."

"That isn't it at all. I'm not sure she'll give you the chance."

"Either way, she didn't kill her husband or have him killed. She's lost most of her friends and she doesn't have a family of her own to stick up for her. She doesn't have *anyone*. *I* want to be there for her even if she and I don't end up together. This isn't 'I'll help you if you'll marry me.' I've never been successful at maintaining a lasting relationship. I'll probably be single for the rest of my life. So whether we work out as a couple is...something else."

"I'm just saying—"

"I *know* what you're saying. It could be dangerous and it's not in my best interests. But I won't be the guy who only looks out for himself. I can't imagine that's the kind of man *you'd* want me to be."

Dylan sank down in a chair. "Of course it's not. I'd rather not see you hurt, that's all."

"Someone has to step up."

"Are you sure it has to be you?"

"Didn't you hear anything I just told you?"

He sighed. "Yeah. I did."

"This doesn't have to spill over onto you."

"If it affects you, it affects me."

"And if you were me, you'd do the same thing."

Nothing.

"Am I right?" Rod asked. "Think of Cheyenne."

After a protracted silence, Rod tried a hopeful grin and his brother reluctantly grinned back at him. "Aw, shit," he said. "Okay. You got me. So...what'd she say to him when he called?"

"Nothing," Rod replied. "She went white as a sheet and dropped the phone. Then she left town almost immediately. And now she's not responding to my calls or texts."

Dylan leaned back. "You don't have any idea where she is?"

"She told me she was visiting her little girl at her in-laws', but I don't believe it."

"Why?"

"She told me they'd hardly let her talk to Cassia for fear the child would ask to come home. So I could see her going over there. She's missing her kid. But I can't see her staying. I doubt she'd feel welcome."

"Where else could she be?"

Rod turned back to his computer. "That's what I'm trying to figure out. I don't believe she's using me to fight her battles, not if she won't even tell me where she is. When I asked her, she said it wouldn't be *right* to involve me."

Dylan rubbed his chin. "I *knew* I liked her."

Rod scowled at him. "I told you, I can't let her fight this battle on her own. Sebastian deserves to encounter someone his own size."

"The thought of it being *you* scares the shit out of me," Dylan said. "Because I don't foresee a good outcome. You can't touch him, not unless he comes after you first, or he comes after her when she's with you, which means he'd probably have a weapon. Either way, there's no guarantee that he'll go to prison. He killed her husband and got away with it, didn't he?"

"I've got a rifle. I'll use it if I have to."

"That's my point! I don't want you to have to kill a man, Rod—even a man like that. However this plays out, it's going to be tricky."

"I agree," Rod said. "But what kind of chance has she got on her own?"

"I care about *you*," Dylan muttered. "I don't even know *her*."

"I have to help, Dyl. It makes me sick to think she might not be safe."

"Already?" Dylan cursed, but then he gestured for Rod to get out of the way. "Fine. Let me use the computer. There are a few sites that might be able to give us the information we need. Anya was telling me she once used them to find a roommate who stole some of her stuff and then took off."

"Wait a second," Rod said. "You said the information *we* need?"

"If you're in, *I'm* in."

Rod shook his head. "Hell, no. You have a family now. I'll handle this on my own."

The house at 211 Birch Street in Hayward was quiet. Although it was nearly three, there were no kids playing in the yard. But it was a hot afternoon. And *someone* was home. None of the cars had been moved. There were other signs, too. If India watched carefully, she could see the flicker of a television reflecting off the glass beneath drapes that didn't quite fit the window.

Knowing Sebastian might be so close made her damp with nervous sweat. But she'd done everything she could to prepare herself to approach his neighbors. She was standing on the stoop of the house across the street from his right now, wearing a dowdy, billowing skirt with a flowing top she'd purchased at a secondhand store. She'd visited a few other shops as well and picked up a briefcase, a short-haired brown wig and a pair of "reader" glasses. Her goal was to look middle-aged and frumpy, so that if Eddie, Sheila or Sebastian happened to notice her in the neighborhood, they wouldn't immediately recognize her.

Her disguise wasn't a lot to rely on, but she was determined to see this through, do something to fight back. These days she had no doubts about the kind of man Sebastian was, felt no sense of obligation to be kind or helpful to him. So at least she knew who and what she was dealing with.

She was going to stay calm and outsmart him. He'd never expect her to go on the offensive like this. She supposed she had that in her favor...

Pressing one hand to her chest as if she could slow her racing heart, she lifted the other to knock. She had no idea who'd answer the door, if that person might be a friend of Sebastian's or how he or she would react to questions, even if there was no friendship involved.

The knob turned and a giant of a man, bald with rheumy eyes and a scraggly gray beard, stared out at her.

"Hi." She summoned what she hoped was a disarming smile, but he interrupted before she could say another word.

"Whatever you're sellin', we're not interested," he said and closed the door.

India was tempted to leave it at that. She didn't have the nerve to push very hard. The tattoos on the man's neck and arms made him look dangerous, despite his age. But this house faced 211, so the people here were likely to know more than anyone else on the street. They merely had to look out a window to observe the comings and goings at Sebastian's place.

Do it for Cassia... Forcing back the fear that welled up, she knocked a second time.

The same man opened the door. "What do you want?" he growled.

A woman called out above the TV that was droning in the background. "Who is it, Frank?"

"If you'll shut up for a minute, maybe I can find out," he yelled back.

Acting as professional and confident as she could, India handed him one of the cards she'd made at an office supply store.

"You're a private investigator?" he said after eyeing the fake name, fake business and other fake information she'd given him. Only the phone number and email address were real. The number was a new Google number that went to a voice mail attached to the email address.

"I don't usually do fieldwork," she said, as if she was making an admission. "I'm a computer geek, working with a firm of investigators, and I'm not quite comfortable banging on people's doors. You can probably tell." She fanned herself as if she was a bit flustered, which should be convincing, since it was true. "But I feel very passionate about this particular case, so I thought it might be worth coming to ask you a few questions."

His eyes narrowed. "What case? What're you talking about?"

"How well do you know your neighbor across the street?" she asked.

"Which neighbor?"

When she pointed, she could only hope there was no one looking out at her. The last thing she wanted to do was draw attention to herself.

"Three people and some kids live in that house," he said.

As she'd guessed. "Is this man one of them?" She pulled out the picture of Sebastian she'd gotten at the library from one of the many newspaper articles on Charlie's murder.

Frank glanced at it, but he didn't take it from her. He scowled as his gaze returned to her face. "Why do you ask?"

"Although I still have to prove it, I believe he's guilty of—" she hesitated as if she was being careful not to go too far "—some crimes against children, and I'm looking for the evidence to prove it."

His manner changed immediately, which was why India had devised that particular lie. Even most drug dealers, addicts, burglars, ex-cons, gangbangers and other thugs were protective of children. "What kind of crimes?"

Again, she pretended to be making a conscious effort not to poison his mind, all the while hoping his imagination would fill in the blanks. "I'd rather not say. He's innocent until proven guilty, as you know, and I'm not here to stir up any negative sentiment."

"This must be serious." He peered more closely at her. "Are you saying he's a pedophile?"

She raised her free hand. "We don't have enough proof to bring charges…"

"He's suspected of it, though? Way I heard it, he was arrested for killing some doctor. The police came 'round asking questions about him last year."

"They couldn't make those charges stick, which is why he's back in the neighborhood. And now there's reason to believe he's done a lot more than shoot one doctor." India hoped this guy hadn't followed the coverage of Charlie's murder too closely. She wasn't sure how well her disguise would hold up. There'd been pictures of *her* in the papers, too. "He's obviously not a law-abiding citizen. I don't condone murder of any sort, but I especially don't condone victimizing children."

"Hell, no!" he said. "The wife and I have grandkids who come over here. He'd better not touch one of 'em."

"Frank?" The woman who'd called out before did so again.

"Be there in a minute, June!"

India hoped "June" wouldn't decide to come to the

door. The fewer people who saw her, the better. "If you could help me, we might be able to put him away for good. He belongs behind bars."

"Yeah, he does. Like I said, there are kids living with him. What do you want to know?"

"First of all, I'd like to make sure I've found the right man. Could you look at this picture?"

"That's the guy who's living across the street," he confirmed without hesitation. "I recognized him immediately."

"How well do you know him?"

"Not well. People come and go in this neighborhood. When he lived here before, I passed him on the street a few times. Then he was gone, probably in police custody. Now he's back."

"When did he return?"

"No clue."

"When did you first notice him?"

"Night before last?"

"So you can't tell me if he has a job."

"No, I'm guessing he doesn't work. They're night owls over there. Sleep most of the day."

"Have you ever spoken to him?"

"Not directly."

"Would any of the other neighbors be able to tell me more?"

"Doubt it. Like I said, people come and go in this neighborhood. Most of these houses are rentals. It's not like anyone's ever going to throw a block party."

India hadn't learned a great deal, but she'd confirmed that Sebastian was living with his wife again. "I understand. Well, if you see anything…unusual, would you please alert me at that number?"

He held up her card again. "You bet."

"Frank, what's taking so long?"

He turned as the woman he'd been hollering with walked up behind him.

India froze. She'd been hoping to get away before she could come face-to-face with anyone else, but she hadn't quite made it. "This gal works for a private investigator," Frank explained. "The guy across the street's some pervert."

"He is?" June, who was obviously Frank's wife, squeezed into the gap between him and the door.

India held her breath as their eyes met.

No recognition. Thank God. Perhaps she hadn't followed all the media coverage…

"What kind of pervert?" she asked.

"I really can't—" India started, but Frank answered. "Sex offender."

June shook her head. "There are so many of 'em these days. They oughta cut off their nuts."

India let her breath seep out. Not only was there no recognition in June's eyes, she was buying the pedophilia story. "I'd be satisfied if we could just get him off the streets," she said. "So if you see anything you think I should know about, anything he could be arrested for—" she indicated the card she'd given Frank "—please feel free to call or email me if you'd rather not contact the police."

"Okay, but…what should we be looking for?" June asked.

"The license plate numbers of any people he seems close to. Whether or not you see him carrying a gun. That sort of thing."

"I remember the cops were looking for the gun he used to kill that doctor," Frank said. "Did they ever find it?"

"I'm afraid not," India told him.

"We'll keep an eye out," June promised. "His wife sits out front with the kids every once in a while. Not that she watches them very well. But I'll speak to her next time I see her, find out what I can."

India reached out to shake her hand. She'd come to this street fearing the neighbors, had judged them by the depressed state of the houses and shabby yards, but she really liked this couple. "Be careful what you say, though," she warned. "He's dangerous."

"Don't worry about me," she said. "I'm a tough old gal. I'll call you if I learn anything."

India turned to go. She got all the way to her car. But she felt so guilty for lying to them, was so afraid that what she'd said would persuade them to stick their necks out too far, she turned back and knocked on the door again.

This time June answered. "Is there something else?" she asked.

India cast a hesitant glance over her shoulder. She wanted to keep herself and her child safe, but she didn't want to put others in jeopardy in the process. "I'm afraid I'm not working for a private investigator who's on a pedophilia case," she said.

June blinked several times. "You're not?"

"No." She clasped her hands tightly in front of her. "That card I gave your husband? It's fake. And this wig and…and the rest of what I'm wearing? It's a costume."

The bewilderment on June's face made India cringe. *"Why?"*

"That doctor you mentioned? The one who was shot?"

Frank came up behind his wife. "Yes…" he said.

"I'm his widow."

"So what are you looking for?" June asked.

India told them the truth. How Sebastian had gotten off and was contacting her again. How she'd moved away and yet feared he might come after her. How desperately she wanted to protect her child. That the police weren't able to do anything to change her situation. "I feel like… like finding more evidence or something else that might put Sebastian back behind bars is my only choice," she finished. "I'm sorry for telling you that big story. If I wasn't so desperate, I would never have lied."

Instead of being angry, as India had expected, June pulled her into an embrace. "Honey, you got nothing to apologize for. I'd lie, cheat or steal to protect my family."

India squeezed her eyes shut. This total stranger was being kinder to her than her own mother-in-law. "Then you won't tell him I came by, asking about him?"

"Of course not!" Frank said. "We have no loyalty to him. The neighborhood would be safer without him."

"Let's make sure he goes to prison, where he belongs," June added.

"Okay." India smiled as she wiped the tears that'd begun to fall. "Thank you. I can't… I can't thank you enough."

"We're going to find that gun," Frank told her. "He doesn't stand a chance against the three of us."

19

India had just reached her motel room and pulled off that itchy wig when she got a call from Rod. She almost answered it, but she stopped herself at the last second. She hated to lie to him again, and yet she couldn't tell him the truth. He wouldn't like what she was doing. He'd try to talk her out of it—any sane person would—even though she had no better choice. Sebastian had her backed up against a wall. Either she defended the life she deserved to live, or she let him destroy it again, and that wasn't an option.

Frank and June Siddell's promise to help encouraged her. She'd left with their phone number, hadn't even approached the other neighbors. They'd told her to let them poke around instead. Having people who belonged in the area ask a few questions wouldn't be nearly as intrusive as a stranger showing up at the door, and the fewer people she approached, the less chance of being discovered by Sebastian. She didn't want to spook him; she wanted him to remain cocky, confident and complacent in the belief that he'd escaped the long arm of the law and had nothing to fear.

As she sank onto the bed, Rod's call transferred to

voice mail. Because she'd had so much to do today—creating her costume, making those fake business cards and finding and printing a photo of Sebastian—she hadn't been able to get much sleep. She needed a nap and planned to take one as soon as she saw whether or not Rod had left her a message.

He didn't; he sent her a text message instead.

I know you're not at your in-laws.

How? You haven't contacted them, have you?

No, but I could. I have their number.

Suddenly no longer tired, she sat up and crossed her legs as she stared at her phone. He *had* to be bluffing. He couldn't have figured out where they lived. She'd never even given him their full names.

But he could've easily gotten them from the newspaper articles on Charlie's murder...

I don't believe you, she wrote and held her breath while she waited.

A few seconds later he sent their name and address, along with their phone number.

How had he come up with that information? They weren't listed anymore. But they hadn't moved since Charlie died. She supposed there was plenty of contact information floating out there in cyberspace.

Don't call them!

Why not?

Because you're right. I'm not there.

Now we're making progress. Where are you?

Oakland. Visiting an old friend.

Bullshit. This has to do with Sebastian, doesn't it.

His response didn't include a question mark. He was making a statement.

She nibbled at her bottom lip while trying to devise a reply. She'd never guessed Rod would bother to look up her in-laws...

I'm taking care of things.

How?

Don't worry. I've got it covered.

Why won't you tell me?

Because it's not your problem.

I'll help if you let me, India. You don't have to go through this alone.

He didn't understand, probably couldn't even conceive of the danger Sebastian posed. She wasn't sure *she* would've been able to if she hadn't experienced what she'd experienced. The ease with which some people could kill hadn't become real to her until she'd witnessed

Charlie's murder and then watched Sebastian lie about it and get off.

Why would I endanger someone else?

Because I don't want you out there alone, doing whatever you're doing.

I have some help.

Technically, that was true, now that the Siddells were handling reconnaissance for her.

You won't owe me anything, India. This isn't an offer based on sex or marriage or anything like that. This is an offer of friendship. I'm sure you could use a friend. Isn't that what you asked for the night we first met? I'm here. Just level with me.

She took so long to decide what to text back that he called her. And this time she answered.

"Finally!"

"I'm sorry. I don't mean to be mysterious. It's not like I wanted to leave you hanging."

"Then tell me what's going on."

She toyed with several strands of hair on the wig she'd purchased.

"Do I have to call your in-laws?" he threatened when she didn't speak up. "Tell them that Sebastian's stalking you?"

"No!"

"Then…"

She doubted he'd act on that threat. But she also knew

he'd keep badgering her, wouldn't back off. "I've found out where he's living, Rod."

"What does that mean? You'd never actually go there…"

"Well, not to the door." When she told him what she'd done this afternoon, he remained silent long after she finished speaking.

"Hello?" she said.

"I'm not sure how to react."

"You could tell me you understand."

"Which would only encourage you. I will admit that not many people have your courage."

"It's more desperation than courage. I don't have any other choice. But…I appreciate that you're checking in with me—and all you've done to help. I'll come home when I can."

"Whoa. Wait a sec. We're not done yet, sweet cheeks."

She had to smile. He'd never called her by a nickname before. *"Sweet cheeks?"*

He ignored that. Clearly, he was more interested in discussing what mattered. "You can't let everything hinge on whether a neighbor might be able to find out what Sebastian did with the gun."

"It has to be somewhere, couldn't have disappeared into thin air. I just hope he didn't toss it into the Bay. I'm not sure we'll ever recover it if he did."

"What are the chances he'll disclose the truth? Unless he's stupid, he's never going to volunteer what he did with the murder weapon, especially to an old couple living across the street."

"He's a talker, brags constantly. It's possible. I was hoping… I don't know. I was hoping I might catch a break. It's time for my luck to change."

"What does he like to do?" Rod asked. "Where does he like to go? A certain strip club or bar? A convenience store or gym? There must be someplace *I* can bump into him. Maybe the Siddells can tell us where I should hang out."

"*You?* No, never," she said. "Stay away from him."

"Why? Unless he's into killing random guys, I should be fine. We've never met, so he won't recognize me, won't have any reason to suspect me, either. Maybe I can befriend him. He'd share things with a buddy that he wouldn't share with a neighbor. Think of all the jailhouse snitches who go to the police with information on their cell mates. This wouldn't be quite the same thing, but I could give him someone to talk to, someone to try to impress."

The idea that Rod would be in the same vicinity as Sebastian made India uncomfortable. "What if you push too hard and he gets suspicious?"

"I'll be careful."

"I don't want you to approach him. It has to be someone else."

"Who?"

"Anyone!"

"You don't think I can pull it off."

It wasn't that. With his build and his tattoos, even his background, she had no doubt he could blend in. She'd initially pegged him as a rough sort, hadn't she? He had that dangerous edge to him. But the fact that he could be believable in an outlaw role didn't change her mind. "I'm too afraid to let you try."

"Watch it," he teased. "You're not supposed to care about me. You've put a lot of energy into trying to avoid it, remember?"

"How can I forget?"

He chuckled. "Give me your address. I'm coming over."

She wanted to see him. The thought of being able to touch him, to kiss him, filled her stomach with butterflies. *I'm pathetic...* If she didn't watch herself, one of them—maybe both of them—would get hurt, and if she let him get involved in her efforts to fight Sebastian, that pain could include more than heartbreak. "What about your job?"

"I can't remember the last time I took a week off. It'll be my summer vacation."

"Dylan won't mind?"

"That's the beauty of working with family. My brothers will step up. I've got this cast slowing me down, anyway. Better I take vacation when I'm a little gimpy than when I'm not."

He managed so well with the cast she wouldn't call it much of a handicap. "Even if your brothers cover for you, I can list lots of things that would be more fun."

"Yeah, well, I guess I'll tour Europe next year."

"Okay," she said with a laugh and gave him the name and address of her motel.

Rod could tell that India had been glad to see him when he arrived. She hadn't tried to hide her excitement. Although she'd just gotten up from a nap, she'd given him a sleepy smile and slipped easily and eagerly into his arms. Then she'd invited him in and proceeded to fix her hair and makeup because they were planning to go out to eat.

He'd been hungry, but he'd also been so anxious to touch her that he'd kissed her as soon as she was finished in the bathroom—and they'd never made it out the door. After making love the first time, they'd ordered a pizza, discussed how to create a situation that would let him befriend Sebastian—and then made love again.

At first the sex had been passionate, almost frantic, as if they'd been apart for too long, even though it hadn't been long at all. But after their pizza, the sex was different, more serious, more meaningful. And that was what he couldn't get out of his head.

He was developing feelings for her. Somehow she fit him—his personality, the way he liked to be touched, the way he liked a woman to respond when he touched her. At last he could understand what Dylan and Aaron must've experienced before settling down. He would've been happy to learn he wasn't incapable of that kind of caring, except that he was worried about where the relationship was heading. He was losing his heart—but did she even want it?

She was still wearing her wedding ring…

"You seem a little tense," she whispered when he thought she'd already gone to sleep for the night. "You okay?"

He couldn't see her face; she was spooning him. It was dark in the room, anyway. "I'm fine. Am I keeping you up?"

"No."

"Then why are you still awake?"

"It's only ten."

"Aren't you ready to sleep?"

"I am. I've had so many short nights in the past eleven months, I could sleep for weeks before I get caught up. I'm just…thinking."

"About…"

"You."

He hoped she'd explain that statement, say something to allay his fears, but she didn't.

"Are you scared to meet Sebastian?" she asked.

He was more afraid of *her*. He could handle himself around other guys, even dangerous ones. But love? That was new territory. "Not really."

"You should be."

He adjusted his pillow. "Why? Far as he's concerned, you and I have no connection. He doesn't have any reason to start anything with me."

"You'll be asking some sensitive questions. If he gets spooked—"

"Relax. I could get hit by a car crossing the street tomorrow. Anything could happen, but we can't be afraid of it all the time. Like I told you, I'll be careful."

She snuggled closer, slid her hand up his chest in a movement that suggested she liked the way he felt. She was growing more and more confident with his body. "Still. I'm not convinced having you come into such close contact with him is a good idea. I wouldn't be able to live with myself if you got hurt. I already feel responsible for Charlie. I'd give anything to go back and…and change what happened."

Would she? Because then *they* wouldn't be together… "Charlie was ambushed. He didn't have a chance. I'm going into this fully aware." He tucked her hand under his chin, reveling in the feel of her bare breasts against his back. "Besides, I make my own decisions. This is my choice. You won't be responsible for anything."

"Maybe I could hire a PI."

"Most PIs don't do that sort of thing. At least not any

I've ever heard about. That's cop territory, and the cops aren't going to do it."

"We could put out a few feelers, see if we can find a PI who'd work with us."

He turned the ring on her finger so the diamond wouldn't cut him. They were naked. There was nothing separating them—except what she felt for Charlie. "That'll take time. And what if we get some guy who says yes but isn't convincing? If Sebastian ever realizes you're trying to put one over on him, he'll be leery of every stranger he meets. The game'll be over at that point. Basically, we have one shot at this, so it's got to be good. I trust myself to handle it more than I'd trust someone whose only interest is in how much he'll get paid."

She kissed his neck, then his shoulder, but she seemed as restless and unsettled as he was.

"You have to have some confidence in me, India," he told her. "I can take care of myself."

"I believe you. That's the thing. I just hope I'm not making a mistake by letting you do this."

Again, he felt her wedding ring as he entwined his fingers with hers and couldn't help hoping *he* wasn't the one making the mistake. "We have to roll the dice," he said.

20

Natasha was still at the body shop. When Mack came home for dinner, she'd already left the house. But that'd been several hours ago. It was getting late and she wasn't back, which was why he hadn't gone to bed. He was waiting up, watching TV in the living room, to be sure she returned safely.

As a sports analyst talked about the latest Giants game, he read over the texts he'd sent her throughout the day. She'd ignored all of them.

You're not going to answer? I said I was sorry and I meant it.

Come on, Tash. Forgive me. Please?

Hello?

You don't have any right to be mad!

Okay, I get it. You do have a right to be mad. But you have to understand that this is hard for me, too.

He felt like a scumbag trying to garner sympathy by pulling the "this is hard for me, too" card. He had nine years on her and a lot more life experience. He shouldn't be complaining. But he was growing desperate. He couldn't bear the thought of her hating him. Why couldn't they find neutral ground somewhere *between* love and hate?

"What're you watching?"

He nearly grimaced with distaste when Anya walked into the room. J.T. had gone to bed over an hour ago. He'd assumed she'd retired with him. *"SportsCenter."*

"Fun." Her sarcasm tempted him to say she should go watch her own TV. She had one in the bedroom. But he bit his tongue. He'd long ago decided it was usually best to ignore her. Now that Natasha had graduated and they didn't have to be so careful to keep life calm and stable for her sake, maybe they could tell J.T. and Anya that it was time to move out. His father didn't particularly annoy him. He sort of liked J.T.—a lot more than his brothers did. But Anya got under his skin like nobody else. Some of the stuff she said to him and Rod and Grady was so overtly sexual it was embarrassing. Grady had once confided that she'd walked in on him when he was getting out of the shower, and he felt certain she'd done it on purpose.

"So Natasha's leaving for college early, huh?" she said.

Mack was surprised she knew. Natasha rarely spoke to her; they weren't close. And *he* hadn't volunteered the information. "Who told you?"

"My daughter, of course. You may look after her like an old hen, but I'm the one who gave birth to her. Why, is her change of plans a secret?"

"No. Just relatively new."

"So she *is* going."

"Yes. In a week." To get a reasonable airfare, they'd had to wait that long.

"Any idea why?"

"You didn't ask her when she told you?"

"I asked. She didn't answer."

He shrugged. "I guess she's eager to get out on her own."

"It's got nothing to do with you?"

When she took the conversation in *that* direction, Mack felt his stomach twist into knots. "Why would her moving out have anything to do with me?"

She slouched onto the ottoman not far away. "Really? You're going to play dumb?"

"I don't know what you're talking about."

"Oh, stop pretending," she said with a roll of her eyes. "You've wanted her since the moment I brought her here."

Mack gripped the remote so tightly he thought he might break it. "Anya, if you'd like to keep living under this roof and enjoying the other necessities we provide, like food, I suggest you keep your mouth shut. I haven't done anything questionable where Natasha's concerned. Matter of fact, I've tried to be good to her. To take care of her." He could've gone on, could've mentioned that he'd had to fill the gap because her own mother had done such a poor job, but he didn't see anything to be gained by turning this into a screaming match. Rod wasn't home, but Grady was. Mack hoped to get through this evening, and the rest of Natasha's stay in the house, without drawing attention to his problem.

He braced himself for whatever she might say, but she surprised him by agreeing. "You think I haven't noticed that? She's one of the lucky few who knows what it's like to be truly loved by a man. You've been better to her than anyone's ever been to me—I can tell you that."

He doubted Natasha could be called *lucky*. But he did care about her. Deeply. "Then let's agree to leave it there."

"Sure, if that's where you want to leave it, although I have a few thoughts on the subject—"

"I don't want to hear them," he broke in. "Thank you."

She got up to leave, then turned back. "I get that you have no love or respect for me. Maybe I've earned that. But I'm going to do you a favor, anyway. She's not a child anymore, Mack. You can have her if you want her."

The front door opened before he could respond and Natasha walked in. She took one look at her mother, shifted her gaze to him, then went to her room without greeting either one of them.

"I'll continue to do what's best for her," he murmured to Anya.

"Even if it's not what's best for you?" She threw up her hands. "Suit yourself."

She acted as if he was needlessly hurting himself *and* Natasha, but if *she* condoned them getting together, there had to be something wrong with it. He never wanted to be on her side.

She had one thing right, though. He loved her daughter.

Mack sat there for another thirty minutes, hoping Natasha would come out and talk to him. But he knew that wasn't going to happen when he heard the shower go on in the bathroom down the hall from her room. She was getting ready for bed.

After turning off the TV, he started for his own room. He had to work in the morning, and the day would be a long one. Since Rod was taking time off, they'd all have to carry a heavier load. But he never made it as far as the stairs that led to the basement. He migrated to Natasha's room, hoping to have a few words with her when she got out of the shower, just to make sure she was okay.

His computer, which he let her use, was on her desk. He sat down to search the internet while he waited, but as soon as the screen saver dissolved, he saw that she'd been on Facebook, scrolling through pictures posted by her fellow high school graduates, who were on a senior trip to San Diego.

She'd never mentioned a senior trip. She probably hadn't wanted to ask for the money.

Or maybe it wasn't a school-sponsored event and she hadn't been invited...

He clicked through the pictures, then got distracted by a message that said, "See how far we've come," which linked to a page that showed the seniors as babies. Natasha's entire graduating class had posted baby pictures alongside their senior pictures. Except for her. She'd sent in a photo of one of Dylan's dogs as a puppy.

Mack remembered hearing her ask her mother for a baby photo a few weeks ago, remembered Anya saying she didn't have one. Anya claimed they'd all been "burned in the fire," but Mack had never heard about a fire, and Natasha didn't recall one, either. More likely, Anya had lost Natasha's baby pictures somewhere along the way, since nothing mattered to her more than drugs, and she used to be even worse than she was now.

But why had Natasha turned in a puppy picture?

He read through the comments. Some guy named "Teto" said she was a cute pup and he'd like to do her "doggy style." Mack wished he could put his fist through that kid's face, but the sexual innuendo didn't upset him nearly as much as some of the comments made by the girls. "And she's still a dog," or "Now we know she's always been a bitch."

"What're you doing in my room?"

Mack had gotten so caught up he'd forgotten to listen for the shower. Natasha was standing in the doorway. She wasn't wearing one of his T-shirts; she'd put on the real pajamas Rod had given her last Christmas. The fact that she'd eschewed his T-shirt was significant, but instead of commenting on that, he motioned to his computer. "Why the dog pic?"

"What else was I supposed to use? It was an assignment. I had to turn in *something* if I didn't want it to affect my grade."

"Dylan's dog—that was the best you could think of?"

"Would you rather I used stock art of some random baby? Pretend I was just like everyone else? I'm not *that* desperate." She waved a hand. "Doesn't matter, anyway. I got the points and the grade I needed."

She had to be hurt by what some of her peers had posted, but, in typical Natasha fashion, she was dismissing it as if she was too tough for that. "What're you doing in here, anyway?" she asked. "Did you come to get your computer?"

"No. I came to tell you that you can take it to school with you."

"I don't need it," she said. "I'm planning to buy my own."

"You won't have the money, not for some time, and you'll need a computer. I hardly ever have to type anything. I text, so my phone's more convenient. Take it."

"No, it's yours. I can rent one."

"Take it!" he insisted.

She shrugged, but he couldn't tell if she was acquiescing or just refusing to argue. "Is that all?" she said. "Because I'm kinda tired."

He scratched his neck. "You don't want to talk about last night?"

She wouldn't look at him. "I'd rather forget it, but every detail is permanently etched in my brain. Ah… Oh!…" she panted, mimicking Bella. "Yes! God, that's good."

He cringed. "Thanks for the vivid reminder."

"No problem. I'm glad you had fun."

"Natasha—"

"Don't. It's fine," she said. "You don't owe me anything. I get that. I'm the one who was out of line."

"Bringing Bella home was a mistake, and I'm sorry. I'm *very* sorry. I wish I hadn't done it. My mind is…not where it should be."

"Couldn't you have waited until I was gone? But… okay." She began straightening her room, which was almost spotless. She'd always been a neat freak, usually cleaned *his* room, too.

"I feel terrible about it," he admitted.

She hesitated. Then, to his relief, she seemed to soften. "Don't feel bad. I was in the wrong to begin with."

Wait. This wasn't what he wanted to hear, either. How was *she* in the wrong? By accurately judging his interest and responding to it? Now she seemed to have convinced herself that she'd been crazy to ever believe he could want her. She was so used to disappointment that she was already trying to accept his rejection—despite the mixed signals she'd been receiving and how upset she'd been just this morning. "Seriously?"

"Of course. Feel free to call whoever it was you fucked

last night and have her over again. This is your house, and I'm a guest in it. I'll stay out of your way."

He had no interest in Bella, wished he'd never touched her. "You're *not* a guest in this house. That's the problem. Why, did Grady say something to you?" That *guest* stuff sounded as though someone had taken her to task for misbehaving…

"No, I just figured out what you've been trying to tell me. *Duh*, right?"

Uncrossing his feet, he leaned forward. "And what is that?"

"I kept thinking that once I grew up, once I was 'old enough,' we could be together. But I was wrong. I'm not too young for you. I'm too *old*."

Mack felt his eyebrows come together. "Can you explain that?"

"To fit into your life," she said. "Now that I'm a woman, I'm sort of in this 'no man's land.' You want to fuck me, but you feel like you can't, so you don't know what to do with me."

That was true. As usual, she understood perfectly— *too* well. He wanted her beneath him, welcoming him inside her. But he couldn't touch her in that way, refused to be the kind of lecher that would make him.

"So I'm backing off, like you asked," she said. "And I hope it's soon enough that you're not sorry you met me. You've done so much for me." Her throat worked as if she was fighting tears. "You've been there for me so many times when no one else was. Thank you."

The chair creaked as he leaned forward again. It was hard not to get up and go to her. "Natasha, I could *never* regret knowing you."

She offered him a sad smile. "Good. Then at least we'll part friends."

Finished with the few things she could put right in her room, she climbed into bed and slid beneath the covers.

She'd put an end to the conversation, but there was so much more Mack wished he could say. He wished he could tell her how beautiful she was, regardless of what those mean girls had posted on Facebook. How hard it was for him to let her go and how much he'd miss her. She'd been such a big part of his life for the past two years—the part he always looked forward to. It'd gotten to the point that he couldn't wait to see her when he got up or got home from work, if she was at school and not at the shop with him.

But admitting any of that would only take them back to what they couldn't have, and it wasn't fair to give her false hope. He felt as though the sexual tension that had developed recently was his fault, because he hadn't been able to mask his interest well enough.

"Good night," he murmured, but he didn't leave. He waited until she'd fallen asleep. Then, with a sigh, he walked out and closed the door behind him.

India sat across from Frank and June Siddell at a café several blocks from where they lived. They'd called first thing in the morning to let her know they had some information, so she'd arranged to meet them for lunch.

Rod wasn't included. He'd asked to come, but as much as India liked and trusted the Siddells, she didn't see why anyone had to know about Rod. If the Siddells weren't aware of who he was or the fact that he was involved, they couldn't give him away, even accidentally.

Rod said she was being *too* careful by keeping them

in the dark, but he could tolerate a higher level of risk than she could. She'd told him to go eat on his own and drove to the café without him.

"It's so nice of you to try to help me," she told Sebastian's neighbors. "The worst part of what I've been through is the helplessness. Waiting for the police to find Sebastian and arrest him. Feeling as if everyone's blaming me, even though I'm telling the truth. Then watching the justice system fail—"

"I can't believe he got off," Frank interjected, sounding thoroughly disgusted.

"I wouldn't be taking matters into my own hands if there was any other way," she said.

June reached across the table to clasp her hand. "We know that. What you're doing is scary, but we'd fight back, too, if we were in your shoes, so we're happy to do our part."

"Thank you."

The waitress arrived with the coffee they'd requested when they sat down, so they ordered their meals. Then June opened her purse, put on her reading glasses and smoothed out a piece of paper. "I wrote down a few things for you, in case they come in handy."

"Like what?" India asked.

"A list of all the neighbors, their addresses and phone numbers."

"I approached a couple of people on our street last night," Frank chimed in. "To see if I could find someone who knows Sebastian better than I do."

"And? Did you find anyone?"

"Guy who lives on the right told me he's partied with Sebastian a number of times, said Sebastian's always hitting him up for drugs."

"Why would he do that? Doesn't Sebastian's brother, Eddie, sell meth?"

"*Sell* is the key word there. Eddie's strict about getting paid, and Sebastian usually doesn't have money. This guy, Mike, said Sebastian's always trying to mooch a freebie."

"Did he mention where Sebastian likes to hang out?"

"Gave me a coupla places. After Hours, a bar that's not far away, and Solids and Stripes."

"A pool hall?"

He nodded.

"Does he take his wife out with him?"

"Hardly ever. He leaves her home with the kids," Frank said. "I don't get the impression he cares about her. Just uses her. Mike said Sebastian beats the shit out of her if he gets mad enough."

Disturbed by this news, India set her coffee down without taking a sip. "And the kids?"

"Sheila wouldn't be nominated for Mother of the Year," June said. "I took some muffins over this morning. Thought it would be a nice gesture—and a way to see if her husband was around. But Sheila didn't invite me in. And I couldn't tell from the doorway if Sebastian was home. The kids were, though. They were running around half-dressed and filthy, like usual."

"Did you feel Sheila might be open to your friendship?" India asked. "That you might be able to gain her trust?"

"She doesn't seem particularly interested in me. Or anyone else, for that matter. I'd bet my bottom dollar she's on drugs, too. All the signs are there."

India finally took a sip of her coffee. Sebastian's life was a mess, and it sounded as if his wife's wasn't any better. "If you could get her to admit that Sebastian wasn't at home the night he killed my husband, that would help. She's the one who provided his alibi."

"I tried talking about the trial," June said. "Told her I'm glad her husband's out of jail. That's when she clammed up."

"Sure wish we'd been paying more attention that night," Frank said. "But maybe we can make up for it. There's an old shed out back. Sometime when they're gone, I'm going to take a peek inside, see if I can't find the gun he used to shoot your husband."

"The police searched the house," she said. "I'm sure they would've included the shed."

"That was before. Might be worth a second look."

"I'm worried you'll get yourself into a dangerous situation. Maybe if you see him drive off one evening, you could call me and I'll have a look."

"Forget that," Frank said. "What if he came back unexpectedly? I'll handle it. We owe it to ourselves, as well as his wife, those kids and everyone else in the neighborhood to get rid of this dude. We have to stop him from hurting people."

When he stated it that way, as if seeing Sebastian put behind bars wasn't just *her* responsibility, India felt better about involving him. "Okay. I appreciate the support."

"I'll check the bar and the pool hall tonight, see if he's at either place."

If Frank was willing to go *that* far, India couldn't leave him feeling he was her only hope. So, without using Rod's name, she explained that she had another friend who also planned to try to connect with Sebastian.

"A fellow in Sebastian's age bracket would have a better chance of getting close to him than I would," Frank admitted. "It's brilliant."

"We'll see. Having two people will allow us to cover more ground. If you could go by the bar tonight and call me if you see Sebastian, that'd be enough. I'll have my friend visit the pool hall."

"Absolutely," he said with satisfaction and sat back as the waitress brought their food.

"Let's call Cassia."

India looked up in surprise. She and Rod were in the motel room, sitting on the bed. They'd been on her computer, pulling up every piece of information they could find on Sebastian. Rod felt he'd have a better shot at befriending him if he had some concept of what Sebastian was like, what he might find appealing and how to approach him. But after several hours of research—which included reading the transcripts of the trial and India telling him everything she remembered about her old boyfriend—the suggestion that she call Cassia came out of nowhere.

"My daughter?" she said.

"Do you know another Cassia?"

"No, it's just…"

"What?"

It was strange hearing her name on his lips. They hadn't talked much about her child. India felt she had to keep that part of her life separate. "You know how possessive my in-laws are with her."

"I do. But I also know that you're missing her, and you have every right to talk to her. Maybe it'll be easier to press the issue if we go over there to visit instead of call."

"There's no time for a visit."

"Why not? They live in San Francisco. We can be there in twenty minutes, stay for half an hour and be back in plenty of time for me to go to Solids and Stripes. That place won't even get going until well after Cassia's in bed."

"I realize that, but...I can't show up with a man, Rod. My in-laws will never believe I loved Charlie if I'm with someone else so soon."

He stretched out on the bed.

"What?" she said.

"Eleven months isn't that soon."

"It's been a *hard* eleven months, which makes it feel like an eternity. I'm with you on that. But I can assure you that eleven months won't be nearly long enough for them."

"Shouldn't they be more concerned with whether you're recovering? Whether you're happy?"

"To be honest, I don't think they care about me. I'm beginning to wonder if they ever did."

"Then who says *they* get to decide if and when you see your child?"

She pushed the laptop away. "I'm trying to respect their wishes."

"Because you care so much about their opinion."

She had cared at one time. She wasn't so sure how she felt these days. Having them doubt her and judge her had hurt too badly. But they were Cassia's grandparents. And she knew how sad Charlie would be if he could see what was happening. He'd always wanted his folks to embrace her, since she didn't have parents of her own anymore. "There's that—and then there's the fear that they'll sue me for custody of Cassia."

Rod scowled at her. "No judge in his right mind would take Cassia away from you."

"Whether the police have really crossed me off their

suspect list remains to be seen. And even if they have, it doesn't mean the Sommerses believe I'm innocent, Rod. They could make me look like a woman who killed her child's father. Once they convince the judge that I might've gotten away with murder, they'll show him what a stable and loving home *they* can provide, and…and who knows what he'll do? They raised Charlie, after all, and look how well *he* turned out."

"That has no bearing—"

"It could," she broke in. "Once I go to court, there'll be no guarantees. Judges have so much power. You can't begin to guess what will sway the man or woman who presides over the hearing. Maybe we'll get a male judge who hates his ex-wife, a woman who happens to look or act like me. Or a judge who was rescued from neglect or poverty by a set of loving grandparents. Or a judge who followed the trial and felt I was to blame. Trust me, once Claudia and Steve decide to go for this, they'll stop at nothing. They'll dig up every stupid decision I've ever made and use it to characterize me as an unfit mother. And even if they can't get any traction at first, they've got the money and the time to hang in there for the long haul. I can't let my life go in that direction. Cassia's all I've got left."

"Then visit her without me," Rod said. "That shouldn't piss them off too much. Tell them you really missed her, so you thought you'd drive over."

"I don't even know if they'll be home."

"So call first."

"I can't. Then they'll be gone for sure."

He sat up. "Are you hearing yourself right now?"

"It's a bad situation." Although she longed to see Cassia, she didn't know if she could tolerate being treated as an unwelcome guest by Charlie's parents. She wasn't ready to return to San Francisco, either. The city was so much a part of her life with her late husband...

"It doesn't have to be tonight," Rod said. "Just think about it. You can see her if you want to. I'll make sure of it."

She smiled as she nodded. His words empowered her, but she couldn't let him *make sure* of anything where her daughter and her in-laws were concerned. "I'll have enough on my mind tonight worrying about you. Maybe tomorrow. Or the next day."

He looked as if something in her response troubled him, made him realize that they wouldn't always be cloistered away like this, that the rest of the world would eventually intrude. "What is it?" she asked.

"Nothing," he said.

She didn't push. "One day at a time, huh?"

"Yeah." He got off the bed. "I guess I should go."

She followed him to the door. "I'm not sure we should do this."

"Quit worrying." He kissed her forehead. "I'll text you. Let you know if I make contact."

She caught his arm. "No. Don't try to text me. If Sebastian happens to see my name or number, he'll link the two of us. Delete all my contact information before you spend *any* time with him."

"My phone is password protected. Besides, I'm not going to give him any reason to get hold of it," he said and left.

India walked over to the veranda and watched him pull out of the lot.

Solids and Stripes was a decent pool hall—not nearly as seedy as Rod had expected. He arrived at ten, bought a beer and hung out around a big-screen TV that was showing NASCAR reruns. Then he played some darts and moved over to the pool tables, where he hoped to scrounge up a game to help whittle away the hours. None of the men he'd seen so far resembled the pictures India had shown him of Sebastian; he wasn't there.

Rod got in on two games, both of which he lost because he wasn't concentrating. More interested in watching the door to see who came and went, he regularly checked the flow of people. Then he'd check his phone to see if Frank was having any better luck at the bar.

At midnight, when he was well into his third game, he finally heard from India regarding Frank.

Frank says he's been at After Hours since nine. Doesn't think Sebastian's going to show. He'll be heading home soon.

In Rod's opinion, it was too early to give up. But Frank was in his sixties. Rod could see why he might call it a night.

"Do you mind?"

Rod moved aside so his opponent, a guy named Dave, could take the shot he wanted and perched on a bar stool to text India back.

No sign of him here, either. I'll stay until one thirty, then swing by the bar on my way back to the motel. Make a last pass before closing time.

Okay. I have to admit I'm kind of relieved.

He wasn't relieved. They needed Sebastian to show up so Rod could bump into him. They couldn't let this thing drag on forever.

Have Frank call his wife to see if Sebastian's car is back at home.

"Your turn."

Rod pressed Send and looked up to find his partner waiting for him. "Sorry. Wife doesn't like me going places without her," he mumbled.

"That's why I don't have a wife," the guy responded with a laugh. "So I can go where I damn well please."

Rod sank two solids but missed his next shot. So while he waited for another turn, he went back to the stool and checked his phone.

Frank says both cars are still gone.

"Shit," he muttered.

"So you're paying attention, after all?" Dave asked.

Rod focused on the game. The guy had nearly cleared the table. Only the eight ball remained. "Yeah," he said, but he didn't care if he lost. He was angry that he'd mishandled the night. He and Frank shouldn't have gone to places Sebastian *could* appear. The bar and the pool hall were supposed to be Sebastian's favorite hangouts, but he could have others. They could waste days, weeks like this.

They should've watched Sebastian's house until he left, then followed him, Rod decided. That made a lot more sense.

"Hey." Dave snapped his fingers in front of Rod's face. "I won, dude. You're done."

Rod didn't even bother to check the table. The guy wasn't all that good; with any real effort, he could've kicked his ass. But he had other things to do. "Too bad," he said and walked out.

Before he got in his truck, he sent India another text.

Give me Frank's address.

She replied right away.

What for?

So I'll have a base while I watch Sebastian's house.

The Siddells have been nice. I appreciate their help and support, but we don't know them all that well. It's safer if they don't ever see you.

Rod climbed into his truck and called her. "That plan isn't going to work," he said the moment she answered.

"Why not?"

"Because it's too inefficient. You're trusting the Siddells. I'm going to have to trust them, too."

"I'm trusting the Siddells with the fact that *I'm* poking around, but I'm already a focal point for Sebastian. We can't trust them or anyone else with *your* safety. What if… What if they mention you to another neighbor they think they can trust, but that neighbor rats us out?"

"That's the chance we're going to have to take."

"No, it isn't."

He started the engine. "India, I'm betting they're listed or I can look them up on the internet, so don't be difficult. I don't need your permission or your agreement."

Silence. Then she said, "Don't make me sorry I ever got you involved."

"Sorry or not, we're both in this now. Give me the address. Let's see this through, get it over with."

After a little more coaxing, she finally provided him with the address.

Since the only car he could see when he arrived was the broken-down Camaro, Rod assumed he'd missed his opportunity for tonight. Sebastian could stay out until morning or even later. But Rod figured it might be worth hanging out for a few hours, just in case he came back and went out again. The weather was warm enough that he wouldn't be uncomfortable sitting on the porch while the Siddells slept, and being that close would give him a great view.

Tweakers like Sebastian often stayed up for days. For a meth addict, the night was young.

21

Boredom set in before exhaustion did. Only Rod's determination to put a stop to what was happening to India kept him on that porch. But by three in the morning, it'd cooled off and he was beginning to wish he had a jacket.

He was about to give up and head back to the motel when he decided to walk across the street and see if he could find out anything that might help them. He'd been playing it safe while trying to figure out who was involved in this game, where they were right now and what they might do. But he hadn't seen any activity at Sebastian's house, or on the street in general, since he'd started his vigil. He was going to have to get closer to make this night count for something. A light in the front part of the house still burned; he had the feeling someone was up and wanted to at least catch a glimpse of whoever it was.

Moving slowly, carefully, he crept around the perimeter of the house, looking for some way to peer inside. Most of the rooms in back were dark, but he couldn't risk trying to peek in the front. What if someone drove by at that moment? Or Sebastian or Eddie came home? The drapes were pulled on the biggest window, anyway, the one with the light gleaming around the edges. So he doubted he'd be able to see anything even if he took that risk. The residents of this house were interested in protecting their privacy, but, fortunately for him, they were also concerned with saving money on their utility bill. Most of the windows were open to let in the cool night air, which provided him with a unique opportunity—if he had the balls to take advantage of it.

Did Sebastian have the gun that killed Charlie tucked under his mattress? In his nightstand? In his closet? The police hadn't found the murder weapon when they searched the house, but Sebastian could've given it to someone else for safekeeping and reclaimed it after he got home. Maybe he felt he had a better chance of keeping that gun out of the hands of the authorities if he retained possession of it himself, instead of hoping no one would stumble upon its hiding place.

According to India, Sebastian thought highly of himself; he just might be that daring. Rod figured it was worth a quick look while he had the chance.

Pulling his phone out of his pocket, he turned on the "do not disturb" feature so that it wouldn't buzz at a bad time. Then he returned to one particular window that seemed more accessible than the others.

Adrenaline charged through his system as he stood in the dark, listening for any sounds coming from within. There was no movement, but he could make out the muted rumble of a TV elsewhere in the house. If he had his guess, this was a back bedroom. He hoped it was the master and not where the kids slept. He didn't want to scare the crap out of Sheila's children by climbing through their window in the middle of the night—but if he was going in, this was his best point of entry.

Since the frame was already bent, the screen wasn't

much of an obstacle. It'd been flimsy to begin with; if necessary, he could've torn the mesh. But hoisting himself through the opening with only one hand wouldn't be easy.

Neither would getting out if someone screamed…

He told himself he'd be quiet, but he ended up making a lot of noise. And he landed on something. It didn't feel like a sleeping child, thank God. He bent to make sure and was relieved when he felt nothing other than some discarded clothes and a tennis shoe. No one stirred or came to see what the hell was going on, which encouraged him. If he could get away with that much noise, he could pretty well do whatever he wanted.

He could see the various shapes of furniture in the moonlight, including the outline of bunk beds. This was a child's room, all right.

He'd just stumbled over some toys while heading for the hall, one of which emitted loud *Battlestar Galactica* music, when he heard a small voice say, "Sheila?"

Shit. He'd awakened one of the kids, after all.

"Sheila? That you?"

It sounded like a boy. Rod felt he had to say *something* or the little guy might panic. "No, bud. It's me. Sorry if I woke you. I was…looking for the bathroom."

"Who're *you*?" he asked.

The other kids didn't seem to be in the room, and this one didn't act alarmed. No doubt he'd seen a lot in his short life, living with the kind of people he did. Rod wondered how far it was to the back door and if he could get there without being seen by an adult. He sure as hell didn't want to climb through the window again…

"Just a friend of your uncle's," he said as if it was no

big deal that he'd be standing in the kid's bedroom at that time of night.

"Eddie?"

"Yes."

"He's not *my* uncle," he grumbled.

Obviously, the kid didn't like Sebastian's brother. How did he feel about Sebastian? "You two don't get along, huh?"

No answer. As far as Rod was concerned, that was a definite yes. Instead of leaving the room, he navigated the messy floor to reach the boy's bed. "What's your name?"

"Van."

"How old are you, Van?"

"Eight."

"You the oldest in the family, then?"

"I'm not part of the family. My mother was Sheila's sister. She's dead now."

Wow. And this was what he'd been left with? "How long ago was that?"

"Don't know. When I was little."

"What happened to her?"

"She fell off a bridge."

Rod didn't want to dwell on Van's mother's death, so he focused his next question in another direction. "You have any brothers and sisters?"

"No, but Sheila has two girls."

"How old are they?"

"Five and three."

"Where are they now?"

"In their room, I guess."

"Do you look out for them?"

"Try to," he muttered as if he didn't feel he was capable of doing a very good job. "When I'm not in trouble."

"What do you get in trouble for?"

"Everything. Not picking up my toys. Not going to bed early enough. Getting up too early. Eating Sheila's food. Not paying attention in class."

"Those aren't the worst mistakes in the world. You seem like a nice kid to me."

"Really?" He sounded doubtful, as if he didn't hear praise very often.

"Absolutely."

"Even though I'm supposed to be sleeping right now?"

"You heard something that woke you up. How's that your fault? I took a wrong turn."

"Yeah, I guess." He thought for a moment, then he said, "Um, you're not going to tell Eddie what I said about him, are you?"

"That he's not your uncle? Heck, no. Why would I tell him that?"

"Because you like him?"

"I'll be honest. I don't know him that well. We're just hanging out tonight. I may never see him again."

"Oh. He has a lot of friends like that."

"Why? Is he an asshole?"

The boy laughed. "Yeah."

"Sorry he's not nicer. Sucks to grow up with people like him around. What about Sebastian? He an okay guy?"

"I hate him even more," Van whispered.

Rod mussed the boy's hair. "The good news is that you're only little until you grow up."

"I can't wait."

Rod was just thinking about how he was going to close this conversation and get out of the room when an idea occurred to him. This was a smart kid. And he had no love for the adults in his life…

"What does Sebastian do that you don't like?" he asked.

Van remained silent for a few seconds, then he said, "Lots of stuff."

"Can you give me an example?"

"I forget." He sounded sullen.

"He was gone for a while, wasn't he?"

"Yeah. When he was in jail."

Rod didn't ask why he was in jail. He wasn't sure this boy would even know. But a second later Van volunteered, "The police say he killed someone."

Obviously, he was troubled by the accusation. "I heard about that. But he must not have done it, if they let him go, right?"

Van said nothing.

"Right?" Rod pressed.

"Maybe he did do it."

That statement was hardly forensic proof, but Rod couldn't help getting excited. "How could he have? Your mom—er, Sheila—told me he was here with her the night that man got shot."

Van muttered a few words Rod couldn't quite make out. He *thought* it was "That's what she made us all say," but Rod didn't hear the boy clearly and he needed to be sure. "What was that?"

"Nothing."

"C'mon, what?"

He wriggled down under his covers. "I better go to sleep before I get in trouble."

Rod tried to keep him talking. Asked if he played sports. What his favorite video games were. How he was doing in school. But it was obvious the boy felt he'd gotten too close to admitting something he shouldn't and that'd spooked him.

So Rod backed off. Maybe once he befriended Sebastian, he'd have another chance to win this kid's trust and really get him talking. That could take Sebastian out of India's life—and Van's—for good.

"Okay, I'll let you go back to sleep," he said and straightened the blankets. But as soon as he got up and started moving toward the hall, he heard voices. Two men and a woman.

"Uh-oh. Don't tell Sebastian I'm awake," Van whispered, his voice full of fear.

India couldn't sleep. She was too worried. She'd been watching the clock ever since Rod left, couldn't imagine what was keeping him, especially because he'd stopped communicating with her. She'd tried texting him. She'd even called several times, but there was no response.

Had something happened to him? Should she keep calling—or was she putting him in a compromising situation?

After another ten minutes with no word, she forgot about the TV show she'd turned on to distract herself and began to pace. "Answer the phone!" she muttered as she risked calling once again.

No response. *Why?*

Sweat rolled between her shoulder blades as memories of the night Charlie was killed pressed closer than they'd been since that terrible event. Allowing Rod to help her had been a bad idea. Had she gotten *another* man killed?

"Please, no…" She had to learn what was going on,

find out if he needed help. She couldn't let anyone else die. She wouldn't be able to live with herself.

But how could she help Rod when she didn't know where he was or what he needed?

Should she go over there?

No. If Sebastian saw her, it would only make things worse. What *could* she do?

She began to scroll through the contacts on her phone. She'd added the number Sebastian had used to her address book so she'd recognize it if she ever received another call from him.

She brought up that information but didn't hit the icon to dial him. She stood there, transfixed, staring at his name. What was he doing right now? Did it involve Rod?

With a curse, she called Frank Siddell. She hated to wake him, but she needed him to check the porch and, if he wasn't there, look around for Rod's truck. Maybe Rod had just fallen asleep.

When Frank got back to her, it wasn't good news. He said Rod's truck was still parked a few blocks away. The engine was cold—it didn't appear to have been moved for some time—and yet Rod was nowhere to be found.

"Should I walk across the street?" Frank asked. "See if he's over there?"

India clutched her phone even tighter. "No." What reason could he give for showing up at four thirty in the morning? "I'll call the police," she said, but once she disconnected, she changed her mind. She was afraid that whatever was happening would be over by the time the authorities could respond. Detective Flores would understand what was at stake, but he lived in San Francisco, and she wasn't sure he'd be able or willing to leave his jurisdiction.

With a deep breath, she scrolled back to Sebastian's latest number and, without letting herself think any further about it, hit the call button. If he had Rod, and he knew Rod was connected to her, he'd say something. Her hand shook as she brought the phone to her ear. Maybe Rod had made contact and they were merely talking, becoming "friends" as she and Rod had planned.

Still, that seemed unlikely this time of night. They couldn't have met at a public place if Rod's truck was where he'd left it when he went to Frank Siddell's. And no one began a friendship by randomly knocking in the middle of the night.

Something had to be wrong...

"India!" Sebastian sounded excited, relieved to hear from her, which made her nauseous.

"What're you doing?" she asked, slurring her words so he'd think she was drunk.

"What do you mean? Nothing. It's almost dawn. I'm about to go to bed. What are *you* doing?"

"Can't sleep." She listened for voices and other noises in the background but heard nothing. And Sebastian didn't seem anxious or upset. Those had to be good signs. "I thought you'd be at a party. You're out of jail now, right? You can go anywhere, do what you want."

The emotion in her voice seemed to give him pause. "Just got home," he said.

"From where? From some other poor woman's house?"

He didn't answer the question. "Have you been drinking?"

"What do *you* think?" She began to sniffle. Now that she'd called him, she had to have a reason. She certainly didn't want him to think she was interested in rekindling their romance. She'd briefly considered trying to play him that way, trying to get close enough to figure out where he'd hidden the murder weapon. But she couldn't stomach the thought of letting him touch her. Her fear and hatred went too deep. She also knew how a pretense like that would be perceived if and when it came out. There would be those, like her in-laws, who wouldn't believe she'd been pretending at all. "Why'd you do it, Sebastian?" she asked. "Why'd you have to *kill* him?"

"I didn't kill anyone," he said.

That he could make such a claim to *her*, of all people, was enraging. He was so careless, so indifferent to the suffering he'd caused and the precious life he'd taken.

Her anger ballooned like a sudden wind filling a sail. "Yes, you did," she nearly screamed. "No matter what you said in court, no matter what you say now, I *saw* you shoot him. You and I both *know* what you did."

"Come on. Don't be like that. Let's not talk about that night. I feel as bad about it as you do! I wish it'd never happened."

So now he admitted it? Dirty liar… "What is that supposed to mean? Am I just supposed to *forget*?"

He lowered his voice. "If I remember right, there were parts of that night you enjoyed as much as I did. But *I* didn't share those details in court."

She covered her mouth as the bile rose in her throat. "Only because it didn't serve your purposes. And I didn't enjoy any of it," she said. "My skin crawled every second you touched me. You murdered my husband, and when you took his life, you ruined mine."

"Look, I'm worried about you," he said. "You need to calm down."

"I'll do exactly as I please! You have no control over

me!" she yelled. "I'll never allow you to have control again."

"Where are you?" he asked.

She slid down the wall, no longer able to bear up under the heartache of the past year. What had started as an excuse to contact him in case he'd gotten into some conflict with Rod was quickly turning into an honest outpouring of her grief and misery. "You killed him!" she moaned. "You shot the man I loved right in front of me!"

"I'm sorry for your loss," he said. "But like I said before, I don't want to talk about it over the phone. Tell me where you are. I'll come get you, take care of you, make it better."

"You can't make *anything* better. You can't even run your own life!"

"India, where are you?" he asked again.

"Where are *you*?"

"Home, where I belong."

"Alone?"

After another brief silence, he said, "Don't tell me you're jealous."

"I just want to know if you're alone!"

"I'll be alone, if that's what it takes to get you back. I'll do anything."

Oh, God… "Home isn't where you belong. You belong in prison."

"And you tried to put me there. I hurt you, and you paid me back. I'm willing to forgive and forget if you are."

"As if you have any reason to forgive *me*! I was trying to help you!"

"At least I acted out of love. You have to understand that."

She started to laugh. "Out of *love*. You acted out of love. You're as crazy as I thought."

"Crazy enough to still want you," he said as though that would flatter or sway her. "Let's meet up and talk, put all of this behind us."

"Never!" she said and disconnected. She was about to call the police. That conversation with Sebastian hadn't told her anything she didn't already know—that he had no idea what he'd cost her or the rest of the world. But while she was drying her eyes, she finally received a text from Rod.

I'm fine. Be there soon.

With a whimper she couldn't choke back, she dropped her head onto her knees.

She was still crying when he came through the door, couldn't seem to stop, but she didn't give him much of a chance to say anything about it. Getting up the second she laid eyes on him, she grabbed him by the shirtfront and pulled him to her. Then she kissed him long and deep.

"Where have you been?" she asked, but as soon as those words were out of her mouth, she was running her fingers through his hair and kissing him again.

The taste and feel of him was pure relief. And desire. And…she didn't know what else. Too many emotions were racing through her to define them all. He was alive and well. She had him back. "I'm so glad you're safe," she mumbled against his lips. "I was freaking out."

He wiped her tears. "Sorry, babe. Didn't mean to scare you," he said. "But I won't lie—I like that you're so happy to see me." When he picked her up, she wrapped her legs around his waist and let him carry her to the bed, where he fell on top of her.

"Don't go over there again," she said. "*Ever.* I don't care what our plan was. Let's throw it out. He's a total psychopath."

"We'll talk about it later. No need to blow what we have going right now."

She would've laughed at the way he could so quickly and easily separate the stress and danger from the desire, except that her feelings were too intense for laughter. The desperation she'd felt while he was gone lingered, making every second she held him seem like a moment stolen from time. "You've been up all night. You're not too tired?"

"I'm exhausted, but I could never be too tired for this."

She slipped off his shirt and licked the warm skin of his muscular chest. "You taste good. Every inch of you tastes good, and you feel even better."

He clasped her chin while he gazed down at her. Something about that look felt significant. She was pretty sure they were diving into a deeper level of intimacy than she could maintain. But she refused to think about that, or the consequences, whatever they might be. She was so badly shaken. The only way she could be significantly re-assured was to hold Rod as tightly as possible. To cling to him while he moved inside her. To feel his heart pounding against hers and hear his breathing turn ragged as their lovemaking grew more intense. Losing herself in his touch meant she didn't have to think of anything or anyone else. As he kissed her again, she slid her hands down to grip his ass and pull the bulge in his pants more tightly against her.

She craved raw passion. Only that seemed powerful

enough to erase everything else. But this kiss wasn't hungry as much as it was achingly sweet, and that nearly undid her. Why did she have to feel more than the simple pleasure of his touch?

"Take me hard and fast," she murmured.

"Why the rush?" he asked. "Why not take time to enjoy it?"

"I feel like I'll die if I can't be with you right now," she whispered, but that was before she could think, could filter her words. Not only did that statement sound over the top, it implied a greater commitment than she could promise, especially at this precarious point in her life.

Everything was so uncertain.

But that seemed to be what he wanted to hear. His expression showed fresh purpose when he pulled off her clothes.

22

Rod could feel India's wedding ring the whole time they made love. He tried to avoid thinking about it, even noticing it, but whenever her fingers slid between his or she ran her left hand over his body, there it was, a constant reminder.

Her ring had never bothered him quite this much. He'd figured she'd take it off when she was ready. There was no need to rush her; she'd been through so much. But he was beginning to care a great deal more for her than he had any other woman, and that was making him reluctant to share her, even with a ghost. He was so focused when he made love to her. He could see that he was acting as if he had something to prove, as if he was trying to outdistance the competition.

He needed her to care enough that she couldn't deny her feelings. Needed to feel she wouldn't let him down in the end. Somehow she'd managed to slip beneath his defenses when no one else could, and now he was vulnerable in a way he'd never been vulnerable before.

When they were finished, he dropped down beside her, heart pounding, short of breath. That was when the exhaustion he'd felt on the drive home hit him again.

"What happened tonight?" India asked.

"For the most part, a whole lot of nothing," he replied. "Until I decided to go over to Sebastian's house and have a look around."

Her hair tumbled forward as she shoved herself up on one elbow. "Why would you take that kind of risk? Don't you believe me that he's dangerous?"

"I believe he *can* be dangerous, which is different from being dangerous all the time. I had my eyes open. I felt we needed to have something to show for tonight—to make some progress. I won't allow this asshole to hold our lives hostage indefinitely. If we could just establish that there's no gun in the house, we could at least cross that off our list."

"The police checked the house when they searched, Rod."

"He could've hidden it somewhere other than the house and brought it back. Or he could have another gun. That would be good to know, too, wouldn't it?"

With a troubled sigh, she rolled onto her back.

"What?"

"I'm mad at you," she said.

"Because I was trying to help?"

"Because you could've been hurt!"

"Come here." He pulled her close and kissed her temple. "I wanted to see what I could find, figure out what Sheila's like, just…get closer. Gain some sort of advantage or create an opportunity. You understand that, right? Winning at what we're doing takes information as much as anything else."

"But you don't seem to be scared!"

He chuckled. "I'm *not* scared." He had been that one moment, when he realized Sebastian was home. If not for the phone call Sebastian had received, which took his attention precisely when Rod needed that to happen, he might not have been able to get out of the house. As it was, he'd worried that Sebastian would hear the back door open and close and come after him.

Fortunately, he got away without incident.

"You should be," she said, unwilling to back down.

"Would you like to hear about my adventure or not?" he asked.

She cast him a sullen glance, but her curiosity got the better of her. "Of course I do."

"Fine, then. For your information, I managed to get inside the house. And I feel it was worth the effort."

She sat up. "No way! You went *inside*?"

"I was after something we could work with, and I think I may have found it."

That minimized her outrage. "Really?"

"Really." Holding sleep at bay a little longer, he explained how he'd climbed in through Van's window and ended up waking the boy.

"Sheila's son *saw* you?"

Learning that almost set her off again. Rod could understand why she'd assume it wasn't good news, but he didn't think meeting the boy would be an obstacle. "Van's her nephew, not her son, and it was dark, so he couldn't see me clearly."

"There's still your voice. Your smell and size. Your cast. *I* would know you in an instant."

"You've had sex with me," he said.

"It's not just that. You have a certain presence. You stand out. People remember you."

"He's a kid."

"Which means he must've been terrified. You don't think that'll *make* him remember?"

"He was just waking up from a dead sleep. And he wasn't half as frightened as a regular child would be. I'd say he's more frightened of the adults he lives with than he was of me."

She drew her legs closer to her body. "That's sad."

"I couldn't help feeling sorry for him," he agreed and went on to tell her what had happened and what he thought he'd heard Van say about the night Charlie died.

She interrupted the story at that point. "Whoa, wait a minute. He told you he was *coached* to say Sebastian was home that night?"

"That's what it sounded like to me. But he was mumbling and wouldn't repeat himself."

"Can we get him to repeat himself to Detective Flores? Get him to tell the truth?"

Rod considered the situation from Van's standpoint. "Right away? I doubt it. What's in it for him, except being punished? He's terrified of Sheila *and* Sebastian. Doesn't like Eddie, either. I got the impression the adults in his life don't treat him like they should."

"I'm so sorry about that. But if we put Sebastian away, he won't be able to hurt Van—or anyone else."

"That still leaves Sheila and probably Eddie."

"I would never purposely put a child in a bad situation. But Van knows the truth! And he wants to talk or he wouldn't have said what he did. He can tell everyone that Sebastian wasn't at home the night Charlie was killed!"

Rod was afraid he might've gotten her hopes up a little *too* high. Even if Van knew something that could help, getting that information out of him would be tricky—

especially since Rod would also want to protect him as much as possible. "Sounded like it."

"Then he *has* to talk," she said. "The fact that he was told to lie should convince a jury, shouldn't it?"

"It lends support to your version of events. But a child's word won't be enough to make the DA charge Sebastian again," Rod said.

"I thought you were excited by what you'd uncovered."

"I *am* excited. But we have to be realistic. My mind's taking a different direction where Van's concerned."

"Which direction would that be?"

"We need physical proof. Forensic proof. Something that can't be refuted."

"Yes…"

He tugged on her hand to urge her to lie back down. "What if Van can tell us what Sebastian did with the gun?"

She took a few seconds to think that over. Then she said, "Why would Sebastian ever trust a boy with that information?"

"He wouldn't. But Van has to have heard a lot, living in that house—if not from Sebastian, then from Sheila or even Eddie. He's so young I doubt they pay any attention to what they say in front of him, especially if they're high."

"Did you ask Van about the gun?"

"I couldn't. Not yet. If I ask too soon, he'll just get defensive. Then he may never tell me. I need to spend more time with him, earn his trust."

"How are you going to do that?"

He ran his fingers through her long, silky hair. "By befriending Sebastian."

"But Van's the person you *really* want to get to know?"

"Why not? I believe I stand to learn more from him. Children trust sooner and, like you said, Van wants to talk."

She rested her cheek on her hands as she stared at him.

"So am I forgiven for scaring you?" he asked.

She didn't answer his question. "I have something to tell you, too," she said.

This came as a surprise. "What's that?"

"I called Sebastian tonight."

A jolt of adrenaline shot through him. "You *what*?"

"I thought he had you. I felt I needed to…to interrupt him, to see if I could find out anything, to stop what I feared was happening."

"Shit, India. I don't want you having *any* contact with him."

"It's not like I *wanted* to call him! I panicked. I didn't know what else to do."

"You didn't ask him about *me*, did you?"

"No. Of course not."

He remembered how he'd found her, crying on the floor when he walked in, and realized how frightened she'd been. It had taken real courage to make that call— and it didn't escape him that without her, he might not have made it out of Sebastian's house as easily as he had. Her call had to be the one that'd distracted Sebastian. "I'm sorry I put you through that. I know how hard it must've been to hear his voice."

She pulled up the sheet. "I've never felt such hate. I don't want to feel that way anymore. It'll only make me bitter. But…I can't seem to let it go."

"You will, in time," he promised. "It's just too close right now."

They said nothing, just continued to stare at each

other—until she broke the silence. "Why are you helping me?" she asked.

He considered all the things he could say but decided to keep his personal feelings out of it. "Because you need it."

"I appreciate everything you're doing. I hope you know that. But…I need you to be careful, Rod. I couldn't take it if…if I was responsible for someone else getting hurt."

"You're not responsible for me, India. I've told you that before. I'm making my own decisions, okay?" He'd been planning to tell her about his almost-encounter with Sebastian, but her worry changed his mind. Knowing he'd had such a close call, and that only her interruption had made it possible for him to get out of Sebastian's house, would upset her.

"What'd he say to you?" he asked.

"Not much," she said with a frown. "I didn't really give him the chance. I completely lost it. You saw me when you walked in. I was so afraid he'd hurt you. That's all I could think about. And then the pain and anger from before sort of…rose up and took over."

"How'd he react?"

"Said he still wanted me. That we should forgive each other."

She was hard to get over. Rod wondered if he might be the one missing her and wanting her back someday. "Unbelievable."

"He doesn't seem to care about what he did. Killing Charlie means no more to him than if he'd swatted a fly."

"We'll get justice for Charlie—and for you," Rod said. "Then you'll be able to move ahead without looking back."

"I hope so," she whispered, but he could tell she was having trouble believing in that dream.

"I promise." He took her hand and, as he threaded his fingers through hers, tried to steer her mind elsewhere, so she wouldn't continue to worry. "Are we going to see Cassia tomorrow?"

"Rod…"

"Fine. Are *you* going to see her?"

She hesitated, obviously tempted. "Charlie's parents won't like it if I show up without any warning."

"Do you care that they won't like it?"

"Might be better to wait until we get this settled."

"Why? Then, if this ever does come down to a custody battle, they can claim you showed no interest. That you didn't visit her once while she was at their house."

"They wouldn't do that."

He slid one finger down her shoulder and over one breast. "Are you sure?"

"No," she admitted.

"Then go see your little girl, regardless of whether they like it. And call her as often as you want."

She'd seemed so remote since they'd had sex that he was almost surprised when she snuggled close. "Don't let me fall in love with you," she whispered.

As India had anticipated, returning to San Francisco wasn't easy. What had happened in the city was simply too heartbreaking.

But Rod had a valid point. As vulnerable and rattled as she was, she couldn't allow her in-laws to intimidate her, to make her feel she couldn't see her own child. Just because she'd been nice enough to let them take Cassia didn't mean she'd also agreed to stay away. Visitation hadn't even been discussed, because India had never thought it would be a problem. Once the trial was over and Sebastian was put away, she'd expected her situation to improve.

Rod had come with her, although they'd taken her car and she was at the wheel, since she was familiar with where they needed to go. He'd said he wanted to spend the day with her, see where she'd lived, but she suspected he was just trying to make it easier for her to drive across the Bay Bridge and enter what she now deemed hostile territory. While there was still a small part of her that loved the city and would've enjoyed sharing it with him, her recent history in this place filled her with dread. She hadn't left her home all that long ago; the memories here were so fresh and disturbing.

"*This* was your home?" he said as she stopped at the curb in front of the house she'd bought with Charlie—the house where he'd been killed.

She nodded. A three-bedroom, one-bath Spanish Mediterranean, it had been built in 1931 with the expansive arched windows, hardwood floors and vaulted ceilings she loved. Although small, it had a fabulous view and wasn't far from West Portal Park, with all the shops and restaurants in that vicinity.

Whiskey Creek wasn't San Francisco, but it had its own sort of charm—at a fraction of the cost. She was holding out hope that she could make the transition. Whether she'd stay would depend a great deal on what happened in the next several months.

"Neighborhood looks expensive," Rod said.

"It is," she admitted. "We paid $1.5 million for the house, and it's only eighteen hundred square feet."

"Wow." He seemed suitably impressed. "Must be hard

to move to Whiskey Creek after living like this," he said. "The pace of life, everything, is so different."

She could tell the differences bothered him, made him feel he was at a disadvantage. "I'll be happy if I can just survive the next few weeks and months and begin rebuilding my life."

"Understood," he said.

She wasn't quite sure what he understood. He seemed to think she'd warned him off. She supposed, in a way, she had. But they didn't have the chance to talk about it. A woman dressed in workout clothes and pushing a stroller came jogging down the street. India recognized her immediately and wished she'd driven away a few seconds earlier, because now it was too late to escape without being seen. Ellie Cox, the friend who'd left her that message, was out for an afternoon run.

"Oh no," she muttered.

"What is it?" Rod asked, but there was no time to explain. Ellie was approaching her window, so she lowered it.

"India!" Ellie cried. "How wonderful to see you again!"

India masked her true feelings with a smile. "Great to see you, too."

Pressing a hand to her chest, Ellie took a moment to catch her breath. "So where are you living these days? I tried calling, but I'm not sure I have the right number anymore."

India stated her name on her voice mail greeting, but she didn't point that out. Neither did she specify her new location—although Ellie might already have heard she was in Whiskey Creek. "I got your message, but life's been so hectic for me, what with all the changes. I haven't had a chance to get back to you. I'm sorry."

"No problem. I was only checking in, making sure you were okay."

India didn't believe she cared. Not for a minute. She'd done nothing to support India through the trial, had distanced herself as much as her husband, Mitchell, had. But for the sake of avoiding confrontation and being polite, India played along. "I'm fine. Thanks."

Ellie's gaze shifted to Rod. "Is this…a friend?"

"My new neighbor, Rod Amos," she said, then introduced Rod to Ellie.

"Nice to meet you." Ellie's words were polite, but her voice seemed to say, "Look at you…with another man already."

Or was that India's imagination? She had to admit she'd become sensitive to criticism.

Rod dipped his head. "My pleasure."

"It's great that you're meeting new people," Ellie said.

India curved her fingernails into her palms. "Yeah. Having a friend has made the transition a lot easier."

Ellie's eyes flicked to India's wedding ring. "I'm happy to hear that."

India turned her attention to Ellie's baby, who was gnawing on his chubby fist. "Grant's getting big."

"He's a handful. He was *such* a colicky baby."

Knowing Ellie, that meant he got up once a night. Ellie had never been one to feel she should have to sacrifice. "He's darling."

"We think so."

The sight of her friend's child reminded India that she and Charlie had been planning to have another baby. They'd initially wanted only one, which was why they'd waited. But about a year ago, India had changed her mind, and Charlie had slowly warmed to the idea…

"How's Mitchell?" India asked.

"Busy, as always. You know Mitch. He's as much of a workaholic as Charlie was."

The mention of Charlie hung so awkwardly in the air that, for a second, India wasn't sure how to react. She felt like a completely different person than when she'd been married to him. As if the murder had somehow exposed her for the pretender she'd been, white trash living a fairy tale with her heart surgeon husband. As if she'd never had the right to live in this house or be friends with Ellie or the other residents on the block.

She started the car. "Sorry to rush off, Ellie, but we're heading over to Charlie's parents' and don't want to be too late."

"You're taking Rod to meet Charlie's parents?" she asked in surprise.

Definitely not. Rod had agreed to hang out at an internet café, where he could grab a bite to eat and surf the web during her visit with Cassia. She'd intended to minimize the fact that she was with another man. Ellie couldn't make a big deal of it if Rod was going to her in-laws' place with her. "Of course," India said. "Why not?"

"No reason," Ellie replied. "Tell them I said hello. It was wonderful to see you."

"You, too."

"Call me soon. We'll do lunch."

"I will," India lied and, with a wave, drove off down the street.

She'd driven three blocks before Rod said anything.

"Is that what you want?" he asked at length. "To be like Ellie? To lead the type of life she does? To have what she has?"

She understood what he was asking. He wanted to

know if what she dreamed and longed for was something he'd never be able to give her.

She considered the implications. Did she need San Francisco, with all the people and connections it offered? The abundance of art? The culture? The wealth and prestige Charlie had afforded her?

No. She could live a much simpler life and be happy. *That* wasn't the problem.

Reaching over, she took his hand. "I wouldn't mind the baby."

23

Claudia couldn't even manage a smile when she opened the door. "India! What are you doing here?"

"I came to the city to do some shopping for the new house and I couldn't go back without saying hello."

"Oh." There was a marked hesitation, but then she stepped back. "Would you like to come in?"

"Mommy!" Cassia came running the second she heard her mother's voice.

India scooped her up and held her close. "Mommy has missed you *so* much, little girl."

"Miss you, too, Mommy," Cassia mumbled, locking her arms tight and pressing her face into India's neck.

Charlie's father got up from his recliner. The coloring books scattered on the floor indicated Cassia had been coloring while he watched the news and Claudia made dinner. India could smell garlic and other aromas drifting out from the kitchen.

"Why didn't you call?" he asked. "Let us know you were coming?"

"I thought it would be fun to surprise you," she replied.

He and Claudia exchanged a look, but India ignored their displeasure. Rod had been right. She'd needed to see her daughter and was glad she'd come. "What have you been up to, Cass?" she asked, pulling back to peer into her daughter's face.

"Making you a picture." She wriggled to get down so that she could lead India over to her spot on the floor.

"Wow! That's beautiful!" India exclaimed as she examined the partially colored butterfly. "You do fabulous work."

Cassia dropped the coloring book and began to tug India toward the back door. "Papa and Mimi bought me a trampoline. Come see."

"A *trampoline*?" India echoed. Wasn't that sort of a large present?

"She's had so much fun with it," Claudia said. "And, of course, it's good exercise."

India couldn't help noticing that neither Claudia nor Steve had really welcomed her. They hadn't embraced her, hadn't asked how she was doing or how she liked Whiskey Creek. They'd said none of the things they would've said back when Charlie was alive, and coming to this house had been such a pleasant experience. "You don't mind having a trampoline in your yard—even though she won't be here that often?" she asked.

Claudia averted her gaze when she responded. "It'll give her something to look forward to when she does come."

The terrible feeling India had had since Charlie's death—the feeling that his parents thought *they* should raise Cassia—made the hair stand up on her arms. Surely that was paranoia talking. They wouldn't even *consider* it... Would they?

The trampoline was huge, a full-size one that took up a large portion of the backyard. "You know the plants below the bed will die from lack of sunlight," she said to Claudia, who'd followed them out.

Cassia scrambled up to demonstrate how high she could jump.

"We don't mind." Claudia checked over her shoulder, as though she expected her husband to back her up, but Steve had stayed in the house.

Again, India told herself it was just her own insecurities, but Steve acted as if he could hardly stand to be around her.

"Jump with me, Mommy," Cassia called out, and India took off her shoes. She'd always loved trampolines, and this one was the best money could buy. They played on it for almost an hour before they were too exhausted to continue. By then Claudia had gone in to finish supper— and hadn't come back.

"Are we leaving now?" Cassia asked as they went inside. "Should I get my clothes?"

India glanced at the table. Claudia had set only three places. The Sommerses weren't going to invite her to join them for dinner. "Not tonight," she told Cassia. "But you'll be coming home soon. In about twelve days."

Cassia's face fell. "No!" she said. "I want to go now."

"But you've been having so much fun with Papa and Mimi. They just bought you that tramp. You don't want to leave it this soon, do you?"

Cassia threw her arms around India's legs. "I miss *you*."

India bent to kiss her soft cheek. "I miss you, too. We won't be apart much longer. I promise."

"Why can't I come home?"

"Because we have so many things planned." Claudia spoke from where she stood at the stove. "You don't want to miss out. Papa promised to take you to the Monterey Bay Aquarium to see the octopuses and the sharks and the eels, remember?"

"Why can't Mama take me?"

"Your mother has to work."

That wasn't strictly true. India could go to the aquarium; she worked for herself. But apparently she wasn't to be included in *any* of their adventures. "Papa and Mimi have been looking forward to visiting with you for a whole month. I can't disappoint them by taking you home early." She smoothed her daughter's fiery-red hair, hoping to calm her, but Cassia wasn't so easily put off.

"You're *leaving*?" she cried as soon as India straightened.

"I have to," India replied.

"No! I want to go with you!"

Claudia's scowl hit India like a dart to the chest, made her hyperaware of her mother-in-law's disapproval.

"I'm getting ready to open my pottery store, remember?" she told Cassia. "That takes a lot of time."

"I'll help you," her daughter promised.

"When you get back."

"No!" she said and started crying. "I want to go!"

Claudia pushed the skillet she'd been using to sauté asparagus spears off the burner and trudged over to peel Cassia away. "This is why we'd rather you'd called," she murmured. "She was doing fine. Why'd you have to upset her?"

"That wasn't my intention."

"Don't, Mimi!" Cassia tried to squirm away from her grandmother. "I'm going with Mama!"

Steve entered the kitchen, lifted Cassia into his arms and carried her down the hall, away from India. "Don't be naughty," India heard him say. "We still have lots of things to do. You'll be glad you stayed."

"I'd rather not leave you with a crying child," India said when her daughter was out of earshot. "I'm happy to take her home with me, if that would be easier. I could always bring her back next week, when she'd probably be excited to stay again."

"I can't believe this," Claudia said. "That's what you were hoping would happen, isn't it? You thought you'd come here and get her all riled up, then you'd take her home early. You couldn't back off and give us one month with our granddaughter, despite the fact that we just lost her father eleven months ago."

So many retorts rose to India's tongue she almost couldn't decide which one to use. "I don't mind sharing her, don't mind letting you enjoy her. That's why I agreed to 'Mimi's Camp' in the first place, Claudia. I was just… missing her. So I came for a visit."

"Why couldn't you have waited two more weeks and saved us this upheaval?"

"I needed to see my daughter!"

"Of course. And, as usual, you put your own feelings first."

"As usual?" India gaped at her mother-in-law. "I'm sorry about the loss of your son." She kept her voice low so Cassia wouldn't hear—although there was little chance of that because she was crying louder than ever. "But I've lost everyone who's ever mattered to me. If you think, for one second, that you've had it harder than I have, perhaps you should consider *my* losses. And I know you don't believe it, but I didn't do anything to hurt Charlie. I *loved* him. I still love him, will always love him. So I'm as much of a victim in this as you are. Maybe even

more. The last time I checked, there was no one pointing a finger at you, blaming *you* for his death!"

Rearing back as if she'd been slapped, Claudia looked stricken. She almost crumpled, almost moved to hug India. India could see her emotions waver, just as she could isolate the moment Claudia realized she couldn't quite overcome her doubts. What she'd heard in court had destroyed all the love and trust that had once existed between them. "I wish I could believe that," she said.

"This isn't what Charlie would've wanted," India whispered. "Please. You're letting Sebastian take even more from us than he already has."

Tears sprang to Claudia's eyes, once again revealing the vulnerability that had threatened to come out a few seconds earlier. "You're right," she said. "I'm *so* sorry. Sometimes the grief gets so bad, and I miss him so much, I…I get angry, need to find someone to blame."

"*I* didn't hurt him," India insisted. "I was telling the truth in court. I was only trying to help Sebastian get to LA, where his mother was, so he could receive the support he needed."

Her torment showed in her eyes. "But why'd you have to do that? He isn't worth your time or effort."

"I once cared about him. And I was in a better situation than he was. I felt it was my duty to help an old friend. That's all. But feeling responsible—for allowing Sebastian back into my life—only makes what I'm going through worse. Can't you understand that?"

Tears began to slip down Claudia's cheeks. "Of course I can," she said and pulled India into her arms. "We'll get past this," she whispered. "Somehow, we'll heal and learn to live without him."

* * *

Since India was smiling when she drove up, Rod could only assume the visit with her daughter had gone well.

"You look happy," he said as he got in.

"I am. You were right. Although the visit got a little rocky there for a while, it also brought all the tension to a head and gave me the chance to tell Charlie's mother—again—that I had nothing to do with her son's death. And she needed to hear it."

"Was she receptive?"

Her smile broadened. "Yeah. She even hugged me before I left."

He squeezed her arm. "That's nice. How's Cassia?"

"Great. They've been buying her toys, *expensive* toys, and taking her all over the place—basically spoiling her rotten. But I guess that's what grandparents are for."

"Then you didn't mind leaving her…"

She merged into traffic. "You thought I might bring her with me?"

"I was sort of hoping."

"Why?"

Because the question of whether she'd ever be willing to include him in her family would've been answered. As long as she kept Cassia separate, she kept part of herself separate, too. But he didn't say that. "I don't like the way they make you feel," he told her, and that was also true.

They came to a stop at the light. "I decided it wouldn't be wise, not with what we're trying to do right now," she said.

"She could hang out at the motel with us, go swimming during the day, to the park."

"But having her means so much to them. I felt I should let her finish out her stay. It was tough to leave her, though, especially when she started to cry."

"I can imagine." Was there more to her decision? Like the fact that she was with him?

She threw him an accusing glance. "You don't think I should've left her."

"I think it's fine, as long as it was your choice and not theirs."

The light switched to green. "My relationship with the Sommerses has taken a turn for the better. I'm feeling encouraged."

Despite those words, Rod sensed that she was experiencing some regret at leaving Cassia, maybe even some fear that they'd be unfair in the end. "At least things are moving in a positive direction." He looked at his watch. "Did they feed you? It's nearly seven. I'd like to head back to the motel, unless you're hungry."

"I can wait."

"You haven't eaten?"

"Claudia was cooking dinner, but she didn't invite me to stay."

"Why not?" How hard could it have been to include one more person—the mother of their grandchild?

"I'm sort of wondering myself. They had plenty. But by the time we had our little…talk, I'd said goodbye to Cassia. Claudia probably didn't want to start that whole mother-parting-from-child process all over again."

Rod tried to give the Sommerses the benefit of the doubt, but he wasn't pleased that they hadn't treated India better over the past several months. "We can stop somewhere. What would you like to eat?"

"I'm not that hungry. I'm still high on relief," she said with a chuckle. "I'll get a quick sandwich from this little place I know after you go to Frank's."

"Okay," he said.

They were busy navigating the traffic vying for the Bay Bridge when India's phone rang. She glanced at her car's computer screen at the same time Rod did, so they both saw Sebastian's name.

"What should I do?" she asked.

"Ignore it," he replied.

"Maybe I could find out where he'll be tonight so you can run into him."

"No. I don't want you to have any more contact with him."

She nodded and they waited. After the call transferred to voice mail, they listened to Sebastian's message.

"What was going on with you last night? You were losing it, babe. I'm worried about you. You okay? I'm doing better now. I can help if you need anything. Call me. Let's not go on like this. You know I'm not a bad person, that I'd never intentionally hurt anyone."

India shook her head. "Can you believe that? He's acting like we're *friends*. As if nothing happened. As if he didn't shoot my husband in cold blood."

The nerve Sebastian had making that call, on top of everything else, infuriated Rod. He thought he could get away with murder. But Sebastian wouldn't continue as a free man. Rod was going to see to it that he was taken out of India's life for good. "I'm glad he's confident," he said. "Confident people are seldom as cautious as they should be."

Mack knew almost immediately that he shouldn't have come. He'd known Natasha would be here—it was eighteen and up on Fridays, this was her last weekend in town, and if there was any fun to be had, it was usually at Sexy Sadie's.

He sat with Grady at a small table in the corner and tried to focus on what his brother was saying, but he couldn't resist tracking her movements throughout the bar. She'd come with someone named Meredith, who was at least twenty-five. Natasha didn't know her all that well because the woman was from Jackson and they'd just met a couple of weeks ago at the shop. Why they'd decided to hang out together he couldn't say, but it meant that Natasha hadn't come with him. She wouldn't be leaving with him, either. That was what had him worried. Although Sexy Sadie's didn't serve alcohol to those with an X on the back of the hand, like the one on Natasha's, she'd gotten alcohol somewhere. More than a little. He was fairly certain she was drunk, and he blamed Meredith, who must've bought it for her. When he'd approached Natasha to say hello, she'd introduced him to Meredith, whom he'd already met briefly at the shop. But then she'd moved away as if he didn't figure into her plans for the evening at all. He hadn't figured into her plans since that night in her bedroom.

He'd thought that was what he wanted—for her to back off. But this was almost worse. The desire he felt hadn't gone anywhere. And now he'd been robbed of spending any time with her. Once she left for college, things would never be the same. He already lamented the changes.

Why'd they have to meet the way they did? Why was his father with Anya?

If J.T. divorced her, maybe then, in time...

Mack didn't dare to even hope. Thinking that Natasha might not be taboo someday only weakened his resolve.

"Do you think you'll ever leave Whiskey Creek?" Grady asked.

Mack was watching Natasha dance. Usually, he liked

the way she moved to the music, but tonight he could see that she'd hooked up with a male partner who was slipping his hands down over her butt.

"Mack?"

He returned his attention to his brother. "What?"

"You're quiet tonight. You okay?"

"Fine, why?"

"Because I have to repeat everything I say to you."

"Sorry. What was that? Something about Whiskey Creek?"

"Do you think you'll ever leave this town?"

He had to fight the urge to look back at Natasha. "No. Why would I?"

"Don't you ever wonder if there's something else out there for you?"

"Can't say I do. This is where Dylan's at, where you and Aaron and Rod are. Where my work is. Whiskey Creek is where I belong. Why? Do *you* plan to move?"

"Not necessarily. Sometimes I wonder what we might be missing, that's all. If Mom and Dad sort of…locked us into a life we might not have chosen. Maybe we would've gone to college, become something, moved to a big city, maybe the east coast. Who knows?"

"Natasha has a shot at all that." Which was part of the reason Mack was leaving her alone. He wouldn't steal those possibilities from her before she even had the chance to choose.

"So you're satisfied."

"Yeah. Our lives could be a lot worse." These days their lives were pretty darn *good*, but Mack wasn't in the mood to discuss it. He could hardly stay in his chair. The guy who'd been dancing with Natasha had her pressed up against the wall and was kissing her…

Curling his hands into fists, Mack willed himself to stay put. "You okay with driving home tonight?" he asked Grady.

Grady looked a little startled. "You said *you'd* drive."

He felt his heart sink. "You're counting on that?"

"Hell, yeah. It's your turn," he replied and grinned as Sally Abernathy, who'd been flirting with him for the past few weeks, came over to ask him to dance.

"Okay, got it," Mack said so Grady could feel free to have a good time, but as his brother and Sally walked onto the dance floor, all he could think was *God, I can't even dull the pain.*

Once again forcing his gaze away from Natasha, who was now making out with that bozo—someone with a receding hairline and a paunch for a belly—Mack clenched his jaw and began to peel the label from his beer bottle, anything to keep his hands busy so he wouldn't go over there, yank that guy off her and smash him in the face. So what if the dude looked thirty-five or older? That was her choice. She was nineteen, he told himself. But he was counting the minutes, hoping Grady would come back and keep him from losing his cool.

Grady didn't get the chance. Before the song could end, the woman he'd brought home from the bar last time—Bella—cut through the crowd with a gaggle of her girlfriends in tow.

"And the night gets worse," he said under his breath. He would've been happy to leave, except he couldn't. Not only had he agreed to be Grady's designated driver, he was worried about Natasha. He was afraid this reckless abandon she'd adopted would get her involved with someone she didn't really want. Who knew what this guy might do to take advantage of her condition and her determination to show one Mack Amos that she was now old enough to act as she pleased?

"Well, look who it is."

When Bella spoke to him, Mack managed a polite smile and tipped his beer toward her. "Evening."

Nose in the air, she said, "I didn't expect to see *you* here."

He found that comment rather strange. *He* was the one who lived in Whiskey Creek, not her. And she'd seen him here last time. This was where they'd met. But he let it go so he wouldn't seem rude by pointing out that she was the one out of place.

"Nothing better to do, huh?" she said when that didn't get a response.

"Not tonight," he replied, but he was beginning to think *anything* would be better than enduring this kind of torture. Natasha had her hands in the man's hair as if she was enjoying herself.

He longed to be that man, to feel her against him, to taste her lips…

"Mind if we sit down?" Bella asked.

She'd been so angry when she left his house this past week. Why would she want to hang out with him now?

He had no clue. Neither did he care to find out. "Not at all," he said as he gave his seat to one of her friends.

He noted the surprise on her face. She hadn't expected him to leave, but he couldn't sit there any longer. For one thing, he had to move around, work off some of the excess energy that was pouring through him. For another, Natasha and her partner had disappeared. He worried that the jackass who'd been making out with her had dragged her into the hallway that led to the bathrooms or outside, where he could get serious.

24

Natasha couldn't feel anything. She hated being so fuzzy and disoriented. It reminded her of her mother, which disgusted her. She'd sworn she'd never be like Anya.

But at least her heart was no longer aching. She'd seen Mack and been able to walk away from him without feeling as though it was tearing her guts out. And if she kept her eyes closed, she could almost pretend he was the man who was kissing and touching her so hungrily.

"God, you're beautiful," the guy said. "I feel like the luckiest man on earth."

"Don't talk," she told him. His voice ruined the illusion. His smell did, too. Blocking that out was hard enough. "And can you kiss me with a little more…force?" she asked.

"I'll show you force," he muttered and kissed her so hard he almost bruised her mouth. Maybe she should've said with more "authority," the way she imagined Mack would kiss. Mack did everything with confidence and precision, wasn't sloppy like this guy. Still, there was something exhilarating about no longer caring, about no longer waiting and hoping. Casting caution aside made her feel powerful. She wasn't going to let her desire for Mack ruin her life. *He* didn't want her, wouldn't touch her—but *this* guy seemed more than willing. Why not allow him to act as a stand-in? It wasn't as if she'd ever have to see him again. He'd told her he was from Angel's Camp.

"Let me take you home," he whispered, "where I can treat you right."

They were in an alcove where they couldn't easily be observed, but she knew why he was asking for more privacy. He hoped to have sex with her, and why should she refuse? Maybe it was time she lost her virginity, learned what all the hype was about. Most of the girls at school had been sleeping with guys for several years. Natasha was beginning to feel odd for saving herself, for wanting Mack to be her first. She was different enough already.

So maybe she'd dispense with all the waiting and wondering and quit hoping her first time would mean something. When she was younger, she'd been molested by some of her mother's boyfriends. Once, Anya had even offered her up for sex in exchange for money. Her mother refused to acknowledge that now, but Natasha would never forget it.

Thankfully, the guy had walked out instead of accepting Anya's offer. But that experience and others like it had given Natasha an education; she wasn't *totally* in the dark. She'd seen her mother having sex with any number of men, understood exactly how it worked. She just didn't know how it *felt*. Despite the fact that she hadn't enjoyed the groping she'd endured when she was young, she could tell sex *could* be good, with the right person.

That was the reason she'd decided to wait. Only now she felt foolish for hanging on to what seemed like a childish dream—the dream that she'd get the man she'd always wanted. Life never worked out that way. She, of all people, should know that.

"Come on. I'll make it good for you," the guy promised, his mouth hot and wet on her neck. "Get you off as many times as you want—do whatever you ask."

He had his hands on her breasts and was kissing the skin that showed above her glittery tank. She kept telling herself those were *Mack's* hands, that he was finally touching her like she'd imagined he would since the day she'd met him. But her ability to fantasize wasn't quite keen enough. Despite all the alcohol in her bloodstream, which had enabled her to take it *this* far, she felt a mild revulsion, didn't think she could go through with it.

"Ready to leave?" he asked when she didn't respond.

"No." This wasn't working, wasn't remotely satisfying. He wasn't *anything* like Mack.

She tried to pull away, to head back toward the dancers and the acquaintance she'd come with, who was sitting with a group of cowboys along the opposite wall. But this guy—Benny he'd said his name was—wouldn't give up.

"Hey, wait." He grabbed her wrist so she couldn't go. "We were just starting to have a good time, weren't we? Come on, you've got my heart pumping like a bass drum, and I've got a major woody." He held her hand to his crotch to show her. "I have to have you."

She squinted to bring him into clearer focus. "I don't even know you."

He kept her hand in place. "So you weren't serious? You were just getting me worked up? *Teasing* me?"

The anger in his voice surprised her. "I *wanted* to feel something," she explained. "But I…don't."

What she'd said didn't seem to make any difference. He ducked his head to kiss her again, as if she hadn't told him no. "Look, see how good we are together? Let's make love, sweet baby—"

"Stop it!" She wasn't enjoying herself at all anymore. She tried to remove her hand from the bulge in his pants, but he wouldn't let her. "I don't want to do this," she said. "It's only going to make me feel worse."

"That's where you're wrong," he whispered. "It'll make you feel better. It'll make you feel like a sex goddess."

She almost gagged when he stuck his tongue down her throat. She would've called for help if she could, but he had her pinned up against the wall so tightly she could scarcely breathe. Then the room began to spin. Was she going to pass out? She could feel his hands slide up her shirt, his mouth move to cover her left breast…

At that point it occurred to her that she *could* breathe, could scream, but she felt so foolish for getting herself into this mess, she didn't feel she deserved any help. And she certainly didn't want to embarrass Mack or Grady— or get them into any more trouble, like what'd happened to Rod when he came to her rescue the last time.

She'd been hoping to hurt Mack, she realized. She was lashing out at him because he'd rejected her. Which just showed her immaturity. She was a stupid fool who'd fallen in love with the wrong man, and this was where it had led—to some stranger groping her in a bar.

Maybe she wasn't any better than her mother, after all. Maybe it was true what some people said, "The apple doesn't fall far from the tree." What did one fuck matter, anyway? As far as that went, what did *she* matter— to anyone?

She let her head fall back and gazed up at the ceiling. She didn't have the strength to fight. She felt sick, disgusted, broken. The list went on. She was ticking each nasty emotion off to herself. Doing that distracted her from what had turned into a nightmare. But the next thing she knew, Benny went flying against the opposite wall and Mack stood between them, looking angrier than she'd ever seen him.

"She's drunk. She can't give consent," he growled.

"She wanted it," Benny cried, covering his head as if he expected Mack to drag him to his feet and punch him out.

Mack looked as though he might do just that, but he turned to her instead. "Are you okay?"

She clutched at him, to make the room stop spinning. "No. Will you take me home?"

Instantly forgetting Benny, he lifted her into his arms and carried her out.

"I'm sorry," she mumbled as he deposited her in his truck.

"Don't apologize."

"Where's Grady?" she asked when he climbed into the driver's side. He and Mack had come together, but she couldn't remember seeing Grady as Mack carried her out.

"I'm texting him right now, telling him to call me if he can't catch a ride home."

She didn't put on her seat belt. As soon as he dropped his phone in the empty ashtray where he kept it when he drove, she lay down with her head in his lap.

He paused before starting the truck to slowly run his fingers through her hair. "Don't worry. Everything's going to be okay."

"I'm going to miss you," she whispered.

"I'm going to miss you, too," he said.

Rod was beginning to think their plan wasn't going to work. He went to the Siddells' every night, and he waited and watched, but Sebastian never went anywhere interesting, nowhere Rod felt he could approach him. Sebastian filled up with gas and bought a pack of cigarettes. He took Sheila and her kids out to some dive for pizza. And he went to the liquor store to grab a six-pack when he had a few friends over. That was about it.

Rod would've been frustrated, except that he liked the Siddells so much. He liked returning to the motel every morning to climb into bed with India even more. Generally, she was up waiting for him, as if keeping that vigil somehow meant he'd return safe. They slept late, lounged by the pool, went out to eat, showered together, watched movies and made love more often than he'd ever made love with anyone else. Being together in a motel for so long felt as if they were on a honeymoon, except for when he had to head over to the Siddells' at night.

There were moments Rod wished nothing would change. He cared about India that much. But there were also moments when he felt a great deal of pressure to fix the problem so he could go home. Guilt, for taking so many days off in a row and expecting his brothers to cover for him, bothered him, but he couldn't go back to Whiskey Creek until this situation was resolved. Sebastian kept calling her and leaving messages, pleading with her to put the past behind them—never mind that he was still with his wife. India couldn't even tell herself that he'd go on about his business and let her go on about hers.

"I have to see this through," he told Dylan a week later, on Sunday afternoon, when he was sitting out by the pool. India wasn't with him. She'd gone to the room to plug in her phone, since her battery was dead, and to get them another cold drink from the vending machine.

"Of course. We wouldn't want you to do anything else," his brother said.

Rod got up and moved his lawn chair so he wasn't directly in the sun anymore. "But it's been ten days, and I haven't gotten anywhere."

"You have a plan. That's something. A lot hangs in the balance. You can't simply waltz into Sebastian's life and expect him to tell you where he put the gun."

"No, it could take *years* to build up that much trust. That's why I'm hoping that boy I told you about, Van, will tell me instead."

"I'm hoping the same thing. We're looking forward to getting you back. But we're willing to sacrifice. Who else is going to help India if we don't?"

Rod remembered a family meeting when he'd heard the same sentiment expressed about Natasha—and look at her now, getting good grades, graduating with honors, heading off to college. They'd made a difference in her life. If only they could help India, too. Supporting her in this way was definitely a joint effort, since his brothers were carrying his workload at home. "I'd like to see Natasha one last time before she goes."

"She leaves tomorrow afternoon. You could come home and drive her to the airport, then return to the motel. She's flying out of Oakland, and you're free during the days, right?"

"I'll do that. How's Mack handling her leaving?"

"What do you mean?" Dylan asked. "He's handling it just like the rest of us."

Rod realized that Dylan really *didn't* know what was going on with Mack and Natasha. "They're closer in age," he said, to cover for the question.

"He had a woman over not too long ago," Dylan said.

"How'd *you* find that out?" Rod asked.

"Dad said something when the same woman stopped by the shop yesterday to bring Mack lunch."

Maybe Dylan *did* know about Mack and Natasha, but he didn't want to get into it any more than Rod did. In any case, Rod wasn't going to ask him directly. "There're plenty of women out there to keep him busy."

"Exactly. Speaking of women, how are things between you and India?"

Rod wasn't sure how to answer that question. He was feeling all kinds of things he'd never felt before, but she was still wearing her wedding ring, still keeping him separate from her daughter. "I like her."

"How much?" Dylan said.

"A lot."

"You two getting serious?"

Rod couldn't tell how seriously *she* was taking the relationship—and he was hesitant to ask, in case she brought up Charlie or her daughter or her in-laws and ruined what they had right now. "She just lost her husband eleven months ago."

There was a slight pause. "You're not getting in over your head, are you?"

"Yeah," he admitted. "I think I am."

Silence.

"No advice?" Rod said with a laugh.

"I knew when it finally happened, you'd fall hard."

Dylan had fallen hard, too—only, it had worked out for him. "Have you heard from Chief Bennett?"

"Yeah. Spoke to him on Friday."

"And you didn't mention it?"

"Why ruin your vacation?"

"What's going on?"

"Liam's pressing charges. Claims you used a baseball bat."

Rod rested his elbows on his knees as he stared at the concrete. "Shit."

"Don't worry," he said. "I've already hired an attorney."

"*You* hired an attorney? This is on me, Dyl."

"No, it's not. Who knows how much it'll cost? The expenses could wipe you out. And it started because you were protecting Natasha. Together, we'll have enough to fight him."

"India said she heard Sharon tell him we have money. He's looking for us to pay his medical bills."

"He can go to hell. He started the fight. He could've killed you when he ran you off the road. You're in a freakin' cast. Far as I'm concerned, he should pay *your* medical bills. And that's what the attorney thinks, too. So we're countersuing. Maybe when Liam realizes he could wind up paying a bunch of attorneys' fees as well as his medical expenses, and possibly even yours, he'll think twice about taking the gamble."

"Are you positive we shouldn't just settle with him, pay up? As much as that galls me, I'm betting it'll turn out to be cheaper than hiring an attorney."

"I don't care. We're standing on principle here. We won't let him get away with lying about you."

Rod would feel equally determined, except he didn't want his brothers to be hurt, financially or any other way. He'd do whatever he had to in order to protect them. "Then I'm paying for the whole thing."

"Don't get your checkbook out quite yet, little brother. We'll see how this goes. With any luck, *he'll* be paying *us*."

At the clang of the gate surrounding the pool, Rod

glanced up. India was back with their drinks. "Everything okay?" she asked, looking concerned.

His irritation had to be showing on his face. He made an effort to clear it. "Of course. Everything's fine." She didn't seem convinced, so he added, "It's nothing money won't fix," and told Dylan he'd talk to him later.

"Is Dylan upset that you're still gone?" she asked when he'd disconnected. "Do you need to go back?"

"No, he's supportive. Quit worrying. I'm not going anywhere."

She sat on the chaise beside his. "I don't want to cause you any problems."

He almost asked if he'd ever be able to compete with her saintly husband. He understood how different he was from the kind of man Charlie had been. He wasn't going to change the world. Wasn't going to save any lives. Wasn't going to take her to any swanky parties. He could only hope love would be enough, but he wouldn't ask. He refused to put her under any more pressure, not with what she was already going through.

"You're getting burned." She pressed a finger into his arm.

"That's why I moved out of the sun."

"When we get back to Whiskey Creek, we're going to look as if we've been sailing in the Caribbean."

"*You're* not," he teased. "You're as pale as ever."

"Because I don't tan," she complained. "I only burn, which is why I always have to wear sunblock or cover up."

He held his arm next to hers and chuckled at the difference, but he didn't laugh for long. He sobered as those pretty blue eyes of hers caught his attention. She was looking at him so intently. Then she leaned in and gave him one of those honey-sweet kisses he loved so much.

Surely that meant something. Or would everything change when they went back to their normal lives?

25

That night Rod caught his first break when he followed Sebastian and his brother to the pool hall. Eddie rode in the passenger seat; Rod had seen him come and go over the past few days, and the Siddells had confirmed his identity. For this trip, Sheila and the kids were left behind.

When Rod walked into Solids and Stripes, he was glad he'd been there before—and that the man he'd played pool with was back, too. Dave remembered Rod and invited him to play, giving Rod a comfortable vantage point from which to observe Sebastian and wait for the right opportunity to initiate a conversation.

That opportunity didn't come for quite some time. He was beginning to think it never would, but shortly before midnight, Eddie went to the bathroom, leaving Sebastian to rack the balls after their last game.

Rod sauntered over with a beer in one hand and a cue stick in the other. "Looking for some fresh competition?"

Supremely conscious of the fact that he'd spoken to Sebastian once before, when Sebastian had called India and she dropped the phone, Rod held his breath. He was poised to react quickly, but Sebastian didn't seem to recognize his voice. He merely waved toward the restrooms. "I got my brother here."

"So?" Rod said. "He can play the winner."

Sebastian was only an inch or two shorter, had longish black hair and swarthy skin with arms almost entirely covered in tattoos. He also had evidence of acne from an earlier period in his life. But he was handsome in a rough sort of way. Rod could see why India might've been attracted to him. The women at the pool hall seemed to like him, too. Rod had seen him kiss one and feel up another without any apparent concern for the fact that he was married.

"Who are you?" Sebastian asked.

Rod had already decided he'd make the answer to that question easy and use his own first name. He figured he'd be a lot less likely to screw up that way. "Rod Cunningham. You?"

"Sebastian Young." He removed the rack, leaving the billiard balls in a perfect triangle. "I don't think I've seen you around here before."

"I'm new in town, from San Jose, but I've been in to play pool once or twice."

"Oh, yeah? What brings you to Hayward in the first place?"

"My job."

"What'd you do?"

"I'm an auto body technician. My cousin owns a shop not far from here." Rod tilted his beer toward him. "What about you?"

"Currently unemployed."

"Okay. Now I know you and you know me." He jerked his head toward the pool table. "We gonna play or what?"

Sebastian grinned. "We gonna put any money on it?"

"Why not?" Rod had no idea how good Sebastian was. He'd been careful not to watch him too closely. But the guy's skill level didn't really matter. Rod didn't care if this cost him $100. He actually felt it might be smarter to lose, even if he had to do it on purpose. No doubt Sebastian would like him better—and that was the real goal.

Fortunately, Sebastian turned out to be a talented player, so it wasn't difficult to make the loss look real. Rod wasn't entirely sure he could beat him even if he was giving it his best, so the game looked and felt authentic.

Eddie had come out of the bathroom shortly after they started and stood by to watch. He smiled when his brother sank the eight ball and Rod slapped his money on the table. But Rod wasn't willing to leave it at that. He didn't have days and weeks to develop a relationship. He had to make this opportunity count, had to get close to Sebastian fast. As soon as Sebastian moved to pick up the money, Rod snatched it away. "Double or nothing?"

Sebastian exchanged a look with his brother, then nodded. "Why not? I don't got to be anywhere else."

Rod gave the second game his full effort and managed to win. He didn't want to fork over $200 and have Sebastian be finished with him. He needed to get Sebastian to ask for a third game—a tiebreaker, so they'd have more time to interact—and it worked. After the twenty minutes it took to lose that last game, Sebastian was clapping him on the back and promising to buy him a shot.

They moved to the bar, where they told stories and drank. Rod couldn't believe Sebastian didn't find his interest a little strange. But most people were egocentric enough not to question the attention they received, and *his* ego was bigger than most. Before long, Rod didn't have to say much. Sebastian did all the talking—to the point that Eddie lost interest and went to throw a few darts.

"What are you doing after this?" Rod asked.

Sebastian rocked back. "Hell if I know. Why? You lookin' for a party?"

Rod grinned. "I wouldn't be opposed to finding one."

"You got any money left?"

"A few bucks."

Sebastian leaned close and lowered his voice. "My brother might be able to score you a little crystal."

Rod couldn't say that he'd *never* taken drugs. He'd dabbled here and there when he was younger, mostly with prescription drugs passed around by kids at school, but not after Dylan caught him smoking a joint when he was eighteen. He hadn't touched anything other than alcohol since, but he knew that acting interested in getting high would be the quickest way to score an invitation to Sebastian's house. "Then what the hell are we waiting for?"

Sebastian let out a whoop. "I like you, man," he said. Then he called his brother over and whispered in his ear.

Eddie, however, wasn't quite as willing to embrace the idea. "We don't even know this dude," he said, and he didn't bother to whisper. Rod suspected Eddie *wanted* to be overheard, wanted to watch his reaction. "He could be a cop."

Sebastian already had a buzz going. Rod could tell he was feeling pretty damn good. "Rod's not a cop," he said. "I can smell a cop from a mile away."

"I'm *not* a cop," Rod confirmed.

"Thing is…we've never seen you before, so how would we know that?"

"Just because you haven't seen me doesn't mean I

haven't been in. Ask Dave over there. I played pool with him the other night."

Dave happened to catch Rod pointing. He looked a little perplexed, then smiled and nodded when Rod waved.

"See?" Sebastian said. "He knows Dave."

"Go on over and ask," Rod insisted.

Eddie acted as if he might do that, but then his face cleared and he shrugged. "I guess a recommendation from Dave is good enough for me. I gotta make money somehow. Let's get the hell out of here."

Nights seemed to drag on forever. India missed her potter's wheel, wished for a better way to distract herself from the anxiety she felt than watching TV. But without Rod, there wasn't a lot to do in a motel room. He always said she should sleep, that she didn't have to wait up, but she was too worried to go to bed without him. She wanted to be alert and near her phone in case he tried to call or text for help.

She scrolled through her pictures, looking at the ones she'd taken over the past ten days. Rod wasn't much for posing. But she'd gotten a few really good shots of him, in which she'd captured his sexy smile or the personality that showed in his eyes. He was funny and gorgeous and strong—and sweet and tender, too. So what if he and Charlie were different? Did they have to be the same? Was she doing her husband a disservice by picking someone completely opposite to him?

"What am I doing?" she asked aloud. She wished she could talk to Charlie, discuss the terrible conflict inside her and the guilt that was holding her back where Rod was concerned. She also wished she could discuss the fear that welled up every now and then. She didn't want to be hurt again. She'd been through too much, and it was all too recent. Charlie had always been a stabilizing influence. She could trust his judgment. But Charlie was gone.

She flipped through more pictures. Was it really only two years ago that they'd been in Scotland, touring the castles? She'd suggested they go to Mexico, had wanted to lie on a warm beach. But Charlie had been too worried about the danger, what with the drug cartels and the police corruption. He'd said he wouldn't risk his family.

Who knew that he wouldn't live much longer than another year in spite of playing it so safe?

It was all because of Sebastian. And here she was, making Sebastian the center of her life, to the point that she was currently living out of a motel. Was she foolish to be doing this? Would she only get Rod hurt, too?

She'd tried to talk him into going home and leaving the sleuthing to her. He wouldn't hear of it. She supposed that was one thing he and Charlie had in common. They were both driven, both stubborn. She'd begun to trust Rod, to depend on him. But she was also *finally* starting to get along with her in-laws again. What would they say if they learned she was seeing another man? Did she dare tell them? How long could she hide it?

She was just trying to think of a way she might be able to break the news when she received a text from Rod.

Met up with Sebastian at the pool hall. Following him to his place.

Her heart lurched into her throat, and she climbed off the bed. It was happening. Tonight. What they'd been trying to achieve.

Was it a mistake?

Are you sure you should be doing this?

Two hours passed.
He never answered.

Rod hadn't intended to get high. He hadn't had any choice. He soon found himself sitting in the living room with Eddie, Sheila and Sebastian, and knew instantly that he'd give himself away if he offered a last-second excuse. He could say he'd just received a text, that a problem had come up at home and he had to leave, but if he did that, if he bailed out, he'd probably never get another invitation.

Instead of leaving, he did what he could to distract the others by acting as if he thought someone was coming to the door, so he could get rid of most of his rock by fishing it out of the bowl and crushing it into the carpet. But he had to smoke some, and he had to admit he'd never experienced such a rush. Pot just wasn't the same. A lot of years had passed since he'd experienced even *that*.

The euphoria streaking through him sent his nervous system into high gear, made his heart race and his senses grow keen and receptive. It would've been easy to succumb to the pleasure, but he knew he had to keep his wits about him, remember why he was here. Sebastian had been high on crystal meth when he killed Charlie. Rod would be a fool to assume he'd be any less dangerous just because he seemed to be enjoying himself. Drugs affected people in different ways at different times.

Truth was, Sebastian could be *more* dangerous. And he had his wife and brother with him, who'd most likely do anything they could to cover up any crime he committed. If the next few hours went badly, they'd probably help bury Rod's body.

Rod made a joke Dylan had repeated to him earlier about two computer nerds, and they all started to laugh. He laughed, too. The laughter came easy, while most of the other pretense had not. So he told a few more jokes.

"I like you, man," Sebastian said. "You're an okay dude."

Rod got up to pace around. He felt bulletproof, as if he could conquer the world, and he supposed that was a good thing. Sebastian liked him now, but if Sebastian turned on him, he might need the added acuity and strength.

"Where you going?" Eddie asked.

Rod gestured at the hallway. "There a bathroom down here?"

"Yeah, on your right."

He didn't really have to go; he just needed something to do, some outlet for all his energy. He also needed to figure out some way to get to Sheila's nephew, to talk to him. But how? He didn't want to be caught in the boy's room, didn't want to be mistaken for a pedophile. And what would he say to Van? "Hey, wake up. It's me again. Any chance you know where Sebastian hid his gun?"

The boy might be young, but he wasn't stupid.

Deciding he'd be better off biding his time, Rod returned to the living room, where Sebastian and the others were continuing to smoke. Since he probably wouldn't get to talk to Van tonight, he was hoping he'd have the opportunity to talk to Sheila. Depending on how disgruntled, trusting or just plain stupid she was, she might be a good source of information. But with every single nerve in his body firing at once, he couldn't sit still. The only thing that kept him from flying too high was the TV. The colors seemed unnaturally bright, which he found sort of fascinating. That gave him something to focus on to help him ride out the drug.

Unfortunately, coming down took much longer than he'd anticipated. The last time Rod remembered glancing at the clock, it was nearly five, and Sebastian and the others were *still* partying. They were like rats, pressing a lever that gave them a reward. They wouldn't abandon the *lever* until there was nothing left.

At least they were no longer paying much attention to *him*. That relieved some of the pressure, even though he couldn't really do anything while they were all there together.

He tried isolating Sheila by asking if she had something he could eat. He wanted to draw her into the kitchen, where they could talk without being overheard. But she waved him off, told him to help himself to anything he could find. She was as much of a tweaker as Sebastian was, afraid they'd smoke the rest of the crystal if she took a break.

Then, just when he was thinking he should probably leave, that India would be too worried if he stayed longer, he must've fallen asleep. Because when he woke up, he was lying on the couch alone with the sun blazing through a crack in the draperies.

A knock sounded, and he realized what had disturbed him. Someone was at the door.

Rod hesitated, wondering if one of the household's regular inhabitants would come from the back to answer. But no one did, so he got up—and found a worried Frank Siddell on the doorstep. As soon as Frank saw Rod, his expression changed—filled with relief. But he said nothing to give away the fact that they knew each other.

"Hey, I live across the street over there." He gestured

as if someone else could see them. "Just wanted to tell you that you have a broken sprinkler that's been shooting up like a geyser every morning."

"I don't live here," Rod told him, "but I'll tell the people who do."

"Great. Thanks. With what we have to pay for water, I thought you'd like to know," he said and walked away as if he was merely doing his neighborly duty.

Breathing a long sigh, Rod stood in the entry. He wanted to text India, but he knew Frank would reassure her, that Frank had come on her request. And he didn't want to be holding his phone if Sebastian walked out of the back bedroom to see who'd been at the door.

He shouldn't have worried. Sebastian didn't appear. Neither did Eddie or Sheila. The noise roused only the kids. Two little girls came out of a room—one dragging a blanket behind her and the other sucking her thumb.

Rod was surprised that they barely looked at him. They didn't approach him the way most kids would, didn't speak to him, either. They showed no curiosity or interest at all. They just found a channel showing a cartoon and sat down to watch.

Obviously, having a stranger in the house was nothing unusual. Rod was considering getting Van out of bed. But that didn't turn out to be necessary. Van appeared of his own volition a few seconds later. Although he seemed groggy—had the waffle-like imprint of a blanket on his cheek and his hair was mussed—he took one look at Rod and then Rod's cast and stopped short.

"Hey, are you the guy—"

Rod interrupted before he could finish. "Good morning. Sleep well?"

He nodded but was distracted when his cousins begged him for food.

Van went to the kitchen and got them each a bowl of cold cereal, which he put down in front of them. Then he offered Rod some.

Rod was impressed. He could tell there wasn't much cereal left. He was afraid these children weren't getting the nutrition they needed. Meth addicts often went without food for long periods, since the drug suppressed appetite. Rod wasn't about to take the little they *did* have. "No. I'm not hungry," he said. "You eat it. Then maybe we can go out and throw a baseball. Would you like to do that?"

His eyes widened. "You mean...*you and me?*"

"Sure. Why not? It'd beat sitting here watching these lame cartoons, wouldn't it?"

He grinned. "Heck, yeah!"

"You have a mitt?"

His face fell. "No. I don't ever get to play baseball."

"Then we can buy you a mitt. There's got to be a store around here somewhere."

"You're going to *buy* me a mitt?"

"If you'd like one."

He looked around as if he thought this must be a setup, and Rod felt terrible that, in a way, it was. "Sure. But I'm not very good, not like the other boys at school."

"All it takes is practice. Why don't you ask Sheila if you can go to the store with me?"

"I can't."

"Go to the store?"

"Ask. She won't be up until a lot later. And I'll get in big trouble if I bother her or Sebastian while they're sleeping."

"Then you'd better stay here while I go grab the mitt. So you don't get into any trouble."

"I can go with you," he said. "They won't care. Not if I don't wake them up."

Rod suspected that was the truth but still felt he should leave him behind. It wasn't right to take someone's kid without asking. But Sebastian or Eddie could be up when he got back, could insist on going out to throw with them or come sit on the porch to watch. That meant he might never have another chance to really talk to Van.

He'd risked this much; it was time to go all in.

"Okay," he said. "Let's get in the truck."

26

Eddie had to meet his supplier. That meant he had to drag his ass out of bed and get showered. "Yogi," as the man called himself, wasn't a thug. He worked downtown San Francisco, in the financial district. Selling crystal meth helped him maintain an enviable lifestyle, one that included owning a yacht and jetting off to Paris at will, and he took all sources of income seriously. He wasn't a user; he was far too much of a health fanatic for that. This dude had his life *in control*. He just didn't have any compunction about making money off those who weren't quite so disciplined.

"What's wrong with people these days?" he'd say. "It's such a lie that drug dealers are ruining lives. We're not forcing this shit on anyone. At what point can we expect people to take responsibility for their own actions? If they're stupid enough to destroy their bodies and brains by smoking stuff they know is harmful, that's their problem. It's not as if people haven't been warned. The dangers of drugs are plastered all over billboards from here to New York City! Sixth-graders have been taught to avoid this shit!"

His philosophy made it easier for Eddie to sleep at

night. But he hated Yogi. The guy was a coldhearted bastard who would never make any exceptions or concessions. When Eddie had shown up late for their last meeting, he'd been put on "probation," which meant he'd be fired if he was ever late again. *Late!* As if that was such a big deal!

Eddie was tempted to take the fat stack of cash he had to turn in and skip town. Losing ten grand might make Yogi think twice about treating his dealers like bottom-feeders. But the money wouldn't last forever, and Eddie was too afraid Yogi would catch up with him. As "civilized" as Yogi pretended to be, Eddie had no doubt he'd resort to very drastic punishment, maybe even murder. After having him killed, Yogi would probably say, "He knew the rules. He chose to break them." With Yogi, it was infraction, punishment, period.

But now that Sebastian was back home, and the cops were driving through the neighborhood all the time, perhaps watching the house, Eddie was afraid he'd be followed. Yogi had warned him that they might try to get him on a drug charge so they could make a deal—information on Sebastian in exchange for a lighter sentence—and that worried Eddie. He could wind up going to prison because he wouldn't rat on his brother. And if he went to prison, he'd be even more vulnerable than the average inmate. Yogi wouldn't tolerate him screwing up like that after he'd been warned; Yogi would be too worried he'd eventually rat him out.

Eddie needed to move, get away from his brother. But he hadn't expected Sebastian to ever be released. That he'd gotten off was a miracle.

Eddie felt better after a shower—until he found out the kids had eaten all the damn cereal. "What the hell?

You didn't save me *any*?" he said, glaring at the two little girls sitting in front of the TV.

Matilda and Peggy blinked up at him but turned back to their cartoon without answering. He hated it when they did that—looked through him as if he wasn't there. What happened to respect? They deserved a good spanking, which he'd be more than happy to deliver.

"I asked you a question. Did you hear me?"

Matilda, the older, flinched when he raised his hand and finally answered. "Van got it out for us. We didn't know we couldn't have it."

"Van's awake?" he said. "Where is that pain in the ass?"

"He went outside with some guy." Peggy still had her hands up, as if she might have to fend off a blow.

"*What* guy?"

"I don't know."

He walked over to the window, parted the drapes and saw a big blue truck parked at the curb. Rod Cunningham, the guy who'd partied with them last night, owned it. He hadn't gone home? Why the hell not? And what was he doing with Van?

A trickle of unease ran down Eddie's spine. Why had that guy taken an interest in Sheila's kids? Was he some kind of sexual pervert?

No way. They'd hung with him last night. He'd seemed cool. A guy like Rod could get just about any woman he wanted. Why would he be interested in kids? And he couldn't be working for the cops. He'd known Dave at the pool hall, hadn't he?

Eddie remembered that little wave, the one he hadn't bothered to check out, and could already feel Yogi's disapproval. He should've been more careful. So what if the dude smoked some crystal with them last night? An undercover cop would go that far, wouldn't he? Undercovers had to do *something* to be believable or they'd be too easy to spot.

"Shit." He went outside to see what was going on, but he didn't have to go far. Rod was teaching Van how to throw a ball in the vacant lot kitty-corner to them. Eddie could hear him yelling, "No, put your opposite foot forward. That's it. That'll give you more power. Now let me see what you've got."

Neither of them seemed to notice that he'd come out of the house, so Eddie walked over to Rod's truck, which blocked him from view, and took a peek inside. Except for a Starbucks cup, a sack and some packaging from the sporting goods store where he'd apparently bought the athletic equipment he and Van were using, it looked fairly clean. The doors were locked, but whoever had gotten out of the passenger door hadn't shut it tightly enough to latch.

Eddie opened it and poked around. Found some papers stuffed under the seat. They were work orders from some place called Amos Auto Body in Whiskey Creek, California. Did Rod work there? Because he'd said his cousin owned the auto body shop where he was working and it was nearby.

They had to come from his work, Eddie decided. They weren't for *his* truck; they were for all different makes and models. So maybe they were from a previous job. But then, why would he keep them?

"Hold on! You're using the wrong foot again," Rod yelled to Van.

Eddie opened the glove box. Inside, he found a pack of gum, an owner's manual, a tire pressure gauge, a box of condoms and the DMV paperwork for the truck. He expected to find Rod Cunningham as the registered owner, but the slip read Rodney *Amos*—like the Amos in the company name on those work orders—and had an address in Whiskey Creek.

What the hell? Why didn't the names match? And where was Whiskey Creek?

He glanced at his watch. He had to get going.

After folding up the registration and one of those work orders, he shoved them in his pocket. Then he put everything back in Rod's glove box and hurried inside the house to brush his teeth and get his keys.

Before he left, he woke Sebastian. "Something's going on with that guy you brought home last night," he said.

Scratching his head, Sebastian squinted up at him. "What're you talking about?" he mumbled, still half-asleep.

Sheila stirred in the bed beside him but didn't wake completely. With a groan, she rolled over as if she didn't appreciate the noise. Eddie didn't care if he disturbed her. It was about time she got her ass out of bed so she could take care of her kids. Maybe Van wouldn't be out playing ball with a total stranger if she was any kind of mother.

"That guy? The guy who said his name was Rod Cunningham?" Eddie said.

Sebastian yawned. "Yeah? What about him?"

"I don't think Cunningham's his real name. It's Rod Amos."

As those words registered, Sebastian sat up—and the sleepiness fell away. "What makes you say *that*?"

Eddie pulled Rod's registration and that work order out of his pocket and threw them both on the bed. "This stuff."

"What is it?"

"The registration on his truck and some auto body work order."

"You checked his registration?"

"I went through his glove box." Eddie had no more time to explain. "I gotta go. I'll come back as soon as I can. Meanwhile, you better hope he isn't a cop."

Sebastian peered at the documents. "He's not a cop. Cops don't work out of their own jurisdiction. And Whiskey Creek has nothing to do with Charlie Sommers."

"Then maybe he's not a cop. Maybe he's another private investigator. Charlie Sommers's parents have the money to hire an army of them, and they've hired a few over the past year. I told you that when you were in jail we had guys sniffing around here all the time, trying to talk us into giving up something that would get the charges against you to stick."

The blood drained from Sebastian's face. "Oh, shit…"

"Exactly. You need to get your ass out of bed and deal with this *now*," Eddie said. "Check him out real good, because if I get arrested, I'm going to tell the cops everything I know. No way I'm going to prison 'cause you let the wrong guy get too close."

"He came right into our house. Smoked some crystal with us, man. That's ballsy," Sebastian marveled, his voice filled with shock.

"Don't let him become a problem."

"Where is he now?"

"Outside, playing ball with Van."

"He's *what*?"

"You heard me," Eddie said and rushed out.

Frustrating though it was, Rod hadn't been able to get any information out of Van.

The boy knew *something*. He was holding back; Rod could feel it. But no matter how often Rod brought up the night Charlie was murdered, Van wouldn't talk about it. Rod guessed he'd been upset when he'd said what he did before, and now that he was calm, he was too afraid to talk about the adults in his life.

Getting him to open up would take some time. He'd have to build the boy's confidence and trust—maybe more than he'd initially believed. He still considered it worth the effort. The anger in this child, the outrage, would eventually cause the truth to come out. But that was more likely to happen when Van was a teenager or an adult and he felt less threatened.

Rod didn't have nearly that long, couldn't keep chasing this on the off chance he was right.

"What're you doing?" Van's face creased with worry when Rod paused to text India. Rod knew Frank would've told her he was okay, but he didn't want her going crazy in that motel room, wondering why he hadn't come home since then.

"Telling someone I care about where I am."

"Oh. You don't have to go home yet, do you?"

The poor kid was so starved for positive attention and so grateful for what Rod was teaching him that Rod didn't have the heart to disappoint him. "Not quite yet."

"Good." He smiled, which wasn't something he did as often as most young boys. But after Rod had thrown him a few more balls, half of which Van missed, Van's smile disappeared. He was becoming frustrated with his own lack of ability. "How long will it take me to get good at this?" he asked.

"It doesn't happen overnight, Van," Rod said. "You have to be patient."

"Will it take a week?"

Rod chuckled as he threw another ball, and this time Van managed to get it in his mitt. "Probably several weeks. But you could improve quickly."

He groaned when he missed another one. *"How?"*

"Practice. The more you practice, the better you'll be."

He hesitated before throwing the ball back. "Are you going to take my glove when you go?"

"No, of course not. That belongs to you. You'll have to work it in, make it more supple. You should write your name on it."

"But who'll throw to me?" Sebastian wasn't likely to take an interest in his wife's nephew.

"Why can't your uncle?" Rod knew that the only person Sebastian cared about was Sebastian. But this gave Rod another chance to bring India's ex-boyfriend into the conversation.

Van mumbled something Rod couldn't hear.

"What was that?" he asked.

"I said, 'He won't.'"

"What about Eddie?"

He shook his head as if Eddie wasn't a possibility, either.

"Your aunt?"

A roll of Van's eyes told Rod he should know better than to suggest any of them.

"There's gotta be boys at school who like to play ball," Rod said.

"Yeah," he agreed. "But they won't play with *me*. I'm no good. I'm always the last one who gets picked at recess or PE."

Fortunately, Rod had never had to go through that. He'd always excelled at sports. He'd had older brothers who were also athletic and had taught him and played with him. In any event, if anyone ever *had* said he couldn't play, he probably would've given that kid a bloody lip. Like Van, he'd been angry—so angry that he'd acted out a lot. Only, he hadn't been quite so beaten down. He had Dylan to thank for that. This boy had no one.

"I'll throw with you whenever I'm around," Rod said.

Van perked up. "You're coming back?"

The last thing Rod wanted to do was hurt this boy in any way, so he felt it was important not to set his expectations too high. "Probably. For the next little while. But I have to move in a couple of weeks, so I won't be around forever."

His shoulders drooped. "Oh."

"By then you'll be playing as well as the other boys, and you won't need me," Rod said, hoping to encourage him.

Van didn't respond. He needed somebody for a lot more than throwing and catching.

It was a hot day, so after another fifteen or twenty minutes, Rod called him over to the sidewalk, where he'd left the sports drinks he'd purchased when they went to the store.

"This is good!" Van said as he gulped half the bottle.

Rod stifled a smile. Van was feeling pretty pleased with the attention he was receiving. "Tell me something," he said.

The boy squinted up at him. "What?"

Rod lowered his voice. "Would you like it if Sebastian was gone?"

His eyes cut to the house as if he was checking to see whether they were being observed.

"You can tell me," Rod coaxed. "You can tell me anything, and Sebastian will never know that you said it."

He kicked at a tuft of grass. Then he nodded.

"Is that a yes?" Rod asked. "You'd rather he was gone?"

Another reluctant nod.

"You understand how that could happen, don't you?"

Van licked the orange drink from his lips. "How?"

"The police want to put him behind bars. They'd like to solve that murder he committed. They just don't have enough evidence to prove Sebastian was the one who shot Charlie Sommers. But you and I know he did it, don't we?"

"*You* know it?" he asked but wouldn't look up.

"I do," Rod confirmed.

He kept his head bowed. "How?"

"I have my ways. So if you can tell me anything that might help—if you've ever seen him with a gun, or you know where he might've put the gun he used, or you remember that he *wasn't* home that night your aunt told you to say he was—you should tell me."

He chewed his bottom lip.

"What is it?" Rod asked.

"Will my aunt go to prison, too?"

Ah, *there* was the problem. Even if he managed to get rid of Sebastian, his life wouldn't improve—at least not by much. "I'm afraid not. She's lying for him, but I doubt they'll put her in prison for it. I know that's discouraging, but we have to think about the lady who lost her husband that night, and how that would help her and her little girl. They're innocent victims. We want to keep them safe, don't we?"

Finally, he looked up. "Are you a policeman?"

Rod had revealed the level of his interest, but he didn't regret it. He didn't see any other way—not if he was going to learn what Van knew before he had to return to Whiskey Creek. Having patience was difficult when one or two sentences from this boy could fix everything that was wrong in India's life. "No. Just someone who cares."

He opened his mouth, closed it and opened it again. "I've never seen him with a gun."

Rod managed a tolerant smile. It wasn't fair to put this boy under too much pressure. "Okay. You can tell me whenever you're ready."

"Are you going to leave?" he asked. "Are you mad at me?"

"Not at all. Get over there. Let's practice while we can. You're getting better already."

Van started to walk back. Then he turned around. "Rod?"

"Yes?"

"I didn't see a gun, but—" his voice dropped "—I heard him tell Eddie something about shoving one under the neighbor's house."

Rod felt his jaw drop. "Which house? Do you know?"

He shook his head.

"That's okay," Rod said. "Don't worry. I'll find it somehow—and no one will ever know you're the one who told me, okay?"

"Okay." He shaded his eyes against the sun. "Can we play for another hour?"

Rod figured he owed the boy that much. To Van's giggling delight, he tossed him over his shoulder and carried him back to his spot. "Why not?"

27

Sebastian had used a search engine to learn everything he could about Rod Amos. There wasn't a lot that came up. Only a few links related to the Rod they'd met and not someone else by the same name. His family owned an auto body shop in Whiskey Creek, a Gold Country town about two hours away. From what Sebastian could tell, it was similar to the towns that were a little larger and more familiar, like Grass Valley, Placerville and Jackson. Whiskey Creek itself wasn't much more than a dot on the map.

So why had this man come to the Bay?

"What're you doing?" Sheila asked after a long, drawn-out yawn.

"Checking on something," he replied.

"Why don't you come back to bed? I'll make it worth your while."

He heard the suggestiveness in her voice, but he wasn't interested. He was no longer attracted to Sheila. She'd really let herself go, especially when he compared her to India, who'd always been so beautiful. But he wasn't always as indifferent as he was today. Usually, he felt a piece of ass was a piece of ass, and at least this piece of ass came with a place to stay. He needed somewhere to hang out until he could get a job and decide what he was going to do with his life.

"Would that be a no?" she said, sounding pouty.

"Quit being a stupid bitch," he snapped and returned to the website for Amos Auto Body. The business looked legit. Nothing he saw led him to believe that Rod Amos was anything more than an auto body technician. He wasn't a private investigator. Eddie had to be wrong about that, and Sebastian couldn't wait to tell him.

But Sebastian was still concerned. He found nothing that explained why Rod had lied about his last name and where he worked…

Maybe those lies had nothing to do with Charlie's murder. Maybe Rod was moving from one family-owned auto body shop to another. And maybe he didn't get along with his father, so he was using his mother's maiden name. People did shit like that all the time.

The buzzing of his phone interrupted his concentration. As soon as he saw his brother's number on the screen, he picked up. "You prick!" he barked. "You scared the hell out of me for nothing."

"I like the sound of this already," Eddie responded. "Rod's okay, then? We don't have anything to worry about?"

"Not that I can see. Whiskey Creek is just some Podunk town in the Sierra Nevada Foothills. And I've searched the internet. I can't find a single private investigator by the name of Rod Amos *or* Rod Cunningham."

"Then what does he want with *us*?"

"I guess he wanted to party, right? He smoked some crystal, didn't he?"

"I didn't see him smoke much. But whatever. Does he know you're checking him out?"

"No, he's outside with Van."

"Still? Don't you think *that's* strange? That he's got so much interest in an eight-year-old boy who's no relation to him?"

"So the dude likes kids. It's not like he's molesting him. They're not in some dark room. They're outside where everyone can see, playing ball for Christ's sake."

"Sometimes it starts there."

"Yeah, well, it's going to end there, too. If he tries anything with Van, I'll kill him."

"Okay," Eddie said with a sigh of relief. "Anyway, that's good news about Rod. I was freaking out."

"You had me going, too!"

"We have to be careful. We can't let strangers get too close, Sebastian. We took a risk last night, a risk we shouldn't have taken, and it could've cost us."

"Agreed. So how'd it go with Yogi?"

"I hate him. But he's the only reason we can pay the mortgage. And I wasn't late, so we didn't have any trouble today."

"All right. See you when you get here." Hungry, Sebastian shut down the computer so he could get something to eat. But, on a whim, he decided to call Amos Auto Body first, just to see if he could find out anything more. He didn't have to say who he was, doubted anyone there would recognize his name from the papers even if he gave it.

"You going to smoke again?" Sheila asked.

She wasn't even out of bed and she was already at him for more dope! "No, and neither are you," he grumbled while he dialed.

"You woke up in *such* a bad mood," she complained and got up to go to the bathroom. Meanwhile, someone in Whiskey Creek answered his call.

"Natasha at Amos Auto Body. How can I help you?"

"Rod there?" Sebastian asked.

"'Fraid not."

"Should I call back this afternoon?"

"No, he's out for a few days. I'm not sure exactly when he'll be back. Can I take a message?"

"This is a friend of his, Jimmy…er…Smith. I met him at a bar last night. We hung out with a couple of girls I know." He was about to add that Rod had stayed over and forgotten his wallet, when she interrupted.

"With a couple of *girls*?" She sounded shocked. "I thought he was on vacation with India."

Sebastian's blood ran cold. India's name was distinctive enough that there could be no confusion. Rod wasn't a cop. He wasn't a private investigator working for the Sommerses. But Sebastian had little doubt that he wanted the same thing—to see him go to prison for the rest of his life. Why else would a friend of India's approach him at the pool hall and pretend it was a random occurrence? No way could it be random, not if he had ties to her.

And now Sebastian understood why Rod was spending so much time with Van.

He was after information.

A door slamming somewhere else in the motel startled India awake. After Frank's call, assuring her that Rod was okay, she'd dozed off. But judging by the light coming through the crack in the drapes, that'd been some time ago…

Acid poured into her stomach as she scrambled to

check the digital clock on the nightstand. It was noon and Rod wasn't back yet. Why? Where could he be now?

She grabbed her phone to see if she'd heard from him and immediately fell back against the pillows. Yes! She'd received some texts. One had come in a few minutes ago. He was playing ball with Van. He'd be home soon. Not to worry.

Weak with relief, she closed her eyes and breathed deeply. Once she'd calmed down, she allowed herself to get excited for the first time in a long while. If Rod was with Van, maybe he was learning something important— or *would* learn something important. If that happened, it could change her whole life.

Could they actually win this war they were waging? Was it possible that Rod could come up with some detail that would convince the police to drag Sebastian back into court? Would Sebastian be punished for his crimes?

India remembered the night she'd come upon Rod striding angrily down the road with his hands curled into fists. She'd assumed he was someone she should avoid, had warned herself against him. And yet *he'd* been the one to believe in her when almost no one else would, at least not completely, not without reservation. He was the only person in her corner, ready to help her fight despite the danger. Everyone else, people who'd known her much longer and supposedly cared about her, had simply gone on with their lives as if she must deserve what was happening to her.

The past two weeks would've been so much more difficult without him. She couldn't wait to see him, couldn't wait to hear how he'd managed to strike up a connection with Sebastian…

But as the seconds ticked away and fifteen minutes

turned into thirty, and then another hour passed with no word, her excitement began to wane.

Something was wrong or he would've been back by now.

"He's up to no good. Maybe he's even looking for the gun."

Sebastian hated to hear that, but Eddie had to be right. What else could Rod be doing? He'd brought Van home, said his goodbyes and driven off with a vague promise to catch them at the pool hall sometime soon. But he hadn't left the area. Sebastian had put Sheila's iPhone, which her bedridden mother paid for so she could contact Sheila and the kids, in Rod's glove box. That meant he could track him on the computer via the Find My iPhone app. Once Rod had stopped a few blocks away, and his truck didn't move again, Sebastian had asked Eddie to drive by that location on his way home to see what was going on.

Eddie had called back a few minutes later to say the truck was parked at a fast-food place, but Rod wasn't inside the vehicle or in the store.

The conversation continued when Eddie got home.

"Van swore that Rod never asked him anything about me, Charlie, India, the trial or the murder," Sebastian said. "They just played ball."

"And you believe him?" Eddie asked, incredulous.

Sebastian raked his fingers through his hair. Why not? *He* hadn't said anything to Van about what happened that night at India's. Why would he?

But he supposed it was possible that Van could've overheard him talking to Eddie—if the little shit was listening in when he shouldn't be. Van wasn't someone

Sebastian would tell, but he also wasn't someone he'd worry about.

"Get him back here," Eddie snapped. "*I'll* ask him this time, and I bet he has a bit more to say."

"Can't. Sheila took him and the other kids to that assisted living place to see her mother. If she doesn't do that once a week, Vickie'll call Child Protective Services, and if CPS takes the kids, Sheila's welfare check will be cut in half."

"Then text her, damn it! Tell her to make it short. We have to figure out what this Rod bastard is up to."

"I can't text her. I took her phone."

His brother began to pace in quick, agitated movements, which made Sebastian's anxiety worse. What the hell could he do?

He wasn't going back to jail. He knew that much. He'd do whatever he had to in order to make sure *that* didn't happen.

"The kid told him *something*," Eddie insisted. "I *know* he did."

Maybe that was true. No matter how many times Sebastian had asked, Van had maintained the same story, but Sebastian couldn't question him *too* forcefully, not right before he went to see Grandma Vickie. Sebastian benefited from the money Sheila received. Besides, what good would it do to get himself reported for child abuse? That would just give the cops another reason to knock on his door, to watch him closely.

"Van doesn't have anything to tell," he said, but he wasn't as convinced as he pretended. He was merely trying to calm his brother so he could think straight.

That attempt fell flat and only made Eddie angrier.

"Are you willing to stake your life on that, brother? Risk going back to jail?"

"Hell, no. But pressuring Van's not the answer." The last time he'd started in on the kid, Sheila had said she'd call CPS herself if he didn't stop. *You get him taken away, we lose eight hundred bucks a month*, she'd screamed. *How will we get anything we need then?*

"So what *is* the answer?" his brother demanded.

"If you'd give me a second, maybe I could come up with something!" he shouted back.

Eddie ignored his outburst. "*I* think we have to assume the worst, which means there's no time to waste. Let's go get Rod. We'll lure him into the car, take him out into the sticks and beat him to death."

"I'm not fighting that dude," Sebastian said.

"Come on, don't be a puss! He's got a broken hand, for fuck's sake. And it'll be two against one!"

"I don't care. He looks pretty fit. And he must be able to handle himself, or he wouldn't have come here last night. Anyway, how will we *lure* him into the car? The guy's not stupid. If Van told him anything, he'll be leery."

"We invite him to go smoke again."

"He won't fall for that, not if he isn't who he says he is."

"Then we accuse him of stealing Sheila's phone," Eddie said, obviously developing the plan as he spoke. "When he tells us he didn't take it, we'll ask if we can search his truck. He'll let us, because he doesn't know it's there. Then he'll be shocked when we find it. That'll get us close to him. I'll hold him while you stab him. Make sure you get him two or three times, to be on the safe side. After that we'll shove him in the backseat, jump in the front and drive off."

"In broad daylight?" Sebastian asked.

"What other choice do we have?" Eddie spread his hands in appeal. "We can stand right by the cab, block what we're doing. Anyone who happens to be driving by won't know what the hell's going on."

"And then what?"

"What do *you* think? We take him out and bury him somewhere no one will ever look."

Sebastian tried to imagine that plan being successful but had too many reservations. "They can trace our cell phones—the towers they ping off and shit."

"Then we leave them here."

"What if he's already told India whatever he learned from Van? While we're messing with him, she could come for the gun."

"Then *we* grab the gun first."

As tempting as it would be to reclaim the weapon he'd used to shoot Charlie Sommers, so he could hide it in a safer place—like the bottom of the Bay—he'd been careful not to go near it. No one had found it. As far as he was concerned, it was safer to let the gun stay where it was. There'd been no need to take the chance.

But this changed everything. "Okay. Only, we don't kill him right away." Sebastian came to his feet and began to pace, too. "We sit tight and wait until he leads us to India. Then we settle this after dark."

Eddie lowered his voice. "You mean we make it easy and shoot them both."

He nodded. "I should've done that before, instead of leaving a witness. But if we play our cards right, I'll have another chance. We follow him until we find her, and then we take care of this once and for all."

"You can do that? You can go through with it this time?"

"I don't have any choice. She's gone too far, proved she's no friend of mine." How dare she get him in trouble again. As if what she'd said and done during the trial wasn't punishment enough. She *knew* him, damn it. Probably better than anyone, since she was the only woman he'd ever loved. She knew he'd had a rough life, that what he'd done that night wasn't like him. She could've had a little compassion.

Eddie seemed to mull over his words. Then he said, "I like it."

"Good. Because we better move. We need to be in position, watching from somewhere he won't notice us when he gets back to his truck. If he has the gun, we'll have to use a knife, like you said."

"We can do that. We can overpower him." Eddie pulled out his keys. "He won't be expecting us, so he won't have a chance to use the gun even if he has it."

Sebastian eyed his brother. "I need an eight-ball, man. I have to be messed up if I'm going to do this."

Eddie scowled. "We don't have time."

"It's the only way this'll work. Come on, man. *I need something.*"

"Like a clear head?"

"No, I need to be on top of my game."

"You don't have any money—and crystal isn't free."

"I'm sure Rod's got money on him. We'll take that. When we're done with him, he won't have any use for it, anyway."

"Fine," he said and pulled a baggie out of his pocket.

"If we're careful—if we make it so the bodies are never discovered—today might be the end of it," Sebastian said. He had to psych himself up. Because as angry as he was with India, he wanted to take her to bed, marry her, live with her—not kill her. He'd gotten rid of Charlie, taken that drastic a step, just so they could be together.

"*Now* do you believe India's a bitch?" Eddie asked once they were stoned.

Sebastian felt the drug curling through his veins, filling him with energy and power, turning him into a superman. He could take on Rod Amos; he could take on anyone. "I'll always love her," he admitted.

"You can't think like that, man."

"Yes, I can. Because it doesn't make any difference. It's her or me."

Rod wasn't answering his texts. Did that mean he *couldn't*? Or had his phone run out of battery?

India prayed it was the latter, but he had a charger in his truck… Determined to get help if she needed it, she called Frank, who went out to water his lawn so he could hear as well as see what might be going on at Sebastian's house. Ten minutes later he told her it didn't look as if anyone was home. Both drivable cars were gone. Rod's truck was no longer at the curb, either.

India considered that encouraging, since it suggested that he wasn't in the same place as the Young brothers.

But if Rod wasn't in any danger, where had he gone? And why wasn't he responding?

She texted him again, even though she'd sent him more than a dozen messages in the past hour.

Hello? Rod? Please let me know you're okay.

She waited another fifteen minutes. By then it was well after one, and she was falling into a full-blown panic. Positive something terrible must've happened, she broke down and called Flores.

The detective didn't answer—she got his voice mail—but when she called the station instead, and said it was an emergency, he got right back to her.

Once he heard her story, he told her it'd been a mistake to involve Rod. That was pretty much what she'd expected him to say. What she already knew. But then he promised to call Hayward PD and ask them to send a unit to Sebastian's address, which was what she'd been after from the beginning.

She wrung her hands as she strode back and forth in front of the TV, which was playing some stupid game show. With time moving slower than the continental drift, and still no word, she was afraid she'd go crazy, especially when recent memories of her and Rod began to parade through her mind. The way he touched her. The way he kissed her. The way he laughed and teased her...

Losing Charlie, especially in such a tragic way, had been the worst thing she'd ever been through. There was no question about that. But she had a terrible feeling it would be just as difficult to lose Rod. She hadn't built a life with him, hadn't had a child with him, hadn't owned a home with him. She hadn't actually known him for very long. And yet...she'd fallen for him. Somehow she'd lost her heart, even though she'd been so deeply in love with Charlie she'd thought that could never happen.

Unable to tolerate another second of the agonizing wait, she called Dylan's number. She hated to worry Rod's brothers, but she also hoped they'd had some contact with him today. Maybe there'd been an emergency and he'd gone home to help.

"Have you heard from Rod?" she asked as soon as Dylan answered.

A long pause met this question; Dylan was obviously taken aback. "I got a text this morning, saying he wouldn't be able to take Natasha to the airport today. He told me he was at a sporting goods store, but he'd been up most of the night and needed to get some sleep and check on you. I'm thinking that should've happened by now, but…he hasn't come back?"

Although he spoke calmly, she could feel the deep concern behind those words. "No, he hasn't."

She filled him in on the details, although it wasn't easy to talk. She kept choking up, had to fight back tears.

"Well, he's not here," Dylan said when she was done. "He wouldn't come here without telling you."

Deep down, she'd known that. Rod took great care of her, would never drive off without a word and leave her wondering. If he was going to take his stepsister to the airport, he would've invited her to come along.

"I'll call you as soon as I hear something," she told Dylan. Then she grabbed her keys and left to see if she could spot Rod's truck in or near Sebastian's neighborhood. That was the last place he'd been, which made it the best place to start.

Detective Flores had cautioned her to stay put. He'd said he didn't need her getting involved in whatever was happening. But she refused to hide out in the motel, refused to leave Rod out there alone.

She wouldn't lose him.

28

He couldn't find the gun. Using the flashlight he kept in his truck, Rod had been under every house on Sebastian's street—at least the ones he could get under. Whenever anyone questioned his activities, he said he was a private contractor working with the city to inspect houses for a new type of toxic mold. Thanks to the list of neighbors the Siddells had given India, he was familiar with the names of the residents and claimed they'd all been sent a letter—that they could ask Frank Siddell if they didn't remember getting one. No one he spoke to remembered receiving a letter, of course, but after that, they assumed they'd missed the notice and let him go ahead without even asking for ID.

Unfortunately, being free to search didn't help. He'd had no luck. There were too many places to hide a gun. The weapon that had killed Charlie could be inside a box of discarded files, wrapped in a packing blanket, shoved inside the upholstery of an old couch or slipped among other storage. It could be stuffed in a random nook or cranny or tucked up in the rafters. For all Rod knew, Sebastian could've buried it. And how would he ever find it in the ground? Sebastian had stashed it more than eleven months ago. Rod doubted he'd still be able to spot the disturbed earth.

Learning that the gun was under a neighbor's house had sounded hopeful at first—but that small clue wasn't enough. And he was going on very little sleep, so he was too exhausted to keep looking.

As he trudged back to his truck, he put a hand in his pocket to get his phone. Then he remembered that it was dead. His car charger worked only if the engine was running, and he'd hardly been in his vehicle at all.

He checked his watch instead. Nearly two. Damn. He'd gotten so caught up, he'd stayed too long, considering that he couldn't communicate with India. She must be frantic by now. But he'd had to search while he could. He felt a sense of unease, a certain…disquiet, as if he had to find that gun fast or he'd never have another chance.

After more than an hour of driving up and down each street in an ever-widening circle, India found Rod's truck. She almost couldn't believe it when she saw it sitting there. She would've been relieved, except he wasn't near it, and he wasn't in the McDonald's, either. She went in and showed the employees his picture on her phone, but no one had seen him.

She called Detective Flores to update him and was steeling herself to walk out so she could take another look at the truck—this time to see if there was any trace of blood—when Rod came striding across the street.

The second she saw him, she ran out and let him scoop her up like a child. "Why haven't you called me?" she breathed, feeling the roughness of his beard growth against her cheek.

"What are you doing here?" he asked instead of

answering. "You're not supposed to be anywhere near this area."

She wouldn't let go—*couldn't* let go. Not yet. "I came to find you—to…to get you."

"India, you have to relax, to trust that I know what I'm doing. Or you're going to give me away." He sounded slightly exasperated, but she could tell he wasn't truly angry.

"It doesn't matter, because you're not coming back here," she said, resolute.

"Of course I am. Listen. Van told me that Sebastian hid the gun under one of the neighbor's houses. We just have to figure out some way to find it."

Even that information, important as it was, couldn't distract her. Squeezing her eyes shut, she breathed deeply, taking in his reassuring scent. "Someone else will have to find it."

He pulled back to look into her face. "Why? Why not me?"

"Because I won't risk you again," she said. "I can't do it, Rod. I can't go through another night like the last one, another morning like this one. I love you too much."

He held her chin with his good hand. "Whoa, slow down. What'd you just say?"

"That you're not coming back here. It's too danger-ous. I can't believe I ever let you—"

"No, the other part."

The intensity of his gaze made her rack her brain for anything she might've said that would surprise him so much he'd want to hear it twice. Then it occurred to her. In that gush of words, she'd confessed her love. When she realized, it came as a surprise to her, too. She *did*

love him, but she certainly hadn't planned to tell him—
not this soon. "It's true," she admitted.

"How do you know?" he murmured, resting his forehead against hers. "How do you know you're not confusing love with relief or gratitude or…a sense of obligation
because I'm helping you? Your emotions have to be
scrambled right now. And we *are* sleeping together, which
could make you feel more…connected to me than you
otherwise would."

"This morning when I thought you weren't coming
back, it became pretty obvious to me. It's too soon for either of us to get serious. But that doesn't change anything.
I'd be heartbroken if you got hurt. You *have* to be safe.
So, please, go home to Whiskey Creek, to your brothers."

"I'm not going anywhere," he said, "not without you."

"Rod—" She was about to tell him that she'd called the
police, that they might already be at Sebastian's door, asking about him. Their time playing undercover investigator
was over. But he interrupted before she could get that far.

"After we get out of this mess, we'll go home together," he said.

Sebastian wasn't a cold-blooded killer, not like those
psychopaths he saw in the movies and on TV. He didn't
take *pleasure* in hurting others, so he couldn't see how
more prison time would reform him or do a damn thing
for society. Why couldn't India understand that? If only
she could find it in her heart to forgive and forget, maybe
he could be whole again, like the man he used to be when
she loved him. The real Sebastian would never hurt any-
body. He wouldn't have killed Charlie if he hadn't been
in the depths of despair and not thinking straight.

She hated him these days. But a single night shouldn't

define his whole existence, should it? He'd done good things, too. He'd spared her *and* her little girl, didn't hurt them at all. Considering the rage pouring through him at the time, it was remarkable that he'd managed to retain *that* much control.

She had no concept of how lucky she'd been, how kind *he'd* been. When he'd shown up that night, he'd planned to kill them all in one last, desperate act before turning the gun on himself.

Too bad he hadn't been able to go through with it. He would have, except she'd been there, telling him she'd come back to him, that they'd be together. When she'd touched him, when she'd let him make love to her, it reminded him of how great they were together. She'd convinced him he'd have someone he loved and respected to help make his life easier.

But that had been a lie, a manipulation.

And she thought *he* was bad…

"You see that?" Eddie spoke as if he'd known from the beginning that Rod wasn't someone they could trust. His "I told you so" tone irritated Sebastian, but what could he say? His brother had shown more caution than he had.

"Yeah, I see it." Sebastian couldn't look away. India was kissing Rod in the parking lot of McDonald's as if the rest of the world could burn to the ground for all she cared.

The sight of them so caught up in each other turned his stomach. They were coming after him together. She didn't care about him, never would—even though he'd reached out and tried to apologize, tried to rekindle the friendship.

This was what his willingness to forget the past and move on had brought him. She was determined to see him destroyed. Never mind that taking his freedom and his dignity for *decades* wasn't fair, not for something that was more of a mistake, a screwup than anything else.

She'd left him no other option, he decided. He had to finish what he'd set out to do eleven months ago, or he'd soon be locked away in an eight-foot cell, where he'd become some bigger man's bitch.

Although he'd rather die than tell anyone, especially Eddie, he knew what being raped by another man felt like and would never allow anyone to humiliate him in that way again—no matter how many people he had to kill in order to avoid that fate.

"Should we hit 'em now?" Eddie asked. "While we've got the chance?"

Sebastian eyed the cars pulling in and out of the parking lot. There were too many people around. If they were going to do this, they were going to do it right. "No. We wait until dark, like I said."

It was time for Natasha to go. Mack had already hauled her luggage out to Grady's Chevy Tahoe, since Grady was the one who'd agreed to drive her to the Oakland airport instead of Rod. Mack had made up an excuse as to why he couldn't go, claiming he had plans for the evening. He felt it'd be easier to say goodbye here at home, where they'd have some privacy. He'd bought her a necklace and was waiting for the right moment to give it to her.

But Grady was hollering through the house that they had to leave.

Mack was beginning to worry that she wouldn't come to tell him goodbye, when she knocked on his bedroom door.

He opened it immediately. Then he had to step back

for a minute. She was so beautiful. She was going to drive all those college boys crazy—a bittersweet thought for him. "You all set?" he asked.

"You weren't going to see me off? You were just going to let me leave?"

He'd wanted to walk her out, but he knew better than to give her the necklace in front of Grady. Had it been a simple farewell gift—the kind he *should* be giving her—he and his brothers would've gone in on it together. But he hadn't mentioned the purchase to anyone else. He'd known Dylan and the others would find his gift a bit too telling. A heart-shaped pendant with a small diamond in the upper left side was the kind of thing a man bought for a wife or a lover—not a stepsister. "I was hoping you'd come to me."

"And if I hadn't?"

"I would've had to mail you this." He opened his dresser drawer to retrieve the small velvet case he'd tucked in there yesterday.

Some of the sadness she'd been carrying around evaporated the moment she saw it—and hope, although tentative, brightened her eyes. "You bought me something? Is it just from you, or—"

"It's just from me," he broke in.

When he handed her the box, she flashed him a smile for the first time in days, a smile that broadened as soon as she opened it. "Wow."

"Turn around. I'll put it on for you."

"I love it." She lifted her hair as he fastened it around her neck. Then she looked down at the golden heart as if he'd tossed her a lifeline—something she could cling to while she was gone. "Thank you."

"You're welcome. You mean—" his voice broke and

he paused to gain control of his emotions "—you mean a lot to me."

"God, Mack," she whispered. "Just *say* it. Please? You love me."

He stared at the pendant, nestled perfectly in the valley between her breasts. He knew if he didn't focus on that, he'd focus on her lips, because he wanted to kiss her more than he'd ever wanted to kiss her before. "Take advantage of every opportunity at college. Live life to the fullest. Embrace all the opportunities that come your way. But be careful. You can be a ballbuster, but once someone manages to get past that defensiveness, you're all heart. That's why I got you this necklace. It reminded me of you."

"You're not my dad, Mack," she said. "God knows who my dad is, but I'm an adult now. I'm not looking for a father figure anymore, and I certainly don't want *you* stepping into that role. It's bad enough that you consider yourself my 'brother.'"

"Our parents are married, Tash."

"Our parents are completely dysfunctional and have totally fucked up our lives!"

"You really have to watch your language."

She ignored that, too intent on what she was trying to say. "We have a chance at happiness—with each other. Why don't we take it?"

"For a lot of reasons. You're too young, for one. Anyway, you're going to be fine."

"Because of you and your brothers. If you hadn't taken me in, I have no idea where I'd be right now. I doubt I'd be heading to college. I'm so grateful and yet everything you've done for me is what stands between us."

"*College* stands between us. Go and enjoy the next

four years. And don't let your feelings for me hold you back."

"Natasha!" Grady's voice boomed down the stairs. "What the hell? You're going to miss your plane!"

"I don't care about catching my plane," she whispered, ignoring Grady. "I'd rather stay here with you."

"Don't make this any harder," he said. "You'd better go before Grady comes down."

"No one knows about this necklace?"

"No one can know. If Grady sees it, make up something to tell him."

"I will." She clasped the necklace as if it meant everything to her. "If you didn't feel anything, it wouldn't matter if he or anyone else saw it."

"Natasha?" Grady called. "Are you down there?"

"Yes! I'm saying goodbye to Mack," she called back. "Be right there."

"Be safe," Mack told her.

She slid her arms around his neck and pressed her cheek to his, but he didn't respond. He couldn't.

Wearing a wounded expression, she eventually dropped her arms and turned to go. But it was that wounded expression that beat him. He couldn't let her leave so sad.

Before he could stop himself, he caught her elbow, spun her to face him and kissed her like he'd always dreamed of kissing her, with an open mouth and plenty of tongue. With all the passion he'd kept bridled for so long. In seconds he had her up against the wall, and he could tell she liked it. She wrapped her legs around his waist as if she'd welcome a lot more than that and shoved her hands in his hair.

He knew she hadn't kissed many guys, but she was a natural. He loved the way her passion rose so quickly to match his, the way she parted her lips and welcomed his tongue, the way she tasted.

He wasn't sure how much further he would've taken it if Grady hadn't called for Natasha again.

"Now!" Grady yelled, thumping the wall near the top of the stairs and startling them enough that they broke apart.

They were both breathing heavily as they stared at each other.

"I love you," she whispered.

"I love you, too," he finally admitted.

With an expression of pure relief, she gave him another quick squeeze. "I knew it! I'm coming back to marry you as soon as I graduate," she said, then hurried upstairs.

Rod didn't think he'd ever been more exhausted in his life. He fell asleep almost as soon as he hit the mattress and didn't wake up for hours. When he did come around, he couldn't see anything except darkness, but he could feel India tucked up against him.

The steadiness of her breathing indicated that she was asleep. He told himself he shouldn't wake her. She'd been on an exhausting roller coaster of emotion the past few weeks—the past *year*. But he couldn't help remembering those few minutes in the parking lot of McDonald's, when she'd declared her feelings for him. He wanted to hear her say it again, say that she loved him. He wanted to thread his fingers through hers without feeling Charlie's ring.

He waited for what seemed like an eternity, hoping she'd wake up on her own. But when she didn't, he couldn't resist touching her. He slid his hand up over the swell of her hip as he kissed her neck, and she accommodated him by turning onto her back.

"I can't believe you're awake," she murmured. "It's the middle of the night, and you've had even less sleep than I have." Her voice was still husky, but she molded herself to him as if she wasn't unhappy about being disturbed.

He cupped her left breast through his T-shirt, which she'd pulled on after removing her makeup. "It's not easy to sleep with you lying beside me."

"You haven't had enough sex?" she said with a laugh.

"I could never get enough of you. But I'm not looking for sex. Not right now." He took his time kissing, touching her.

"Then what?" she whispered.

Maybe he did want to make love. Then he could tell her with his body what he wasn't quite ready to say. He'd never felt so protective or possessive of anyone, but he was also a little superstitious—afraid to express those emotions for fear of jinxing the closeness and intimacy that was developing between them. He'd never been quite so happy. The last time he'd felt this complete was before his mother died.

But he needed more time before he could trust what he was feeling—and what *she* was feeling. Once they got beyond the problems they were facing now, maybe he'd be able to let down his guard.

"It's weird. You make me want to give you everything I've got—and yet I can feel myself holding back," he said.

"You're trying to play it safe, to prepare for all eventualities."

"I'm not trying to prepare for all eventualities."

"Yes, you are. But you can't fall in love and remain in control at the same time. They're opposites."

"You're still wearing your wedding ring, India."

She said nothing. She stared at him for several seconds. Then she removed the ring. After putting it on the nightstand, she ran her hand gently down his face. "Is this better? Is that what you were waiting for?"

He smiled. "It certainly helps.

"Then stop holding back."

"I'm not."

"Yes, you are. You don't have to make a commitment, but at least give yourself permission to let go, to embrace what you're feeling, let it carry you away if it's powerful enough to do that."

It was plenty powerful. But letting go, giving himself permission to love her as much as he was afraid he could love her, was a terrifying thought. What if, in the end, he wasn't enough for her? "I'm just an auto body technician from a small town, India."

Propping herself up on one elbow, she drew a heart on his bare chest. "I know who and what you are, Rod."

Her hair tickled as it fell against his shoulders. He'd yanked off his shirt but hadn't bothered with his pants. He'd been too tired. "Is it enough for you?"

She studied him for several seconds. "Can't you tell?"

He linked his left hand with hers. "That's not an answer."

"My feelings aren't based on your profession or where you live, Rod."

He might've told her he loved her right then. The words were on the tip of his tongue. He opened his mouth to do exactly that—when he heard a loud thump and the sound of breaking glass.

29

At first India thought there'd been an accident. Some drunk had stumbled on the way to his room and smashed into their window. Or a thief was trying to break in. Not until she heard Sebastian curse did she realize what was *really* going on. Then her whole body went rigid. This was exactly what'd happened eleven months ago! Sebastian had come out of nowhere and invaded the sanctity and privacy of her bedroom.

Determined to put up a fight sooner this time, before Sebastian could get any more of an advantage, she managed to overcome the debilitating terror and regain control of her body. Even then it seemed as if she could move in only slow motion. She attempted to throw herself over Rod, to stop any bullet meant for him, but he wouldn't allow her to act as his shield. And he was strong enough to stop her. As Sebastian tripped and fell, Rod shoved her off the bed.

"Lock yourself in the bathroom and don't come out!" he yelled.

The adrenaline that had enabled her to overcome that first burst of fear worked against her now. Her hands shook as they skimmed the top of the nightstand, searching for her phone but knocking her wedding ring off instead. Help. She had to get help—not hide in the bathroom. But she wasn't sure where she'd left her cell.

Damn it! Where was it? Maybe it'd fallen on the floor...

She dropped to her knees so she could search the carpet and found it. "911," she mumbled in desperation, as if saying the numbers would somehow dial them. "911."

A hand grabbed her by the arm and pushed her halfway across the room. It was Rod. He was trying to get her into the bathroom. She had no idea what *he* was going to do, but he didn't seem to be following her. She had no doubt that they'd both end up dead if she couldn't get help. They were completely vulnerable. And Rod had the use of only one hand. They hadn't prepared for an attack because they'd never dreamed Sebastian would be able to trace them to the motel.

This room had felt like the one safe place on the planet.

The memories of Charlie's death tumbled through her mind—disjointed, terrifying. She couldn't go through this again...

India was shutting the bathroom door when she heard a noise that told her Sebastian hadn't come alone. A quick check confirmed it. A second man was climbing through the broken window. Eddie. She knew it was Sebastian's brother even though she could barely see him in the dark.

"Shoot him!" Eddie shouted. "What the hell are you waiting for?"

There was no time to call the police. Rod would be dead in a second.

"You bastard!" she screamed and threw the blow-dryer.

It wasn't much of a weapon. After glancing off Sebastian's shoulder, it crashed to the floor and broke into pieces. But having an object come at him out of nowhere startled him. Turning, he fired.

India's ears rang from the blast. But she felt no pain, and he couldn't get off another shot before Rod hit him in the side of the head with his right hand, cast and all.

The gun dropped with a solid thud as Sebastian toppled over.

"Get in the bathroom!" Rod shouted again. But if she didn't do something, Sebastian would recover the gun; already he was trying to shake off Rod's blow. And there was no way Rod could stop him. He was fighting with Eddie.

As Rod and Eddie knocked the lamp off the nightstand and slammed into the wall, India launched herself at Sebastian. She'd heard the gun hit the floor but couldn't see it in the dark. She hoped he couldn't see it, either, hoped to kick it away from him.

She was afraid he'd knock her out before she could make much of a difference, however. An image of Cassia rose before her mind's eye, and she felt a deep sense of loss. The Sommerses might get to raise her, after all. But that thought only made her anger burn hotter. She would *not* allow Sebastian to win—even if she died trying to stop him. She refused to face the same agonizing what-if questions she'd faced since Charlie's death.

"No, damn you, not again!" she yelled as she slugged, scratched and kicked for all she was worth.

Sebastian shoved her out of the way so violently she fell and hit her head on the nightstand. The blow stunned her, made it difficult to think. But she could hear voices, and she was fairly certain they weren't in her head. There were people standing outside the broken window, marveling at the commotion.

Why weren't they doing anything?

"What's going on?... I don't know... They've been broken into... Get the manager... There's fighting! Call the police!"

"Help!" India cried. Then, thanks to a glimmer of moonlight, she spotted the gun. She thought she could crawl to it, but Sebastian had spotted it, too, and he was closer. She doubted she'd be able to hold on to it, anyway, even if she could reach it. He'd simply wrest it away and shoot her. Then he'd shoot Rod, before any of their confused onlookers could figure out what to do.

So she did the only thing she could think of. As he turned his back on her, she came up from behind and looped the cord of the blow-dryer around his neck. Then she clenched her teeth and pulled, using every ounce of strength she possessed.

He bucked and fought for breath, gouging at her hands and trying to reach behind him to grab her. But she hung on like a woman possessed. For Charlie. For Cassia. For Rod.

Fortunately, he couldn't get a good grip on her. He switched to trying to pull the cord away from his neck instead, which might've worked had he done that first. But she was too far ahead of him in the struggle, had already tightened it.

Even then she had to fight to hang on and nearly lost her grip when he managed to grab a fistful of her hair. He yanked so hard she thought he'd pulled it out. But Charlie seemed to be in her heart and her head, egging her on, helping her push through the pain.

She'd never known that a few seconds could last so long. Just when she thought she'd subdued Sebastian, her strength began to wane. She couldn't hold on, after all. He was going to get away...

And then there were several people in the room. Rod, his mouth and abdomen bleeding, pried her hands off that cord. Two uniformed police officers restrained Sebastian; someone else removed the gun.

It was over.

"You okay?" Rod murmured and gathered her to him.

Rod needed half a dozen stitches on the left side of his abdomen. Eddie had had a knife, and he'd managed to get in a good swipe before Rod could disarm him. That cut was Rod's only injury, though, aside from the busted lip he'd sustained when he rushed Eddie and their heads had collided in the dark. When he'd landed that blow to Sebastian's head, he'd broken his cast, which had to be replaced, but he hadn't caused any further injury to his hand.

Overall, the incident could've been a lot worse. At least, other than a sore head and a few minor bumps and bruises, India hadn't been hurt. The bullet Sebastian fired had gone into the wall. She was shaken after the ordeal—anyone would be—but Rod was impressed with how quickly she'd rebounded. While the ER doctor finished with him, he could hear her talking on the phone outside his room, as calm as ever. And when she came back in, she was smiling.

"What is it?" He knew she'd just spoken to the policeman who'd arrested Sebastian and Eddie. She'd also notified the detective who'd been working Charlie's case.

"Sebastian and his brother are going to jail for a long time. They've got a whole list of offenses—assault with a deadly weapon, battery, breaking and entering, possession. I can't even remember them all. But I think they had disturbing the peace in there, too."

Rod let his head fall back. The surfeit of adrenaline had drained him. "A long time. That's what I was hoping to hear."

She nodded to the doctor, who had his prescription pad out. "Is he going to be okay, Doc?"

"He's going to be fine."

"Good," she said and rubbed her hands on a shaky exhalation.

"Is that it?" Rod prompted. "Is that all the police had to say?"

She came to his bedside and took his hand. "Not quite. They have the gun. They can't confirm it's the weapon that killed Charlie. That'll require a ballistics test. But I'm hopeful—and so are they. It's the right caliber, so… there's that."

He caught the scent of her perfume as she leaned over to peck his lips. "I'm glad you weren't hurt any worse," she said.

"We have a lot to be grateful for." He took her hand. "You must be relieved to know that Cassia will be safe when she comes home."

"Absolutely." She smoothed his hair off his forehead. "And it's all because of you."

She'd come to the Bay Area first, before he'd decided to join her at the motel. He didn't feel he should get all the credit, but the doctor spoke before he could respond. "That's it, Mr. Amos. You're all set." He handed Rod the prescription he'd been writing. "This is for an antibiotic. Take the whole bottle, as directed. Who knows what kind of germs were on that blade."

"Will do. Thanks."

"You bet. You can get your things and go." The doctor gave his shoulder a friendly squeeze before heading out.

Rod was so exhausted, he'd fallen asleep at various points during his treatment. He wasn't sure he had the energy to walk out under his own power, especially since he was high on painkiller. India had to help him put on his shirt, and she let him lean on her as he got up.

"Is there any chance you know how to make meat loaf?" he asked as they walked out.

She gave him a funny look. *"Meat loaf?"*

The nurse said goodbye to them and they waved before stepping into the bright afternoon sunshine. "Or chicken-fried steak?"

"You want me to make you a meal? *Today?"*

"Not today. I'm just wondering if you can cook."

She held him tighter when he stumbled. "Is that a prerequisite to being with you?"

He winked. "Let's say it'd be a nice bonus."

"You liked my cookies."

"You got anything else to show me?"

"Fortunately, I do—since that sounds important to you."

He associated homemaking skills with a different part of his life, back when he'd had his mother. He missed her, missed the type of home they'd had and the care they'd received, but he'd missed that for a long time.

India directed him to the passenger side of his truck. "I'm sure I can manage dinner here and there. You've earned a few home-cooked meals." She shot him a wry glance. "But just so you know, ironing is out of the question."

He grinned at her. *"I'll* do the ironing."

"I'd like to see that."

"You got me. I probably won't be doing any ironing," he said with a laugh.

She waited for him to climb in, then closed the door and circled around to the driver's side. Before she could put on her seat belt and start the engine, however, Dylan called.

"What room are you in?" he asked as soon as Rod answered.

"What *room*?"

"At the hospital."

"I was just released."

"So we came for nothing?"

"You're here?"

"Of course. We dropped everything as soon as it came on the news."

Rod twisted around to see if he could catch a glimpse of Dylan's Jeep, but the parking lot was too big. "Who's we?"

"Me, Cheyenne, Aaron and Presley. Grady and Mack are in Grady's SUV. We got a sitter for the kids because we didn't know how long we'd be gone."

"No Dad or Anya?"

"We conveniently forgot to tell them you'd been hurt. Are you okay?"

He lifted his shirt to take a look at the bandage covering his stitches. "Yeah. Nothing a few stitches won't fix. But since you're here, can someone follow us to Whiskey Creek in India's car? I'm too drugged up to drive."

"We can drive both vehicles, if you need us to. Let the two of you relax."

Rod nudged the woman who'd come into his life so unexpectedly. "Would you rather have someone else take the wheel?"

"No. I'm happy like this," she replied, and he understood that she was content to be alone with him for a while, to process what they'd been through and reassure herself that it was really over. She wasn't ready to put on a social face for people she'd barely met.

"She's got it," he told Dylan. "Just hold on so we can give you her keys."

After they handed off the keys to her Prius, and his family had left, Rod reached over to caress India's cheek. "Let's head home, huh?"

30

The next few days felt like a dream. Rod stayed at India's house, because they had more privacy there, and she kept busy creating pottery while he was at work. In the afternoons, she'd scour various cookbooks and prepare the best home-cooked meal she could—something she enjoyed because he acted as if cooking was the kindest thing anyone could ever do for him. He always attacked her food with gusto, then sat back with satisfaction. Having him come home to eat the meals she cooked soon became one of her favorite parts of the day.

But evenings were also nice. After dinner they'd walk along the riverbank, visit his brothers or go to town for dessert.

Rod was wrong when he wondered if she needed a more sophisticated or better-educated man in order to be happy. And if *she'd* ever wondered about that herself, the happiness she felt with him proved otherwise. He made her feel whole, complete, despite all the damage of the past, and it had nothing to do with his profession or whether he had a degree. She was proud of him for being who he was, proud to be with him.

He hadn't told her that he loved her. He never mentioned

how he felt, but he treated her as if she was important, and she was fine with letting the relationship develop from there. She wasn't in any hurry to receive a commitment. She wasn't in any hurry to give one, either. She loved him, but their relationship was so new. He hadn't even met Cassia yet. Although she was impatient for that to happen, she was also a little uneasy. She wasn't looking forward to the moment her in-laws would arrive, partly because she'd had to tell them about Rod. All the major news networks had shown a video clip of him escorting her out of the motel with his arm around her, protecting her from the cameras and gawkers. The confidence and authority with which he'd shepherded her through the gathering crowd, and the eagerness with which she'd climbed into the ambulance that bore him off to the hospital, would've given her away—even if the various news anchors hadn't reported that the widow of Dr. Charlie Sommers and her boyfriend, Rod Amos from Whiskey Creek, were attacked while sleeping in a motel room by the same man who'd killed her husband.

That Sebastian was back in jail, awaiting trial, and the police had the gun he'd probably used to kill Charlie made the Sommerses happy, on the one hand. But India knew they were disappointed in her on the other.

So much for that little heart-to-heart with Claudia in the kitchen… Now that conversation only made India look manipulative and insincere. The fact that she was already with another man at that point and hadn't bothered to mention it made her seem deceitful.

Suddenly, India realized that she'd been pressing the pedal of her pottery wheel farther than she should have. Jerking herself out of her thoughts, she looked down to find that her current project was off center as a result.

"Darn it!" Disgusted by her lack of focus, she scrapped the project, turned off her wheel and got up to wash her hands. She couldn't concentrate right now. She was happy as long as she wasn't thinking about her in-laws. But she'd have to deal with them soon, and until she did, she knew she'd have that dark cloud hanging over her.

Her phone buzzed in the pocket of her baggy cutoffs, which were about the most comfortable thing she had for working, especially when it was so warm outside.

After drying her hands, she pulled out her cell to see Rod's picture on her screen. Knowing it was him chased some of her concerns back into the shadows, where they'd resided since that night in the motel.

"Hi, Rod."

"Hey, gorgeous. What're you doing?"

She frowned at the lump of clay that was supposed to be a teapot. "Not much. You?"

"I'm off for lunch. Want to grab a bite?"

"Sure. Are you coming here?"

"I thought we could meet in town."

He didn't like her to see him in his work clothes. She got the impression he wasn't comfortable making it so obvious that he was "just" a blue-collar guy. He even showered at his place before coming over every night. So she was encouraged that he'd offered, felt maybe he was starting to trust her feelings for him.

"Where?" she asked.

"Just Like Mom's? They serve great apple pie."

"Okay. Let me change, and I'll be right over."

He was waiting for her when she arrived. He had paint flecks in his hair and was wearing a pair of faded jeans, a white T-shirt and his work boots, which also had paint specs and spatters. He certainly wasn't dressed up, but he was *always* easy to look at. She waved as she approached him at the entrance to the restaurant.

"What?" he asked, his eyebrows coming together when he saw the expression on her face.

"You look…tempting."

He glanced down at himself. "I haven't even cleaned up."

"When you're that handsome, it doesn't matter."

With a laugh and a shake of his head, he kissed her. Then he hooked his arm playfully around her neck and guided her into the restaurant, where they were seated.

The place was busy, but then it usually was.

"You always check in once or twice during the day, but this is the first time we've had lunch," she said. "To what do I owe the pleasure of your daytime company, sir?"

He leaned forward. "I have something to tell you."

She laced her fingers in her lap. "I hope it's something good."

"It is." He waited until the waitress had delivered their water and menus. Then he said, "Liam's dropping the charges."

"*Really?* Why?"

"I guess he didn't want to deal with the countersuit. He realized he could lose a lot more money that way."

She reached over to squeeze his hand. "That's wonderful, Rod! I'm so happy for you."

He picked up his water glass and tilted it toward her as if in a toast. "It's been quite an adventure since you came to town."

"I had nothing to do with that fight."

The waitress stopped at their table again, and India chose a Cobb salad, while Rod ordered a pastrami sandwich.

"Cassia comes home tomorrow," he said. "You excited?"

"Of course," she replied, but he must've been able to tell that not everything was as positive as she made it sound.

He grimaced. "You're worried, aren't you?"

"I need to put some distance between me and the past. Need a chance to get my feet under me again, especially where Charlie's parents are concerned. But I'm afraid they'll keep pushing, keep asking for her to come and stay. They're so involved in her life—*overly* involved. It's almost as if they're trying to replace Charlie with his daughter, and I don't have any idea how far they might push it."

"They know you're a loving mother."

"They think they can love her better."

"Still, they can't accuse you of mistreatment or neglect. They don't have a case, even if they're certain they can do a better job. You call to check on Cassia just about every day."

That was true, but a lot of those calls were due to him. He was the one who encouraged her to brave the negative energy that blew through the phone like a gale-force wind. Since they still put her off more often than they let her talk to Cassia, she would've preferred to wait out the remainder of the month. Once Cassia was home, she could try to put everything behind her—not only the loss of her husband, but the loss of her husband's family, too, since they were now excluding her. As it was, India felt sick after every call. She'd sit there and stare at her phone long after Claudia had disconnected. But then Rod would pull her into his arms and kiss the top of her head. He wouldn't say anything; he didn't need to. He knew that what they were doing hurt, and he hated being the reason. He just couldn't do anything to fix it.

"I'll be glad when she's back, and they're gone," she said.

"I hope they'll leave it at that."

"Me, too. I could go weeks without talking to them."

She happened to catch sight of Theresa, who was sitting across the restaurant with a small group of friends, gazing at Rod with such longing it almost broke India's heart.

"Don't look now, but Theresa's here," she murmured. "She's got her eye on you, and she seems quite tormented."

Rod scratched his neck. "Maybe I'll go visit her tonight. It's time to return her basket—and break the news."

"What news?" India asked, feigning innocence.

He narrowed his eyes. "You need me to lay it out?"

"That'd be nice. I took off my wedding ring for you. I haven't worn it since the motel. But you haven't said anything."

"I've been making love to you every night—and waking up with you every morning."

She gave him an arch look. "None of that explains how you plan to handle other women."

"I'm not handling them at all," he said wryly. "I'm not available."

She grinned at him. "That's what I wanted to hear."

He helped himself to a big bite of her salad. "I'm glad. Because you're off the market, too."

They were watching the news that night when a story about three brothers living in an orphanage made Rod get up and turn off the TV. He couldn't see the images they were showing, couldn't hear about the children who needed a home. He was already struggling to keep his mind off Van and his situation.

The boy reminded him too much of himself. Rod had been so hurt and lost after his mother killed herself and then when his father went to prison. Fortunately, for him, he'd had a big brother to fill the gap, and Dylan had done a remarkable job, considering that he'd been only eighteen at the time. But even with Dylan, those years hadn't been easy. And Van had no Dylan. Van had no one except his drug-addicted aunt, who didn't seem to care much about him.

"You tired?" India hid a yawn. They'd spent the evening snuggled up on the couch, watching a movie before the news had come on.

"Yeah. I guess those long nights last week are catching up with me."

She peered at him a little more closely. "Is that all?"

"What do you mean?"

"You've been quiet tonight. Have you heard from Natasha? Are you worried about her, since you didn't get to see her off?"

"No, I'm not worried. I've talked to her here and there, and we've texted a few times. She arrived safely and is settling in." In his last conversation with his stepsister, she'd been happier than he'd expected. But she was already planning a trip home for Thanksgiving. And, of course, all she could talk about was Mack.

Rod was more concerned with how Mack was tolerating *her* absence. The past few days he'd barely spoken at work. It was almost as if he was grieving.

"She's a tough girl."

"Yeah." He ambled over to the table that held photographs of Cassia—from birth to her current age.

"Are you nervous about meeting my daughter tomorrow?" India asked.

"Not really." He was more worried about how the Sommerses might react to meeting *him* and whether they'd threaten India with a custody suit. He knew Cassia meant everything to India. Could his relationship with India withstand the pressure the Sommerses might put on it?

He and India did great together when they were in their own little world. He'd never enjoyed anyone more. But that could all change when she had to be a mother again and put her daughter first.

"I've never brought this up, but I should probably ask," she said.

The somber note in her voice made him turn.

"Does it bother you that I have a child, Rod? And that she came from someone else?"

"*Bother* me?" he echoed. "God, no—on both counts."

She frowned. "Then what's going on with you tonight? Stop making me guess. The way you suddenly jumped up to turn off that TV as if you couldn't sit still another moment… I can tell *something's* wrong."

"I can't quit thinking about Van," he said with a sigh.

Understanding registered on her face. "Oh. I get it. That orphanage story hit a little too close to home."

"There are *so* many children who don't have what they need."

"And not enough people to help."

He straightened one of the picture frames. "It's disturbing."

Her lips curved into a gentle smile, which he saw when he looked back at her. "What's behind that smile?"

"You're a lot more sensitive than all those muscles and tattoos might lead someone to think."

"I feel I need to *do* something."

Curling her legs underneath her, she pulled one of the couch pillows into her lap. "Like what? Sheila will never give up custody. I'm sure she needs the money she gets from the state."

"That's the part that makes me sick. I honestly believe money's the only reason she took him in."

She nibbled on her bottom lip while she watched him wander around the room, examining her various decorations. "Okay, so…if you *could* help, what would you do?" she asked.

He thought about Natasha and how much he'd come to love her. It had been a difficult decision to take her in, considering how unhappy she'd been at first. But he was so glad they'd done it. He felt they'd gotten as much out of it as she had. "I'd like to be a big brother to him. Spend some time playing ball. Teach him how to ride a bike. Take him shopping for school clothes and help him with his homework. You know…be someone he can trust and lean on."

"What about Sheila's other kids? You told me she has two girls."

"She does, but at least they belong to her. That bond can make a big difference. They don't have to feel as if they're unwanted guests until they're eighteen."

"And we can't take over for every mother who does a poor job," she mused, "or we'd be quickly overrun."

"Exactly. I'd be satisfied if I could just help Van."

"Then why don't you approach Sheila? Tell her you'd like to help?"

"I doubt she'll be excited to hear from *me*. Because of us, her husband's going to prison."

"It's because of *him*. We didn't do anything wrong. And I bet she won't hold that against you forever. I can't imagine Sebastian was easy to live with. She'll get over him sooner or later and hook up with someone else, someone who may not even want Van around. Then she'll probably be grateful that you're willing to help."

"I can't wait until later. He needs me now."

"Then you could pay her to let you take him once in a while."

"She'll just spend the money on drugs."

"We can't control what she does with the money. At least you'll have some one-on-one time with him."

He pictured Van squinting up at him in the sunlight, like he had that day they'd played ball. "It'd be good if he could come here every other weekend."

"That's a big commitment."

"I'm willing to make it—if you are."

"You want me to be part of this?"

When their eyes met, he felt a powerful surge of emotion. "I want you to be part of everything."

She got up and came over to him. "Then I'm in." She took his hand to lead him into the bedroom, but he gave her a slight tug to get her to turn. Then he held her face as he kissed her.

"It scares me how much I love you," he said.

She stood up on tiptoe to kiss him again. "Why?"

"It doesn't seem like it could be real. It happened so fast, and I've been single for so long. I'm not sure I can depend on it."

Her thumb grazed his bottom lip in a tender caress.

"It's real," she whispered. "You don't have anything to worry about."

"And that's not going to change, even after the Sommerses come tomorrow and make you feel like shit for being with me? Or threaten you with a custody battle?"

A troubled expression settled on her face. "Let's hope that doesn't happen."

31

Rod hadn't been able to sleep very well. He'd tossed and turned, then he'd gotten up early to wait for Claudia and Steve—and Cassia—to appear. India had slept late, but he didn't think she was really resting. He figured she needed to be alone. If he'd gone to work, as usual, she would've had all the solitude she could ask for. But he hesitated to let her confront her in-laws without him, felt he should have the opportunity to defend being with her. He knew India felt vulnerable. He didn't want her in-laws to talk her into waiting until Cassia was older to get serious with anyone, hoping she'd cut things off with him and later meet someone more "suitable." He'd finally fallen in love; he was willing to fight for the relationship. The question was, would *she* fight to be with *him*?

He couldn't begin to guess how far they'd push her. They held the trump card; they could make her do almost anything to maintain peace, so she could raise her daughter without any trouble or interference.

He glanced at the clock as he carried his coffee cup to the sink. A few minutes till noon. They'd texted her when they left two hours ago and should be arriving any minute.

Did she love him as much as she said?

He was about to find out.

"Are you sure you want to be here for this?"

At the sound of India's voice, he looked over his shoulder to see her standing in the kitchen doorway. "Yeah." He was positive. *She* was the one who seemed to be experiencing some doubt. They'd decided it would be best for him to meet the Sommerses right away, to confront their bias before it could become any more entrenched. Why let Charlie's parents assume he was just a fling, a passing love interest who wasn't worthy of becoming a father to Cassia?

"We have to be careful," she said. "We can't shove our relationship in their faces."

"I realize that. But now's the time to show some solidarity and strength. We need to let them know it'll be a real battle—and ultimately a futile one—to try to get custody of Cassia."

"I hope they don't mistreat you."

"Don't worry about me. I can take it if they do." What he couldn't take was seeing them mistreat *her*—or seeing her give in to them. He needed her to be decisive and strong, to demand that they accept him as part of her life.

But that could potentially cost her custody of her child...

The doorbell rang. Clutching the door frame, she glanced back as if the Big Bad Wolf had just come to call.

"How do I look?" she asked.

"Like a stranger."

She blinked at him as if she didn't quite understand, but she'd reverted to the "doctor's wife" he'd met the day she moved in.

The doorbell rang again before she could question his

comment. "Here we go," she said and threw back her shoulders as she crossed the living room.

Steeling himself for whatever might happen, and trying to arrange his expression into something that didn't look challenging, Rod finished rinsing out his cup before following her.

The little girl he'd seen in the photographs, with the shocking orange hair, came barreling into the house and nearly bowled India over as soon as she opened the door. "Mommy!" she cried, throwing her arms around India's legs.

Cassia was wearing jeans, tennis shoes, a Giants jersey and a baseball cap—nothing frilly. From a distance, he might've mistaken her for a boy.

India peeled Cassia's arms away so she could kneel down and give her a proper hug. "You're home," she said. "Mommy's so glad. I've missed you more than you'll ever know."

The trepidation Rod had been feeling edged up a notch. No matter what, India and Cassia could not be separated...

"This is where we live now?" Cassia asked.

"It is. Don't you remember? I brought you here just after I bought it."

"It's different."

"Because it's not empty anymore."

"I remember the river outside."

"Yes. You'll have to be very careful to stay away from it when I'm not with you."

"I will. I'm not a baby!"

Rod looked up to find a woman with streaks of gray through her dark hair and stern lines around her mouth glaring at him. He'd pulled on a long-sleeved shirt even though it was summer because he'd thought it might improve her impression of him if he hid his tattoos. He knew how some people felt about them.

Her look said he was trash, regardless.

Overcoming the temptation to react negatively, he strode forward and stuck out his hand. "I'm Rod Amos. I live next door. You must be Claudia."

Claudia's attention *immediately* shifted to India, and Rod felt India's gaze shift between them as she straightened. "This is the man I've been seeing. Rod, allow me to introduce you to Claudia and Steve Sommers, Charlie's parents."

Steve didn't accept his hand, either, so Rod let it drop. "Would you like to sit down?"

Claudia didn't respond. Her eyes were riveted on India. And neither she nor Steve moved toward the couch. "I can't believe you'd have him here," she said.

"Who is he, Mama?" Cassia studied him curiously.

"A good friend of mine," India replied. "He's helped me a lot since you've been gone, and I care about him a great deal."

"You *care* about him?" Claudia scoffed. "That's supposed to justify jumping into his bed? You couldn't have met him more than a month ago!"

"We've spent so much time together," India said. "You get to know someone pretty fast when you're together all the time."

Steve made a sound of disgust. "And you claim to have loved our son. He's only been gone a year."

Rod bristled at the acid in Steve's voice but held his temper. What happened here had to be up to India. He had to trust her to protect what they'd found with each other. Nothing he did could compensate for a lack of commitment on her part.

But she was holding his heart in the palm of her hand...

India maintained a smile for the sake of her daughter but gave Cassia a little nudge. "Honey, I have your room all ready. Why don't you run and see what it looks like?"

"Where is it?" she asked.

"Just down the hall."

"Oh, I remember!" She slapped her forehead as if she should've remembered sooner, then her eyes narrowed. "My room isn't pink, is it?"

"No, it's blue. You're going to like it."

Her daughter's expression cleared. "Yay!"

As soon as she ran off, India turned back to her in-laws and lowered her voice. "As I've told you before, I'll always love Charlie. But that doesn't mean I can't love someone else, too."

"Love?" Claudia echoed. "You loved our son and yet you could take off your clothes for his killer?"

The blood drained from India's face, so Rod stepped in. India had been afraid Sebastian would talk. This confirmed that he had. He was trying to lash out, take her down with him.

"That didn't happen," Rod said.

"Sebastian says it did."

"Sebastian's a murderer. It's not too much of a stretch to think he could lie."

"It's not true?" Claudia demanded, looking back at India.

India's voice was so soft, Rod could barely hear her. "No, it *is* true."

Stunned silence met this admission. Rod was as surprised as the Sommerses were. "You don't have to tell them anything," he said to her. "They haven't treated you right since Charlie died. You owe them nothing."

"But I'm tired of lying," she said. "I want to tell the truth, be completely honest. Yes, I had sex with Sebastian. But it was the hardest thing I've ever done—the worst thing I've been through, other than seeing Charlie get shot. Only my love for Cassia made it possible for me to do what I did."

Claudia closed her eyes. "That's disgusting."

"How dare you judge me!" India said. "You have no idea what it was like that night."

"I know that Charlie's been gone for a year. And in those twelve months, you've been trying to convince us that you *didn't* let Sebastian touch you, just as you've been trying to convince us that you've been miserable since Charlie died—so miserable and traumatized you fell right into this man's bed. Someone who looks like he's on Sebastian's wavelength."

Rod felt his muscles tighten and his jaw clench, but he said nothing.

"Rod's one of the best men I've ever met!" India snapped in outrage.

"Of course," Claudia said. "After all, *you* know how to pick 'em."

India's eyes glittered with anger. "I picked Charlie, didn't I?"

Claudia's lip curled. "No, you didn't. Charlie picked you. Although I can't imagine why."

India brought a hand to her chest as if Claudia had shot her.

"That's enough," Rod said quietly. "I won't allow you to disrespect India. If you can't be decent, it's time for you to leave."

"As if *you* have any right to tell us to go!" Steve said.

India shook her head at Charlie's parents. "Don't you realize you're forcing me to choose between the man I love now and you?"

"Maybe it's time you showed us what Charlie saw in you," Claudia said. "Maybe it's time you stood up and took charge of your life instead of going back to your old pattern of being with one loser after another. I don't know what happened that night, if you really had to do what you did, but I do know I won't allow you to raise Cassia with a string of men in her life. I'll fight for custody myself, if I have to."

India laughed without humor. "Of course you will. You've been searching for any excuse to do that, haven't you?"

Claudia looked startled. "What are you talking about?"

"Your son would've expected more of you," she said. "But now that I know exactly where you stand, I think it's important for you to know where *I* stand. If you can't accept Rod, *you'll* be the one who gets cut out of my life—and Cassia's, too."

"I love it, Mommy!" Cassia called from down the hallway and came rushing back to show them her enthusiasm.

They all turned to stare at her.

India managed a smile for her daughter's sake, even though Rod could tell that she was trying to hold back tears. "That's wonderful, honey. I'm so glad."

"We'll fight you," Steve murmured to India. "And I'm not sure you want to go down that road. If I were you, I wouldn't want my less-than-stellar record—including what happened the night my husband was murdered— brought out for close examination."

"I've made my mistakes," India said. "I'll admit that.

But this time I've chosen well, no matter what you think. I won't let you cost me my future happiness."

The pressure in Rod's chest eased as he put his arm around her and stood close, hoping to lend her some comfort as well as support. "You'll be wasting your money as well as disappointing your dead son if you go after the woman he loved," Rod said. "We'll be good to Cassia, make sure she has more love than she knows what to do with. So keep that in mind. Because if you fight us, we'll fight back. And we'll win."

"I can't believe you've turned on us!" Claudia cried.

"Mimi, why are you being mean?" Cassia asked.

India picked up her daughter. "You're the ones who turned on me," India said, and Rod showed them to the door.

When they were gone, Rod put his arms around India and her little girl. "You were wonderful."

"Mommy, what's wrong?" Cassia asked. "Why are you crying?"

She rested her head on his shoulder. "I'm just happy you're back," she told Cassia.

"Are you mad at Papa and Mimi?"

"A little," she admitted.

"Why?"

"They mean well, but…they're confused right now."

"Oh."

Rod tugged on her baseball cap to get her to look up at him. "You like baseball, huh?"

She nodded.

"Good," he said. "So do I."

Epilogue

Three months later...

India stood at the window, looking out at Rod, who was playing catch with Van and Cassia. Cassia was too young to be very good, but what she lacked in skill she made up for in enthusiasm. She had to be in the middle of everything Rod did—and he loved it. He doted on her so much, India now feared *he'd* be the one to spoil her instead of her grandparents. She hadn't heard from them since they'd dropped Cassia off, but at least they hadn't acted on their threat to sue for custody. And she hoped they'd come around eventually, for her daughter's sake.

When Van caught a particularly difficult throw, his smile stretched almost from ear to ear, which made India smile, too. So it surprised her when she felt tears running down her face. A lot had changed in the past fifteen months. She'd had to completely rebuild her life. All she had from before was Cassia, the money Charlie had left her and a few treasured pieces of art she hadn't been able to part with. The rest she'd sold. Putting it up in her new house just hadn't felt right—smacked too much of hanging on to the past. She didn't need it to feel close to Charlie, anyway. In spite of everything, she could sometimes feel his presence as if he stood beside her, looking on in approval.

This was one of those moments, probably because she'd just heard from Detective Flores. The ballistics tests had finally been completed on the gun Sebastian had brought to the motel. They had the weapon that killed Charlie.

God, she missed her husband. Still. If not for Sebastian, she would've continued to be happy with Charlie and the life they had together. She remembered being fulfilled with her art and her interests, the importance of his work and their little girl.

But now she was fulfilled in a different way, a much more personal way. Rod's job wasn't nearly as demanding, so he was able to invest much more of his time in her and Cassia. Never had she felt more important to someone.

Dashing a hand over her face to dry her cheeks, she went to blow her nose. Then she carried a jug of lemonade and paper cups from the house.

"Ready for a cold drink?" she called.

The kids rushed over, so she poured them each a glass before carrying one over to Rod.

"Careful, I'm sweaty," he said when she leaned in to kiss him.

"I don't care," she said. "I'm so happy to have you in my life."

"Look at them *kissing* each other," Cassia whispered loudly to Van.

India was chuckling at her daughter's reaction as she pulled away, but Rod caught her hand. "That was nice," he teased. "I must be doing something right."

"You make me happy," she said.

"You don't mind living out here in Whiskey Creek?"

"I'll live anywhere with you."

"You're in it for the long haul, aren't you?"

Sometimes he still seemed surprised by that.

"Absolutely." After what his mother had done, she knew he had some deep-seated abandonment issues. Although he never acted needy, if he believed he might get hurt, he tried not to care. But she knew he liked to hear her say she wasn't going to change her mind or suddenly stop loving him.

The kids were already finished with their lemonade and calling for him to throw the ball. She thought he'd set her aside and continue the game. Instead, he kissed her again. "I've never loved anyone like I love you," he said.

* * * * *

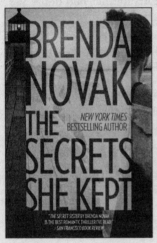

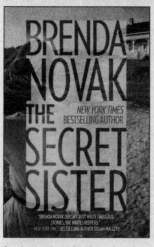

Turn your love of reading into rewards you'll love with
Harlequin My Rewards